RICHARD DANSKY

FIREFLY RAIN

WIZARDS OF THE COAST
DISCOVERIES™

Firefly Rain

©2008 by Richard Dansky
Cover Photograph ©2008 by Noah Grey

Book designed by Matt Adelsperger

First Printing: January 2008

9 8 7 6 5 4 3 2 1

ISBN: 978-0-7869-4856-7
620-21724720-001-EN

Library of Congress Cataloging-in-Publication Data

Dansky, Richard, 1970-
Firefly rain / Richard Dansky.
p. cm.
ISBN 978-0-7869-4856-7
1. North Carolina—Fiction. 2. Ghosts—Fiction. 3. Psychological fiction. I. Title.
PS3604.A55287F54 2007
813'.6—dc22

2007021309

U.S., CANADA,
ASIA, PACIFIC, & LATIN AMERICA
Wizards of the Coast, Inc.
P.O. Box 707
Renton, WA 98057-0707
+1-800-324-6496

EUROPEAN HEADQUARTERS
Hasbro UK Ltd
Caswell Way
Newport, Gwent NP9 0YH
GREAT BRITAIN
Save this address for your records.

Visit our web site at www.wizards.com

DEDICATION

For my wife, Melinda,
without whom
all the best stories
would remain
unwritten

Acknowledgments

I'd like to thank the following people, without whom *Firefly Rain* would have remained no more than a light drizzle:

Bruce Baugh, Zach Bush, Olivier Henriot, and Mur Lafferty, for their superb feedback and suggestions

The Bastard Sons of Mort Castle and extended family thereof, for their support and encouragement

Geoff Grabowski, for much-appreciated assistance with shotguns

Janet Berliner, James A. Moore, and Alexis Nolent, for all of the professional encouragement and help along the way

My coworkers at Red Storm and Ubisoft, for putting up with the crazy writer in their midst

Susan Morris and Phil Athans at Wizards of the Coast, who were wonderful, incisive, and most of all, very patient with me

My agent, Robert Fleck, for all of his hard work, advice, and friendship

And my family, who aren't like that at all. Honest.

PROLOGUE

I remember a night when I was six years old the way some folks remember their first kiss. Six years old and full of fire, wandering around the field behind the house with an empty jam jar in my hand. I caught my first firefly that night—pulled it out of the air just a little too hard and crushed the life out of it with fingers that shouldn't have been able to do so. I didn't know what I'd done, of course, so I took my prize and set it in the jar. It slid halfway down and then stuck to the side, its legs moving slowly, its gold-green glow fading to nothing.

"Shine," I told it earnestly, and screwed the cap of the jar on tight. I'd punched air holes in the top with scissors, the way I'd thought you were supposed to, and I figured that down in the jar the firefly could hear me. "Shine for me," I told it.

"Son, don't do that," my father said. He was a large man who kept getting larger, with a shock of black hair that never got around to turning gray. Mother had broken him of smoking the year I turned five, but she'd never be able to stop him eating instead, and it showed from year to year. When I was six, though, he could still move like a cat, and I never knew he was behind me until I heard those words. "Don't do that," he said, and I turned to face him.

"Don't do what?" I asked, and held the jar up before me as an offering. "Want to see my firefly?"

He pushed my hands down gently. "No, son, I don't. You shouldn't catch them that way."

"Why not? I made air holes," I said, and I tapped on the lid of the jar for emphasis.

He took a deep breath. "Do you know why fireflies light up?" he asked.

"No," I replied.

"It's because they're looking for other fireflies. The ones in the air are looking for the ones on the ground. See?" He pointed to a spot in the grass that was all alight. "That's how they find one another. The ones that shine the brightest find the others the fastest. But if you catch the brightest, because they're the ones you see the best, well, that means the best fireflies don't get to meet their friends. And that's wrong, you see?"

I stared up at him and blinked. "No," I said. "I just want to catch fireflies."

He opened his mouth to try to explain further, and Mother hushed him. "Let me explain, dear," she said, and Father's mouth shut like a shed door swinging closed.

"Of course, dear," he said, and he walked off. She watched him go without saying a word, and then she turned back to me.

"The problem isn't with you wanting to catch fireflies, you know," she told me as she bent down to put her face near mine.

Her voice was a whisper that just the two of us shared, her face a blur in the evening darkness.

"Oh?" I said. "Then why is Daddy upset?"

"He's not upset. He just doesn't want you to keep the fireflies from doing what they have to do," she said. "You see, fireflies are how angels find things when they come down from heaven. If you catch the fireflies, then the angels get lost and they can't take the good souls back to heaven with them. That's why you can't catch fireflies, honey. Is that okay?"

I nodded at her, my eyes wide. "Can I still chase them, if I don't catch them? Is that all right?"

She kissed me on the forehead and laughed. "Of course, sweetheart. Of course that's all right." She took the jar from me, unscrewed the lid and gently shook the dimming corpse of the firefly onto the grass. Then she screwed the lid back on and headed for the back door to the house, her brown dress making her almost shapeless in the twilight.

My father caught up with her right outside the door. I could hear their voices rising, each in turn, but I paid no attention to their words.

I was too busy chasing fireflies.

Dear Son,

Your mother just informed me of your intention not to return home for the holiday season, and I have to say, I am disappointed in you.

I'm sure you have plenty of reasons that seem good to stay at school over Christmas. You have your friend, you have a life up there, you maybe even have a girl. I don't know—these aren't things you've shared with us since you've been away. I can understand wanting your own place and your own life, and I'm sure the house where you grew up seems boring and quiet compared to all of the excitement of the big city, but it's where you came from, and that ought to mean something to you, at least at Christmas.

I have a certain amount of sympathy for wanting to find something of your own, especially at your age, but that should never come at the cost of causing pain to others, especially not to those who love you. I cannot count the number of times you've promised your mother that you would be home for Christmas this year. Needless to say, she misses you terribly, and the news that you are not coming home has hurt her badly.

You're a grown man now, or close to it, and I'm sure you think you can make your own decisions. Part of being a man, though, is understanding those decisions, and weighing what they cost. There's more in this world than you and your wants, Son. You'd do well to remember that.

We'll leave a place for you at the table, just in case you change your mind. Your mother would be pleased if you did.

Father hadn't signed the letter, hadn't needed to, really. There was no one else it could have come from. I'd read it when it first arrived, then tucked it away in a place where I couldn't find it easily when the mood struck me to throw it away.

And now, here I was holding it in my hands, the last thing that was mine in a place I'd lived in for years without leaving any kind of mark. I was leaving, heading back to Carolina with my tail between my legs and the memory of a failed business behind me. It was time to go somewhere else, to regroup and recover.

Even if that meant going back to a place I thought I'd never see again. In Boston, the wounds were too fresh, the failure too new. It would just be a temporary visit, I told myself. I'd be in and out, recharged and ready to take on the world again, somewhere else.

So my belongings, the few I'd wanted to keep, had gone on a moving truck headed south, and here I was ready to follow. "A retreat," a former employee of mine had called it, and she was right. I was falling back.

The letter was still in my hands. I felt the rasp of the paper under my fingers—old, heavy typing paper that hadn't aged well. It was dry and brittle, and carried with it an unpleasant weight of memory and expectation. It was the last letter Father had ever sent me, and the notion of bearing it back to its point of origin seemed suddenly, deeply wrong.

I crumpled it up and threw it on the floor. Then I turned out the lights, hung my key on a hook over the kitchen sink, and went out to where my car—and the road back to Carolina—waited for me.

That letter had been written on the occasion of my not coming home for Christmas my junior year of college. It was the first time I'd felt brave enough to stay away, to make sure that miles stayed between me and that house, that land. It wasn't that I hated my parents. I loved them both, and they'd loved each other, but in a way that cost them for loving. I never really fit in that house, and living there was like being stretched over a too-tight frame.

Father'd died six years after sending that letter, five years after I'd graduated and announced I'd be staying in Boston for good. It was his heart that finally gave out, but I had to figure the rest of his organs were just disappointed they lost the race. Liver, lungs, kidneys—the doctors told me they were lined up one after another, ready and willing to go.

Mother went ten years after Father's passing. I think I was partially to blame for that, though no one ever said as much to my face. My visits home grew shorter and shorter, and I made them less and less often. There was a business to run, after all, and quiet evenings in North Carolina farm country didn't offer much compared to the nightlife on Lansdowne Street. Besides, there was always a sense of expectation when I did make it home, an unspoken question hovering in the air of when I was going to come back for good. Mother never asked, so I didn't have to answer, but it hung there between us every time.

I nearly missed her funeral because we were closing a deal for distribution with some Japanese firm that week, and they wanted me there for the signing. There would be plenty of time to make it back after the meeting, I told myself, and I almost believed it.

In my darker hours, I wonder if Mother chose that moment to die deliberately, to see if just once I'd choose her over whatever it was I'd found up north. As it was, it was a near thing, and I made it home with only hours to spare. I remember driving like a madman from the airport in a rented car that was too big for my needs and too slow for my wants, but which had been the only one left on the lot. I also remember cursing everyone and everything else for my lateness.

They buried her out back, next to Father but with enough space between them that it was clear they didn't always see eye to eye. Afterward, we gathered at the house to share memories and reassure one another that we wouldn't forget her. Friends of the family asked me a dozen times and more if I was all right, if there was anything I needed, if there was anything they could do. I thanked them all, told them gravely that I was fine, and promised them I wouldn't sell the property. "Family land stays in the family," I told them, and I'm pretty sure I meant it. And since there was no other family, no aunts or uncles or cousins out there to maybe cast their eyes on the property, that meant it stayed with me.

Before the last of the well-wishers drifted away, I made arrangements with a man named Carl Powell, a friend of Mother's, to serve as caretaker on the property in my absence. Carl was weathered and lean, and I couldn't even guess how old he was. He still had all his teeth and most of his hair, and he'd been an occasional visitor at the house for as long as I could remember. I knew that he had been a big help to Mother in her declining years, and I felt good giving him the key and a check to cover the first year's worth of maintenance.

"Keep your money," he'd told me at first, when I'd asked him if he was willing.

"Carl, it's an old house, and it's going to need some work," I replied. "And it's a fifteen mile drive for you to get here from your place. I can't not give you money for doing this."

"Fine," he said, but there wasn't a lot of joy in his voice. "I'll give you an accounting at the end of the year."

"I trust you," I said, which was probably the worst thing I could have said. "Let me know if you need any more."

"I will," he said in a voice that promised just the opposite, and he stuffed the check into his pocket. Carl left without another word to me, and hardly any to anyone else.

Reverend Trotter, an old family friend, was the last to leave. He'd given a fine and gentle eulogy for Mother, and he'd been sharp enough to make sure I didn't have to speak more than a few words about her. Like everyone else in that church, he knew that a few words were all I had.

"Jacob," he told me, and he wrapped his hands around mine, "the times ahead are going to be harder than you think. You've lost both parents now, and that's the sort of thing that hits a good man hard. If there's anything you need, or if you just have to talk to someone, don't hesitate to call."

"Thank you, Reverend." I squeezed his hands for a moment, and then pulled mine away. "I think I'll be all right, though."

He gave me a look that said, clear as day, he didn't believe me. "That's a big house full of memories you'll be staying in, Mr. Logan, and those memories just might come knocking harder than you think. I don't like to think of you out here by your lonesome in the middle of the night, realizing deep down that she's gone and you've got things you never had a chance to say."

I smiled at him. "Don't worry, there's no chance of that. I have to go back to Boston. I'm leaving the day after tomorrow."

He blinked and took a step back. "So soon? You sure you don't need more time here, just to pull yourself together?" He leaned in close and added, conspiratorially, "Besides, some folks might take that as disrespectful."

My smile got a little harder. "I know how to show respect for Mother, Reverend. Other folks can say what they like. Carl Powell's going to be taking care of the house, and I'm better equipped to handle the legal paperwork back home. Staying here wouldn't do anyone much good."

"*Staying* home might do you more good than you think," he corrected me, and then he shook his head. "I'm sorry, I'm speaking out of turn. Chalk it up to worry, Jacob. That offer stands, even if you have to call me from the big city in the middle of the night."

I held the door open for him. "I do appreciate that, Reverend. Thank you."

"You're welcome. You take care of yourself, Jacob Logan. Come back some time." He walked across the porch and down to his car without looking back, without expecting an answer.

"Some time," I said softly, after he'd gotten in his car and driven off. The sun was going down as he did so, and long shadows marked my way as I walked back down to where they'd buried Mother. As the sky got darker, the fireflies came out to light my way.

I sat down there by the graves and waited, reading the headstone's inscription a dozen times and wondering why I wasn't feeling more. It wasn't until full dark came that I stood and cleaned off the fireflies that had landed on the stones.

Only then did I walk away.

The drive took two days. I could have made it in one but I didn't see the need. The truck with the rest of my belongings was following well behind, following the sort of route that let it leave earlier and arrive later than I would, without any way to check on it in between. In practical terms, that meant that there wasn't any sort of schedule for me to keep, which was the sort of practicality I liked. I hadn't called ahead to let Carl know I was coming and I liked it that way. There was a vague notion in my head of drifting back into town and making as light an impression as possible. Maybe I could be gone before anyone noticed I'd come.

Ten o'clock had come and gone by the time I turned off of the state route and found my way through the little town called Maryfield. Mother and Father's house lay on the other side of it, well outside the city limits, and driving straight through was the only way to get there. There were more lights and shops than I remembered, but not many, and I didn't feel like stopping to consider the differences further. Two days on the road had me bone tired. There'd be time enough to explore later, if I felt the need.

A quick left onto Harrison Farm Road led me right back out of town and into the dark. The road had been mostly gravel when I was growing up; now the asphalt extended farther, and the houses and street lights with it. But soon enough the last of the lights faded behind me. The town had crept closer to the house, but it still had miles to go before it was knocking on the door—my door, really. For that I was thankful, and there was a smile on my face as I drove off into the dark.

The road narrowed to one lane of hard-packed gravel, bounded on each side with a drainage ditch. Strangers had trouble with the road if they drove it after dark; watching neighbors winch station wagons back up onto the road had been a common pastime in my youth. I knew it, though, knew it well enough to take in the landscape as I drove. I could see the outlines of the trees that lined the road and not much else. The only things visible beyond them were the lights from the few houses I passed and the fireflies in the fields.

It was going to be a good summer for them, I could tell. Already the ground was thick with gold-green light, and the air above the fields danced with those cold sparks. It had been a long time since I'd seen fireflies in that kind of abundance—Boston isn't partial to that sort of thing—and for a moment I was tempted to pull over and catch one in my hands. Then I thought about the two stones standing out past the pine trees and the empty house waiting for me, and all temptation fled.

The driveway came up on me suddenly, and I had to jam on the brakes to avoid overshooting the turn. Only the mailbox on the side of the road had let me know where the driveway was, and even then I'd nearly missed it. A dark house set well back from a dark road on a dark night is easy to miss, I told myself, and then I realized how truly dark it was. Even with the sky mostly clear and a half moon shining down, the house I called mine was just plain wrapped in shadow. It had the look of a place that had gotten used to being ignored and liked it that way.

And not only was the house dark, but so was the land it stood on. From where I stood, I could just see the road and the neighbor's property beyond it. There, in the distance, I could see little specks of light dancing in the air. A turn to the east, where the old Tolliver farm was, and I could see the same thing. Mr. Tolliver had been a mean son of a bitch and put up wire along the top of the fence at the property line, and near as I could tell, there were even fireflies crawling their way along that. And I was sure without looking that if I turned back west, toward town, I'd see them there, too.

But on my land, nothing. I could hear the frogs out there in the dark, but sound wasn't the issue. Light was, and I couldn't see any clear over to the boundary. No fireflies crossed the line that separated my land from anyone else's.

I stayed out on the porch for an hour, watching, but none of them ever did.

I finally got tired of waiting on the fireflies and decided to do something useful with myself instead. The hour was late enough that I didn't feel like unpacking everything from the car, but I could certainly manage enough to get me through until daylight. With a bundle of clothes and a toothbrush tucked under my arm, I slid the old brass-colored key into the lock on the porch door. It went in smoothly, with no sound and no resistance. I unlocked it, looked around, and laid my hand on the knob.

Feeling the weight of years, I twisted it and shoved the door open. It swung smooth and silent on the hinges without making so much as a single creak. I think I would have preferred the noise.

Stepping through into the kitchen, I pocketed my keys and dropped my clothes on the kitchen counter. Even without turning on the light, I knew where everything was—counter to the right, kitchen table farther on and to the left, and light switch on the wall by the door.

It felt the same, too. Ten seconds under that roof and it all came flooding back. Just big enough to feel hollow and just small enough to feel cramped; that was my parents' house. Hot in the summer and cold in the winter, dark in the daytime and noisy at night—the sensations all came flooding back.

I forced the thoughts out of my head and went back out to the car for a small bag of groceries I'd picked up at a convenience store on the way in. It wasn't much, just enough to get me through a couple of days as I settled in. The fridge was running, much to my relief, so I tossed the entire bag in there—bread, beer, pre-packaged cold cuts, and all—with the intention of sorting it out in the morning.

I shut the door and, after a moment's hesitation, locked it. It felt strange to do so here, where you never locked your door unless circumstances were strange and dire. It would have felt stranger not to, though. It would take more than one night to break a decade and a half of Boston habits. The car was locked up tight, too. There were things in there worth stealing, I was certain, even if there wasn't anyone around to steal them.

Satisfied and exhausted, I grabbed my clothes and toothbrush again, and let memory guide me to my old room. Tossing the toothbrush on the dresser, I swept the dust off my childhood bed and found a clean blanket to wrap myself in. There'd be time enough in the morning, I figured, to set myself up properly. Weary from the road, I turned out the lights and lay myself down.

And no light came in through the window.

CHAPTER 2

I woke up at half past nine, a positive luxury to a man used to angry alarm clocks at five thirty. It took me another lazy, enjoyable hour to make myself presentable to the world through the application of cold water and hot coffee. It was nearly eleven before I felt like shrugging into the clean clothes I'd brought in with me the night before. No shoes, though—I kept my feet bare as I walked out to the car to unload a few more armfuls of clothes and essentials. The grass and gravel felt good under my feet, and the occasional sharp stones bothered me less with every step.

The clock said it was noon by the time I called Carl Powell, and I was halfway to waiting until supper or beyond when I did so. My memories of Carl were of a man who was a friend to Mother and Father both, but one with little use for their son. We'd had a few communications since Mother's funeral, most of them brief and to the point. I sent him checks, he told me the house was fine, and most years I remembered to send him a Christmas card. That was about it, and both of us seemed happy with the arrangement.

I'd wrestled with the decision not to call Carl a time or two before I started on the road. Warning him I was coming would have been the sensible thing to do, but the businessman in me told me not to do so, that I'd do better to get a look at the place before he knew I was on my way. That way, I'd see its real condition, see what sort of job he'd actually been doing and whether I'd gotten my money's worth.

That's what the rational part of my head said, anyway. It was good cover for the fact that Carl scared the crap out of me, and that I wanted time to establish the house as mine again before I talked to him.

Carl's phone rang nine times before he picked up. I'd been just about to hang up when I finally heard his voice on the line, low and suspicious. Carl was not a friendly man, nor had he ever been. "Who's there?" he said by way of greeting, and he sounded like he begrudged me the words.

"Carl, it's Jacob Logan," I said by way of reply. "I have a question for you."

"You're back, ain't you," he said. It wasn't a question. "Might have let a fellow know you were coming."

"I'm sorry," I said. Manners were everything with Carl. I remembered that too late, and knew I'd pay for the mistake. "It was a last-minute idea to come back here."

"Last minute and too late, but you came back anyway." There was silence at the end of the line for a good thirty seconds. "So, why'd you call?"

I cleared my throat twice, a nervous habit I'd picked up ten years previous and never managed to break. "Like I said, I have a question for you. Did you ever go out to the house at night?"

He made a sound that I assumed was him sucking his teeth

for a good moment or so. "A couple of times, yes. When the house needed fixing. Why'd you ask?"

"I noticed something odd last night, and I was wondering if you'd seen it, too."

"Odd, you say? Now let me think." He gave a dry chuckle. "There's a few odd things in that house, son. Only one out in the fields, though. Is that what you're asking about?"

"So you've seen it," I interrupted. *The hell with manners*, I thought. Carl knew something. "What did you see?"

He brought his chuckle under control and hid it behind a wheezy cough. "It's not what I saw, you understand. It's what I didn't see, and what I haven't seen on that land since the night they put your mother in the ground. You think on that. I'll drop the key off by nightfall."

I started to say that I didn't want him to return the key, but the line went dead, and I realized Carl had said all he wanted to say to me. The receiver felt heavy in my hand, so I set it down gently and went scrounging for one of the energy bars I'd brought in from the car with my clothes. By daylight, the bag of groceries I'd brought with me seemed even smaller and more pathetic in the empty expanse of the refrigerator. I'd have to rectify that, I realized. I'd have to do a lot of things to make the house livable, even for a little while.

Originally, I'd been planning on finishing my unpacking after breakfast, then running into town for some groceries, but my conversation with Carl somehow shot all that to hell. Instead, I spent a few hours simply wandering through the various rooms of the house, letting my memories wake up, holding favorite knickknacks, and admiring Carl's housekeeping.

As houses went, it wasn't much, though some of our neighbors had grumbled about it being a little extravagant. Grandfather Logan had built the heart of it back before the Second World War, even as the house he'd grown up in was crumbling to the ground. That was the way it went; one came down and another went up to take its place, and the children played in the old ruins when their parents weren't looking.

He hadn't built it all himself, of course, though he'd done more work than one might think in raising it. Family legend had it that when it was finished, Grandmother Logan took one look at it and said, "Not bad for a first try. Where's the one we'll be living in?" What Grandfather Logan said in response was not recorded for posterity.

Regardless of the opinion of grandmothers long dead, it was a well-built house, and more than adequate to the needs of Logans past. Modest upkeep was all it took; new paint every so often and a fool up on the ladders to clean out the gutters when they clogged with pine needles.

Grandfather Logan never liked people much, and as such the house had been built facing away from the road. Truth be told, the road side of the house had almost no windows in it at all, nor did it have any doors, or indeed any real evidence that the house wasn't long abandoned. Two generations of Logan women had planted flowers there so that the view from the road would at least be pleasant, but their efforts were never more than half successful. The house blocked the good light there, so most of what grew wasn't that pretty. They sure tried, though, every year without fail.

The outside of the house was painted a faded red that had

once been the color of brick. The sun had beaten the strength out of the color, though, and what was left was barely darker than the Carolina clay it rose up out of. A faded wood porch painted that same clay red came off the kitchen door and faced the driveway, three steps above the ground. Most of the house was set over a crawlspace, partly because the land sloped away toward the back of the property, and partly because the water table was high enough to turn the neighbors' root cellars into foul-smelling ponds after a few days of rain. Grandfather Logan had been the cautious type, so the whole house was raised up on brick supports, with a fence in between and a locked gate that you could open up to let the plumber crawl through when you couldn't do the job yourself.

The porch had been Father's favorite place. He liked sitting out there of an evening with a beer, watching the road out of the corner of his eye, at least when Mother would let him. The porch was wide, wrapping around the kitchen and to the back, and it had a high wood rail that was broad enough to rest a flowerpot or a beer bottle on. The kitchen door led out to that porch, and as long as I could remember, that was the main door we used to go into or out of the house. There was a front door, certainly, but it, like the shotgun Father had kept in the trunk at the foot of the bed, was used only on very rare occasions. I could recall the front door being opened twice, both times for funerals. Everyone who knew us knew to go round the side, and as for people who didn't know us, well, they could stand out there all day if they wanted to.

The kitchen was small by some standards, but it served well enough for us. A fat white gas stove sat on the wall by the door. Mother had always set her teakettle on the back left element, and I was not surprised to see it there when I walked in. There was a window over the sink, flanked by yellow curtains Mother had stitched herself, and an expanse of white counter that had been put in with great fanfare back when I'd been about twelve. Cabinets filled with pots and pans lined the walls, but the cast-iron skillet lived on top of the stove. In the corner was a round kitchen table that had rarely been graced by a tablecloth. It was Formica, with long metal legs and flecks of gold in the plastic of the tabletop, and the chairs that came with it were just as ugly. Father had bought it, brand new, when I was very young. When Mother expressed her disapproval, Father said calmly that we'd get a new one just as soon as this one wore out. Now they were ten years gone and more, and the table was still here. Father would have laughed at that. Mother, not so much, I think.

The rest of the house was on the same level, all built spinning off a long hallway that ran out the back of the kitchen. Down at the end was the family room, which doubled as the dining room when we had guests. As a result, the table spent most of its time shoved against the outside wall and covered in papers. There was a fireplace, rarely used but still functional, and a ceremonial pile of firewood in front of it that looked like it would fall to dust with a touch. There was more out back, I knew. There was always more out back.

The left side of the house, facing away from the kitchen, was Mother and Father's side. Their bedroom was there, as was their bathroom. Those doors were not to be opened by the likes of me, and it was only on rare occasions that I had ever even knocked. My room and the bathroom that served the rest of the house were on the side of the house nearer the road. There was a small guest room as well that doubled as Mother's sewing room. More often than not when we had company, however, I moved into the guest room, and the guest took mine. My room was the more comfortable of the two, and by far the cooler.

What we called the attic was really more of a crawlspace over the long central hall. The attic door was set flush into the hallway ceiling, and you could pull it and its foldaway ladder down with a long white cord that dangled from one end. Being able to jump high enough to grab that cord had been a goal of mine from early childhood, and I spent years of frustration leaping from a crouch every chance I got, only to fall short.

It was much later that I learned that Father had been steadily snipping the cord shorter to encourage me—so he said—to jump higher. He only stopped once the string got so high he was having trouble pulling the thing down himself. Mother was more practical. She just stood on a chair to reach the pullcord, and once she had yanked it open, told Father to go up there instead.

Everything unusual and unloved was up in that attic. Shells for Father's unused shotgun sat in a box next to baby clothes and stacks of magazines from before the war. Toys went up there when I outgrew them, to be stored against the day when I had children of my own. It was the family history, to be opened up again for each successive generation in turn.

I'd thought about cleaning it out after my parents died, but had never gotten around to it. Instead, I simply left instructions with Carl that the attic was not to be disturbed unless the roof needed work. I might not have had the time to touch that stuff, but that didn't mean anyone else had the right to do so.

The last room in the house was a mudroom that had been added in the sixties, more of a shed tacked on to the main building than anything else. It held the washer and dryer, things Mother had insisted on, and about a thousand half-empty bottles of household supplies. Most of them were no doubt worthless, but I figured they had squatter's rights. After all, they'd been there longer than I had. A door led to the outside, a relic of the days when the washing went outside to dry. To my knowledge, it hadn't been used in years.

There had been a shed once, but it had long since fallen in on itself. No barn, either, and don't think the neighbors didn't tut-tut about that. Good land going to waste, that's what they thought about our place, but Father made enough money that he didn't need to work the land. "Let it rest a few years," he told me when I asked about it. "It's certainly earned it." And so the long grass grew tall and the pine trees and black locust grew up when they didn't think anyone was looking. It would take a full summer's worth of hard work to make the land ready for farming. Trees would need to be cut down, stumps would need to be pulled out, and a whole lot of soil would need to get turned. Father had left that job for me, and I figured to leave it for whoever came after. In the meantime, though, it made things what might be called "scenic," and that was good enough for me.

It was nearly suppertime when I finally stepped out the kitchen door and onto the porch to do the day's labor. It was hot and the air felt thick as the cotton ball clouds that lurked in packs overhead. It put a smile on my face—good old North Carolina weather. I'd always laughed when the people I'd known in Boston complained about the summers there. It was like hearing a rich kid complain about how he got the Porsche instead of the Mercedes. They wouldn't know real heat if it wrapped them up and squeezed tight.

I filled my lungs with some good, clean country air and started down the stairs to the driveway. Two steps down, my footfall made an unexpected sound. I pulled up short, looking down to see what I'd done.

An envelope rested there under my toe, now marked with the print of my shoe. The dirt outlined half the imprint of a key, no doubt Carl's. He had indeed said all he meant to say to me, it seemed, so I pocketed the key and crumpled up the envelope for later deposit in the trash. The fact that I hadn't heard Carl's truck in the driveway was puzzling, but I put it down to the fact that sound didn't carry well through Grand-father Logan's walls. With a shrug, I went back to the business of unloading the car—without Carl's help.

Not that I'd actually expected help, mind you, but I hadn't *not* expected it, either.

Most of what was still in the Audi were odds and ends—the bits and pieces I hadn't trusted to the truck or found a safe carton for. There were more clothes, a few pairs of shoes that I could still wear and several others I didn't dare try, and more handkerchiefs than one man should probably own. Bookends, desk accessories, and a wallet full of CDs; that was the sort of thing I'd stuffed into the back seat and trunk. Somewhere in there was a box full of papers and a laptop, but I didn't feel any great urgency to rescue either one. They reminded me of Boston more than the desk lamp or the old Red Sox cap did. So I puttered and fidgeted and took all of the useless stuff in, one small armload at a time. Some of it I found places for, some of it I just dumped in what I pretended was a neat pile in the guest bedroom. There was no need to find a permanent home for anything, so mostly it was just a matter of figuring out new definitions for "not underfoot" and "out of the way."

It was getting on nine by the time I'd shifted the piles of goods to my satisfaction. When the last trip had been made, I wiped the sweat out of my eyes, and then I went into the kitchen to make myself a sandwich for dinner. The movers were due to arrive late that evening, and I thought that once I'd finished eating, I'd sit out on the porch and wait for them.

But as the dark crept up with no sign and no phone call, I got restless. A couple of glasses of water gave way to a couple of beers, which didn't help my mood any. Eventually, I resigned myself to the fact that they weren't coming and took myself for a walk.

The property was large enough that a man could ramble a good ways in any direction he chose, though most of the land had long since been left to grow wild and could be tough going as a result. The plot where they'd buried both Father and Mother was about as far back as the cleared land went. The rest was all tall grass clear to the edge of the woods, and if it had been left to me, no doubt the weeds would have claimed the graves as well.

Carl hadn't let that happen, though. I walked past the curtain of pines and saw he'd been diligent in keeping the gravesites clear. Green grass cropped close was all that grew there, that and a flowering vine that wound its way up Mother's stone. There had always been a rumor that Carl had been sweet on her, and I didn't doubt it, not that I cared. *Didn't do either of them any good*, I thought. Instead, I just let myself drift as I walked along, and I didn't think about Carl or Mother any more.

I was almost feeling peaceful when the jangle of my cell phone brought me back to myself. Hastily, I dug it out of my pocket and answered, "Logan."

A woman's cold voice answered me and let me know I had new voicemail. The light on top of the phone blinked red at me, slow and steady. With a shake of my head, I dialed up the message and put the phone to my ear.

"You have. One. New message, recorded today at two. Thirty. Five. PM." That's what that robot voice said this time, and then it spewed out a gibberish phone number as the source of the call. I took a deep breath and silently cursed the voicemail system for taking its own sweet time to get the message to me. Then, all the best profanity out of my system, I punched up the message itself, and wondered why my gut was suddenly twisting.

The call turned out to be from the moving company, as I had been hoping, but that was where things turned grim. They had some bad news for me. The truck with my furniture on it had been involved in what the man on the phone called "an incident," where "incident" meant "getting caught too close to a jackknifing tractor trailer." The truck, and just about everything on it, had been wrecked beyond any hope of salvage. The man, who gave his name as Jason Proctor, hastened to add that their insurance would cover the value of the goods I had lost, and that I was welcome to drive up to Baltimore, where the crash had occurred, to look through the remains myself. He was, of course, very sorry for the inconvenience. He also left a number I could call any time, day or night, to discuss the matter. A few more apologies followed, and then he hung up.

I said a small prayer for the man who had left that message before saving it. The poor bastard sounded like he was about to start crying by the time he was done. I wondered if he'd had anything on that truck himself, or if he'd just had to deliver the bad news to one too many customers over the years. I resolved to ask for him by name, and dialed in the number he'd given me.

Mr. Proctor had gone home by the time my call was finally connected, but I got patched through to a man who sounded almost exactly like him. This was a Mr. Douglas or some such, who apologized twice before reassuring me that a check would be coming soon to cover my losses.

"How much?" I asked, and he gave me a number, backed by a bunch of gobbledygook about the terms of loss under the contract.

"That'll be fine," I said, cutting him short midphrase. "Didn't like most of that furniture anyway, to be honest."

"It will be?" he said, and he sounded surprised. "I mean, excellent. We'll need a few days to process things, of course, but hopefully this will be resolved—"

"Call me when the check is coming," I told him. "No excuses, no explanations. I don't care if you have to have it signed by the company president and his sixteen dancing virgins. Just let me know when the check is coming, and if you did manage to salvage anything. Do I make myself understood?"

There was silence on the other end of the line—the sound of a man who's been interrupted in the middle of a memorized speech and doesn't know how to get his brain back in gear. "Umm, certainly, Mr. Logan," Douglas finally said, and he coughed. "I'll do everything I can to get that check to you in a timely fashion."

"You do that," I agreed, and I asked after the health of the driver.

"He should make it," Douglas said. He sounded surprised that I'd ask, which I regarded as an indictment of his position. It's common for people to ask after money and not men, I knew, but I wasn't raised that way. It was a damn shame that most of the people Douglas talked to had been.

I hung up on Douglas while he was still finding new ways to say he was sorry and started the walk back up to the house. I could see it from where I stood, a darker shadow against the night sky, long and low against the horizon. Not much of mine would be in that house, not much at all.

The notion didn't bother me as much as it might have. Indeed, I was almost disturbed by how little the news had shaken me. The house was already furnished, and Carl had seen to it that everything was in fine repair. I'd slept the night before in my childhood bed and it had done me the favor of not collapsing beneath my grown-up weight. I suspected that it would be fine for the foreseeable future as well, which was a good thing. I'd long since decided that I'd be sleeping every night in my childhood bedroom instead of the master. Spending a night in my parents' marriage bed was not something I could ever do.

And with that thought, I trudged up the stairs and onto the porch. With one hand I picked up the beer bottles for transportation in to the sink, and then I went into the darkened house.

There were no fireflies that night, either, at least not that I could see. Lord knows I was looking for them.

Morning came and went while I lay in bed and stared at the ceiling. I'd finally drifted off around five, which is to say, just about the time the sun was coming up, and had slept fitfully at best after that. I'd had dreams, dreams of previous homecomings, and they gave me a cold fear I didn't quite understand. None of the dreams were what you would call a nightmare; far from it. They were just flashes of good times had long ago, and of Mother and Father mentioning how good it was to have me home. But each time, I woke up with my heart hammering in my chest and sweat dripping off my brow.

Home. That was the one word that kept echoing through those dreams, the last word I heard every time before my eyes flew open. And that was just plain foolish. There was nothing here to fear, no history of abuse, pain, or blood. I'm sure my hindbrain had to work hard to find those good memories, but that was the worst I could say on the matter.

Besides, this house hadn't been home in a long time, and I had no intention of letting it become so now. Just a couple of weeks of relaxation and recuperation were all I asked of that building and of the land it rested on. I wanted it to put up with me long enough to let me get my footing back and cash my checks. Then I'd be moving on, my load even lighter than it had been before. Carl could have the place in perpetuity for all I cared.

With that thought, I lay myself back down and got a solid hour's sleep before I woke up again, screaming.

No one heard me, though, and for that I was grateful.

Midafternoon I finally forced myself out of bed and stumbled around the house. I'd made some vague plans the day before about going into town and exploring a bit, but that seemed pointless now. Instead, I made myself a couple slices of toast then sat on the porch and watched the fields until the sun went down.

This time, I didn't stay to look for the fireflies that I was afraid wouldn't come. Instead, I went inside, pulled down the shades, and drank the last of my beer. It didn't help me sleep.

I slept late again the next morning, if you could call it sleeping. Around the fifth time I counted to ten and told myself that, yes, it was time to get moving, I finally heaved myself out of bed and got a start on the day. Yesterday's laziness could be excused as road fatigue or re-acclimation, but today there was work to be done. The rest of my life had to come in from the car, the temporary storage solutions I'd improvised needed to be given a bit more thought, and I needed to get myself in gear before moss started growing on me.

Besides, I was hungry.

I was mostly done yawning by the time I made it to the kitchen, but there wasn't much waiting for me in the icebox.

Empty beer bottles I had plenty of, but food? Not much, especially not in the breakfast department. Angry with myself, I scavenged what I could and then went stumbling back into the bedroom to get myself dressed for the day. On occasion Father had roamed around the backyard in his bathrobe, but on the off chance anyone was watching, I didn't need to add to the Logan reputation for eccentricity.

My jeans held up to the sniff test well enough, though the t-shirt I'd worn yesterday didn't do quite so well. I shrugged into a new one, slipped my feet into sneakers without socks, and headed out to the driveway. I was angry with myself. Why was I spending so much time in bed if I wasn't getting any damn sleep? I pulled out my keys and mentally planned the loads left to take in. It shouldn't take more than two or three trips, I decided, and then I could get a move on. Put them away, then drive into town for a slightly more efficient supply run—that would be a good day's work. And in the evening, I could shake the cobwebs off the laptop and start planning my next move. There wasn't any net access out at the house—hell, there wasn't even a television in the place—but that wasn't necessarily a bad thing. It would cut out the distractions and let me focus. In any case, it wasn't as if anyone was rushing to e-mail me these days. At least nobody I wanted to hear from.

The car was sitting where I'd left it, the paint job trying to shine under a faint coating of white road dust. I made a mental note to hose it clean as soon as I could find where Carl kept the hose, and I clicked the door unlocked. With a beep and a flash of lights, it answered the keychain, and I decided that unpacking could wait. Clearly, the car had sat still long enough. It wanted to be driven, and I found myself wanting to drive it, to get away from the house for a little bit and just let myself stretch out. Besides, there wasn't enough of my gear left in the car to interfere with the supply run. There was plenty of room for everything.

I slid into the driver's seat, the leather steering wheel grip cool under my fingers. "That-a-baby," I told the car. "You're gonna run a little bit today. Let's see how fast we can get to town." Grinning, I put the key in the ignition and turned it.

Nothing happened.

"Son of a bitch," I swore, and I tried it again. The engine coughed but failed to turn over. A third try, and it didn't give so much as a click.

I sat there for a while, then tried it one more time.

Nothing. After another minute, the battery just plain gave out, like someone had stuck a knife in its back. The lights dimmed, the indicators keeled over, and the car sat there like very expensive roadkill.

I swore, and then I got out. Too late I heard the keys jangle in the ignition as I slammed the car door shut. A quick tug on the handle told me that it was in fact locked, and that I was out of luck. So I swore some more, kicked the car door—gently, on account of the paint job—and sat myself down against the front tire.

"Goddamn," I said, and then a few stronger things, as I tried to figure out what to do next.

Angry with myself, I pulled the cell phone from my pocket. There was one person in town I figured I could call for help, though I was sure he wouldn't exactly want to hear from me.

Still, I figured, he couldn't begrudge me his assistance on this one. It might cost me dear in pride to make the call, but that was the sort of payment Carl seemed to like taking.

Pride, however, was something I was divesting myself of more or less freely. With just a small wince, I dialed Carl's number. It rang twice before Carl picked it up.

"So what do you want now?" he asked without preamble when he picked up the phone.

"Carl, I need some help," I said, and I got a cackle for an answer.

"Of course you do. All alone out there at that great big place and you don't know what you're doing. I'm surprised it took you this long t'call me."

I felt myself growing angry and swallowed it back as best as I could. Let Carl have his fun; I needed his help and that was worth a little ribbing. It wasn't like I didn't deserve it, either. This time, at least.

"It's not like that," I said slowly. "My car won't start and I'm out of groceries. I was wondering if you could recommend a good garage, maybe, or come out here to give me a lift into town."

"I'll bring you something t' eat," he said, and he hung up.

"That's not what I—" I started to say, but he was already gone. I stared at the phone. It blinked a blank screen at me, and then went dark. The connection was gone, and so was Carl.

"That know-it-all son of a bitch," I said with sudden anger, and I threw the damn phone off into the tall grass like I was tossing Carl out with it. It spun high and caught the light before arcing down behind the green and hitting with a quiet thump.

"Fat lot of good that did you," I told myself, hoisting myself to my feet. A quick brush of my backside scared up a lot of dust, and I looked around as if Carl might already be coming up the road.

He can't get here that fast, dumbass, I told myself, *and you might want to go find that cell phone fast, before it rains or something.* But it felt good to just leave it there in the tall grass. It was something I'd done, after all, instead of having done unto me. I could go find the damn thing later. I'd call from the phone in the house and listen for the ring in the yard. I'd find it fast and easy. But I'd do it later, because right now I was just plain pissed off.

Pissed off, I hiked myself onto the porch and sat myself down. And pissed off, I waited for Carl.

CHAPTER 4

Like the devil himself, Carl showed up when the sky was turning red just above the horizon. Tall, angular, and weathered, he hopped out of his truck and grabbed a sack of groceries from the front seat. "Can I help?" I asked him, but he ignored me, marching right in my porch door and putting the bag down on the kitchen table.

"How much do I owe you?" I asked, placing myself between Carl and the door. This way, I figured, he'd have to speak to me, if only to ask me to get out of the way. He stopped and stared at me in disbelief.

"Nothing," he finally said. "You owe *me* nothing." He put a curious emphasis on the word "me." "I'm just keeping a promise, that's all."

"What are you talking about?" I took a step back to block the doorway with my body. "We have a contract, and you didn't promise me anything."

Carl shook his head. "Contract's over with you back in town, but you're right. I didn't promise you a damn thing. That don't mean I didn't make a promise to someone else." He jerked a thumb over his shoulder. "You've got enough there to keep you for a while. I'll be back with more in a few days."

"I'm hoping my car will be fixed before then, so you won't have to do that, Carl," I said sharply. "I don't intend to rely on your help."

He grinned at me, his lips thin and set tight against his face. "You can intend anything you damn well please. I just figure I'll save you the embarrassment of another phone call by telling you I'll be by presently. Don't eat it all at once, y'hear?" And with that, he brushed past me and out of the house.

I stood there and watched him go. He drove off quickly, his truck raising a trail of dust behind it as he sped off down the road, back to town. Meanwhile, my car, the car I'd been so proud of in Boston, just sat there, immobile and useless. It looked ugly and out of place, and I suddenly felt the same way.

"Well, *do* something," I said to the lump of machinery sitting there, more out of frustration than anything else. It didn't respond, not that I'd expected it to. I stared at it a moment longer, then went inside to see what Carl had brought me.

It was obvious, I saw after I unpacked the sack of groceries Carl had provided, that he didn't think much of me. There was no beer in that bag. That much had been obvious when he set it down on the counter without the reassuring clank or clunk that you get from bottles or cans. Instead, there was a gallon of milk and, tucked in next to it, a squeeze bottle of Bosco.

I felt my cheeks get hot with embarrassment. Milk and chocolate syrup? I slammed the Bosco down on the counter and ripped open the icebox door. It swung open hard enough to bounce back and catch my arm on the elbow as I tried to shove the milk in. The pain nearly made me drop it, which would have been a disaster. I could only imagine calling Carl again to explain that I'd spilled the milk he'd brought me, and could he please fetch me some more? I'd be able to hear his laughter without the phone, and so would have half the county. The thought was unbearable.

Moving with considerably more caution, I put the milk on the top shelf and the Bosco on the bottom. No sense leaving the two of them together to get any ideas, after all.

I turned my attention to the rest of the bag, the contents of which proved considerably less inflammatory. There were a few packages of Oscar Meyer cold cuts, a loaf of bread, some eggs (which sat miraculously uncrushed down at the bottom), and a few other essentials. A tin of instant lemonade mix was the heaviest thing in there, sandwiched between a fat stick of butter and some sausages. Some cans of beans and a couple of thin, tough-looking steaks wrapped in butcher paper rounded the whole thing out.

In my head, I added the whole thing up and gave a low whistle. It wasn't exactly gourmet fare, but it still had to have cost Carl a pretty penny. And he said he'd be coming back in a few days with more.

It didn't add up. Or, more to the point, it did add up, and it would keep adding up. I had paid Carl nicely to keep the house in good repair, but not to keep me fat and fed. And as for that promise he mentioned, well, the less I thought about that particular statement, the happier I was. Sighing, I washed out my empties and put them in the paper sack, then put it next to the trash can. I'd recycled in Boston. Here, I was just getting them out of the way.

CHAPTER 5

Morning came slowly after another sleepless night, and the car was no longer where I'd left it.

I found myself standing out in front of the house, too angry to speak. The car was gone. Sure, I had been five kinds of fool to leave the keys in the ignition, but that car hadn't been capable of moving under its own power, keys or no.

And now it was gone. Somehow, some way, someone had come in the middle of the night and taken it out of my driveway without so much as a whisper or a rattle. Hell, if I hadn't known better, I'd have thought there'd never been a car there in the first place. The empty spot beside the house looked . . . well, it looked like it was supposed to be empty, not that it made me any more pleased that my car was gone.

And it had happened here.

Here, where I got laughed at for locking my car door. Here, where the front doors weren't locked except when there was a door-to-door salesman in the vicinity. Here, where this sort of thing was not ever supposed to goddamn happen.

I'd never had my car stolen in Boston, that was for damn sure.

Taking deep breaths, I walked over to where the car had been and stared at the ground. There was nothing of what I was looking for—no heavy tracks that spoke of a tow truck's presence, no broken glass from a smashed-in window, not even any footprints that weren't my own. What might have been the Audi's tracks leading back to the road were so faint that I wasn't sure they were there at all, and walking their line back and forth a few times didn't make me any surer.

"This is just plain stupid," I told myself, and I went back into the house to call the police. The officer I eventually talked to was polite but not terribly helpful when I finally got him on the line, but he promised to send someone around to take a look at things soonish. Meanwhile, if I didn't mind, if I could write up a statement on my own, it would make things awfully convenient.

"Of course, Officer," I heard myself saying, much to my own surprise. "Is there anything else I can do to help?"

"Thank you, Mr. Logan," he said, "but I think that'll do it. We'll let you know when someone's on their way. Have a nice day."

"You, too," I said, and I hung up even as my jaw dropped. "Good God," I said to no one in particular. "Even when I was growing up, the police weren't *that* goddamned Mayberry." I checked to make sure that I had in fact cut the connection, then added a few more choice curses about goddamn gooder hick cops who wouldn't know how to do an investigation if it bit them on the collective, fat, Krispy Kreme-loving ass.

As a matter of fact, I got so warmed to my subject matter that I barely heard the noise outside over my ranting. For a second I couldn't place it, but as I shut myself up to listen, what it was became clear.

Wheels on dirt on gravel, that's what it was, and as I walked to the window I saw Carl's battered old pickup pulling in off the road. I ran outside, arms waving to stop him, but he either ignored me or just plain didn't see me. He lurched to a halt right where my car had been, then swung his long legs out of the cab and came striding around the front of the truck.

"You son of a bitch!" I yelled, even before he reached me. "What the hell do you think you're doing?"

"Delivering your mail," he said calmly. He thrust a fat envelope at me. "I took the liberty of cashing the check those insurance people sent you. The folks at the bank remember your mother fondly."

My jaw dropped and my mind went blank, but my hand reached out and took the envelope. Without thinking, I stuffed it in a pocket.

"You could say thank you," Carl grunted then turned away. "Sorry to hear about your car," he added, striding off.

He hadn't taken more than two steps before I tackled him. He went down hard, his hands barely out in time to break his fall.

"How the hell did you know about my car?" I howled in his ear. "I just called that in five minutes ago."

Easy as a duck shrugging off water, he threw me off his back. I landed awkwardly, a *whoof* of air shooting out of my lungs, and scrambled back. Carl looked at me over his shoulder, and he had blood in his eye. He looked grim as death, and in that moment I knew, sure as Christmas, that he could kill me if he wanted to.

A small part of me thought he just might.

"You get one of those, son, and that's all." With a lanky man's grace, he climbed to his feet. I stayed down in the dust. "It's a small town. People talk, even police. And you'd best have some proof before you accuse a man of stealing around here. That's something you didn't learn at your Boston college, now, is it?"

Without another word, he strode off, back toward his truck. I watched him go—heard the cab door slam and the engine growl to life. He threw it into gear ungently, and I saw the tires on his truck churn up the dust and rock where any clues might have been.

Stop him, a voice in my head screamed, but I didn't move. Couldn't, really. He might have stopped the truck, after all, and gotten out, and Lord knows what would have happened next. But I still hated myself for my cowardice.

An uncomfortable pressure in my pocket reminded me of the payment that had brought Carl out here. A whole batch of questions hopped into my mind, most of them about how exactly he'd managed to cash a check made out to me that he shouldn't have known about in the first place.

The whole thing stank to high heaven, but I didn't know where to start pulling at it. So I did the only thing I could, which was stand up, open the envelope, and count the money.

A fat wad of bills was waiting for me when I popped the envelope—sealed so recently the glue was still wet—open. There was a lot of money in there, more than I expected. I pulled the cash out and riffed through it. Twenties, fifties, hundreds—there was quite a bit of money in my hands, though that would have been true even if it had been all small bills. I did a fast calculation in my head, got a number that had some round numbers behind it, and whistled. With the house long since paid for, it was enough to live on for a good long while. Good fortune had surely smiled on me, at least in this hour. I hadn't thought my furniture was worth quite so much, but if the insurance company did, who was I to argue. I counted the money again, came up with a number that was slightly larger than the one I'd guesstimated, and started back toward the house. Whistling.

It was only then I remembered the conversation I'd had with the man from the moving company. He'd given me a number. I'd agreed to it. And there was far more than that in my hands.

Insurance companies didn't make mistakes like that, and they sure as hell didn't give you more money than they had said they were going to. Carl, the money, the things I'd been told by that man Douglas—the pieces didn't even start to fit.

I nearly called the police again right then and there, but common sense stopped me. What could I accuse the man of? Giving me money? Driving into my yard to do so? Stealing a car that couldn't move? I'd just get laughed at, and I'd had enough of that already. I put the whole matter aside and went back in the house, stashing the money in a biscuit tin for something approaching safekeeping. There was a pitcher of lemonade in the refrigerator—I'd made it the night before—and so I poured myself a glass and thought about chasing fireflies.

If there was nothing I could do about Carl, I reasoned, I might as well chase the other mystery of the place. So very carefully, I took down one of Mother's old mason jars from a high shelf in the kitchen. I rinsed it to clear out the dust then used an old screwdriver to punch holes in the lid. When night fell, I was ready. Jar in hand, I walked up to the road and my property line.

Here the difference was stark and plain. Out in the road, fireflies danced. On my side of things, they didn't. You could draw the line with a stick in the dirt, and it would be straight and true.

I put the jar down in the driveway and reached my hands out across the line. Slowly I cupped them around a firefly, a poor little fella who was minding its own business in midair. Then, quick as lightning, I snapped my hands shut around it. I could feel it crawling around in there, signaling frantically through the cracks between my fingers.

And, slow as I could, I pulled my hands back to my chest. Would it know, I wondered. What would happen when it crossed the boundary onto my land? I got my answer soon enough. As soon as my cupped hands crossed that line, the light went out and did not return. I could feel the little thing go frantic, ramming against my hand as hard as it could, trying to get back to the road.

I was cruel and didn't let it go. Instead, I held my hands there against my chest for a long minute, until the wiggling stopped. Only then did I open my fingers to find a dead firefly resting on my palm. It made no motion, and its tail lacked the fading glow every child comes to expect. Instead, it just lay there like a thing long dead.

Respectfully, I set it down back in the road. Then I

unscrewed the top of the mason jar. With the empty jar in my hand, I stepped into the road and started catching fireflies.

It was harder than I remembered. When you're a child, you have a knack for these things. Once you get older you forget, or maybe the skill just leaves on its own. In either case, it took me a good half hour to get the dozen fireflies I wanted into the jar, even though the fields were ablaze with them. Maybe they saw what had happened to the other one.

Once the last one went in the jar, I screwed the cap on tight. Inside, the insects flared up like fireworks, one after the other. The light from them was bright enough to read by, or to walk without fear in the dark. One by one they shone out, brighter than even the remembered prizes from when I was a boy. I held them up for a moment, just to see them. They might have been beautiful. I don't know; it's not a word I ever used much.

And then, careful as I could, I set the jar down on the boundary between the county's land and mine. The bottom of the jar barely hit dirt before all the fireflies flew to one side like the other was on fire. There they stayed, crawling all over each other and flashing franticlike, fast on and fast off.

I watched for a while, then nudged the jar a half inch farther onto my land. They crammed closer still, lights flickering on and off fast. Every few seconds one would slip and fall onto the unwanted side. As soon as it hit glass, it would scurry back across like a scalded cat, pushing and forcing its way in with the others until another one fell.

Another half inch. There wasn't space for them all now, and they knew it. One after another they slammed themselves against the glass, against the lid. They tried, wings flapping, legs flailing, but there just wasn't enough room, not any more.

Me, I watched until the losers stopped moving, and the winners barely twitched for fear of being shifted again. "I'm sorry," I told them, and I pulled the jar all the way over my property line.

It didn't take long. Fifteen seconds later, I was pouring dead fireflies onto the ground, out on the road. Not a one recovered like I'd been hoping they would. Not a one moved.

"Goddamn," I said, and I threw the mason jar off into the night. It hit a rock somewhere down the road and shattered, and I found myself hoping Carl would cut a tire on it.

I had proof, now. It wasn't something about the foliage, or the soil, or anything else a scientific mind might have proposed to me. Fireflies hated my land, hated and feared it. If brought onto it, they'd flee. If they couldn't flee, they'd die. But under no circumstances would my parents' graves ever see their light.

The thought started me moving. I didn't believe the story Mother had told me all those years ago, but I did remember lights dancing on those tombstones. They'd flown over this land once, lighting it up so the angels in Mother's mind could see it. Something had changed, had changed hard and unkind, and the only place the answers might be was at the foot of those graves.

Wind whispered through the pine trees as I walked past them. The needles rustled against each other like the sound of Mother's housedress when she walked, soft against the ear. Off at the back end of the property, I could hear the tree frogs calling, high and sharp. Underneath them was the noise of the bullfrogs, deeper and hungrier.

Mother had joked that Father was part bullfrog, especially when he was eating. He stopped finding that funny after a while.

I took the last few steps to where the gravestones were. Mother and Father were the first ones buried on this land, even though it had been in Father's family for generations. My great-grandfather had farmed it, and so had his father before him. Fathers passed it down to sons, living here, marrying, growing old, and dying, but not a one had chosen final rest here. A church ten miles distant held most of my ancestors in its cemetery, though a few could be found in long rows of markers at Chickamauga and the poppy fields of France. That's what I'd been told growing up, and I found no reason to disbelieve it now.

Father chose to be buried here, though, or so I once thought. Years later, I learned it had been Mother's decision to lay him to rest out back, keeping him near so she might not be so lonely. Maybe she'd felt guilty for the way they'd fought when he was alive and wanted to make it right after he was gone. I refused to speculate. All that mattered was that he was here, and that she was laid to rest beside him.

All this ran through my mind as I looked down on their markers in the moonlight. There was enough to read the inscriptions by, though years of heat and summer thunder had long since scoured away the tombstones' shine. "Joshua Jeremiah Logan," said Father's. "Beloved Husband and Father. He Will Be Missed." Mother's read "Elaine Stoudamire Logan, Wife and Mother. Her Soul Rises to Heaven." No dates marked either one. Let the ages try to figure out when they lived and died. Here in this place, they were timeless.

Their graves had been lit by fireflies once, fireflies I'd brushed away sure as I'd killed the ones out in the road. No fireflies lit the graves tonight, though, and if what I'd seen in the mason jar was any indication, they might never light them again.

All around me, the night got still. The wind hushed and the frogs held their tongues. It was silent, quiet enough that I could hear the rasp of my breath and the thump of my heartbeat, and nothing more. I turned and blinked in surprise. Off in the distance I could see the wind moving leaves. Not here, though. The silence was just around me.

And around those graves. I took a step forward, away from that hallowed soil, and then I cast my words out over the fields.

"What do you want?" I asked, in a voice just this side of shouting. *"Just tell me what the hell is going on here!"*

Nothing answered me, not that I'd expected anything or anyone to do so. My words faded into the distance, swallowed up by the silence. I stared after them, and eventually the world came back to noisy life around me. It wasn't much, just the wind in the pine trees and the frogs in the distance, but it was enough to drown out the beating of my heart.

Lacking anything better to do, I lay down on the cool, wet grass at the foot of those graves and slept.

CHAPTER 6

Morning broke and carried away with it the strongest memories of the night's dreams. Some stayed long enough for me to recognize them, though, and I found myself clinging to those fiercely.

They were images from when I was small, before Mother and Father were too tired to hide their fights from me. Saturday morning pancake breakfasts and games of catch out back, afternoons spent helping Mother with her strawberry patch and pushing a hand-powered mower across tough crabgrass and clover.

Good memories, mostly, and pleasant ones. I'd missed those—I hadn't thought about them in too many years.

Right about then I realized I still rested on the ground. A blade of grass was tickling my ear, but otherwise it was as fine a bed as a man could ask for. Stretching out my legs, I decided against getting up quite yet. I could smell the tang of the red clay, sharp and cold and mixed with the sweet scent of the crushed grass underneath my head. The dew off the leaves had soaked through my clothes here and there, but it wasn't uncomfortable so much as it was refreshing. It was as if my skin were drinking it in, taking water directly from the land that had cradled me.

I rolled over and stared straight up at the sky, a swath of true Carolina blue framed by the dark green of the pines. Thin lines of white cloud drifted past, grace notes on the music of the heavens. As for the stones, they hung there just outside my field of view, but I could feel them. There was no heaviness to the knowledge, though, just an awareness of their presence as something right and proper.

And sleeping in their shadow had felt right and proper, too—at least for one night.

I stood and dusted myself off, more out of habit than out of hopes of brushing stray blades of grass off my legs. The rational part of my mind cursed me for a damn fool, but its voice was small and tiny, and I didn't listen to it long.

The lemonade was still on the counter when I walked back into the kitchen, so I poured myself a glass and took a sip. It was warm, of course, and sharp. I was amazed that yellow jackets hadn't found a way to get into it. They, unlike the fireflies, had no problem with the homestead, and there was a nest some-where on the property that had spit out plenty of the damn things every time I wandered around outside. Still, the drink refreshed me, and I found myself feeling stronger than I had in days. Yesterday's problems didn't seem so puzzling. In the light of day, Carl's figure shrank in my mind. He was just an old man trying to do right by his own code, never mind that his code was thirty years out of date. I'd find a way into town today and talk to the police, then maybe get another car. Seeing me on the land clearly pained Carl somehow, so it was just the honorable thing to do, to make sure he didn't have to see me here any more. I'd release him from his promise, whatever it might have been, and we could go our separate ways.

As for the fireflies, they were still a mystery, but one I was willing to live with by the light of day. I wasn't willing to kill any more fireflies to satisfy my curiosity, and they wouldn't give up their secrets. Let them stay away, then, and I'd live without them until the time came for me to move on. After that, they could do what they pleased.

"Moving on." The words sounded strange to my ear that morning, and I felt in no hurry to do that. At first, I'd wanted to stay here two weeks, no more. Now my thought was more of fall. Summer here had always been pleasant, my memories told me, and there was money in my pocket. I could easily stay here through the heat and the long slow days, recovering from Boston at my own pace. Sure enough, it would take me out of the game for a while, but by the end I'd admitted the game was not something I'd ever enjoyed that much. No, it was better to stay here for a few lazy months, sipping lemonade and looking out over the black fields at night.

The door to my parents' bedroom remained resolutely shut as I walked past it and down the hall. For all I knew, it had been shut since the day after Mother's funeral. I had closed that door and walked away, and if Carl had ever opened it, there was no sign. Perhaps today I'd look inside, take possession of it and make it my own.

First, though, I needed a shower and a clean change of clothes. I ducked into my bedroom and rescued the last clean pair of boxers from my travel bag then took a pair of jeans and a shirt to go with them. Socks I'd find later, I decided, after I'd had a chance to walk on the grass barefoot. I'd need to do laundry today, I realized, and that was not something I looked forward to. The washing machine was ancient but serviceable, but the dryer had the look of a fire waiting to happen. Best to hang up a line out back, I decided, and let nature do its part.

The shower refreshed me further, hot water washing the last of the night's worries away. I wouldn't even call Carl for a ride, I decided. I'd walk toward town and hitch, and maybe meet another of my neighbors that way. I needed someone besides Carl to talk to. That much I knew, and hitching a ride seemed as good a way as any to find some conversation. My friends in Boston had mostly melted away when the business did, and no one had called me since I left. I had expected that to continue, even before I'd lost my cell phone in the underbrush. So, if I wanted to hear human voices, I'd have to find them here.

The air dried me off almost as fast as the towel did. It was promising to be a hot day, unseasonably hot, and dry as well. I shrugged into my jeans and buttoned down my shirt, ran a comb through my hair and a brush across my teeth, and pronounced myself fit for human company. I took a pair of socks from my dresser—too small for a grown man, both the clothing and the furniture that held it—and my shoes from the floor, and then I went outside to feel the grass between my toes.

Forty-five minutes went by before I'd had enough of that to declare myself ready to go. Father had always frowned on walking barefoot on the grass, though he loved to do it himself. Snakes worried him, and so did ticks and chiggers and every other biting creature on God's green earth. Mother was more practical, and often talked him into going without shoes so he couldn't caution me when I did, too. The grass was thick and tight, with no bare patches or dandelion stands. Carl had been doing good work, it seemed, and it felt like heaven under my feet.

Enough was finally enough, though, especially if I wanted to make good progress toward town before the day's full heat came up. With one last look down at my toes, I sat on the porch and pulled my socks onto my feet. I wiggled my toes one last time then slipped the tennis shoes on over them. They were scuffed and old, but with the laces pulled tight, they fit my feet well. I'd used them for just about everything except tennis back in Boston, and they'd been the first things I'd packed. They were dirty and worn and softer than cotton, and somehow they belonged here.

I locked the door behind me, a big city habit I suspected I wouldn't be able to break. Fortunately, I'd kept the house keys on a separate chain from the ones for the car, and so they hadn't vanished along with it. Even if they had, I still had the keys Carl had left, but I was just as glad not to need them. I'd tucked them in a kitchen cabinet and fully expected never to need them again.

And so, with the sun coming up over the tree line behind the Tolliver farm, I took the long walk down the drive to the road. When my feet hit gravel, I turned to the right, toward town and all the wonders it might hold. With a last look back at the house—just in case, though I couldn't see the damn door from where I stood—I started walking.

Town had in fact gotten closer since my last visit, moving out into the countryside in bites and chunks. Still, it had mostly advanced on a line that didn't take it straight in my direction. What that meant for me was that my property values had gone up a bit, but that my walk into town stayed long. Best of both worlds, that was the way I figured it, and on a fine morning like the present, I was happy to test myself against the distance.

The town had a name, of course. It was called Maryfield on the maps, but to everyone who lived outside it, it was simply "town." Hell, most of the kids I'd gone to school with, even the ones who lived in town, called it that, too. It was the core of our world, the place we went to see movies and buy baseball cards. In the same way New Yorkers of my acquaintance referred to "the City," it was "town," and that was all that need be said.

Mind you, my upbringing had not been entirely parochial. Father made sure we traveled on occasion, and so I got to see beyond Maryfield's borders. There had been plenty of long car rides: to Memphis, to Washington, to Atlanta, and beyond. Lengthy drives and short visits were most of what I remembered, and being the envy of my classmates when I got back with souvenirs and stories. Those little tastes of life outside might have been the start of it, now that I thought on things. If I hadn't had those moments, I might never have needed more. I might have stayed.

Such were the thoughts I had as I took long strides up the road toward town. It wasn't paved out here, just hard-packed dirt with a thick coating of white gypsum gravel. The road surface didn't change to pavement until you were just outside the limits of the town proper. Once you got onto the gravel, it rattled itself off the undercarriage of your car like bullets spat from an old gun. The gravel sent up dust, too. Get on that stretch of road and a gray cloud rose up behind you like a rooster tail. You could see a car coming a half mile away, easy, and on a clear day even farther.

I saw a cloud just like that boiling up in the distance now, a good ways off. "Carl," I guessed out loud and kept on walking. The remnants of the mason jar lay scattered on the ground to my left. Embarrassed, I swept a few of the larger fragments off the road with my foot as I passed. Everything you do at night is still there come day, I told myself. It was a hard lesson, and one I'd often forgotten, but here was the truth of it sitting out in plain daylight.

The car coming down the road was closer now, though the dust obscured it beyond recognition. I made up my mind not to pay any heed to it, even if it was Carl coming out for some reason of his own. I'd just keep walking, and, to prove my resolve, I edged over to the side of the road, as close to the drainage ditch as I dared.

Another dozen steps and I could hear the sound of tires on gravel and a tired engine growling. It was Carl all right, hunched over his wheel and looking upset. I smiled and waved, and he scowled harder.

The truck skidded to a stop right in front of me, so close a shower of stones bounced off the tips of my shoes. I could see Carl work hard at rolling down his window as I stepped to the side and prepared to walk on past.

"Get in," he said, and he coughed from the dust in the air.

"You're headed the other way," I said brightly. "I'm walking into town, and I wouldn't want to put you out. So, I thank you for the offer, but I feel I must decline." I even raised a finger to my brow in imitation of a salute.

"I'm going back into town," he replied. He swung his door open to block my way. "I'll take you."

I poked my head through the open window. "But you just came out here. I wouldn't want to take you away from whatever business brought you out this way, Carl. So, again I thank you, and I'll get moving now." I sidestepped around the door, making sure not to step in Old Man Tolliver's drainage ditch, and then I started moving again.

Footsteps crunched on gravel behind me and a heavy hand landed on my shoulder. I spun around, half under my own power. "You'll get in the truck," Carl said, "and I'm not taking no for an answer."

I frowned at the hand he still had on me, and after a second it dropped away. "Look, Carl," I said in a much more sober tone, "let's be straightforward here. I don't know what you're up to, but I know you're up to something. As such, I'm not very likely to accept your invitation, however kindly it's meant. The fact that you clearly drove out here just to pick me up and maybe turn around doesn't make my mind any easier about the whole thing. So, let's deal with this like men. You drive back into town, or take care of your business out here. I'll keep walking, and if I find someone else and they're friendly, I'll hitch with them. Otherwise, it's a good walk, the sort Father might have needed back in the day."

I saw him stiffen at that, and the lines of his face tightened. "Now isn't the time to be talking about that sort of thing," he said in a low, sharp voice. "It's a long walk into town, and a longer one back. I just thought I'd save you the trouble."

"Hopefully, I won't be walking back," I said. "If the police can't find my car, I'll need a new one, and I don't think I can wait for the insurance company to settle before I get one."

"The police won't find your car," he said flatly. He climbed back into the cab of his truck. Gravel shot out from beneath the wheels as he did a three-point turn as fast as anyone I'd ever seen. The right corner of his front bumper barely missed knocking me into the ditch, and then he was gone. The truck rumbled off into the distance, leaving me choking on the dust and fumes.

"Now that's interesting," I said as the cloud slowly settled back on to the road. Then I started walking again.

I finally caught a ride about two miles farther on. It was a younger fellow I didn't know who stopped, pulling his pickup over to the side of the road and telling me to climb in back. He'd offer me a seat in the cab, he said, but his dog was sitting there and it had precedence. His face was open and broad, and he had a black sweep-broom mustache underneath a nose someone had broken a couple of times. I decided I liked the man right off, and settled into his cargo bay next to a couple of bags of cement and some ornamental bricks.

We spoke, when the ride wasn't too noisy, through the window in the back of the cab. His name was Samuel, and he'd moved in to town proper a couple of years before Mother died. He'd heard about my house and was interested to see who lived there. It, and Carl, it seemed, had become a local legend. Kids told stories about it, about how it was supposed to be haunted. No one had ever actually seen a ghost, of course, but that didn't stop the talking. The brave ones would drive out there at night in the summer and conduct my experiment with the lightning bugs. That didn't make me feel any better for what I'd done, but it told me the fireflies had been acting strange for a while.

At least, that's what Sam said, and I believed him. There didn't seem to be any reason for him to lie. His dog was a tick hound named Asa, sad-eyed and slow moving. It just sat in that front seat and watched me all the way in. It was a well-trained dog. It never made a sound the whole time we rode together.

When we finally hit town, Sam—he said he preferred it to his given name—pulled over in front of the police station and let me hop out. "If you ever need another ride, you can call me," he said, and then he drove off. I realized after the fact that he hadn't given me a last name or a number. Calling him would be difficult if I had the need. Then again, I was in town to make sure I didn't need to make that call, or any others I didn't want to make. I turned to the building and made my way inside.

I had only vague memories of the police station from my youth, but what I saw before me matched them pretty well. The building was two stories tall and made of brick, with a sign over the doorway that proudly announced that this was in fact the home of law and order in our town. There had been three policemen back in the day—one for day shift, one for night, and one to serve as backup whenever and make sure anyone in the holding cell didn't get too cute. Crime pretty much consisted of domestic disturbances, drunk and disorderlies, and the occasional kid busted for shoplifting bubble gum and a Coke.

I hoped, as I pushed my way past the heavy wood doors, that not much had changed.

The first thing I saw when I stepped in was a heavy woman sitting behind a heavy wood desk. She looked up at me the way a cat looks up at a squirrel on a too-high branch: like I might be interesting if I moved a little closer.

"Morning," I said, taking those steps. "I called in yesterday about a stolen car, and I was wondering if I could talk to somebody about it."

"Hang on one moment, honey," she said, and she started riffing through the thick piles of paper on her desk. Behind her were a few other desks, mostly unoccupied, and an office door with a nameplate that read "Chief Harper." The whole place was painted pink for no reason I could understand, though there was still some good hardwood molding up here and there.

The woman caught me looking at the walls over her shoulder. "It got painted that color ten years ago. Some state study said that pink was a calming color and it would help make felons less violent. What they forgot to mention was that it would drive the rest of us nuts, and there's no money in the budget to repaint it for another five years. Until then, you've never seen so many policemen trying to get back to walking a beat." She laughed, the sort of cackle we used to call a witch laugh when I'd been growing up. The few policemen working at their desks looked over at her then shrugged and went back to whatever it was they were doing. Several had computers on their desks, I noted. Progress reaches everywhere, or so it seemed.

"Here it is, sugar," she said after the echoes of her laugh died away. She opened the file on her desk, and a meaty finger traced down the scribbles of writing. "One car, stolen from the old Logan place yesterday morning. Mr. Logan—and I assume that you are the Mr. Logan in question—called in to report a 2006 Audi missing. Audi. We don't get many of them around here." She leaned forward, her voice dropping to a conspiratorial whisper. "Between you and me, I don't think it was stolen for parts."

"I don't really care much what it was stolen for," I said, "so long as I get it back. Can you tell me whom I need to talk to, Miss. . . ." I let my voice trail away.

"*Officer* Hanratty," she corrected me. She extended her hand to shake. I took it. Her grip was strong, though she stopped short of actually trying to crush my fingers to peanut butter. "And you talk to me. The rest of them would just figure it for a joyride and start asking around the high school cafeteria. Which, come to think of it, ain't all that unlikely. A pretty little car like that would have been one heck of a temptation."

"It would have been one heck of a walk," I retorted. "You don't get out to my place by walking, and I didn't hear another car out there."

"Your place," she said. Her eyes got a little wider. "Interesting. Tell you what. Why don't we do this properly? You pull up a chair and I'll take a statement all policelike, and then you can pretend like you're back in the big city." She threw a glance over her shoulder that could have cut steel. "Seriously, I heard what they told you over the phone. We don't all do things like that, you know."

"I appreciate that." There were two chairs near the entrance. I hooked one with my foot and dragged it over then sat myself down. It creaked a bit, but that was all. I looked around. "Should I be sitting here like this? I mean, I might block the entrance."

Officer Hanratty laughed again. "Don't you worry about that. Nobody who comes in here gets past me unless I say so, and if we need to get out, well, you'll be the first one running."

I grinned along with her. It was hard not to. She saw my smile and nodded. "Good. Now you're in the mood, let's talk about your car. When did you last see it?"

"The evening of the twelfth, just before bed. I'd tried to start it to go into town that morning—well, that afternoon, really—and it didn't even turn over. So I got out and went inside. I called Carl Powell to see if he'd give me a ride into town. Instead, he brought some groceries out to me. We talked a bit, and then he left. The car just sat there until night, and when I got up in the morning, it was gone."

"Uh-huh." Officer Hanratty nibbled on the end of her pencil. "And you say you didn't hear a thing during the night?"

I nodded. "No footsteps, no engine sounds, no voices. I've been up late anyway, keeping . . . an eye on things. Getting used to the place again. It would have been hard to sneak onto the property. And in the morning, after the car was gone, I checked around where I'd parked it. There weren't any footprints and no broken glass. No tracks from another car or a tow truck, either."

"Interesting." She leaned back in her chair, and it made a weary sound. "So what do you think happened to it?"

I shrugged. "I don't know. It wouldn't start when I tried it, wouldn't so much as cough. I can't see anyone driving it off, even if I did leave the keys in it." As I said that, I could see her wince.

"You did what?"

"I left the keys in. Locked, of course. It's one of the reasons I called Carl for a ride into town. I wanted to see if there was anyone around here who did AAA and who could let me back in." Even as I said it, I knew it sounded hollow. Still, there was no reason to admit I'd just been plain steamed and had locked the keys in by accident. That would make me look like even more of a damn fool in front of this woman, and from what I had seen, she did not suffer fools of any kind gladly.

"That complicates things," she said, shuffling a few papers on her desk. "I take it no one's been out to your place to take a look at things?"

"No," I replied bitterly. "Wouldn't do any good, anyway. Five minutes after I hung up with your people, Carl Powell came screeching up in his truck. Parked in the exact spot where my car had been. Between his coming in and pulling out, he pretty much wiped out whatever might have been there. Like I said, there wasn't anything on the ground that I could see, but maybe your people could have spotted something."

A cup of coffee appeared from somewhere, a mug marked with hand-painted letters that declared the owner's undying love for the late Intimidator. She took a sip, made a face, and put it down. "Any idea why Carl was out there to see you?"

I licked my lips, well aware it made me look like I was hiding something. "You're not going to believe this, but he mentioned he'd heard I'd had my car stolen."

"Oh did he, now?" She leaned forward, her bulk making the desk creak ever so slightly. "And did he say how he'd heard about that?"

"He didn't." I couldn't keep all the bitterness out of my voice. "Pardon me for making a guess here, but he almost sounded like he was rubbing my nose in it."

Hanratty took another sip of coffee, slow and measured this time. "Mr. Logan, a word of advice. Carl Powell's better liked around these parts than you are. You might want to keep comments like that to yourself, at least for the time being." She looked left, then right. "Some around here might even say you deserve to have your nose rubbed in things, just a little bit."

"Oh, might they?" I got up out of my chair. "So you're saying that I deserved this, and Carl can get away with it just because he's got some friends?"

"Keep your voice down and put your ass back in that chair," she said affably. "I'm saying that you've been away a long time, and you seem to have forgotten the way this town works. Now, before you go getting yourself too worked up and make yourself more enemies, why don't you tell me what happened when Carl came to visit you, and then I can get to work on this?"

It was phrased politely, but there was no mistaking the iron behind her words. I sat myself down, breathing hard. I could tell my face was flushed. The comment about having forgotten how this town worked stung far more than I wanted to admit. I'd adapted to city life pretty well, I thought. I'd made myself into something of an urbanite, even if some of my friends up north had thought it funny to call me "Country Mouse" on occasion. I thought I was able to deal with pretty much any situation calmly and well. Now, to come back here and be told that the town I'd left behind moved to rhythms too complicated for me to figure right off, well, it got my dander up.

Letting my temper show wasn't going to get me anywhere, though, at least not there and then. I took a deep breath, swallowed, and knotted my fingers together like I used to do in church. "Carl came out to deliver my mail," I said in slow, even tones. "I admit I yelled at him about where he'd parked, and we talked about what had happened to my car."

"Talked?" She quirked one eyebrow and smiled at me in a good imitation of a child asked about the whereabouts of a plate of missing shortbread. "Is that what you did?"

"I didn't accuse him of stealing my car, no, though it did get a bit heated." I shook my head to clear it. "Then he got back in his truck and drove off."

Hanratty made notes on some papers in front of her. "That's all I need to know for now, but I'll probably need to ask you some follow-up questions. I take it you gave the officers on the phone a description of the missing vehicle?"

I nodded. "Silver Audi A6, Massachusetts plate TMB-324. Just in case they misplaced it." She wrote the information down with a grunt that might have been approval. "It still had half my stuff in there, too."

"I'm sorry to hear that." Hanratty sounded singularly unsorry, at that. "I assume you didn't have your furniture in the car?"

"Nope." I grinned without smiling. "That was all on a moving truck."

"Was?"

"Was. It got in an accident up in Baltimore, and everything on board the truck was damaged beyond repair. The moving company settled." I shifted in my chair. "So with the car missing, all I've got in this world is what's in that house."

Hanratty harrumphed and scribbled something on her paper. "There are worse fates." A meaty hand plucked the form she'd been marking up off her desk and waved it in the air. "I'll need you to sign this. Look it over first, if you like."

"I'd like," I said, and I took the paper from her hand. It was my statement, more or less accurately written down. I pulled a pen from my pocket and scribbled my name on the bottom.

"Thanks," she said as I handed it back to her. "I'll look into this myself. In the meantime, you might want to go back out to the farm and wait for some news. I'll call you when I have anything."

Shoving the chair back, I stood. "Thank you," I told her. "I'm actually going to try to find myself another car in the meantime, I think."

Hanratty snorted with laughter. "Good luck. There's no car dealer, new or used, for twenty miles. You probably want to go back to your house and make a few calls, see if a dealer's willing to pick you up to bring you out. Either that or try shopping on the internet. I hear people buy cars that way sometimes up in the big city."

"My laptop was in the car," I said, mainly to cover the

sinking feeling in my gut. "If you want, I can come up with a list of what else I lost."

"That might be a good idea," she said neutrally. "Do you have a ride home?"

I shook my head. "Nope."

She smiled like a mean old porch cat. "Then I guess you'd better start walking."

CHAPTER 7

I did walk then, all the way back to my front door. Anger fueled me for the first few miles, but after a while that faded and just left me with a long, slow road. A few cars passed me—a very few, truth be told—but none of them slowed. I saw curious faces looking out through their windows, but that was all. I thought I recognized one or two, but I couldn't be sure. It had, like the woman said, been a long time.

The first part of the walk was easy enough. Some smart man in Raleigh had designated the stretch of road out of town a state highway. Near as I could tell, that meant that it got paved every so often in order to keep some construction company or other working. Still, it made my walk easier, at least for a while. Eventually, the pavement went away and the road turned to white stone gravel. The houses that lined the road grew farther apart; the fields more frequent and larger. There were stands of trees I walked past large enough to hide a small army or a herd of deer, and more than once I startled a covey of birds into exploding into the sky. It was nice enough to look at, I thought, but a trifle dull. After an hour and a half of heat and dust, I was even ready for Carl to pull up next to me and order me to get in. No such luck, though. It was just me and the road.

As I walked, I reflected on my conversation with Officer Hanratty. There were things I had left out of my story and I wasn't sure why, for they surely didn't paint Carl in a good light. The envelope full of money, for one thing, and the fact that he'd opened my mail, for another. I'd left the fight, if you could call it that, out as well, but that was a bit more understandable. You don't want to tell a police officer that you attempted to assault the man you think stole your car. You especially don't want to tell a police officer that the old man in question kicked your ass when you tried.

Officer Hanratty herself confused me. At times she'd seemed almost friendly, like she and I shared some kind of special view on the rest of the town. Other times, she'd been as tight with the old-timers as I could imagine anyone being. There had been an implied threat there at one point, and a sense that she knew more about things than she was telling. Had she talked to Carl already? I couldn't rule it out, and I had no way of knowing what he might have said. It was a lead-pipe cinch, though, that anything Carl said would be believed over anything I said. Carl was *from* here, after all. I was the boy who went away.

The fact that she made me walk back to the house angered me as well. Whatever the good law enforcement officers back in town might think, I wasn't some spoiled city boy who expected the police to drop everything to ferry me back home. I had not expected Officer Hanratty to give me a ride back to the farm, even though it would have been the work of minutes for her to do so. But the unrestrained glee when she told me I'd be walking, well, that was something else again. The woman could have at least called me a cab, assuming there were any cabs to be had, or sent me out with an officer who could at least pretend to look at the site. Maybe she, too, was trying to teach me something about the town I'd come back to. If so, she'd done a piss-poor job. All I knew was what the sights along one particular road looked like these days. Hell, I hadn't even bothered to walk around town.

Still, some aspects of the conversation did cheer me slightly. If this was just Carl—or one of Carl's friends—trying to put me in my place, then I had every reason to believe that the car would reappear soon. I didn't hold out much hope for recovering the contents, but they were all insured. So was the car, and I chuckled to think about Carl trying to provide cash for *that* particular transaction. The image of the old man walking up to my porch with another envelope stuffed with twenties was enough to make me laugh out loud, and it sped my steps as I headed back down that dusty stretch.

My knees ached and my feet burned by the time I made the turn from the road to my driveway. I'd belonged to a gym in Boston—I got more business done there than at the office—but there's a world of difference between running on a treadmill and walking down a country road. For one thing, on the treadmill you know you're doing it to yourself. If you want it to stop, all you have to do is hit the switch and walk away. The only thing keeping you on there is pride. Well, pride and the fear of doing less time than the man on the treadmill next to you. Out here, though, deciding that I'd had enough just wasn't an option. If I didn't want to walk any more, that was fine, but I'd be sitting on the side of the road until I felt like walking again.

Therefore, it was with visions of a cool bath to soak my feet in, and a tall glass of lemonade, that I turned my face toward the house. The driveway was empty, which I expected. Even if Hanratty had decided the joke had gone far enough, and called whoever had stolen the car to return it, there was no way they could have driven it past me to get it to the house. More likely it would take a few days to let Hanratty save face and make it look like she was working on things.

My heart skipped a beat, though, when I saw there was a package on the porch. From where I stood at the end of the driveway, I couldn't make out many details. Brown paper, yes, and about the size of a loaf of bread. That was all I could see at a first glance.

"Just a package," I said out loud, daring someone to contradict me. Silence was my response. I felt a fool being suddenly uptight over a box, but with all that had gone on, anything out of the ordinary was enough to get my pulse racing. I hadn't ordered anything, nor did I have any friends or family who were likely to send me something unannounced. That left suspicion and fear to argue it out over where that package might have come from, and neither of them had any answers I liked.

On the other hand, I was tired and my feet hurt, enough so that I didn't really give a good goddamn. I looked around to see if anyone was there, and I didn't see anything else out of the ordinary. No windows were broken, no doors were left ajar, and no one had done any fool thing like paint a warning on the side of the house. Nope, it was just a box in brown paper, sitting on the porch like it was the most natural thing in the world. Which, in hindsight, I had to admit it was.

One last glance over my shoulder told me that there was no dust plume on the road, and no Carl coming up behind me. "Well, screw it," I told myself, and I walked forward. It was only a box. That was all. It probably had mail-order fruit or AOL discs or something equally worthless inside.

But my breath still caught in my throat when I went up those porch steps, and my hand shook when I knelt down to pick up the box. It sat there, unadorned with any stamps or postage. There was no return address on it, just my name scrawled in big black letters. Magic marker, it looked like, and poor handwriting to boot. The box was wrapped in brown paper and tied off with string. Ragged bits of tape sealed the ends and folded over onto themselves. It looked harmless enough, and I nearly opened it right then and there.

My hand was halfway to the box when I reconsidered and pulled myself back. It was probably nothing. I knew that. It was just a box. I knew that, too. But something made me leave it there on the porch and go into the house instead. It took a minute's hunting on the kitchen table, but I found myself a pencil and brought it back out with me. Slowly, I slid the pencil, eraser-end first, under the string. Just as slow, I lifted it up, dangling it ever so delicately as I stepped off the porch and backed into the kitchen. I could see the pencil bending under the strain; that box was heavy for its size. My wrist ached to hold it, and my steps got a bit faster. A turn to the left and I was facing the sink. That's where I put the package, thankful that the sink basin was dry.

The whole time I was moving it, the box failed to rattle,

buzz, or explode. For that, I was deeply grateful, but I knew better than to push my luck. I briefly considered running tap water over the thing, like I'd seen in a movie. That notion only lasted a moment, though. The odds of it being paper or something else that would get soggy were a lot better than the odds of it being something dangerous. Instead, I went to the kitchen counter and got out a good, sharp knife from the block. Knife in hand, I turned to the sink and addressed my problem.

The string was humped up in the place where the pencil had been. Gingerly, I sliced through that spot. Nothing happened, except the twine broke neatly into two pieces.

"You're a paranoid dumbass," I informed myself, and I tugged the string away. It slithered out from under the box and dangled from my finger. Nothing but package string, the same as you'd get at a butcher or use for flying a homemade kite. It was clean and new. There was no dirt or fraying to it, and no smell. In other words, it told me nothing, except that whoever had wrapped the package had done it not too long ago. Nodding at my own perceptiveness, I put the string down on the counter and turned my attention to the box itself.

I stared at it for a moment. Then I tucked the point of the knife under one of the corners where the tape came up. A little shove and the knife went through the paper. Then, carefully, I sawed along the line of the box edge, cutting the paper as I went. When I'd made it all the way across the top, I turned it and did the same down the short side. The knife caught in a couple of places on particularly thick layers of tape, but a moment's patient back-and-forth with the edge cut through even that easy enough.

With half the paper on the top flapping free, I put the knife down and lifted the corner up. Underneath was an old cardboard box. It smelled musty and looked frail, and I found myself reluctant to tear away the rest of the paper for fear the whole thing would just fall apart.

I settled for pulling the stuff on the sides away, then sliding the rest out from under the bottom. Whoever had wrapped the box hadn't been too interested in being neat. They had just swaddled that thing in paper and tape as best they could, probably to keep it from spilling its cardboard guts when they set it down.

The top of the box was a flap that ran lengthwise. An old piece of scotch tape, long since gone yellow, held it shut. The knife took care of that. That left opening the lid.

I looked around. Most of the day had gone, and shadows crept across the kitchen. Outside, birds made their evening calls, getting ready to bed down for the night.

Night. I definitely did not want the mystery of what the box had in it gnawing at me all night. Sleep was hard enough to come by, without adding another round of "what-ifs" to keep me restless and pondering. Bare-handed, I leaned forward and flipped the lid open.

I don't know what I expected. Maybe I'd seen too many bad movies. Even as that lid came up, I thought I might see, I don't know, maybe a dead animal. Maybe some kind of threat, or a piece of my Audi someone had hacked off. Maybe a body part from someone I knew, though I wasn't sure what good that might have done.

Instead, there were toy soldiers. They were the good kind,

too—molded lead with broad, flat bases and the sorts of guns that someone would call a "choking hazard" today. Their paint jobs were chipped, scarred, and dented from a thousand hours of play, but I still recognized them. Red for Wellington's British, blue for Napoleon's French—I'd seen these before. Slowly and with reverence, I took the first one out of the box and turned it over.

There, on the bottom, someone had carved three letters.

J. J. L. So small you could hardly read them, but still there. Still telling the world who these had belonged to, once upon a time.

Joshua Jeremiah Logan. Father. And after him, they'd belonged to me.

I'd spent more hours than I could count fighting old wars in the backyard. I'd send the French advancing past Mother's roses, or line up the British to guard the edge of the driveway. I'd built and smashed a hundred dirt forts, buried a thousand toy casualties and dug them right back up again. They'd been my companions and friends through some long summer days, and when I thought about my childhood, I often thought of them.

Father took them away from me when I was nine. There'd been a fight with one of my playmates from school over one of our pretend battles, and a couple of the precious soldiers got thrown. None of them hit anyone and nobody got hurt, but that was enough for Father. He came storming out of the house like the wrath of God, his eyes shooting lightning and his face dark as thunderclouds.

"If you cannot treat these properly," he'd said in a voice just this side of a shout, "you cannot have them to play with. Do I make myself understood?" Without another word, he scooped them all up, even the ones we'd thrown at each other in anger, then took them all inside. I stood there, tears leaking down my cheeks, and stared into the house. Mother didn't come and help me, though. As for my friend—one of the Jericho boys from in town, I do believe—he just watched the whole thing with his mouth curled into a big wide **O**.

He made his excuses and called his momma for a ride home not long after that, I recall.

As for the soldiers, Father put them in a big, long cardboard box and carried them off to the attic. That's where they went and that's where they stayed, and he never did get around to bringing them back down again.

All except one.

As Father stomped his way around the yard, I moved my foot to cover one of the fallen men. I stood there stock-still and hoping he wouldn't count. There were twenty men on each side, just enough for a good battle, and just enough that a missing soldier could go unnoticed.

I held my ground there in the yard as Father packed the rest of them away and carried them off to the attic. I prayed I hadn't broken him, or bent the tip of his gun. And when Father was at last out of sight, I bent down and, quick as a cat, scooped my lone soldier into my pocket. I didn't let him out until I got to my room and slammed the door, and then I hid him on the floor of my closet, behind a big pile of comic books that both Mother and Father knew not to touch. He was my talisman, my good luck charm, and for years I'd carried him with me whenever I could. Even in high school, sometimes, I'd tuck him in a pocket. My lone British soldier, come along for luck.

I held the soldier from the box up to the fading light and admired it. Stamped lead it might have been, but there was a craftsmanship to it, an attention to detail that caught the breath in my throat. No wonder Father had been so protective. They'd meant as much to him as to me.

And just as suddenly as that realization came, a dark suspicion flew in on its heels. Forty soldiers. Twenty on a side. And one gone with me to Boston.

I grabbed the box from the sink and hauled it over to the kitchen table. It hit the Formica with a dull jingle, as the soldiers jostled against each other. Father would have been mighty steamed, but I didn't care. There was something I had to know.

One French soldier was in my hand. I set it down on the table. That was one. I reached into the box and pulled out a fistful of his comrades. They spilled out of my hand and I separated them by allegiance—three red, two blue.

Six.

Another fistful; five more Brits this time.

Eleven.

The next handful caught only two, one of each.

Thirteen. Unlucky number. I winced and took out a double handful to make up for it.

Eleven more. It brought the tally up to twenty-four, and the box was still about half full.

Four in the next handful—all French. One had a big strip of missing paint down the center of his back, and I promised myself that if I found time, I'd do something about it. Not now, though.

Twenty-eight.

Five more soldiers spilled out. Thirty-three. The box was getting empty. The table, on the other hand, was getting crowded. I reached into the box, more careful this time.

Three more. Two French, one English. I set them down carefully with their respective sides. My hand went into the box again. I didn't dare look.

Three more again, but this time with their sides switched.

Thirty-nine. Twenty on the French side, nineteen on the British.

One was missing, like it ought to be.

One soldier had been my good luck charm. I'd taken it with me to Boston to serve as my luck there. When I got a car, I looped string around it and hung it from the rearview mirror. Every time I'd traded in or traded up, I took that soldier with me.

The last time I'd seen it, it had been hanging from the rearview mirror in the Audi.

I took a deep breath.

Put my hand in the box. Felt around.

My fingers closed on a toy soldier.

At midnight I was still sitting at the table with the toy soldiers in front of me. I'd arranged them half a dozen times, and now they stood in four ranks of five, each side facing the other like they were getting ready to fight Waterloo all over again. The box sat behind them, guarding their rear against surprise attacks. Who knew? Maybe my old Barrel of Monkeys would appear next to upset the balance of power.

There was no electric light on anywhere in the house. I hadn't gotten up to turn on the switch, and so everything was as dark as the look in my eye. A little moonlight came through the windows, but it didn't stay long enough to illuminate much of anything. I hadn't even bothered to shut the door behind me. Now it swung back and forth in the breeze, creaking every so often when it thought I wasn't paying enough attention to it.

There were facts here—facts I didn't like putting together. Fact number one was that those tin soldiers had been in the attic since long before I left this house. Fact number two was that only one man besides me had held the key to this house since my Mother had passed on, never mind that he'd been told not to go up in the attic. Fact number three was that one of the soldiers had been in my car the last time I'd seen it. Fact number four was the increasingly irritating knowledge that my car had disappeared in the recent past. And fact number five was that Carl knew for sure I had been out of the house today.

Now, a logical man could take those five facts and make something of them. He could say, well, the man who had the key would be the only one who could have gotten the toy soldiers. That would also make that man a prime suspect in the disappearance of the car, since he'd gotten that last soldier from the missing vehicle. Knowing I was in town would have given Carl plenty of time to leave the box behind, easy as pie. And if Carl was up for theft and trespassing, he was up for going—unwanted—into the attic as well.

The more I thought about it, the more red rage boiled up in my gut. It all made sense, too much goddamn sense to ignore. More pieces started fitting the puzzle, and when they wouldn't quite fit, I jammed them in anyway. Maybe Samuel was one of Carl's friends, sent to drive me into town so I wouldn't make it back to the house any time soon. Maybe that was why Officer Hanratty had made me walk back, to buy Carl the time he needed. Maybe the whole town was against me, the outsider, the boy who went away. Maybe that's what this was about, and the toy soldiers were a subtle way of letting me know it.

Well, the hell with the town, I decided. The hell with all of them. If they didn't like me because I'd gone away, well that was too damn bad for them. I wasn't going to be driven out or made to feel the fool by any damn thing they could do. If they wanted to alternate Christmas presents with grand theft auto, that was just fine. I wasn't budging until I decided it was time to go, and that would be on my timetable, not Carl's. And when I left, I'd find a new caretaker, too. The thought of him anywhere near my parents' marriage bed had started to give me shivers, him with his too-possessive attitude on Mother.

And that got me thinking about how much time he had needed, and what he might have needed it for. "Don't be stupid," I told myself. "He returned the key. There's no way he could have gotten in and done anything. You're being a fool."

Mind you, that's just when I had to go remind myself that he could have made a copy of that key any time in the past ten years. Just because he'd given me one key to this house didn't mean he'd given up all of them.

The wind got real cold then, and blew in through the open door like it knew where it was going. Without saying another word, I got up from my chair and shut the door. Then I turned the deadbolt lock and hooked the chain.

He wasn't here. With every thinking atom in my body, I knew that. But my gut didn't listen to the bits that did the thinking, and they were screaming at me to unlatch that door and run.

Instead, I turned on the light. The kitchen suddenly seemed too bright and too ordinary. White counters were empty and the white floor was swept clean. On the table, the soldiers suddenly looked scuffed and old. The cardboard box they came in seemed to be about to collapse.

Cursing myself for a coward, I picked up the knife I'd used to open the package and moved deeper into the house. Every light switch I passed, I flicked on. The rooms got smaller in the light, got older and shabbier and less frightening.

Mother and Father's bedroom I saved for last. With every light in the house blazing and a knife in my off hand, I pushed the door open. Light spilled in from behind me, revealing a perfectly plain rectangle of wooden floor. The rest of the room was hidden in darkness.

I felt along the wall for the light switch, found it, and flicked it on. The light fixture overhead flickered to life. Half the bulbs were burned out, but there were enough remaining to paint the room with a yellow glow. I took a cautious step in and looked around.

The far wall was dominated by an ancient chest of drawers that had been in Mother's family since time out of mind.

The drawers were empty now, I knew, but her collection of knickknacks still rested on top. A small parade of porcelain figures, most of them some kind of dog or other, sat there and waited under a fine film of dust. To the left was Father's rocking chair, dark wood painted with black lacquer. It had worn away in places, the mark of his hands still here long after he was gone.

But the biggest thing in the room was the bed. It had been a present to my parents from my father's father, a big four-poster with a canopy. Night tables flanked it on either side. On the right side, the table was bare. That's where Father slept. The other side was Mother's, and her table had a washbasin on it. For a moment it looked like there was actually water in there, and my nerves jangled bad enough that I needed to look twice.

Mother loved that bed. Father had often joked that it was her oldest child, and I remembered half-thinking he was serious. I could see the polished oak of the columns, still standing straight and tall despite years of neglect. The canopy was there, too, and the bed was made up with Mother's favorite quilt. Fluffed-up pillows rested at the head of the bed, two on each side.

It all looked freshly made up, and I knew I hadn't been the one to do the making. With a frown, I ran a finger along the edge of Father's night table. Only a little dust came away with my touch. There should have been more, much more. Someone had been in my parents' bedroom. I could guess who, and the thought didn't make me happy.

Again, the washbasin caught my eye. I took a slow walk

around the foot of the bed, my feet landing soft on the Persian rug Mother had been so proud of. Mother's night table didn't have any real dust on it, either. Still frowning, I turned and looked at the bed.

From here, I could see a shadow. On Mother's side of the bed, there was an indentation, a place where a body had been. With my empty hand, I reached out toward it, but then I pulled away. *Let it stay there for the police,* I thought. *Let Carl try to drive his truck over that.*

Shoulders tight, I turned and walked back out. I moved the knife from hand to hand and put my left hand on the light switch. One last time, I turned and looked over my shoulder.

For an instant, I though I saw a second indentation on the bed, next to the first. Then the lights came down, and I shut the door behind me.

CHAPTER 8

The rain started an hour before dawn; fat drops drumming on the roof like soldiers marching. I lay awake in my bed and listened to them. The sound of the storm didn't bring back any childhood memories. It didn't bring with it anything at all.

By seven, I stopped trying to fool myself about the possibility of getting any sleep and rousted myself out of bed. The floor was cold, which was a change, and for that matter, so was the rest of the house. It felt as though twenty degrees had gone wandering off somewhere during the night, and maybe taken another ten with them. *Must have been the rain that did it*, I thought, and I shuffled off to the bathroom.

The bathroom floor was wet, which I discovered by nearly falling on my ass when I set foot inside. Idiot that I was, I'd left the window open the night before. The wind had taken advantage of the opportunity, blowing the rain straight through the screen and onto the tile. The bathmat, scraggly old thing that it was, had soaked through, so I balled it up and tossed it into the tub to drain out a bit. It hit the porcelain with a wet slap, and I went to close the window.

It wouldn't budge. I tried harder, grunting with the effort, but no dice. The window wouldn't move for me no matter how hard I shoved.

I took a step back and looked closely at the problem. Near as I could tell, the rain had made the wood of the window swell up, so all I'd accomplish by tugging on it would be splintering things that ought not be splintered. Best to wait, then, for the rain to stop and the humidity to go down, or so I decided. Then I'd be able to close the window. But for now, I'd have to settle for pulling the curtains across and letting them catch the brunt of the storm, then waiting for things to dry out later.

A couple of steps on the wet floor brought me right up close to the window, and I shivered. The rain blowing through the screen was cold, and it splattered on my chest with each gust of wind. The air was chilly, too, with a nasty bite to it. I marveled that I hadn't felt the temperature drop during the night, and I wondered how the animals outside were handling it. Probably better than I was, I decided, and I pulled the curtains closed. They were a cheerful sort of yellow, a bright shade I'd always hated. Mother had made them, though, so I never said a word. Up they went and up they stayed, and that was the end of it. I was pleased, however, to see the fabric start to darken immediately with the impact of the first few raindrops. Even as I watched, streaks of a deeper gold ran through them, ultimately joining together to paint the curtains altogether.

It wasn't doing much to keep the water out, but I liked the way it looked a hell of a lot better.

Another gust of wind shoved the curtains aside for a moment and reminded me of how damn cold it had gotten all over again. That was enough to convince me that I could wait to take a shower until things warmed up a bit. It also told me that I needed to get out from in front of the window. That wind was fierce, and the raindrops had started hitting with the force of cold needles.

I grabbed the toothbrush and did a quick swipe across my teeth that didn't fool anybody, then turned and wandered back to my bedroom. My bathrobe—too short, and frayed at the elbows—hung on a hook on the back of the door. I tugged it down and wrapped it around myself, double-knotting the belt to keep the robe tightly shut. It was some kind of plaid that was best described as plain old ugly—red and black lines criss-crossing on a white background—and it fit my mood perfectly. Thus fortified against the temperature, I jammed my feet into slippers that hadn't fit properly since I was fourteen and made my way into the kitchen.

The rain beat against the windows of the porch door as I made myself a cup of coffee and heated the iron skillet in preparation for making a couple of eggs. There were a couple of sausage patties left in the fridge, so I threw them in the pan as well and went looking for some bread to soak up the grease with. Looking in the icebox had been sobering, though. Despite Carl's odd generosity, there wasn't that much left in there. One way or another I'd need to get more supplies soon. Food, yes, but I was running out of other things as well, toothpaste and the like.

And lest I forget, there was the little matter of a stolen car to deal with.

I looked at the clock over the sink. It read seven thirty. Damn. Too early to call the insurance company. With a frown for the phone, I grabbed a spatula and moved the sausage around in the skillet, then cracked a couple of eggs and let them fry up proper. The bread, of course, was right next to the stove, so I undid the tie and pulled out a piece. It was wheat bread, Mother's favorite back in the day. Father bought white bread and usually got scolded for it.

Once again I thought about Carl and whatever odd feelings he might have had for Mother. It was unhealthy, I decided. Unhealthy was the right word for it. He was holding tighter to the torch of her memory than I was, and I was her own flesh and blood. Next time I saw him, I'd have to talk with him about that.

That was, of course, assuming that I didn't just haul off and belt him instead.

I stopped thinking about that long enough to drop the bread into the pan, where it immediately started absorbing the grease and turning itself a nice shade of golden brown. I watched it for a while, then flipped the bread and slapped the eggs on top of it. The sausage kept sizzling off to the side, which was just fine as far as I was concerned.

Leaning over the skillet, I told the sausage that you can't do right by a busy day without a good breakfast. It gave no sign of believing me, but it did keep crisping up nicely, which I took as a good sign. And it was going to be a busy day. That much I'd already decided. I'd call the insurance folks and the police department. I'd explore the house a bit further—maybe go up to the attic to see what the footprints in the dust up there might tell me. And I'd make a call back to Boston to see if I could maybe get myself some reinforcements. Maybe I was letting myself get spooked too easily, but I was starting to get the sense I'd need someone else lined up on my side.

The smell of breakfast hit my nostrils just then, along with the scent of the coffee, and they drove any other thoughts out of my mind. I slopped the skillet contents onto a plate and killed the heat, then poured myself a cup of coffee. It came out as black as my mood had been last night, which was about all I could hope for at this hour of the morning. Setting the plate and mug down on the table, I got myself a fork and sat down to eat.

It was a fine little meal, and for a moment I almost forgot about everything else that was going on. The egg yolk dripped down into the toast and mixed with the grease from the sausage to give it taste that was just short of heaven, and the coffee was strong enough to kick down a door. In short, it was just what I needed, and I ate like a condemned man who knows the rope's waiting for him in an hour or so.

A harsh rattle broke my concentration, and I looked up. The wind was whipping raindrops hard against the glass of the kitchen windows. Both the glass panes on the porch side and the windows along the side facing the road were taking some kind of pounding. The rain hit hard then slid down the glass in thick sheets. Looking through those windows was like looking into a funhouse mirror. Everything I saw was distorted by the water as it found its way down, and old familiar sights were suddenly new and strange.

The more I thought about that, the less I liked it, so I pulled the shade down on the door and went back to my breakfast. The house was silent, except for the sound of my knife and fork on the plate and the beating of the rain trying to get in. No voices, no music, no babble. It was something a man could get used to, if he didn't have other things to do with his life.

I sighed, thinking of the cell phone I'd never bothered to find in the tall grass. Finding it now wouldn't do me any damn good, unless I needed an odd-shaped pie weight one of these days. That, I figured, was highly unlikely, so I wrote it off as another of the week's losses. They'd certainly added up. No more, though. I'd had enough.

When I finished, I put the dishes in the sink. There'd be plenty of time to do them later, since going out wasn't looking like much of an option. Instead, I turned back to the table and gently laid the soldiers, one by one, back in their boxes. "Apologies for doing this to you, gents," I told them when the last one was securely packed away. "But I'd rather get you out of harm's way. Or at least, out of the kitchen." Then I took the box, and, cradling it in my arms like it might either explode or start crying, I took it back to my bedroom. There I tucked it into a dresser drawer, safe and sound and hidden under old clothes that no one would ever need to disturb again.

"There we go," I announced. "Nobody's going to be pulling you fellas out of *there*." At this point, it occurred to me that most of the conversations I'd had recently had been either with inanimate objects or with myself, and that wasn't a good sign. It was time to maybe talk to someone else, hopefully someone a little friendlier than Hanratty or Carl.

When the kitchen clock showed a quarter after nine, I figured I could make my phone call without being considered rude. Now I found myself wishing for the cell phone after all.

It had all my numbers in it, and once those numbers had been punched in to the cell's phone book, they fled my brain like spooked horses. After a few false starts, I worked the number I wanted out of my memories, or at least a near approximation of it. A little worried that I'd be calling some angry housewife in Dorchester, I pulled the phone off the wall and dialed the digits in.

It rang twice, or beeped, or whatever people call the noise that cell phones make while the owner's deciding whether or not you're worth talking to. Then, suddenly, a familiar voice came on the line.

"Hello?"

"Jenna?" I said, and I made a silent prayer to whoever watched over fools who lose their telephone books. "This is Logan. How are you?"

"Mr. Logan, I do declare! It has been an awfully long time since y'all called me." Her attempt at a Carolina accent was plain awful, and she knew it. So she chuckled, and I grinned to hear the sound.

Jenna had been with my firm briefly before judging (correctly) that the heart had gone out of both the business and the owner. She'd jumped ship to a consulting firm in Cambridge a few years back, but she stayed in touch. We'd become friends, not lovers—not that there weren't folks who didn't leap to all sorts of conclusions. I'd been indignant on her behalf. Jenna had just laughed and said that one of us should take it as a compliment, though she wouldn't say which one.

That was her great gift to me, you see. It wasn't that she was whip-smart and good looking to boot; she could always make me laugh. Come to think of it, it was a good thing she'd left my firm. A few more weeks of her working on me at the office and I might have regained interest. Lord knows what that might have produced.

"You haven't answered my question," I reminded her when the laughter died down. "Believe it or not, I am interested."

"I thought you might be," she said, and she paused. "I'm fine, really. Same old, same old. However, I'm guessing the reason you called is that you're not so fine. What's the matter? Miss the big bad city already?"

"A trifle," I admitted. "But not enough to give it another shot right now. I think I'm going to be staying here for a while."

"A while," she said, and I could hear doubt in her voice. "Define 'a while' for me."

"Well," I said, stretching the sound out. "At least until I find out what happened to my car."

Her voice rose to a near screech. "Your car? Someone stole your car? I didn't think they were allowed to do that in Winston-Durham, or wherever you are."

"Maryfield," I corrected her, a little more sharply than I'd thought I was going to. "Northwest of Winston-Salem. And yes, they steal cars here, too. That's not why I'm calling, though."

"Well, good. There's not much I can do about it from here."

I grinned again despite myself. "I trust you to work miracles, Jenna. Speaking of which, I'm going to try for one here. How would you feel about taking some time off to experience the simple life? Country breakfasts, nature at its finest, and lousy cell phone reception—what more could you ask for?"

She *hmmed.* "An explanation, for one thing. You wanted to get away from everything up here, remember? So why invite me down?"

"Because I miss your sparkling conversation, and your one hundred percent accurate bullshit detector. How's that?"

"Closer," she admitted, "but still not quite good enough. My time's valuable, Logan. Out with it."

I shrugged, though I knew she couldn't see me do so. "I need someone," I said. "I need someone down here whom I can trust, and who will tell me if I've been sniffing too much fresh air and seeing things as a result. I'm spooked, Jenna, spooked bad, and I need someone to watch my back until I get my head screwed on straight again."

There was silence on the other end of the line. For a moment, I was afraid she'd hung up. Then, softer, I heard her voice, all the wisecrack drained out of it. "You're talking like a native again. That's spooking *me,* Logan. What the hell is going on?"

So I told her. I told her about Carl and the missing car and my run-in with Maryfield's finest. She sputtered like a half-opened fire hydrant when I told her that bit, and threatened to send a good lawyer down to me instead.

She stopped sputtering when I told her about the fireflies and the soldiers. But Mother and Father's bed? I didn't tell her about that. There'd be a time and a place for that, if it came to it, but the secrets of my parents' marriage bed weren't for sharing. At least, not yet.

"So," she said when I finally finished. "Either you've gone completely off your rocker or spooked is an understatement."

"I won't venture a guess," I replied. "All I know is that only a fool doesn't ask for help when he sees a problem too big for him, and right now this is looking too big for me. I'm alone, I'm isolated, and I don't know the lay of the land any more. And that's leaving out all the spooky stuff. Hell, I'll take on a million fireflies acting weird and lock the tin soldiers in the attic and be just fine, if I can get the human side of this straightened out."

"That's not it," Jenna said decisively.

"It's not?" I blinked with surprise.

"Nope. You just want me down there to deal with that lady cop. She scares the hell out of you, doesn't she?"

"She's one impressive woman," I confessed. "But honestly, I think if push came to shove, I could probably handle Officer Hanratty on my own. Slip a mickey finn in her Krispy Kremes or something. I'm clever that way."

Now it was Jenna's turn to laugh. "Attaboy, Logan. Keep thinking like that, and you'll have those local yokels wrapped around your finger in no time."

I felt a sudden lurch of worry at her words. "Does that mean you're not coming?"

"Easy, Logan. Let me look at my schedule, see what's coming up, and maybe you'll get a visitor." I started to tell her how great that was, but she hushed me. "No promises, mind you. Five minutes from now I may decide you're on a moonshine bender and forget the whole thing."

"You're not the forgetting type," I said, and I was deadly serious. "Call me when you know what you're doing."

"I will," she promised. "Find that cell phone, though. I don't want to think about you being at the mercy of country phone wiring."

"Yes, ma'am," I said, and I threw her a salute across the miles.

"Miss," she said, and she hung up on me.

"Missed indeed," I told the phone, and I hung up myself.

CHAPTER 9

I drank another cup of coffee, and then I dialed up my auto insurance company. Ten minutes of punching in my policy number and the pound sign followed, until I finally managed to convince the computer on the other end that I needed to talk to a human being of one sort or another.

"Good morning, how can I help you?" said the voice of the chipper young thing I finally got connected to. I told her she could help me by processing my claim for a stolen car, but all that inspired was the *tap-tap-tapping* of some computer keys.

"Hmm," she said after a while. "It says here, Mr. Logan, that we haven't received the police report on the theft."

"I asked them to send it," I said, thinking that I probably had done so at some point. "You mean to tell me they didn't?"

The voice sounded a bit less perky now, and a little irritated. I could only imagine what she was thinking: *Nine thirty in the morning and already I got myself a crazy.* But she tried to keep it out of her voice. "They were supposed to give you a copy of the report, Mr. Logan, and you were supposed to send it to us. Have you done so?"

"No," I admitted, even as I started pacing in slow circles

around the kitchen. "And that would be because they didn't give me a copy of the report."

"Then technically," she said, and there was just a hint of righteous indignation seasoning her words, "the car isn't legally considered stolen, and there's not much we can do about it."

"But," I started, but she interrupted me.

"I'm sorry, sir, I can't do anything without a police report." No doubt about it now; her voice was shot through with smug. "Is there anything else I can help you with?"

"You have no idea," I told her, and I hung up. "If that's what my premiums were going for," I said out loud, "I've been wasting my money for years." No one chuckled to approve of my witticism, but no one booed, either, and that was as good as a man could hope for.

I turned to pour myself another cup of coffee, but I never made it that far. Outside, I could hear the sound of an approaching car splashing up the road, and I went to the window to see who was fool enough to try to drive in the torrent that was coming down.

The first thing Father taught me when I was learning to drive was the difference between gas and brake. The second was not to try to drive our road in the rain. In theory, the gravel was supposed to hold the road surface together, even when rain came down in solid sheets like a river falling from heaven. In truth, it didn't do the job quite so much. The gravel would just sink into the mud or get itself spit up by tires, and the end result was that the rain turned the road into a rutted swamp in no time flat. A downpour like this was liable to turn the road into quicksand, and I'd seen more than one truck bogged down in what its driver swore had been solid roadbed a minute before.

Smart people stayed home when it rained in Maryfield, at least those of us who lived out past where the pavement ended. Smart people sure as hell didn't drive out this way when the rain was coming down in black sheets and the wind was howling like even it wanted to come inside and hide. Even the bravest usually gave up after a while, pulling over and waiting for the storm to blow itself out. Not this fool, though, or so it seemed.

I lifted up the shade and peered out into the morning. It was dark, so dark a man could be forgiven for thinking the sun hadn't properly come up yet. I wanted to see who was foolish enough to be out on a morning like this, who was unfortunate enough to need to be on the road while I was safe and snug inside.

The car's headlights cut through the dark as it came up the road toward the house. The rain was so thick that it looked like fog, the beams of the headlights showing up distinctly against the clouds. Whoever it was, they were moving fast, and into the teeth of the storm.

The car crested the slight hill that marked the end of Tolliver property and moved into view. For a second I couldn't see its outline or its shape because of the rain. Then, suddenly, the patter of the drops on the roof slowed and it was almost clear, like God had wiped clean the glass of the world so for a moment all His creatures could see plainly. I squinted out at the road, looking to see if I could make out the car, maybe get a look at the unlucky bastard who was driving.

It was silver; that much I could see. And the shape, well, the shape reminded me of something.

Ten seconds later, as it roared past the driveway on its closest approach, my brain put two and two together and got an answer it didn't like.

Unless there was another silver Audi loose in the hinterlands of Cackalacky, that was my car out there, kicking up gouts of water as it charged through the puddles on the road. That was my car doing an ungodly rate of speed down a poor excuse for a dirt road through a thunderstorm that promised tornadoes or worse.

"Son of a bitch!" were the first words out of my mouth, and then my jaw just hung open. I thought for a second about calling the police to tell them, but I could already hear the words coming down the other end of the line. "Well, sir, are you sure it's your car? Lots of cars look alike in the rain, after all." And then in the background I'd hear Hanratty's laugh, like something out of a Disney cartoon, and a click as the line went dead.

Besides, even in a best-case scenario, the car would be long gone by the time anyone from town got here, sirens flashing or no.

Outside, the timbre of the engine's growl changed. I peeked through the blinds. The car had slowed to a crawl right in front of the house. It was barely moving as it sat there taunting me.

I saw red. I'm not proud of it, but that's what happened. Everything in my brain above caveman level just locked itself in a box and hid, and all that was left was an angry monkey saying, "Son of a bitch, that thing's *mine!*"

I grabbed my house key, yanked the door open, and pelted out into the rain. The sound the door made slamming shut behind me was lost in the storm as I pounded down the steps and up the drive.

Whoever was in the car saw me. The car, mud splashed up dark on its silver sides, rolled forward at a slow pace, just faster than a man could walk.

I ran and got within ten feet of the bumper. Then I reached out like I was going to fling myself onto the trunk.

The car sped up. With a snort, it jumped forward and put maybe another fifty feet between me and the license plate. Then, it slowed. Sat there. Waiting.

I kept coming. The gap closed. Rain came down, and thunder and lightning split time, slicing through the clouds.

When I got within fifteen feet this time, the car sped off again.

I stood there waiting. I looked back at the house to see how far I was getting from it, and thought briefly that maybe someone was using this as a way to bust in while I was gone. I put the thought out of my mind, though. If they wanted in, there were easier ways to do it. Besides, I wanted my damn car.

Slower this time, I started forward. It was an angry man's pace, deliberate and righteous. Little wisps of smoke puffed out of the tailpipe as I came forward, the engine letting me know it was still alive.

I closed within a dozen feet. Looked back over my shoulder at the house again. It was hiding behind a curtain of rain, barely visible. If I kept going forward, I'd soon be out of sight of it entirely.

I didn't care. A few more steps brought me closer. Still the car sat there. Little rivers streamed off the back and around the tires.

I kept walking. *My car,* I said to myself. No doubt about it. This was my car. The Massachusetts tags were plain to see. The brake lights glared at me, angry red eyes through the storm. I didn't care. I pulled my robe tighter around myself and started forward.

The driver waited until I was maybe five feet behind the bumper and gaining before stepping on the gas. Mud and cold water spun up behind the wheels and caught me full in the chest as the car jumped forward.

I stumbled. A flash of lightning sizzled the air just overhead, searing everything into an image of stark black and white. I could see the shape of the driver up ahead, outlined against the blinding light. Then the thunder came and knocked me to my knees. The rain hammered into my back like it was trying to push me down into the mud, bury me, and hide any trace of my existence.

I fought it off, stood against the wind and started forward again. My robe was soaked, my legs covered in cold mud, but I didn't care. Through the sheets of rain I could see the taillights of the car, but nothing more. Two red lights shining through the storm, taunting me.

Another flash of lightning cut the sky ragged, a little farther away this time. I braced myself for the thunder and started moving forward. One thought filled my mind: I was going to kill the man who was driving it. I was going to reach the car, pull the door open, and wrap my hands around the neck of whoever was inside. This I knew with a calm certainty, the same way a preacher knows that the Lord is up there and watching.

Twenty more steps. The car just sat there in the rain, thunder shaking the air around it. Ten. I could almost see him through the solid sheets of water coming down.

The engine roared to life as that son of a bitch threw the car into reverse and came screaming back up the road at me. I threw myself to the side just in time, landing in the drainage ditch in half a foot of red-brown water. My shoulder took the impact, slamming hard into the mud. Water splashed up as I hit, mixing with the splashback from the car's passage in a curtain of muddy spray. It hid me from the road for a moment, long enough for the driver to throw the car into first and gun it. I could hear the engine protest and grind, but it obeyed and charged forward. More water spattered down on my back and neck, mixed with pebbles and clots of mud. I shouted something then—curses I can't remember—as the car rolled off into the storm. The rain came down double hard, like Heaven wanted to hide the sight from me. After a minute, even the sound of the engine was gone, drowned out by the wind, the thunder, and the rain.

A sensible man would have gone back inside then, I think. I never claimed to be sensible, though. Just proud sometimes, and stubborn.

Facedown and on my hands and knees, I waited in that ditch for something to tell me what to do next. Cold water flowed around me, the chill of it getting under my skin. My robe was soaked—clinging wet to my legs and back. I shivered and clenched my teeth to keep them from chattering. Even if the damn car was gone, I wasn't going to give the driver the pleasure of seeing me shake.

Slowly, I stood up. Shook myself to get the worst of the mud off.

The car might have been out of sight. It might have been out of earshot. Hell, it might have been swallowed by the mud or the storm or the sky, for all I knew.

But I had seen it go off into the distance, and for as long as I could, I would follow.

With one last look back at the house and a quick check of my pocket to make sure the keys were still there, I climbed back onto the road. My fingers tore gashes out of the mud as I hauled myself up, but eventually they found rocks to cling to that would hold my weight. Red water ran off me in streams as I stood, puddled around my feet and sliding down my legs as I stared off into the distance.

Then, I started running. My slippers slapped against my feet for maybe a dozen steps before I kicked them off and my bare feet hit the road. Cold mud spread around my toes with each step, but I kept running, water and wet dirt flying up behind me. My face was a mask of reddish dirt and my hands were caked in mud. My footsteps sank into the surface of the road, leaving prints that the rain washed away before I'd gone another twenty feet. Gravel from the roadbed tore at my feet, but if they drew blood I didn't see it.

I just ran.

Lightning flashed again, and through a sudden lull in the storm, I saw lights up ahead on the road.

Red lights. The taillights on my car, sure as sunset.

I ran faster. Fence posts went past, their outlines blurred by the rain. Trees were distant shadows, fading through shades of gray. I knew I was off my land now, was farther down the road than I wanted to think about. It didn't matter.

Up ahead, I could see the lights had stopped moving. Maybe the thief was waiting for me. I didn't care. The road felt good under my feet, each footstep splashing in rhythm. The rain didn't feel cold any more. My breath steamed up in front of me, then trailed away in thin streaks.

I could hear the car now. The engine's rasp cut across the noise of the storm. And above it, another sound; the high-pitched whine of tires stuck in mud.

Now I knew why the lights weren't moving. I could feel my lips curl up in a wolf's grin.

Stuck. The bastard was stuck. And I was coming for him.

The car got closer. It was pinned at the bottom of a slight rise, a place where trucks had long since spit all the gravel off the road and left ruts in the hard-packed dirt. Now it was deep mud, and the Audi was trapped in it. The engine roar got louder. If the thief kept that up, he might burn the engine out. Mud spray flew up and coated the taillights, dimming the lights that had drawn me this far.

It didn't matter. I was close.

Lightning flared again in ragged forks from east to west. If the driver was looking, he would have seen me in the rearview mirror. I was that close. My hands had gone numb and my lips were thick with the cold, but it didn't matter. I'd open the door. I'd pull the thief out. I'd take care of business.

And suddenly, there it was. My car. Right in front of me. The wheels were still spinning, digging it in ever deeper. The figure inside turned, looked over its shoulder at me through cold-misted glass, and then hunched over the wheel. He was big, whoever he was, too big to be Carl. For a second, I worried that I'd read the man wrong, then I put the thought out of my mind. Carl had a lot of friends, as Hanratty had reminded me. No doubt I was just about to find out who one of them was.

I put my hand on the trunk. It felt warm, like the rain hadn't touched it. That didn't matter, though. What mattered was that I'd touched it. I took another step forward and pressed my palm against window glass.

The thief rocked back and forth in his seat, no doubt trying to shake the car loose. I could have told him he was wasting his time. That car wasn't going anywhere. I was sure of it. The engine howled as he floored the gas pedal.

I put my hand on the driver's side door. Wrapped my fingers around the handle. Tugged it up.

Lightning hit a tree at the top of the hill. I pulled my hand away to cover my eyes.

And the car leaped out of the hole it had dug for itself and roared away.

I sank to my knees, watching the taillights fade like the devil's eyes into the distance. Tired. I was tired. If I'd had anything left in me, I would have cried, but there wasn't any point to it. The house was somewhere behind me, but I didn't care. It was too damn long a walk. I didn't have it in me. Not now. Not after that.

I managed to get to the side of the road before collapsing, sliding and tumbling down into the drainage ditch. Cold water wrapped itself around me, running past like it was in a hurry to be somewhere I wasn't. It felt good—the chill of it sucking the pain and warmth out of me by degrees. I closed my eyes and waited. *Silly thing to die over, really,* I told myself. *I could have bought another car.* Didn't even really like that one so much when I thought about it.

The noise of the rain went away, and the thunder with it. All the cold left me, too. *Freezing to death in Carolina rain,* the last waking bit of me said to myself. *Isn't that funny?*

Yes it is, I agreed, and I went to sleep.

CHAPTER 10

Light.

Strong arms, lifting me.

A voice, saying "You've had enough adventure for one day, Mr. Logan. Rest easy now."

Hands stripping away my robe, something I knew I should find disturbing. A warm blanket, rough to the touch, slipping over me instead.

"Tsk-tsk-tsk" and "My God, look at his feet."

And Officer Hanratty saying, "How the *hell* did he get all the way out here?"

These were the only things I remembered.

I woke up the next morning in my own bed, stark naked under blankets I hadn't used since I was a boy. My head hurt, and so did my hands and feet, but I felt bruised rather than broken. The smell of scorched coffee was in the air, and I could hear someone whistling in the kitchen.

My brain started coming online then, and so help me God, for a minute all I could think was: Sweet Jesus, Carl took my pants off. Then the rational part of my brain, or at least the part that had other things to worry about besides who'd seen me naked, woke itself up and told me I should probably get out of bed. Wrapping the blankets around myself, I sat up and tried to take its advice.

I looked around the room, but my bathrobe was nowhere to be seen. My clothes were in the dresser against the far wall, but the door was open, and there were footsteps coming down the hall. Heavy ones, too, by the sound of things, and my nose told me someone was bringing coffee.

I decided that the better part of valor involved not having my balls flap in the breeze in front of a stranger. So, rather than make a mad dash for my boxers, I just settled in and wrapped those blankets tight.

After maybe ten ticks of the clock, Officer Hanratty came around the corner and stomped into the room. That woman walked like a cat I used to have, which is to say that she may have moved with authority and dignity, but someone had left grace out of the package. In her left hand was a steaming mug of what my nose told me was freshly brewed coffee, and in her right was a paperback novel about as thick as my wrist.

"You," she said without preamble when she saw I was awake, "are a goddamned idiot. You're also lucky as hell, and don't you forget it."

She shoved the coffee into my hands. I took it gratefully and slurped at it while she dropped herself into the chair in the corner. It groaned in protest, but not too loud.

"Thank you," I said, and I took a long swig of the coffee. It was too hot and too strong and it burned going down, but my, it was wonderful. I came up grinning and saw she was looking at me over the top of her book.

"You seem to be feeling better," she said neutrally, flipping a page.

"I am," I said. "Do I have you to thank for bringing me back here?"

"In part." She looked down, skimmed another few lines, and then lowered the book, a thick finger holding her place. "What the hell were you thinking, running five miles along that road in that storm and dressed like you were going down the hall to take a leak?"

I shifted myself backward a few inches, so my back was against the wall and my weight helped pin the covers around me. "I had good reason," I said. "And as much as I appreciate the coffee, I'm a bit surprised to see you in my house."

"Well," Hanratty said, leering at me, "it was me or Carl Powell. I figured you'd be happier with me. Besides, the door was open."

"Funny, I thought I'd closed it."

"You did," she said. "At least, maybe you did when you went out. Then again, things have happened since then."

"Whatever that means, I guess." I rubbed my forehead with the back of my hand, trying to wipe away the headache that had decided to wake up with the rest of me. "Tell you what. You tell me how you got me back here, and I'll tell you why I was running down the road in my skivvies. Deal?"

"Bathrobe and skivvies," she corrected, but she was smiling. "Fair enough. Here's what happened, at least from my end.

"Carl Powell found you laying facedown on the side of the road, half drowned, and damn near dead of hypothermia. I still don't know why I agreed to let him bring you home, by the way, instead of taking you to the hospital. I may yet change my mind."

"Carl?" I asked. "Now how about that."

She snorted. "I'm glad to see you're taking interest. Don't go starting with any crazy talk about Carl now, not until you at least put some pants on. You see, he said he'd come out here to talk to you. Said he wanted to clear some things off his chest about what was going on."

"Must have been pretty important, for him to come out here in that weather," I said.

"Well, it *is* Carl. Once he sets his mind to something. . . ." Her voice trailed off, and she shrugged. "But in any case, I was telling you what happened. Carl came by and found your door open and the rain blowing in. He stuck his head in and hollered for you, but got no answer. So he walked in and poked around, and he still couldn't find you. That's when he got worried. He called the station from your kitchen, then he got in his truck to look for you. Since he hadn't seen you coming in, he kept going out, and that's where he found you. I got there about three minutes later, and by then, he'd gotten you off the ground and wrapped you in a blanket. Wouldn't let me take you to the hospital, though, like I said. Insisted you'd do better at home. I tell you, I think when I suggested an ambulance he was ready to haul off and hit me."

I sipped my coffee and didn't say anything. Hanratty watched me do it and didn't say anything either.

"So what happened then?" I finally prompted.

"About what you'd expect. We brought you back here and threw you in a hot shower for a while. It works for the drunks, so I figured it would work for you. After that, we threw your sorry butt into bed, and Carl stayed up all night watching you. I came by about an hour ago to relieve him. That's about it."

"He stayed all night?" I blinked. "Seriously?"

Hanratty nodded. "Seriously. Which means if he wanted to do something unpleasant to you, or take something out of this house, he had plenty of time to do it in." She looked around. "If you ask me, it doesn't look like he did, now, does it?"

I shook my head. "It's just a little confusing, that's all. I'm not accusing anyone of anything anyhow, at least not until I have another cup of coffee. Don't you go jumping to conclusions, either."

She threw her hands up in a gesture of surrender, her finger still holding her place in the book. "You got me there," she said, and she chuckled. "Now, tell you what—you tell me what on earth possessed you to go running down the road like that, and I'll get you another cup of coffee."

"Seems fair to me," I said, holding out out my cup.

"Cream and sugar?" she asked.

"Neat," I replied, and I got another witch-cackle. She put her book down with the spine cracked then marched off back down the hallway. I took the opportunity to shut the bedroom door and find myself some boxers and a pair of jeans. No time for socks, though, and I took the first t-shirt I could find, one that read "Braintree HS Athletic Department." I shrugged into that, ran my fingers through my hair, and dropped back onto the bed just as Hanratty knocked.

"All decent?" she asked.

"Yep," I answered.

"Well, damn." She pushed the door open, grinning. "And here I was hoping for a nice view."

"You could have had all you wanted while you were bringing me back here." I pointed out.

"Yes, but I get as much of that as I want helping out with autopsies." She snorted at my expression, shoved the overfull mug into my fingers, and sat herself back down. "By the way, you might want to learn to put away your toys before you go running around in the rain."

"Toys?" I blinked. "What toys?"

She shrugged and jerked one thumb in the direction of the kitchen. "There was a toy soldier in the middle of the kitchen floor. Aren't you a little old to be playing with those?"

"They were Father's," I heard myself say. "Where did you say the soldier was?"

She thought for a moment. "Middle of the floor, like I said. Facing the doorway, like he was guarding it. Not that it was going to do much good if someone came bigfooting through there." She lifted one booted foot then set it down fast, to make sure I knew what she was talking about. "I picked it up and put it on the table, so you can thank me later. If they were your father's, you might want to take better care of them."

"I thought I had," I said mildly, but my thoughts were racing. More than anything, I wanted to go check the box I'd left in the drawer to see if—no, how—it had been disturbed. But I wasn't going to do that in front of Hanratty. For all her newfound cheer, talking to her was still not something I was all that comfortable doing. The last thing I wanted was to have to explain why I was going through my old socks like a dog digging for a bone. No, better to check later.

If, mind you, I decided I really wanted to check at all.

Instead, I breathed in the aroma of the coffee for a moment, reluctant to start the real conversation. I could feel Hanratty's eyes on me, questioning.

"Just one question before I start," I asked her. "Are you listening to me as Miss Hanratty or Officer Hanratty?"

"Didn't know there was a difference," she rumbled. "Everyone in this town wears two hats, at least."

I shrugged and took a drink, barely managing to avoid spilling from the overfull mug. Definitely from the bottom of the pot; I could feel the grounds on my tongue.

Still, I didn't want to seem ungrateful, so I gulped it down, wiped my mouth on the back of my wrist, and started talking. Hanratty listened, nodded, and grunted a couple of times when that was called for, but mostly she just let me ramble. I told her about seeing the car out on the road and about going after it, and about the start-and-stop chase that we'd had halfway to the county line. I wasn't proud in the telling, but I didn't leave anything out, either.

"Did you see the driver?" Hanratty asked, when I finally wound down.

"Nope." I looked sadly into the empty mug. "Best I got was a silhouette against the lightning."

"And?"

I shrugged. "And whoever was in there must have had a hell of a time fitting into the front seat, because they were not thin. Not thin at all." I thought for a moment. "I'm pretty sure it was a man. Seemed to be shaped like one, anyway, though you spend enough time in Cambridge and you learn not to make assumptions on that sort of thing."

She didn't laugh, nor did she offer to get me another cup of coffee. Instead, she crossed her legs—a damn impressive sight to see, I might add—and scrunched up her face in the sort of "I'm thinking" look you usually only see on small children and Elmer Fudd. When she spoke, she didn't sound happy.

"So you're telling me that out of all this, out of Carl's story and your story and your run in the rain, we've got nothing but the shadow of a fat man to go on?"

"That's about it, yeah. Unless someone saw the car driving out here, or driving off once I was dusted."

Hanratty snorted loud enough to rattle the window. "Mr. Logan, you were not dusted. You were *mudded*, not to mention played. I'd tell you that you did something stupid there, but that wouldn't be true. You did so many stupid things that I don't even know where to start the list."

To my surprise, I felt a genuine twinge of embarrassment. "I know, I know. But I saw the car and . . ." My voice trailed off. "I just got mad."

There was no sympathy in Hanratty's voice as she creaked to her feet. "You nearly got dead, is what you got. Look, here's what I want you to do if your car comes around again. I want you to call me, and then I want you to lock your damn door and sit the hell down. You got lucky this time, Mr. Logan. Your little friend could have just thrown the car into reverse after you went down, and then we wouldn't be having this conversation. Hell, he left you there to die. Next time, I want you to take this seriously."

"I had been," I said mildly. "Last time I was in town, I got the impression that you weren't."

Her face got hard, and I knew I'd said the wrong thing. "You get a lot of wrong impressions, Mr. Logan. I'll be going now. Nice to see you back on your feet. If you remember anything else, give me a call."

I opened my mouth to say something, and a look from Hanratty shut it. "I'll show myself out," she said, and she stalked off. The slam of the kitchen door told me she had indeed found the exit on her own, and furthermore, had done so with style. I waited to see if she was really going, or was instead going to stick her head back inside my door to yell something else.

The part of me that bet she was coming back in would have lost if there'd been money on the table. Even through the closed door and down the hall, I could hear the thump of a car door closing, and then the angry cough of a big sedan's engine coming to life. By the time the gravel was spitting out from under her wheels, I'd already stood up and started heading for the last place I wanted to be.

The door to my parents' bedroom was firmly closed when I reached it. The floor didn't show any water, or any footprints. If Carl had been there, he'd mopped up after himself pretty well.

Gingerly, I put the coffee mug down on the hallway floor then nudged it against the wall with my toe. My hand reached out for the doorknob then hesitated. My hand just hung there in the air, not moving where I told it to.

"What the hell?" I said to myself, and I closed my fingers into a fist. They curled themselves into shape easily, but when I tried for the doorknob again, my hand froze in midair. I pulled my hand back, and it went easily. Tried to move it forward, though, and it stopped halfway there.

"Well, goddamn." I stopped trying to move and stared at my hand. It didn't do anything interesting, so I watched it for a minute, and then was struck by a thought.

"Stupid," I told myself, and I knocked. Three times on the wood of the door, one after another.

There was no answer, of course, not that I'd been expecting one, but suddenly my hand felt lighter and I could rest it on the knob. Moving quickly, before whatever it was that had stopped me could change its mind, I turned the knob—old crystal, something that Mother always fretted over whenever I ran through the house—and stepped into the room.

No looking around this time. I knew what I was after. No words, either. If there was something in that room—and considering what I'd been through, a mysterious dent in a pillow didn't seem like so much—it would have to get by without my conversation.

Instead, I made a beeline for the chest at the foot of the bed. It was cedar and filled the air with its heavy scent. Grandfather Logan had made it with his own hands—had stained the wood and given it to my grandmother on their wedding night. Filled with blankets and lovingly tended, it had been off-limits for hide and seek all my life.

"Don't play in there, honey," Mother would say, but she'd never mention the real reason.

I flipped open the lid and started digging through quilts. It was a gamble, I knew. If Carl hadn't taken care of it, if Carl hadn't known it was there, then the thing I was looking for would most likely be a useless piece of junk. But I was banking that Carl knew more about that house and its belongings than I did, and that he did the same thing for Father's things that he did for Mother's legacy.

My hands closed on metal. "Well, hot damn," I whispered, and I pulled the weight up and out.

It was a shotgun, Father's old Fox Savage 12 gauge. I unwrapped it from its cloth cover and looked at it.

It was perfect. Oiled, cleaned, and looking better than it had when Father had owned it. I cracked it and saw two #6 shells sitting there, pretty as you please. Hell, even the twin triggers gleamed. Clearly, someone had been expecting trouble.

Or had figured I would be.

I closed the gun, then smoothed the quilts I'd ruffled in my search. Whatever I'd run into trying to get into the room, I didn't want to give it any more reason to get upset. Carefully, I shut the lid. There'd be enough time to look through Father's things for more shells later. Right now, I just wanted to go sit on my porch with that shotgun. I wanted to sit, and watch, and wait.

And when the son of a bitch who stole my car came back, I wasn't going to lock myself inside and call Officer Hanratty.

I was going to shoot him.

CHAPTER 11

I sat out on the porch all morning with the shotgun in my lap. During that time the barrel of the gun got hot under the glare of the sun, four cars headed into town and two trucks headed out, and an ugly dog trotted along the edge of the drainage ditch on its way across my property. I yelled at it to shoo, and it lifted its leg before moving on at its own pace.

Served me right, I suppose. As the sun burned off the last of the clouds, I slowly came to the conclusion that neither car nor driver was likely to show. Still, I didn't want to go inside. Doing that would have made me feel like a quitter as well as a fool. But the sun got hotter, and the mud dried and cracked, and not a damn other thing happened.

Finally, I compromised by letting myself take a trip to the bathroom. Shotgun in hand, I went back into the house and locked the door behind me, then set the gun down on the kitchen table. Carefully, I lined it up to point both barrels right at the center of the door. The toy soldier, I noted with approval, was already posted in that direction. "Sentry duty," I told him, and I patted the gun as I stalked off toward the john.

I knew it was paranoid. Crazy, even. It wasn't like I was going to rush out of the bathroom with my peter hanging out to defend the homestead from someone knocking on the windowpane. But I can't deny it felt better to have the gun barrels be the first thing any intruder might see.

I didn't bother to shut the door behind me as I went into the bathroom. It seemed silly, me being the only one in the house and all. I did, however, try to shut the window that had been open the day before. It was still cracked a couple of inches, and the wood of the sill was still moist. Carefully, I put my hands on the frame and pulled down.

It didn't budge. I cursed a bit under my breath and tried harder.

Still, nothing.

"Time to do something stupid, I guess," I announced to the sink as I flipped the toilet seat down. It had amused me to no end to see that Hanratty had no doubt propped it back up.

That being said, the toilet backed up against the wall with the window on it, and if I wanted to get more pressure on the stubborn thing, the only way to do it was to climb up on the bowl and push down.

Every kid climbs up on the toilet when he's a kid, and every kid's mother yells at him to get down. I'd been no exception, and neither had Mother. And so, I took a look over my shoulder and out the open door, just like I had when I was nine, before stepping up.

The seat groaned under my weight, but held. Carefully, I placed my feet directly over the lip of the bowl—no sense punching through and getting my shoes soaked—and leaned down on the top of the window.

It held fast. I pushed harder, throwing all my weight into it.

It creaked a little, and some paint flaked down, but that was it. No movement, unless you counted the ominous creaking of the toilet seat under my feet.

"One more time," I told myself, in part because I didn't want to quit just yet, and in part because I was feeling the need to use the bathroom for its intended purpose. I dusted my hands, planted them at opposite sides of the window, and tensed my shoulders for the push.

Behind me, the bathroom door slammed shut then kicked back open against the wall with a sound like a gunshot.

I looked around. The bathroom was empty except for me, as was the hall beyond.

No one else there.

Bullshit. That's what my gut was telling me. The hairs on the back of my neck were up, and I had the cold certainty in my gut that someone was standing right there, watching me.

Slowly, I let go of the window and shuffled my feet around to face out.

The door slammed shut and open again, harder this time.

"Hello?" I called, realizing that anyone who could answer was in the house uninvited and closer to the shotgun than I was.

All things considered, though, that was preferable to the alternative. "Eccentric" ran in the Logan line, and it was too short a hop from there to full-blown batshit crazy.

No one answered, not my "hello" or my prayers. No floorboards creaked, no papers shuffled, nothing.

I was alone. The bathroom door was jumping, and I was standing on top of the crapper with no one else in the house.

No one else alive in the house, a voice in the back of my head said, and I tried to hush it immediately.

It didn't listen. *Think about it, Logan*, it continued. *Who's doing that? What the hell happened when you tried to open the door this morning? Who was sleeping in your momma's bed? It's just plain common sense.*

"I don't call her 'Momma,'" I said angrily. The door swung again. When it hit the wall, I could hear something crack. "And I don't believe in ghosts. Carl, if that's you, I've had about enough. This crap isn't funny anymore."

Carl didn't answer. Neither did anyone else, but as I watched, the medicine cabinet flew open. Behind it, the door started swinging again, banging from open to shut and back again faster and faster.

And behind me, something slammed the window shut. It slammed down loud enough that for a moment I thought the gun had gone off. I half-jumped, half-turned to look, and I lost my balance. For a second, my hands cut the air as I reached for something to hang onto, then over I went.

I hit the bathroom floor shoulder-first, cushioning some of the blow. My head hit the tile a moment later with a crack louder than the one the door had made, and a bright light filled my vision. For an instant all I could see was blinding whiteness; all I could hear was a shrill ringing in my ears. *I wonder if I'm bleeding*, I thought, and was surprised by how calm I sounded. My hand moved to my forehead to feel for blood; it seemed to take an hour to move my fingers that far.

Slowly, imperceptibly, the light and the noise faded, replaced by a sharp pain behind my eyes and a dull one at my temple.

I winced and closed my eyes; tried to sit up and thought better of it. Lying on that cool floor seemed like a good idea.

Something had changed, though, the voice in the back of my head was screaming. Something was different.

I tried to think about it, but it was like putting sandbags on a broken levee. Every time I got a few in place, the water broke through someplace else and knocked them away.

Still, at least it was quiet enough to let me try to think.

Quiet. . . .

And then I knew. Slowly, I looked up from the floor and forced my eyes open against the too-bright light.

The door to the medicine cabinet sat, perfectly still and mostly closed. The door to the bathroom? Open and silent.

Motionless.

An image painted itself in front of me, the picture of the moment I fell and the door swung to a gentle stop.

Right when I'd gotten my feet off the toilet.

"Mother?" I asked the air.

No answer.

Again.

But cool air washed over me. Then I passed out.

CHAPTER 12

I woke up with my face pressed against the floor. Thinking fast, I got myself up as quick as I could. There'd been no telling how many people coming through the house lately, and the last thing I needed at this point was for Carl or Hanratty or whoever to come strolling in on me face down and unconscious. That is, if Carl or Hanratty hadn't been behind what I'd just been through.

Jumping to my feet that fast wasn't too much of a mistake. My head hurt like hell and I thought I distinctly heard my brains sloshing around inside my skull when I turned left and right, but otherwise I felt tolerable enough. Gingerly, I touched the medicine cabinet door. It sat quietly on its hinges, not moving. I rocked it back and forth a few times, just to be sure, but there was nothing to it. No abnormal resistance, no cold chill as I touched it—nothing. Nor did the door seem weighted oddly, or inclined to fall open or slam shut of its own accord.

It was just an ordinary medicine chest door that, the last time I'd seen it, had been swinging like the wing of a drunken bat. Doing it all by its lonesome, too.

"This is crazy," I said out loud, mainly to hear my own voice in the silence. "I need to get out of this house." I looked around and then added, "Just for a little bit."

Nothing answered me.

Quickly, before I could change my mind, I grabbed the shotgun and went out the kitchen door.

It was, I decided as I half-shut the door behind me, time to go down into the Thicket.

The neighbors had unkindly referred to the land past the pine trees by that name for as long as I could remember, and it was as good a name as any for it. Since Father hadn't used the land for what they thought God intended it for, it had grown up right thick, and the passing years had made it even thicker. Thanks to Carl, the land right by where Mother and Father were buried was passable enough, but once you got beyond it there was less grass and more briar with every step. Here and there trees punched up through the knee-high weeds, a mix of pine and black locust grabbing for chunks of sunlight.

You could look back into it a good ways, a few hundred yards at least, until the trees got too thick and the weeds got too tall for good seeing. There were deer down there, I knew, enough that men from town had paid Father for the right to go hunting on the land. No doubt there was other wildlife in the Thicket as well, coyotes and rabbits and God knew what else. Copperheads, most likely—you couldn't swing a stick without hitting one anywhere else in the area. Still, copperheads and rattlers weren't a problem as long as you had a good pair of boots on and made enough noise that they knew you were coming.

For my part, I was wearing ratty sneakers and saying nothing as I went. I did, however, have a shotgun with the safety off cradled in my left arm. No shells in my pocket—hell, I didn't even have my damn keys—but I didn't figure I'd be needing any. The Thicket ran deep into the property and was bounded by the back ends of a few of the local farms. No roads ran back there; no trails for dumbass kids to ride their ATVs or their BMXs. I don't think Father had been back there more than a couple of times, and then only when Mother made him walk the property line.

But the Thicket was where I was going, and part of me was hoping some damn fool coyote would pop out of the trees, just so I could unload on it, literally and figuratively.

That wasn't why I was down there, mind you, or at least not entirely. No matter what was going on in the house, I needed to be away from it for a while, needed some clean air to clear my head before I landed on it again. The house was small, close, and old, and I was feeling hemmed in within its walls. Hemmed in, but not safe—apparently someone was coming and going as they pleased, while I just watched and yelled and got made a fool of.

Town was out. I was feeling better than any man who'd been rained on, dropped in the mud, and smacked with a bathroom floor had a right to be, but that still didn't mean I was up to the walk. Nor did I feel like calling Sam for a lift. I was hoping Sam and I would be friends, and I didn't want to presume on short acquaintance.

Heading down the road the other way, of course, was simply not an option.

Which left me with the Thicket, and in truth, that was just fine with me. It was a still place, a private place, and it was far more mine than the house could ever be. Neither Mother nor Father, nor anyone else, now that I thought about it, had ever spent any real time down there. Which meant that it was nobody's, and if it was nobody's, then for a little while I could make it mine.

Whistling a song I'd heard on the radio on the drive down—something about a cheating woman and an angry man, not that I could blame her for running around on a man who sounded like that—I made my way down from the house and past the curtain of pines by my parents' markers. The urge to look at the gravestones was strong, but I resisted. That wasn't why I was out there. Besides, paying my respects with the shotgun in hand seemed a mite disrespectful, all things considered.

Instead, I focused my eyes on the Thicket looming up ahead. The sun was well up, but that just made the shadows darker under the gathering trees. A little wind was coming in from the west, just enough to make the grass bow down before it while the other weeds stood tall. Bird calls came from every direction. They sounded surprised, like they didn't expect a human down here on this part of the land. Come to think of it, they probably didn't.

A few more seconds of walking and scanning found me what I was looking for. While it had been rare for deer to get up near the house on their own, occasionally Mother had put a salt lick up behind the house. Then they beat a path to our door, one after another. Sometimes we'd have half a dozen or so just milling around back there, and in their coming and going they trampled a few routes into the Thicket pretty thoroughly.

I had a hunch that, since Mother had done it back in the day, Carl had kept it up after she died. Sure enough, there was a game path cutting through the scrub at an angle, and it was easy to find where it came out. After all, there was no sense walking through the stickerbushes if I didn't have to. Letting the deer do the work for me was the sensible thing to do.

The dead weeds made a soft *crunch* under my feet once I moved onto the deer path. It ran pretty straight back toward the cover of the trees, intersected here and there by other trails that led off toward whatever the hell deer found interesting. I ignored the trails and headed toward the line of trees. Already I was passing the outliers, pickets standing watch for the rest of the forest. They were thin trees, but wiry, growing up fast. They had probably only been there for fifteen years, but they looked like they'd been there a century.

Still, my business, if indeed I had any, was farther back. It wasn't that I had any particular memories of the Thicket from my childhood. I hadn't had a tree house, secret place, or a rock fort tucked into the heart of the woods. It was just the Thicket, the part of the land that wasn't the house and wasn't in sight of it, and that's what I needed.

Something scuttled through the grass to my left, and instinctively I moved the gun into a good firing position. The sound moved away, no doubt a rabbit that saw a trespasser a couple times its size and wanted no part of it. I paused for a moment, listening for further movement, but didn't hear any. Up above, a red-tail hawk circled silently; in the trees, his songbird cousins made noise; and the grass whispered with the wind. No footsteps, though, no footfalls or rustling through the grass.

"Perfectly goddamned normal," I said, but as I started walking again, I kept the gun ready. The house had already disappeared back behind that first wall of trees, but now those were vanishing as well, hidden by a new line of green. Up ahead, the pines were getting thicker, promising less scrub on the ground and more shade overhead. It was as good a reason as any to pick up the pace, so I did.

A rustle of squirrels in the branches announced my arrival in what looked to be the Thicket proper. It was young forest, I could see. None of the trees were more than four or five inches thick, and the cover of needles and leaves on the ground was patchy. Here and there, shrubs and weeds defended bare spots in the soil, often in places where beams of sunlight found their way through the leaves overhead. Vines wound their way up a few trunks; poison ivy, thankfully, not kudzu.

I took a deep breath, surprised to find myself relaxing just a little bit. The woods felt good in a way the house hadn't, and I could feel myself responding. They felt friendly in a way a lot of woods I'd been in hadn't. The trees were still far enough apart that a man could walk easily, not crowding against each other. You got the feeling in old woods that you were intruding on the trees' business, like as soon as you left, they'd go back to pushing and shoving and fighting for sunlight, and they were mighty annoyed with you for making them stop for just a minute. Here, they were just starting to figure that out, and the air hadn't gotten toxic with it yet. It felt nine kinds of fine.

I kept the shotgun ready, though, and I didn't flick the safety on.

Somewhere farther on, a woodpecker took aim at a tree trunk and went to work. The sound echoed under the leaves—*ratta-tatta-tatta-tat, ratta-tatta-tatta-tat*. It seemed like as good a direction as any, so I made a guess as to the source of the sound and headed off toward it.

The slope of the land evened out a bit and the shade got darker. It was cool under the leaves, even with the trees keeping out the breeze. All around me, I could hear things moving away—running for cover in the dead leaves, scuttling up tree trunks, flapping away. The woodpecker kept going, though, the sound stronger than ever, so I let it pull me along and stopped wondering about anything else hiding in the woods. The leaves crunched under the soles of my sneakers. I tried walking quietly, but gave up that idea in about a minute flat; the woods themselves were having none of it. You couldn't take a half-dozen steps in any direction without making noise—a *crunch* for the leaves or a quieter *whoosh* for the pine needles. Where they mixed, you got both put together and louder than either.

The *ratta-tatta-tat* stopped. Up overhead, there was an explosion of wings and leaves. I caught a glimpse of the bird—red head, white beak, black and white body—as it leaped from the tree in search of what I guessed was a less busy place to dine. So help me, the damn thing looked offended that I'd interrupted it.

"Be thankful I don't charge you rent," I called out after it, though I'm reasonably sure it didn't listen. The woods swallowed my words in just the way they hadn't chewed up the woodpecker sounds, and left me standing there in silence.

Maybe twenty yards off, I heard the sound of footsteps on leaves.

I didn't think, which is probably for the best. Instead, I pressed my back against the tree, putting it between me and whatever—whoever—had taken that step. The shotgun I held ready. I could feel the sweat on my fingers.

Probably just a deer, I told myself, waiting for another footstep. *Probably just a goddamn wild animal, doing exactly what it's supposed to here in the goddamned Thicket.*

But I didn't believe that, even as I mouthed the words.

Another footstep announced itself. It was cautious and slow, like a man putting his heel down first and rolling toward the toe. Like a man trying to walk quietly on a carpet of leaves.

I breathed shallowly, trying to make as little noise as possible. My right hand held the stock, my left the barrel, and the gun was pulled close to my body, to make sure there wasn't any shine off it. Each breath made a cloud of moisture on the steel of the barrel that faded away in a heartbeat.

More footsteps, some on leaves, some softer on exposed dirt. The snap of a twig came across like a whip crack, and I could feel my finger squeeze on the lead trigger involuntarily.

All around us, the squirrels and the birds went about their business, calling back and forth and generally oblivious to the fact that someone was stalking someone else in the heart of the Thicket. The problem was, I couldn't figure out who was stalking whom.

The footsteps got a hair louder and a touch closer. My heart pounded, the blood in my ears almost as loud as the sound of footfall on forest floor. Another step, a crunch so close I could swear it was right in front of me.

And then nothing.

I counted to ten. To twenty. Told myself that he—whoever he was—was probably waiting for me to show myself. I counted to thirty then counted down backward. There was no sound of movement, no sound of breath moving in and out.

"Damn fool," I whispered, and I rolled out from behind the tree to see who waited for me.

"You need to pick a thicker tree to hide behind, boy," said Carl from behind me. "You were showing on both sides."

Before he was done speaking, I spun and brought the gun down like it was the most natural thing in the world. He was faster, though, his hand coming down to knock it low and away.

I tell myself that it was the shock of his hand against the barrel that nudged my finger hard against that trigger. Sometimes, I even believe it—that I wasn't about to shoot him in the gut without thought or apology.

Doesn't really matter now, I suppose. He slapped the barrel out of line and my finger closed on the trigger and a load of #6 came screaming out of the shotgun with a sound like mountains coming down.

Two trees went down, young ones sawed off about a foot off of the ground by the buckshot. The sound punched my ears and the kick of the gun drove the stock into my belly hard enough to make me grunt. All around, animals scattered like water on a hot skillet, calling out warnings and running as fast as they could. Ragged furrows appeared in the earth, showing the red clay hiding under the soil. Leaves kicked up by the shot danced in the air, slowly coming down to hide the scars I'd inflicted.

And Carl, for his part, stood there like a man carved from wood and stone, watching me watch what I'd done.

"You need to be more careful with a piece like that," he said when I stopped blinking. " 'Specially when you're not used to guns. Someone might get hurt by accident."

I looked at him. He seemed calm, his voice mild as if he were telling me I was holding a hacksaw the wrong way going after a tree branch. He was wearing a blue button-down work shirt, jeans, brown boots, and a hat that might have said John Deere back when it had been green instead of gray with age and use. It was all perfectly normal, really, except that he had no business being in the woods on the ass end of my property in the middle of the day.

That, and the fact that no man I'd ever seen could have moved the way he just did.

"Afternoon, Carl," I finally said when I figured my voice wouldn't crack. "Nice day for a walk, isn't it?"

"Tolerable enough," he agreed, and he nodded back toward the heart of the Thicket. "There's something back here y'need to see." He turned and took a few steps deeper into the woods.

I didn't follow.

"No," I said.

He stopped, turned, and looked over his shoulder. "No?"

I laid the gun down and crossed my arms. "No. Not until

you tell me what the hell you're doing here, Carl. Not until you tell me what's going on."

His face screwed up like fruit left out too long in the sun. "You ask a lot of questions for a man who won't look for answers, son. I'm trying to show you."

I shook my head. "No you're not. You're asking me to follow you on your say-so after I find you out here in the middle of the day for no good reason. I don't even know how the hell you got here, and I've half a mind to march back to the house to call Hanratty."

He cracked a smile. "You could do that, I suppose. Wouldn't do you much good. Time you got back to the house and called and she told you to calm yourself down, and you threw enough of a fit to get her out here, I'd be long gone. And don't be thinking you've got it in you to drag me back to the house, boy. Not on your best day."

I sat down. "Maybe. But you've got something you want to show me. All I have to do is sit here and you're screwed."

"I'm trying to help you, boy," he said, and it was like he was looking down the barrel of a gun and pulling the trigger. The words came out like bullets, one after another. "You come back here and you know nothing, nothing at all about what's going on, and yet you got your smart mouth and your stupid ideas, and you go around sticking your tallywhacker into every damn hornet's nest you can find. This is bigger than you, you know. There's other people waiting on you to get your head out of your ass, but it seems plain to me we're gonna be waiting a long damn time. You can think on that while you sit there, if'n you want. I'll be back in a month or two to see if you've grown up any." And then, he shut right back down and started walking away.

"Wait," I said. He didn't.

I stood. "Carl. Wait!" He kept walking.

"Carl!"

He stopped and turned halfway around with a look that could sour milk.

"Yes?" was all he said.

"Two questions," I said. "Answer those two, and I'll follow you, I swear."

He considered it for a moment. "The answers you get might be 'go to hell,' you know."

I gnawed my lower lip. "I know," I said. "It's a good enough answer for me."

"Fine." He stood there, arms crossed on his chest. "What's so all-fired important to know that you'll jump up and follow me into the dark of the woods if I tell you, when you wouldn't pay me no heed before?"

I swallowed and took a deep breath. "You said before you were keeping a promise. What's the promise?"

He chewed the air as he considered the question. "None of your damn business," he said finally. "Though it's a sensible question for you to be asking. What's the other one?"

"How the hell did you get back here?" I asked.

He grinned. "Walked on over from the Tolliver property. Damn fool waste of a question, if'n you ask me."

And with that, he headed back into the deep part of the Thicket. Grabbing the shotgun in my off hand, I followed him.

I was thoroughly lost by the time Carl led me to our destination. I knew the Thicket was big—I'd seen the acreage of the property on the deed, after all—but it's one thing to see it as a number on a piece of paper, another to actually walk it without a hell of a lot of faith in where you're going.

The walk itself took maybe twenty minutes, though I couldn't tell you which direction we'd gone in or if we'd just hiked in a big circle. A couple of times I asked Carl how far we were from where we were going, and he didn't answer. Come to think of it, that's not quite true. One time, he grunted, and another he shot me a look. Neither was what you'd call real helpful.

Finally, we came through a thick stand of trees into a little bit of a clearing. Carl took a few steps in, then turned and stopped.

"This is it," he said. "This is where I needed to bring you."

I stopped too, right on the edge of the opening in the trees. A couple of feet between me and Carl still didn't seem like a bad thing, though I also figured that if he really wanted to do me harm, there wasn't much I could do to stop him. So I did the next best thing and looked around.

The clearing was maybe thirty feet across, shaped more or less like a circle. The trees that ringed it were among the tallest and, if I had to guess, the oldest in the Thicket. There was barely space enough between them to pass through.

The floor of the clearing was covered in greenery, most of it ferns and the like. Nothing was more than a foot or so tall, and I didn't see any saplings growing out there. A gap in the foliage overhead let the sun beat down on the clearing, and, despite myself, I was impressed.

"Very nice, Carl," I said, and I leaned up against the nearest tree. Sweat dripped off my forehead, and my arms had started to ache from lugging the damn shotgun around with me. "So, what is this place?"

"It's where everything else ain't," he replied, and he took a couple of steps back toward the center. "Come on closer. It ain't gonna bite you none."

"You sure?" I said, and I looked around, left to right. There was nothing but greenery and Carl, but neither looked particularly threatening at the moment. So I shot a short prayer straight up through the trees then walked out to join him.

He wasn't smiling when I reached him, but he wasn't frowning neither, which I regarded as a small victory. "I'm here, Carl," I said to him. "Talk to me."

"I'll tell you what I can," he said, and he scratched the back of his head. "I can talk to you here, I think."

I *think*? Uncertainty from Carl was a new thing to me, and I looked around again to see where it might have grown from. There was nothing strange that met the eye, but I'd been saying that a lot lately.

"What's so special about this place?" I asked. "I mean, there's no trees, but there are a lot of places in Carolina these days that don't have any trees. Of course, this one doesn't have a mall being built on it, so I guess that makes it different."

Carl shook his head. "For a minute, I thought I'd gotten through to you, but I see I was mistaken. You spent too much time in that city, boy. Too much time forgetting who you are and where you came from."

My temper started rising when he said that, and I shoved

it back down as best I could. "That's not fair, Carl. I am who I am. I'm from here just as sure as anything else."

"No." He shook his head. "You were born here. But you ain't from here. You decided not to be a long time ago."

I could feel my face getting red and could see that Carl saw it, too. "Give me a break. I'm not the only kid who left this town to go to college."

"You're reading it too simple. You're right, you ain't the only one to go. But some of them came back and chose to be here. And some left for good and never looked back. But then there's you."

I squinted at him. "And then there's me what?"

In answer, he reached out and took the shotgun from my hands. "You know how to fire this, boy?" I nodded, flushing with embarrassment. Carl plowed on. "You know how to lock and load it, how to take care of it, how to clean the choke and how to put a snap cap in there?"

"Yes," I said, irritation growing in my voice. "So what?"

"So how many of your friends in Boston town could do that? Not a one, I'd reckon. Am I right?"

I snorted. "You're right. So? It's not exactly a useful skill up there, at least not in the neighborhoods you want to be in."

He nodded sagely. "I'm sure. But you were proud that you knew it, weren't you? Proud and just a little bit standoffish, right? 'Cause when push came to shove, you knew those people couldn't survive ten miles past the city limits, but you could."

"Maybe," I said, still guarded. I thought back to the years I'd spent in the city, how I'd always found myself lingering on the outside of any circle of friends I found. Great people, all of them no doubt, but there was always a distance there, a shared experience I couldn't bring to the friendship.

And when it had all fallen apart, I'd come back here.

"Maybe," I repeated. "But what does that prove?"

Carl grinned at me, looking like the world's happiest death's head. "Let me ask you another question. How many cars like yours are there in this town, you think?"

"Who cares? Other people's cars are their business."

He waggled a finger at me. "You ain't answering the question. How many cars like that you think there are? How many people are there used to being able to go out shopping in the middle of the night, or find a fancy restaurant, or do any of them big city things you're carrying back with you in your custom?"

"It's different, okay?" I turned away and studied the trees, just so I wouldn't have to look at him. "It's a change, but everyone goes through those changes when they move. I'm not planning to stay that long, anyway."

He cackled. "Now you're getting near it, Mr. Logan. Now you're starting to get near it."

"Get near what? I'm right here."

"That's right," he said calmly, "and that's the way it's going to be for a good while."

I took a step back. "Are you talking about keeping me here against my will, Carl? That's not exactly what I was paying you for."

Carl spat on the ground, right between my feet. "Boy, if it were up to me, which it ain't, I'd say sell the land to someone who wants it and leave now. Hell, I'd help you pack and drive you to the airport if that's what it took. But it ain't up to me, and it hasn't been, not ever. So do both of us a favor, and just shut up for one minute, while I try and tell you a few things that might be useful to you in keeping your mind and your soul in their right proper shapes. That is, if you think they're worth keeping that way."

I bit my tongue and counted to ten, then waited a little longer before I trusted myself to respond. "I'd be very grateful for anything you could tell me, Carl," I said in as pleasant a voice as I could manage. "As for the state of my mind, well, all I can tell you is that what's going on right now isn't helping it any."

Carl looked at me then—really looked at me in a way that said he was seeing me, instead of Mother's son or some snot-nosed punk from the big city who'd intruded on his farm. He blinked twice and suddenly he looked very old and very tired.

"It's real simple," he said. "You don't belong here, not really. But you belong enough to fool some folks who ought to know better, so they're going to keep trying to fit you into a life that ain't yours."

"By stealing my car?" I asked.

"Stealing ain't the right word for it, no. But that's a little bit of what's going on, just the smallest part. The fit ain't right. And you know what happens when a man's got a part that don't quite fit into the slot it's supposed to, right?"

I frowned. "You get a different part?"

He gave me a sad little smile. "A sensible man does that,

maybe. A clever man tries to shave off a few bits so it'll fit easier. And a stubborn man gets a hammer."

Thinking about that for a second or two gave me all sorts of unpleasant images. I looked up to meet Carl's eyes and he was nodding. "Now you're starting to get it. You think on that, all right, boy? You think on that for a few days, and maybe we'll have something else to talk about."

"All right. But I still don't know where you fit into all of this."

He grinned. "I'm the caretaker, remember? Now go home. Groceries are on the front porch. You'll want to bring them in before they spoil." He squinted up at the sun. "It might have been cold yesterday, but the heat's back today, you know."

"Wait a minute." There was an edge of panic in my voice that I hadn't put there. "How do I get back to the house?"

Carl grinned a purely evil grin and tossed the shotgun to me. I caught it, barely. "It's your land," he said. "You should know it."

With that, he turned and walked off into the deeper wood. He looked like he knew where he was going.

Me, I waited until Carl was gone, then took a look at where the sun was hanging in the sky and made my best guess at a direction that would lead me back to the house. That worked fine, in that in short order I hit the fence that served to mark the back property line, and I followed that around the long way until I got my bearings again. It didn't take me more than another hour or so, give or take another half hour I didn't really want to spend. I spent the time wiping sweat off my forehead, wishing the damn shotgun were lighter, and thinking about what Carl had said. As pleasant as he'd been—for Carl, anyway—I wasn't convinced. If there was anyone in Maryfield who had an interest in messing with my head, it was him, and he'd had plenty of time to rig whatever the hell he wanted to in the house. He'd had ten years of access, he had the closest thing going to a motive, and I had no doubt he could put together any sort of door-swinging, window-jamming doodad he wanted to.

On the other hand, he'd just had his second chance to get me out of the picture permanently, and he hadn't taken it, not even when he could have rightly called it self defense. Besides, the shape I'd seen in my car couldn't have been Carl, not unless he'd squeezed three of himself into the driver's seat.

But if it wasn't Carl, who was it? I had no answers, and all of a sudden concentrating on how damn heavy the shotgun was seemed like a real good idea.

The groceries were right where Carl had said they would be. And this time, he'd brought beer.

CHAPTER 13

The phone rang twice while I was putting the groceries away. I ignored it both times, figuring that if it was important they'd call back, and if it wasn't I didn't want to talk to them anyway. Carl had given me a lot to think about, and very little of it was good.

It rang again as I was closing the door—with more urgency than you'd give an old push-button credit for. I considered just letting it ring then decided that persistence ought to be rewarded.

"Hello?" I said as I picked up.

"Jesus, Logan, about damn time." Jenna's voice washed down the line with the force of a spring flood. "Where the hell have you been?"

"Out back," I said in my best exaggerated drawl, though I realized as I did it that it didn't take that much exaggeration. "Damn, it's good to hear your voice. How are you?"

"Frustrated," she answered, "because the man who calls me up telling me how much trouble he's in can't be reached due to his sudden need to take nature hikes. Other than that, pissed off at American Airlines, irritated with Hertz, and not entirely thrilled with the MBTA. How are you?"

I almost laughed, but managed to hold it in. "It's been eventful lately," I told her. "Let's just say that I've been out in the rain more than I should have."

"Sounds ominous," she replied. "Care to tell me about it?"

I pulled up a chair and sat myself down, near where the empty shotgun leaned against the wall. "Not particularly, but I have a feeling you'll beat the answer out of me anyway."

That got me a laugh, at least. "Good boy. You're learning. But the good news is, you don't get your beating right now."

"I don't?"

Her voice was full of satisfaction. "Yup. Because I'm coming down to see you, like you asked. I'll be coming in to RDU on Friday and staying a week. If these directions are right, I'll be hitting your place around seven thirty, and I fully expect there to be a jug of moonshine on the table and a barbeque going in the backyard. Banjo music is optional."

"It's not all like that, you know . . ." I started, but she shushed me.

"Of course I know that. But you get so puffed up whenever anybody says anything like that to you that it's absolutely adorable. I'll bet you're bright red right now."

"Pale pink," I replied, "and that's because of the sun."

"Whatever you say, dear. Just make sure that you're ready for me come Friday. Is there anything you want from Boston? I can pack up some Buzzy's roast beef sandwiches if you want—it's not like they can go bad on the trip."

I opened my mouth to tell her that I didn't want anything when it hit me that I meant it—I didn't want anything, and I wasn't even sure I wanted her to come down any more. There was silence on the line for a moment while I tried to figure out how to say it.

"Look, Jenna, I'm very pleased to hear you're coming down," I finally stammered. "But I know you're busy, and really, this is a long way for you to come. If it's a hassle for you, it's all right. We can make it another time, if that's easier for you. Better, even."

Now the silence started on her end, and when she finally started talking, her voice was clipped and a touch nasty. "Are you saying you don't want me to come down?"

"Well," I started, and then I paused. "I just know it's a big hassle."

"No. A big hassle would be trying to get the money back for the tickets and canceling the rental car and trying to get my vacation time back from our HR department. Coming down to see you when you're in trouble is not a hassle.

"What the hell is going on, Logan? Last time we talked you sounded like you were caught in a cross between *Deliverance* and the *Amityville Horror*. Now you're dropping hints about strange North Carolina rain dances and acting like there's nothing going on. Next thing you're going to tell me you got that bruise when you fell down the stairs, and that it's all right, Daddy really does love you but he just gets mad sometimes."

"You have no idea what you're talking about," was all I trusted myself to say. "There's a hell of a lot of stuff going on that you know nothing about, and that you can't know a damn thing about, and I'll thank you not to say things like that about Father."

"Look, Logan, I'm sorry. But you're sounding so strange and, hell, I'm worried about you. You never did mood swings in Boston, but now you're going like a metronome. All I know is what you tell me, but that's telling me something's really wrong, and you sound like you could use a friend."

"Sometimes friends know when to stay away," I said softly.

"And sometimes they know enough to ignore bullshit protestations that everything's fine." She let out a short, sharp breath. "Here's the deal, okay? I'll be there Friday night. When I show up on your doorstep, if you don't want me there, I'll turn around and go right back home. But I'm betting you will want me there. You're just too proud and stubborn to admit it."

I swallowed hard. "Deal," I said, was all I could say, really. A moment passed, and then I added "You don't have to do this, you know."

"I know," she said. "But something tells me I ought to. See you Friday, General Lee."

She hung up. I stared at the phone for a minute then did the same. Friday. I had two days to figure out what was going on before she got here, otherwise things could get right ugly fast. Once Jenna sank her teeth into a problem, she didn't let go until it was solved or in pieces, and if she tried bulldozing her way through Carl and Hanratty, there's no telling what would come of it. She'd come down here, thinking that the same act she pulled in Boston was going to bowl over the locals, but she'd learn soon enough that things were different down here—learn the hard way good and sure.

Jesus. I caught myself. What the hell was I thinking? For a minute there, it sounded like Carl was living my skull, not me. I shook my head to clear it and made a silent prayer that I hadn't pissed off Jenna too badly. Right now, I wasn't sure what was worse—if she took my words to heart and cancelled the trip, or if she came down mad. Either way, it wasn't going to go well for me.

But one thing was for damn sure. I wasn't going to figure anything out sitting at the kitchen table and worrying. I needed to get off my butt and do something.

As I sat there, the phone rang again. "You've got to be kidding me," I said, and I stared at it suspiciously for a moment before lurching to my feet to answer. I caught it on the fourth ring, right around the time most sensible people start thinking about hanging up. Figuring it was Jenna calling back to argue some more, I launched right in.

"Look, you really don't have to come down here. I'll even cover the cost of your tickets. I mean it."

"Damn, you're good. I hadn't even asked if you wanted me to swing on by yet," said a faintly familiar male voice. "But, since y'all feel that way about it, I guess I don't have to ask. This, in case y'all are wondering, is Samuel Fuller. I gave you a ride into town the other day."

"Yeah, right, of course," I stammered. "I mean, let me start again here. Thank you kindly for calling, and you do have my apologies. I, well—let's just say that I thought you were someone else."

"I had made that guess, yes." You could hear the smile in the man's voice. "Apology accepted. Now, would you like me to tell you why I called, or do you want to feel like an ass for a while longer?"

I felt myself grinning. "Can I do both? You do the talking.

I've gotten real good at the being-an-ass thing lately."

"Sounds fair to me," Samuel said, and he chuckled. "Anyway, me and Asa were going to head into town in the morning, and it occurred to me that you might be wanting to ride in with us. I mean, I hope I'm not pokin' my nose where it don't belong here, but you didn't seem to have a car last time we talked, and I'm thinking that walk is mighty long. All of which is a roundabout way of sayin' that if you'd like, we'd be more'n happy to stop and pick y'all up along the way."

I gnawed my lower lip for a minute while I thought about it. "That's mighty friendly of you, Samuel—"

"I told you, call me Sam," he interrupted. "The wife does, and what she says, goes."

"Sam, then. It's very friendly of you, but I'd hate to put you out. If you and Asa have business in town, I don't want to hold you up."

"I told you, Logan, you won't be putting us out none. You're on our way. My place is about three-four miles past you, down the Harrison Farm Road. We pretty much have to swing by. Ain't more than a minute to stop for you." He chuckled again. "Or if'n you want, I can just slow down and you can try to hop in. Just try not to land on the dog."

I had to laugh out loud at that. "Well, keep Asa in the cab, and I won't. All right, you talked me into it. What time should I expect you?"

Sam *hmmed* a bit. "I'm thinking 'bout maybe ten thirty, if that's all right with you."

"You're the one driving, Sam. Whenever the hell you feel like getting here, I'll be ready."

"Mind the language, Logan. This here is a God-fearing phone." There was no heat in his voice, though, and I didn't take him seriously.

"Your phone has my deepest apologies, then," I said. "See you in the morning, then?"

"Morning it is," he said, and he hung up.

I busied myself doing nothing important. Making the bed, tidying up the towels, cleaning a wad of hard toothpaste off the side of the sink—the sort of housekeeping a man's got to think of when a woman might be paying his house a visit. By myself, I'm sure I would have got around to it sooner or later, most likely later. With Jenna coming, though, I needed to start getting the place in order.

Mother always liked a neat house, the voice in my head whispered. *It's good of you to keep things the way she liked them.* I frowned and shook it off. Slamming doors were one thing, but voices in my head were proof, right and proper, that I'd gone bughouse. Answering would have just put the cherry on top of the sundae of crazy I was making myself.

Besides, if I'd said anything, I would have had to say that I was doing it for Jenna, and I was afraid that somehow I'd get an argument.

The sun was going down before I'd finished all the little chores that I'd been neglecting. That was fine with me. There was no mystery in the washing up or in doing some laundry in the sink with help from an ancient bottle of Woolite. No sense in mucking about with the washer, I decided, not if I was only washing a few things. Besides, it felt good to be doing something with my hands that I could see the results of, even when those results were wet socks and dirty suds.

I hung the clothes outside as the sky went purple and the first sparks of yellow light appeared on the road. "Not this time," I told them as I went back into the house, and I tipped two fingers to my forehead in a salute. "You fellas stay over there where it's safe. You decide to come back, well, I'll be waiting."

They didn't answer, not that I'd expected them to. Besides, I'd seen what I needed to from them. Right now, I had other concerns.

The toy soldier was still where I'd set it, right next to where the gun had rested on the kitchen table. Something Hanratty had said—that the poor little fella looked like he was standing guard—struck a chord with me. It gave me an idea.

Not a good idea, I'd have been the first to admit, but an idea just the same.

I made my way back to the bedroom and to the drawer I'd set the box of soldiers in back before I'd gone chasing my car out into the rain. It was still there, but I could see proof that it had been moved and then replaced. Wrinkled clothes, curled corners, that sort of thing. Or at least that's what I told myself.

Wasting no time, I emptied the box out on top of the dresser. The little men spilled out, their clatter the loudest thing in the house. "Sorry, boys," I told them as I sorted one from the other, "but you're going to have to work together for a little bit."

Like I said, it was a damn stupid idea. I didn't think it was going to work; hell, I didn't even know what half the idea was. But doing something felt good, and doing something to watch my back felt even better.

Even if the ones doing the watching were little lead toys.

"Here's the deal," I said, picking up one blue soldier and one red. "You're going to watch out for me. I'm going to put you where you can keep watch, and you stay there, you hear me?" A few steps, a turn into the bathroom, and I found myself in front of the window that had caused me so much trouble. Carefully, I put the soldiers down on the sill, facing out. "Don't you let anything in, neither."

They didn't say anything, nor did they suddenly snap to attention, salute, or do anything else a lead soldier was supposed to be unable to do. They just stood there, facing out, and a great peace came over me.

Sometimes a man needs his old friends to look out for him.

With those two in place, I went back for another handful, and then another. I placed them around the house, on windowsills and facing doors and one in front of the fireplace on general principle, in case Santa came early and in a bad mood. Like I said, I didn't actually think this would do anything, but I felt better for doing it, like I was staking out my borders. They marked my fence, sure as wood and stone would have, and stood as a warning to anyone who'd cross it.

The only door I didn't place one in front of was the one in the mudroom. I'd be going out that way to fetch the laundry, and didn't want to risk stepping on anything I ought not to. It didn't bother me much, though, to leave that place unguarded by tiny painted eyes.

After all, it was just the damn mudroom, and once I finished with the laundry, I'd take care of it, too.

A wind came up around ten, howling around the house while I sat in the kitchen reading one of the books off Father's bookshelf. It was some two-fisted detective novel, a Hammett or a Chandler or someone who wanted to be like them. There were plenty of mean streets and meaner people walking down them, some shooting and some tough talk, and not a whole lot of decency or human kindness. It was a good read, but not the sort of thing a man would necessarily want to live, I decided, and I put it face down on the table as the wind shook the windows.

A few minutes more of listening told me that it was time to bring the laundry in before it all flapped away down to the Thicket. I put my shoes back on—I'd slipped them off when I'd sat myself down at the table—and went out back, trusting there'd be enough moonlight for me to see.

There was, more or less. With the moon looking down and the wind picking up, I gathered my things and brought them in. Somewhere in the distance, a dog was barking. I cursed the sort of cruelty that would leave a dog out in bad weather, and then I went back inside.

I shut the door, blocking out all sound except that of the wind, then took myself to bed. For once, dreams didn't follow.

CHAPTER 14

The wind left and morning arrived, and I got myself up and ready to go to town. The lead soldiers were all where I'd left them. So was the laundry, which I rectified after getting a cup of coffee and some cereal in me.

By ten o'clock I was ready to go. More than ready, really, which meant I was banging around the house like a lizard in a jar. "Calm yourself down," I said. "It's just a trip to town." But I wasn't listening. For one thing, it looked less likely I'd run into Carl in Maryfield than on my own property. For another, there were things in town that I missed, that I'd wanted to do and hadn't yet. Pieces of childhood were waiting to be revisited, and I'd been tardy.

A quick check of my watch told me that I had maybe five minutes before Sam arrived, so I quickly scooped the gun out of the kitchen and shoved it under my bed. No sense having it be the first thing he saw if he came in, after all. He was a sensible man and would probably disapprove of the way I was handling it. Then it was just a case of grabbing my keys and wallet and heading out the door. I locked the door behind me, and then I tried the knob five or six times to make sure I'd actually done so.

I was on attempt number seven—just in case, you know—when Sam rolled up. Asa was in the truck bed this time, head hanging over the side and eyes watching me steadily. "Come on," Sam yelled through the open window on the passenger side. "Time's a-wasting."

I gave the knob one last twist, fought off the urge to try once more, and trotted up the driveway to where the truck was pulled in on the roadside. I scratched Asa's head, which he didn't seem to mind too much, then hopped into the cab.

"Howdy," Sam said, and he shook my hand.

"Howdy yourself." I gestured over my shoulder with my thumb. "You didn't need to get Asa out of his seat for me. I'm just a passenger."

Sam made a dismissive gesture then clamped his hand on the gearshift. "He's been wanting some wind in his face for a while now. Had to keep him in on account of the rain, you know. Now hush up and enjoy the ride."

"Yessir." I grinned. "Thank you again for the ride, Sam. I do appreciate it."

He snorted and threw the truck into gear. " 'Course you do. That's why I offered." The landscape started rolling by. "And don't you worry no more about putting me out or nothing. If I offer something, I mean it. You understand."

"I do," I said, a little subdued. "Just not quite what I'm used to any more, you know what I'm saying?"

He nodded, his gaze fixed on the road. "I guess people are a little different where you've been spending your time. But you're here now, and y'all would do best to remember that." A sudden grin flashed across his face, to let me know he wasn't disapproving. "Save you any number of fox paws, you know what I mean?"

I thought about Carl for a minute. "I think I might," I allowed. "But there is one thing left to say about this."

"Yes?"

I reached into my pocked and pulled out my wallet. With Sam watching out of the corner of his eye, I opened it up, and pulled out a twenty. "This is for the gas," I said, and gave him a glare when he opened his mouth to say something. "Uh-uh. You're doing me a big favor, and the least I can do is chip in a bit."

"I ain't a taxi," Sam said, and there was genuine discomfort in his voice. "You don't need to pay me none, and if you insist, I might get offended."

Irrationally, I felt hot eyes on the back of my neck. I turned to look for a second, and saw Asa staring in through the glass of the back. He didn't look friendly.

I turned back to Sam. "If you don't take it, Sam, I'll get offended. I ain't trying to buy your services here. I'm thanking you for a favor and making sure it doesn't put you out none. If you don't take it, I feel like I'm freeloading, and I get enough of that from other folks around here. *Please.*"

He glanced over at me, his face troubled. "I don't know. It don't seem right." In the back, Asa growled. I refused to look back.

"Let me save a little pride here, Sam," I said, softly. "Man's got to have a little pride."

"Pride's a sin," he answered, but without conviction. "All right, if it makes you feel better, I'll take it. But don't be making this a habit, you hear?"

"I'm hoping not to," I said, and I meant it. Folding the bill up, I stuck it in the cup holder.

"Fair enough," Sam said, and he reached over to turn on the cassette player. Toby Keith's singing started up low, with a faint tape hiss behind it. My arm out the window, I tapped my fingers in time against the metal of the door.

"Didn't figure you for a Toby Keith fan," I said, trying to make conversation. In return, Sam spun the volume up, loud enough to make conversation impossible.

I stopped tapping my fingers, and neither of us said another word until we got into town.

Sam pulled in on Main Street, two blocks down from the police station. I looked over my shoulder at it as I got out, and caught Sam doing the same.

"Thanks again for the ride," I said.

"As I said, it wasn't nothing." He coughed into his hand then went looking in his pockets for a pack of cigarettes without much success. "Got any plan for what you're doing today?"

"Not especial," I said. "Thought maybe I'd see a few places I've been meaning to go back to, maybe pick up a paper and read the classifieds. There might be a car I can get my hands on so I don't have to put Asa out no more."

Hearing his name, the hound began barking. "Easy, boy," Sam said, and he moved over to scratch him behind the ears. "Ain't nothing to get excited about." But the dog didn't settle down much, and he kept himself fixed on me the whole time. His muzzle was practically quivering, and I could hear the scrape of his nails on the truck bed liner as he pawed it. I half-figured that if Sam hadn't been there, Asa would have jumped out and gone after me, and all for no reason that I could think of.

I was pretty sure Sam noticed that, too.

"Sounds like a plan," he told me. "Well, I won't keep you here no more. I'll be heading back in a couple-three hours, and I've my own business to tend to. So I guess I'll meet y'all back here in time? Don't worry none, I won't go leaving you here."

"No worries on my end," I said. "And again, thank you. Two or three hours it is."

"We're agreed, then." He gave a sharp nod then turned to the dog. "Asa, stay." Without checking to see if the hound had listened, he turned on his heel and walked off.

"Good dog," I said, as much to convince myself as anything else, and chose the opposite direction. I didn't have a destination in mind, but giving Sam some space seemed like a real good idea, and I was having few enough of those lately that when one came along, I'd follow it.

A half a block down, I got an itch between my shoulder blades, the sort of thing a man's supposed to feel when someone's looking down a gun at him. I knew that was a foolish feeling, but I stopped and looked back anyhow.

Asa was staring at me with the sort of intensity you could feel over distance. I was a rabbit to him, that and nothing more, and if he got a chance he'd be on me. Of that I was now certain, though I had no idea why.

And Sam was going in the front doors of the police station.

"Well, damn," I said softly, and I turned back around.

Giving Sam some space seemed like a good idea indeed.

A couple of blocks and a couple of turns farther on, I finally began to give some thought as to where I might actually be going. Carl had taken care of the most urgent of my needs, and while I did want to get a paper, doing so wouldn't take a couple of hours. That left me at loose ends, as I didn't particularly feel like window shopping, or proper shopping neither. Asa probably wouldn't look kindly on my dumping a load of stuff into the truck bed with him, for one thing, and for another, I wasn't sure if bringing more things into the house was a good idea. Not until I figured out what was going on, in any case.

That got me thinking about the house, though, and about what had happened down in the Thicket. Carl's words hadn't cleared up too much for me, but they had reinforced the notion that there was something in the house—hell, anywhere I went—that just wasn't right.

I chewed that over in my mind for a bit, then felt the sun coming hard down on me. It was hot and getting hotter. I looked left and right and saw I was across the street from Hilliard's Pharmacy. Next to me was some coffee chain shop or other—what some marketing boy was thinking when he put one of those in Maryfield was beyond me. Given a choice between the two, there wasn't any. Hilliard's soda fountain was the mecca of my youth, and part of me still harbored the suspicion that the idea of Vanilla Coke had been stolen from one of Hilliard's soda jerks. Untrue, I knew, but with a stubborn third-grader's fury I held onto the notion. You need to defend what's yours, after all.

I crossed the street (*Maynard*, memory told me without

looking at the sign. The mental map was re-drawing itself nice and easy now), making sure not to jaywalk. No doubt Hanratty would have popped up out of a mailbox or trash can to give me a stern talking to if I had, so I watched the light, waited, and walked over when it was legal to do so.

Hilliard's hadn't changed much from the outside, at least. Its sign, its green letters hand-painted on a field of faded gold, hung down over the door, and the breeze had a hard time convincing it to sway even a little bit. The window was still filled with huge glass vessels of all shapes, loaded with a variety of mysterious fluids in strange, bright colors. The paint on the glass was still gold edged with black, proudly announcing that Hilliard's Pharmacy had medicines, supplies, sandwiches, soda, and ice cream. Underneath, in smaller letters, were the words I was hoping for: "L. Hilliard, proprietor." Old Man Hilliard had been called that when I was a kid, and I had a sneaking suspicion Father had called him that in his boyhood as well. He'd been one of the defining figures of my youthful imagination, a big shaggy bear of a man with a white head of hair and a gray beard that hung halfway down his chest. He didn't look like a pharmacist ought to, according to the television, but he'd been there as long as anyone could remember, and he was as good mixing up medicines and prescriptions as he was making ice cream sodas. Every kid wanted a job at Hilliard's after school or come summer, but he didn't take many, and he expected perfection. Screw up something as simple as a root beer float and you were out on your duff, no questions asked. Old Man Hilliard expected perfection and, by expecting it, nine times out of ten he got it.

I hadn't even gotten the chance to fail, but that hadn't made a dent in my enthusiasm. And when I pushed open the door and heard the familiar bells jingle overhead, for a moment I was nine again and counting my pocket change in hopes of having enough for what my greedy little heart had settled on desiring.

It was Hilliard himself who looked up when I came in, looking more like a sheepdog than ever. His mop of hair had grown down over his forehead so that his eyes were nearly hidden, and his beard had gone pure white. His hands were still steady, though, as I saw when he reached up and adjusted the spectacles hidden in all that hair.

"Can I help you?" he asked as I threaded my way through the narrow aisles. The products were new, at least in part, but the layout was the same. Fat men didn't do well in Hilliard's, that was for certain.

"Mr. Hilliard? I think I could go for a vanilla cola, if you're still serving."

"Huh. I know that voice." He looked down on me over his glasses. "Now let me think a minute . . . you're the Logan boy, aren't you?"

I nodded. "That I am."

"Well, then. Vanilla cola it is. You want a scoop of ice cream in that?" He moved over to the soda pumps, as shiny and bright as the day they'd been put in. "That used to be your favorite, as I recall."

"You're good," I said, grinning. "No ice cream this time, I think, but thank you. I'd hate to spoil my lunch."

"That never bothered you before," he said, and he drew the

soda for me with a surgeon's precision. He set it down in front of me on the counter as I slid onto a stool, resisting the urge to spin around just for the sheer heck of it.

I said a heartfelt "Thank you," dunked a straw from the antique container on the counter into the glass, and took a delicious sip. "How much do I owe you?"

"Two sixty-five," he said. "Prices have, of necessity, gone up a bit."

"I can imagine." I dug out my wallet and slapped a five on the counter. "Up in Boston this would go for four or five bucks, easy."

"Good thing I'm not in Boston, then," he said, and he turned away to make my change. "There's enough change going on right here for me, thank you."

"I noticed." I gestured in the rough direction of the coffee joint. "When the heck did that move in?"

"Not that long ago." Coins landed on the counter, and he shoved the pile across to me. "Folks don't seem to be taking to it, though, which I find to be a good thing."

"Me, too," I added, and I meant it. The level in my glass, I noticed, was going down rapidly. "So, how are things doing? Do all the kids still line up to work here?"

"Some of them," Hilliard said with a shrug, and he pulled out a rag to wipe the condensation off the counter. "Most aren't that interested in hard work and doing things right, but then again, neither were you. So I guess things haven't changed that much. It's good to see you back, though. How long are you staying?"

"I don't know," I answered, surprising myself by meaning

it. "It depends on a lot of things. Right now, I'm just trying to figure out what to do next."

"That makes sense. If you're back here from Boston now, with all your kin gone, it's because you've got nowhere else to go. Not that I'm judging you, mind."

I sucked at the straw, which made crackling noises as it pulled the last few drops of soda up out of the bottom of the glass. "No offense taken. And I'm glad to see you're still here."

He snorted, then he stuffed the rag back in his pocket and went off to fiddle with a pile of papers by the register. "Young Mr. Logan, I ask you where else should I be? This pharmacy is my right and proper place. No matter how many big-city coffee shops they try to install on my doorstep, I am not going anywhere until they carry me out of here on a stretcher. Maybe not even after that." He suddenly flashed me a grin. "I'd love to haunt whoever bought the place after I passed on. I'd look over his shoulder from the other side, just to make sure he was doing things right. And if he wasn't, well, it would be my bound and duty to let him know, don't you think?"

I pushed the empty glass away, suddenly uncomfortable. "You don't have a son to take over?" I asked, trying to change the subject.

"If I did, he'd be answering your questions instead of me, now wouldn't he?" He turned, spotted an invisible smudge on the mirror on the wall behind him, and rubbed at it with another cloth he pulled out of somewhere. "I never married and never had any children. I just wasn't lucky that way, though in a sense every child born in this town for forty years has been a little bit mine. At least, the ones with the sense to enjoy an ice cream soda now and then." His work at the mirror done, he turned back to me and tucked the cloth into his sleeve. "Can I make you another? You've got a few years' worth to catch up on, as I recall."

"No, thank you," I said. "I need to get back into training before I can handle two at a time."

Hilliard snorted out a laugh. "A smart man knows his limits. All right, then, no loitering in the store. Go on, and good luck with whatever you do with the rest of your day. If, of course, you've figured that out as well."

"Nope," I confessed, and I slid down from the stool. "But I'm sure I'll come up with something."

"A man lacking direction could do worse than to go see the preacher," he said. "You might want to think about that."

"You know, I just might." Still chewing on the idea, I went back out into the sunshine, the bells jangling behind me.

A smart man, when there's something going on in his house that ain't ought to be, goes to talk to his preacher. That's a simple fact. Usually it's just something like strife between a husband and wife, or a man and his conscience, and that's what a preacher is for, to tell you what the Good Book says about the matter and to set you straight. But all things considered, this trouble of mine was most likely a preacher's responsibility as well. Even if it was just my mind playing tricks on me, it made plain simple sense to go to church to maybe find an answer or two.

Fortunately, the church itself wasn't that far away. Three

blocks up Maynard and halfway down Porter: that's where I wanted to go. Back in the day, that had been the edge of town, the sign that you'd walked a long, long way. Now it seemed almost painfully close, like the walk wasn't giving me enough time to figure out what I needed to say.

Then I was at the church, and it was time to stop wondering.

The church we used to go to was still standing, which I suppose surprised me a little. We didn't go often—Christmas and Easter and the occasional Sunday when Mother was feeling bad about how we might have stood with God at that moment—but I remember it as slightly frightening. It was all white paint and pointed steeples and heavy wooden doors, and a simple sanctuary with pews twenty deep on either side. No stained glass—it wasn't that kind of place—and not a lot of other frills. It was a church for people who treated their churching like they did everything else: a serious part of life to be done seriously and without any fuss.

The minister had been a tall, slender man named Jefferson Trotter, but he'd never been anything but the Reverend Doctor Trotter to any of us children. He was a soft-spoken man, firm in his beliefs but with a steady heat, not a raging flame. Doctor Trotter taught Sunday school and ran services and organized covered dish suppers and pretty much was the hub the church's wheel revolved around—and he did it with humor and grace and an unusual tolerance for the misbehaviors of small boys who didn't understand why you had to sit still in church.

Town had caught up to the church, I saw when I walked up to it. It used to sit on a lot all by itself, with the graveyard out back and stretching away. Now there was a sandwich place hard on its right, and a hardware store on the left. But the church building itself still stood, still painted white in the places where the years hadn't turned it gray. The same old sign stood out front announcing the weekly service schedule, and I was pleased to see that the Reverend Doctor Trotter was apparently still in residence. And the doors might have been painted a solemn shade of green, but they were just as heavy as I remembered when I pulled them open and walked into the church itself.

The lobby on the other side of the doors had a tile floor of that same green, as well as double doors leading to the chapel. There were also a couple of doors leading off to the necessaries, and a couple of display cases for pictures and other knickknacks the Reverend thought important. A short hallway led off to the right. If memory served, that was where the offices for the Reverend and the church secretary were, along with the Sunday school classroom and, most important in my memories, the water fountain.

I walked down the corridor slowly, well aware of the sound my heels were making on the tile floor. At the end of it was Doctor Trotter's office, and the door was closed. There was no window in it, either, a change from the old days. Back then, you could always look in and see what he was up to. Now, it was a big, solid slab of wood.

Not quite sure how badly I wanted an answer, I knocked a couple of times. After a few seconds, I could hear the Reverend's voice, calling "Yes? Who is it?" It sounded like it was coming from way far away.

"Reverend Trotter?" I answered. "It's Jacob Logan. I don't know if you remember me."

The door opened. "Oh, yes," Dr. Trotter said. "I remember you. You're quite the topic of conversation these days. Come on in."

He'd been honed by the years rather than worn down, that much I saw as he stood there in the doorway. His face was thinner, his nose sharper, and that knife of an Adam's apple he'd always had stuck out farther. But the lines on his face were still few, his eyes were bright, and he didn't look a day over fifty. He looked like he was ready to go out and play a round of golf, and beat you handily if you were fool enough to challenge him.

"Come in, come in," he urged, and then he turned back into his office. I followed him in and sat myself down in the hard wooden chair opposite his desk. For his part, he sat himself down behind the desk, a thick wood thing made from trees that probably went extinct before the dinosaurs did. Neat stacks of paper covered the desktop like the skyline of a young city, with a tower of books at one side. Something about that desk bothered me, and it took me a minute to realize that it was the first one I'd seen in years that didn't have a computer on it.

"So, what finally brings you back to Maryfield?" he asked once I'd made myself comfortable. "Missed the home cooking?"

"Just taking some time to relax and pull myself together," I answered. "I thought I'd come back to where I'd started."

He leaned forward. "A lot of men have thought that. It's

worked out better for some than for others. I noticed you haven't been back to church since you've arrived."

I chuckled. "Well, I figured not to break any old habits, Reverend. No sense doing now what I didn't do back then."

He chuckled softly. "That's one way to look at it. But you're here now. It's been, what, five years?"

"Since Mother's funeral, yes." I nodded. "Thank you again for that. It was a lovely service."

"Your mother was a lovely woman. Kind, loving, tolerant to a fault—you could have done a lot worse for a parent, you know. So, what I'd like to know is whether the lessons she taught you stuck?"

I blinked in surprise. "I figured you'd want to know how I was with Jesus."

Doctor Trotter shrugged. "You know where you stand with Jesus, and if you didn't listen to me about that when you were nine, you're not going to listen now. Your mother, on the other hand, made a right strong impression on you, and a good one. I'm hoping that held."

"Actually," I said, and I coughed. "It's about Mother—and Father—that I'm here to see you."

"Really?" One of his eyebrows shot up in a move I'd spent hours trying to imitate as a kid. "Something troubling your conscience?"

"Something troubling my house, more like it." I looked up at him, into those sharp blue eyes. "You know I moved back into the old family place, I reckon?"

He nodded. "Jacob, everyone in Maryfield has heard that, with the possible exception of you. It's a lovely house, and a sturdy one, too. What seems to be the matter with it?"

"I don't know," I told him. "Someone seems to be trying to drive me out of it. I just haven't decided if it's land speculators or Carl doing it."

Doctor Trotter chortled to himself. "Land speculators? Lord, you have been away for a while. All the building's going on a good long way from here, and it's liable to stay that way. Someone tried to come in a few years ago and build big fat McMansions out on the old Hayter place a few years back. They chopped down a few trees, made a hole in the ground, and then promptly lost their shirts." He paused, and looked thoughtful for a moment. "Never filled in the hole, either, but a bunch of folks from town took care of that. Replanted the trees, too, while they were at it."

"What happened?" I asked.

"That depends on whom you ask." His eyes were twinkling. "If you ask the bank, they were unable to get infrastructure improvements necessary to make the project viable and profitable. Meaning, of course, they weren't able to get the town or the county to pay for four lanes of blacktop going to and from the Hayter farm, and devil take the hindmost."

I laughed. "That must have been some town meeting. I can just imagine some city lawyer trying to flim-flam folks into voting to spend their tax money on that."

"It did not go quite as they expected," the reverend agreed, and he scratched his nose. "I think you can probably understand some of the . . . culture shock they might have been dealing with."

"A little," I confessed. "Less every day, though. At least, that's what I'm hoping. So what did everyone who didn't work for the bank think happened?"

Doctor Trotter folded his hands in front of himself like a sphinx and gave a half-smile. "That depends. The men working construction had all sorts of equipment failures. Mechanical breakdowns, paperwork snarls, all that sort of thing. Other folks just said it was plain bad luck." He nodded knowingly.

I sat back in my chair. "Industrial sabotage? Here?"

"Hmm. I wouldn't say that. Things just ... didn't go as planned. Mind you, I think it worked out for the best. The town didn't need those houses or the people who'd buy them. They'd come out here looking for the country life, as long as it came with all the conveniences of the big city, and when they didn't find them they'd import them. If they want that, there's Raleigh or Charlotte. Maryfield's best off being Maryfield."

"That it is," I said neutrally, and I thought about my car. Gone now, it had fit in about as well as those homes would have.

Just plain bad luck.

Doctor Trotter coughed once, gently, into his hand. "I'm sorry about that, Jacob. I do go on a bit, but that's a necessary trait in a man who has to give sermons."

"And eulogies," I added.

He nodded. "And eulogies. I did both of your parents', as I recall. But we're off the subject, or might be. And since we've eliminated land speculators"—he gave a little chuckle at that—"tell me why you think Carl Powell might be trying to drive you off your land."

I rubbed my eyes, trying to imagine the list of all the strange things that had happened, that could only be traced back to Carl, if you bothered to trace them at all. "Little things. My car getting stolen, and Carl knowing way too much about it. My mail getting intercepted. Doors slamming open and shut, things showing up in places where I didn't leave them. Stuff like that. And since Carl's the only one besides me who's got a key to the place, I figure if anybody's behind this, it's him."

There was silence for a moment, and then for another. Doctor Trotter sat back in his chair, steepled his fingers in front of his face, and looked down at me past them. "Do you really believe that?" he finally asked, in a tone that indicated that just maybe, he didn't.

I thought about it. "I don't see any other way it could be, Doctor Trotter. He's had that place to himself for a long time, he seems mighty protective of Mother's memory, and here I come setting up house in a place he's kept like a shrine. Why wouldn't he want me out?"

"Maybe he's got more going on in his life than just you and that house?" he inquired gently, and I felt myself flushing. "You're doing a fine job of putting together something from what you know, Jacob, but you don't know everything. Leap to too many conclusions or leave out too many things, and you'll find yourself jumping into things you'll need some help to climb out of."

"Okay, fine." I waved my hands to indicate surrender. "I did leave a few details out, things that maybe don't fit with my ideas about Carl. But I'm not seeing anything else that it could be. I mean, no one's in that house but me, and no one's been in that house but Carl."

Reverend Trotter frowned a little bit, the sort of frown that used your face and half your body, too. "That's not true, Jacob. Your mother's been in that house. Your father, too, though he's longer gone. You might want to think about them before you go imagining what's going on in your life."

A slow suspicion crossed my mind, and made its way to my mouth before I could stop it. "Are you saying that my parents' house is haunted? That it's Mother who's spooking me? Oh, come on, Reverend. If it's not Carl, it's Carl and his buddies doing the same number on me that they did on that construction project. You shouldn't have told me about it."

"You should have listened more closely," he replied. "You're assuming it's Carl, and you're assuming that whatever it is wants you gone, and you're assuming a whole lot of other things, all of which revolve around you. Try thinking about things from your parents' point of view. Maybe there's something someone wants from you."

"Yeah, they want me gone." I snorted, but the fire was out of me. I thought about what he'd said for a moment. Objects that moved on their own, doors that slammed open and shut, the fireflies—those were all things Carl would have had one hell of a time rigging. Maybe, just maybe. . . .

"Wait a minute." I sat up a little straighter. "Leaving out the whole question of what Mother would or wouldn't approve of, are you telling me you do believe in ghosts?"

"The Witch of Endor called up the Samuel's ghost, after all, and if ghosts are good enough for Saul, they're good enough for me. The Bible's sort of the original ghost story, when you think about it. With that in mind, why shouldn't I believe in ghosts?"

I blinked. "Well, when you put it that way, I suppose it makes sense. Just a bit of a surprise, really."

The frown faded. "You'd be surprised less if you thought more, you know. I'm not one of those fire and brimstone preachers who thinks anything that isn't wearing white and playing a harp must be the devil's work. You want one of them, I hear there's a church over in Stem that's got a fine one. Me, I prefer to think God understands shades of gray, and that His creation is capable of more than absolutes. So that leaves plenty of room for ghosts."

"Okay, I can see that." I shifted in my seat, feeling like I was twelve and in trouble all over again. Reverend Trotter always had that effect on me—you never wanted to slouch in front of the man, lest he be disappointed. He was like everyone's grandfather, the one you wanted to make proud of you.

Even when he was echoing my crazy talk about ghosts right back at me.

"So," I continued, "let's say maybe you're right—not that I'm necessarily saying so. Seeing as you, unlike Officer Hanratty or my one lifeline back to civilization, don't think talking about ghosts or other high strangeness is pure crazy, what does the Bible recommend for ghosts?"

He waggled a long, thin finger at me. "I'm not saying you're not crazy, and don't assume Officer Hanratty is. She didn't seem to think so when she came by earlier to ask about you. As for the ghosts, I'd suggest clean living. Ghosts are usually unhappy about something, and if you live right, you might make whoever it is happier."

"There aren't a lot of suspects for who it might be," I argued.

"My family built that house. My family's the only ones ever to live in it. And there weren't ever any ghosts in it before. If it isn't Mother, I don't know who it might be."

"It could be your father," he said mildly. "Or your grand-father, grandmother, or a spirit who wandered by and found it hospitable. It might not even have anything to do with the house at all—God works in mysterious ways, and the devil works hard to imitate Him. That being said, your mother does look like a likely candidate. Any idea why she might decide to suddenly start haunting you?"

I shook my head. "Not really. Something I should think about, really."

He stood. "Yes, it is. When you're done thinking about it, you might want to come back and talk to me again. And if you're feeling truly ambitious, you might want to come by on Sunday morning. I hear there's something worth hearing around these parts if you do."

I grinned, and then I stood and shook his hand. His grip was still strong, I noticed, and his fingers curled around to the inside of my wrist. "I just might do that," I said. "If I can get my hands on a car, I just might."

"The Lord will provide," Reverend Trotter said as he guided me to the door, "and if he doesn't, you might want to look in the classifieds. Good day, Jacob Logan. It's good to have you back."

With that, the door shut behind me in a way that said my business here was done. Faintly through the door I could hear Doctor Trotter humming. So help me, it sounded like a Johnny Cash song. "Folsom Prison Blues," if I wasn't mistaken. Not the sort of song you'd expect a preacher to know and love. *To each his own*, I guessed, and took a sip of water from the long-cherished fountain. It was warm and tasted faintly of copper, just like it always had.

I smiled, wiped the extra water off my chin with the back of my hand, and headed out. Bits of the conversation stuck in my head as I took myself to the door. The fact that Officer Hanratty had been asking the Reverend about me set off alarms. I wasn't too pleased that Reverend Trotter didn't take the time to reassure me he'd told her that I was a fine, upstanding citizen and a good Christian to boot. I tried to think of anything I might have done back in the day—frogs turned loose in Sunday school class, sermons slept through, Bibles highlighted in red crayon—that might have earned me poor marks in his book, and I couldn't come up with anything.

I also couldn't come up with any reason Hanratty would be sniffing around my roots like this. Sure, I was worth looking into as part of the case, but to ask the preacher? That was just plain odd.

With a push, the doors to the church swung open, and I stepped out into the sunshine. As the light hit me, something else did, as well.

Hanratty.

She wasn't the only one who could ask questions.

What the hell did I know about Officer Hanratty, and who was she to go poking her nose into my past? I had no god-damned idea and that worried me.

With a silent apology to Reverend Trotter for taking the Lord's name in vain on church property, I hit the sidewalk and turned left. Something else the Reverend had said to me resonated, gave me a direction I could follow.

Check in the classifieds, he'd said when I mentioned my need for a car. The newspaper wouldn't be a bad place to start looking for information on Officer Hanratty, not a bad one at all.

The library was three blocks down, the local newspaper one up and another one over beyond that. I started walking faster.

CHAPTER 15

The library, being closer, was my first target. In all honesty it wasn't much of a library—just a little brick box of a building with a set of glass doors out front and a sign liberated from a closed church that announced what the week's programs were in changeable white letters. The building was one story tall, with a half-sized basement tucked underneath for microfilm, magazines, and other things that started with "M." All the books and the main desk were on the first floor, the better to make sure no one stole anything. Not that book theft was a huge problem in Maryfield, mind you, but the librarians—a pair of elderly spinster women named Miss Lillian and Miss Rose—weren't taking any chances. It was said that they'd defended that book collection against Sherman, and a couple of people believed it until it was pointed out that the Army of the Cumberland had never come anywhere near our town.

Nobody argued that the two Misses hadn't been there to give a sigh of relief when it passed by, though.

A sign in the window told me that the place was indeed open, though the lighting inside was dim enough to give the opposite impression. I pushed for a moment, got no response, and then I pulled the door open. "Brilliant," I told myself as

I stepped inside. "That's a hell of a way to make an entrance, Logan."

Unlike Hilliard's, the interior of the library had changed. Gone were the dingy old lamps and faded orange panels on the wall. Instead, there were fluorescents overhead and new metal shelves that were densely packed with titles, some of which had actually been published in the last ten years. A small reading area had been set up dead center, with a few overstuffed chairs around a low, round table. Against the back wall was an honest-to-goodness computer terminal, right next to the paper card catalog.

Behind the desk was a woman who most certainly was not either Miss Lillian or Miss Rose. She was maybe twenty-five at the outside, short and slender and, truth be told, lovely in a wholesome, schoolmarmish sort of way. Her hair was dirty blonde, done up in the sort of bun you only see on librarians in the movies, and she had glasses with thin black rims resting a little too far down her nose. She was wearing a white cotton blouse, very conservatively cut, and reading a magazine. I leaned over the counter to get a better look—at the magazine, mainly—and noticed as she turned the pages that there weren't any rings on those fingers.

The magazine, incidentally, was *Discover*. They hadn't subscribed to that back when I'd lived in town.

"Can I help you?" she asked, and I suddenly realized that I was still leaning over the counter.

"Umm, yes," I stammered, and I leaned back. My cheeks felt hot. I figured they were one of the colors at the back of the red section of the crayon box. "I'm here about an overdue book."

"Really?" One of her eyebrows shot up. "And how long overdue is this book, Mr. . . ."

"Logan," I answered. "And about sixteen, seventeen years, I think. It was a copy of *The Hobbit*. I, uhh, I lost the book."

That part wasn't strictly true. I hadn't lost the book; I'd kept it and taken it with me to Boston, and packed it up on the truck with most of my other belongings. Still, admission of open theft of library property did not seem like the best way to make a good impression on this woman, and I felt that making a good impression was a wise thing to do.

Besides, the longer I looked at her, the more I decided I liked schoolmarms.

"Well, Mr. Logan, let's see." She pulled out a pocket calculator and started tapping numbers on it with the well-chewed end of a pencil. "At five cents a day, times three hundred and sixty five days a year, times sixteen years—I'm giving you the benefit of the doubt here, you see—plus an extra twenty cents because of the four leap years—we're looking at two hundred ninety-two dollars and twenty cents. Plus administrative fees, of course." She looked up from the calculator with serious gray eyes and stared at me, hand out. "Cash only."

I must have gulped hard, because she let loose a peal of laughter that would have gotten a whole slew of nasty looks from Miss Lillian back in the day.

"No, no," she said, and she giggled rather nicely. "Oh, my, did you think I was serious? Worst case scenario, you would have had to pay the replacement cost, that's all. Besides, we had a general amnesty three years ago. All is forgiven, honest, though if you want to make a donation we won't say no. My *goodness*, you should have seen your face."

"Heh," was all I could offer. "Very clever, Miss. . . ."

"Moore," she said, pulling her hand back before I could shake it. "Adrienne Moore. Now, seriously, how can I help you?"

I tried to will the blood out of my cheeks and my eyes above her rather modest neckline. "Actually, I was hoping to do a little newspaper research. Do you still have the microfilm archives downstairs?"

She nodded. "*The New York Times, Raleigh News and Observer, Winston-Salem Journal, Charlotte Observer,* and the *Maryfield Administrator.* All of them go back at least ten years. The readers are a little tricky, though, if you don't know how to use them."

"That's great news," I said, and I glanced around the room in hopes of locating the stairs to the basement. "Are they the same readers that were here twenty years ago?"

"They are indeed. So you won't have any trouble with them?"

"Nope." I took a few steps toward the basement steps. "Thanks for the help."

"Oh no," she said, and she came out from behind the desk. "You're not done with me yet."

"Beg pardon?"

She swept on past me, a jangling ring of keys in her hand. "Unless you've got a lockpick in your wallet, you need me to open the microfiche cabinet for you. Mind the second step; it's a little loose." And with that, she bounced down into the basement, all business and daring me to follow.

"Still?" I asked the air, and then I followed her down.

The basement, like the upstairs, had been refurbished a bit. There was new carpet on the floor—or at least newer carpet than I was used to—and the walls had been painted a cheery shade of yellow. The same old microfilm readers sat on the same old heavy-legged tables, though, and if the chairs were new, they were the sons and daughters of the ones that had been there all those years before. A massive metal cabinet the color of "sick and hung over" squatted against the wall, each drawer labeled with the name of a different paper. This was where Miss Moore walked, sizing it up like it were a puzzle.

Me, I sat myself down at the first reader and fiddled with it, just to make sure I remembered what the heck I was doing. It all seemed to come back pretty quickly, which was a blessing. After the mishap with the door and the stupidity with the library fine, I didn't want the librarian to see me screw up again. A man can only stand looking foolish so many times in front of a pretty girl.

If she noticed my fumbling, she didn't say anything. "What paper and what year are you looking for, Mr. Logan?"

"Please, call me Jake. And I guess I'll go with the *Administrator*, maybe five years ago and working my way forward."

"I think we can do that, Mr. Logan." She popped the top drawer open and pulled out a couple of spools of microfilm. "Five and four years ago. I can't let you have more than two at a time. Library policy, you see."

I gave her my best puppy dog eyes. "Look, I'd hate to have you running up and down the stairs every few minutes, just because I'm not sure where to look. I promise I'll take good care of it if you just let me have all five years."

She looked at me long and hard. "You're pulling something here, aren't you?"

I shook my head. "Nope. Just trying to find out a piece of town history that I missed while I was living in Boston. I was hoping to be as little of a pain in the ass as possible while I did it. Not that I don't enjoy your company, but I figure you've got things to do—better things than to constantly unlock your drawers for me."

"I'll pretend you didn't just say that," she said with a frown, but not with a big one. "Fine. To keep you from rattling, as you put it, my drawers, I'll give you the other three. But don't you tell anyone about this, and you take good care of them. Otherwise, so help me, I will . . ." She thought for a moment to come up with a suitable threat. "I *will* institute that fine, and whatever else I can think of to make your life miserable. Do you understand me?"

"Why does everyone in this town keep on asking me that question?" I asked, even as she pulled the rest of the microfilm out for me. "And yes, I understand, and I do appreciate your letting me do this. Thank you."

"Maybe they keep asking because you don't seem like you understand much, and you're welcome." She closed and locked the drawer, then pivoted and put the microfilm on the desk next to me. "I'm going to trust you here. Don't make me regret that. Oh, and I'm going to assume that you *do* in fact know how to use the reader?"

"I do," I assured her. "Used to come down here all the time when I was a kid."

"I'm sure you did," she said, gnawing on her lower lip. "All right. Yell if you need help or another roll. For the *Times* or the N&O, you're going to have to switch to microfiche—that machine over in the corner. Good luck with whatever you're hunting."

"Thank you," I said, and before I finished she was already thumping back up the stairs. I very deliberately kept my focus on the roll of film I was threading, and only took one whiff of the lingering scent of her perfume in the air before deciding to breathe through my mouth for the rest of the day.

The *Administrator* was a local paper of the purest sort; thirty or so pages thick on its good days and based entirely on advertising from stores everyone knew about already. It had gone through a series of name changes over the years, from the *Maryfield Democrat* (boycotted by the local Republicans) to the *Maryfield Republican* (ditto from the other side) to the current one, which everyone agreed was an awful name whose only saving grace was that it didn't piss anyone off. With the name controversy out of the way, everyone in town had—and I assumed still did—renewed their subscriptions, as much to show local spirit as anything else. The lead stories were mainly about farming, high school sports, and local politics, with the occasional neighborhood crime getting front page coverage for weeks. It took a mighty big national or international story to make the front page of the *Administrator*; the editors figured you'd get that news elsewhere, but Dan Rather wasn't going to tell you if Maryfield Regional matched up well with Black Mountain in the state football playoffs, Class A.

The focus on local news would serve me well, though, in my

search. The debut of a new police officer, especially a female one, was always big news. No doubt Hanratty's hiring in Maryfield would have been splashed all over the front page for a good long while. And with the *Administrator's* reporting style being best described as "nosy neighbor peeking in your window," I was bound to find out all that I wanted about Hanratty and probably a bit more.

The days sped by in a blur. 2002 was replaced by 2003 and 2004. I saw football games won, basketball games lost, mayors elected and hassled and replaced. Stores opened and closed, paving projects started, dragged on and finally ended, and occasionally someone got themselves shot in a hunting accident. There was no sign of Hanratty anywhere, though. Ten or fifteen times, I cursed under my breath and wished for an online version of the paper with a searchable index.

I was midway through 2005 when the librarian came trotting back down the stairs. "Need any help?" she asked.

"I need some inspiration, I think," I replied. "I'm looking for a bit of local news, but so help me, I can't dig it up."

"Well," she said, and she pulled up a chair next to mine, "what exactly are you looking for? I might be able to help."

I looked over at her. Legs demurely crossed under a long navy skirt, chair a genteel distance away, eyes on the scratchy display; she seemed oblivious to the fact that I was staring at her, for which I was thankful. "I'm trying to find out about a police officer."

"Oh, are you now?" Now she looked at me, her eyes catching mine. "And why, pray tell, are you doing that?"

We locked gazes, and then I looked away. "Well, I've had

some reason to talk to the police lately, and I figured I'd just like to know who I'm dealing with."

"Dealing with the police . . ." She snapped her fingers. "Wait a minute, I know who you are. You're that man who had his car stolen, right?"

"Guilty as charged," I said with a shrug.

"You know, between that and the drawers comment, you might want to think a bit harder about your word choice," she said mischievously. My face must have fallen, because she leaned forward and patted my hand like a grade-school teacher reassuring a nervous student. "Oh. Don't look like that. I read about that just the other day, and that's how I know. Someone stole it right out from in front of your house, didn't they?"

"Right." I nodded. "I'm surprised the paper didn't send someone out to interview me."

"It would have been too much work," she said in a stage whisper. "Besides, they're down the block from the police station, so what more do they need?"

"What indeed?" I shoved my chair back from the reader and narrowly missed going over backward when the feet caught on the carpet. "A few leads might be nice."

"I'm afraid I can't help you there, but I might be able to help with the other matter. Who are you looking for?" Her voice was prim, her manner all business, and she slid her chair over to the space mine had just vacated.

"Officer Hanratty," I told her. "I know she's not from around here, and I don't remember her from the last time I was back in town. So I was wondering when she joined the force and if there was anything about her background. You know, where she came from, if she was on the police force anywhere else first, maybe why she came out to Maryfield."

"And her home address so you could wrap toilet paper around her shrubs?" To my horrified look, she said, "I'm just joking. You are *so* easy to tease. Now hang on one minute." She sorted through several rolls until she came up with one I'd already looked through.

"Ah," she said. "This is it."

"I've already been through that one," I protested.

"You were looking for the wrong thing," she said with a hint of triumph in her voice. "Hanratty's her maiden name. When she came here, she was Officer Lee."

"Oh," I said, feeling like a fool as she spooled up the tape. "Did her husband die?"

Her response was distracted, her fingers full of microfilm. "He ran off two years ago. Probably running for his life, if you believe half the stories they tell, not that anyone around here repeats them. At least, not where she can hear them."

"That's probably smart," I agreed.

"Probably," she echoed, and she started whipping through film. "Here you go. If I understood you correctly, this should be what you were looking for." She scooted her chair half out of the way, and I scooted mine halfway in. One long finger tapped the screen.

"Next time," she added with a prim little smile, "just ask for help."

I thought about answering, and then decided against it and bent my head to see what Miss Moore had uncovered for me. The headline read, "New Additions to Local Police Force," and underneath was a picture of a man and a woman smiling uncomfortably in Maryfield police uniforms. The date in the corner was June 16, 2002, and lower down on the page were stories about the upcoming election and the exploits of a local boy who'd just been promoted to the Double-A Greenville Braves.

I studied the picture for a minute. The woman was much thinner than the Hanratty I knew, but now that I understood what I was looking at, I could see that it was indeed the woman I'd talked to. You could see that same determined look in her eye, that same set of the jaw, even across the years and the lousy quality of the picture reproduction.

"Wow," I said. "What happened?"

Miss Moore shrugged. "Nobody really knows. I don't like prying into other people's private lives, but the best guess I have is that she liked the town and he didn't, and when he left town she stayed. Other people have ideas that aren't quite so nice, but that's just gossip." She made a chipmunk face that explained exactly how she felt about telling tales out of school and crossed her arms.

"Hmm," I said, and I studied the picture. "She seems . . . determined."

"Even more so now," the librarian agreed. "You do want to be on her good side."

"It's too late for that, I'm afraid." I skimmed the article. There was a lot about how Maryfield was very happy to have two new officers with experience in the Durham County Sheriff's Office and police departments. They were out here as part of a new state initiative to share expertise with rural police departments, blah blah blah, and nothing more useful. There were absolutely no biographical details on either one of them, except that vague mention of their previous employment.

That had me curious.

"Read enough?" Miss Moore asked. "I'm afraid there isn't much else to see, at least not in the *Administrator*. When Officer Lee left, it was regarded as tasteless to report on it. There's maybe a column inch or two, but it's buried a couple of pages in. No pictures, of course."

"Of course." I turned to her. "When did that happen?"

She shrugged. "About two years ago. That's also when she, well, it's just not polite to talk about that sort of thing."

I thought about the woman I'd seen in the picture then compared it to the police officer who'd sat in my bedroom and told me how Carl had helped save my life. "I understand, I think." With a click, I disengaged the reader and rewound the film. "I think I'm going to need to switch to the N&O. You don't have the *Durham Herald-Sun* by any chance, do you?"

"I'm afraid not." With a shake of her head that didn't dislodge her bun one little bit, she pulled the microfilm out and shut the reader down. "Give me a minute to put these away. I'll meet you at the microfiche reader."

"I'll bet you will," I said, in my best Groucho Marx, and then I cringed when she gave me a look of non-comprehension. "Never mind. And again, thank you."

"You keep thanking me like that," she said as she slammed one drawer shut and opened another one, "and I might get the wrong idea about why you're down here. There's such a thing as being too polite, you know." Before I could say anything in response, she held up a manila sleeve with half a dozen sheets of microfiche in it. "Start looking in here. I'll be upstairs if you need me. It's not likely anyone else will be in today, but if the head librarian stops by, she does like to see me at the front desk."

She slammed the drawer shut and locked it and was halfway back to the stairs before she remembered she was still holding the microfiche. I got up out of my chair to take it from her and, accidentally, my fingertips brushed hers. Our glances locked again, and this time I couldn't look away.

"Well," she said, and she let go of the envelope. Before I could say a word, she was back upstairs, and the door had slammed shut behind her.

"Idiot," I groaned to myself, and I sat back down. The fiche reader was actually simpler than the film reader was, for which I was most appreciative. Shaking hands aren't good for working machinery, at least not if you want the damn thing to work.

With a look at the closed door, I slid the first sheet of microfiche in and flipped the machine on. *The News and Observer* was an order of magnitude thicker than the *Administrator*, but some kind soul had chopped it up into sections that let me scan it faster.

On the fourth sheet I found what I was looking for. In black and white, it read "Sheriff's Office Scandal Probed," and underneath was a picture of a very unhappy looking Sheriff's Deputy Walter Lee. The article danced around words like "financial improprieties" and "prisoner mistreatment" in a way that left no doubt that there was a fine stink that had settled over the whole affair.

Once I'd located the first article, the trail was easy to pick up. More allegations here, witnesses coming forward there, and then, abruptly, the end. March of 2002 brought a resignation, a short notice, and a disappearance. It looked as if Deputy Lee had cut a deal and left town as part of it. No doubt his wife had resigned her post and followed him.

It made sense, really. Getting away from the big city and burying themselves in a small town that wasn't likely to know much about what Deputy Lee might or might not have done was perfectly sensible. And if the rural police assistance program was invoked as a justification, there was even less reason for people to ask questions.

No wonder Hanratty—I couldn't think of her as Lee, no matter how I tried—looked so grim in that photo. This wasn't something she'd planned on doing, or even wanted to do. But she'd done it anyway, and stuck to it even when the man who'd brought her here wanted to go.

There was something admirable in that, and also something sad. One of these days, I'd have to figure out the balance.

A quick look at my watch told me that it was getting on time to meet Sam back at his truck, so I tucked the microfiche back in its sleeve and shut the machine off. It had been a productive day, and I'd gotten a lot to think about. Heading back to the house to do that thinking seemed like an excellent idea.

The lights went out.

"What the hell?" I asked, and I froze. The basement was pitch black. No light came in down the stairs, not even under the door.

"Well, God dammit," I said. Immediately, my hand went

to my mouth, as if to keep any more cussing from leaking out where the librarian could hear it.

I sat in the dark and the quiet for a second then flicked the fiche reader back on so I could see by the glow of the screen.

Nothing.

"First brownout of the year. Just my luck." Carefully, I put the fiche down and shuffled my way over toward the stairs. The dark felt heavy, pressing in on my eyes like it wanted to blot out even the memory of light, and the air that carried it was no better. With the air conditioning out, it had a sluggish weight to it, soaking up heat and smell and God knows what else until every breath felt like sucking weak tea through a straw.

Every few steps I banged into a chair or table, imaginary sparks of pain lighting up nothing but the space behind my eyes. I took each collision as a sign that someone wasn't happy with me, as well as evidence I was going the wrong way. And so I took small, shuffling steps in small, shuffling circles, praying that sooner or later I'd hit the stairs or something like them.

Even the emergency exit sign was out, which worried me more than I would have liked to admit. Moving slowly, I advanced.

Somewhere between ten seconds and ten hours later, I found the banister. Leaning on it like a drunk with his new best friend, I called up the stairs. "Hello? Miss Moore? Could I get a flashlight or something down here?"

I got silence back, silence and a sense of deepening gloom. "Ah, hell," I told the darkness, and I felt for the first step with my foot.

I couldn't find it.

I tried again, more frantic. Nothing was there. It was as if the banister led up into nothingness, resting on thin air.

But that was impossible. It had to be resting on something, or at least that's what the logical center of my mind told me.

Of course, it was also working overtime to remind me that the stairs had been there a minute ago, before the lights had gone out.

"Don't panic," I breathed. "You'll be fine. There's nothing to worry about." I took a deep breath, held it, let it out. "The stairs are there. You just missed them, that's all. Now let's try again."

Slowly, I dropped down to my knees, sliding my left hand down the banister post. It went all the way down the bottom, and I nearly let out a sob when my fingers found the junction between metal and carpet. Steeling myself, I slid my hand to the right, tracing the bottom of the post in hopes of crossing the boundary to that first stair.

It wasn't there. The banister was just next to nothing. I pushed forward, and nothing stopped my hand. There was no way out of the basement.

I fell back, rolled, got myself onto my hands and knees. The floor still felt solid enough, and I needed that. Full of fear, I crawled backward, away from where I thought the steps used to be. The basement was crowded, after all. I'd bump into a chair or a table or wall soon enough. I'd find something solid as an anchor.

Two steps back. Four. Six. My breath had a rasping edge to it now, like I'd been running hard.

Eight steps. Still nothing.

"Hello?" I called out. "Somebody? Anybody! Can you hear me?"

No voice answered me. Two more steps, slower now, from the fear of not finding anything. Two after that, even slower. I felt nothing behind me, nothing to the side. There was just the darkness and the rough knap of the carpet under my bare hands, and that was all.

Suddenly, I was aware of light.

Not bright light. It was the twilight you got an hour before dawn, when the first rays of the sun are just starting to think about coming over the horizon, the light you're not sure you're actually seeing.

I blinked. The light was still there, and it was coming from all around me. Overhead, the lights remained invisible in the shadows. This light came from somewhere else, from the walls and from the air.

Ever so slightly, it got a bit brighter, almost bright enough to see my hand in front of my face. I froze, sat back, looked around. Yes, I was sure of it now. The light was growing. Not steadily, though. It surged and pulsed, one side of the room momentarily brighter than the other, then going almost completely dark while a ripple of dim lightning darted across the opposite wall.

Green-gold lightning.

"Oh, no," I breathed. "Not here. Not now. Not possible."

All around me, the light grew, and now I could see it for what it was. A living blanket of fireflies covered the walls, swarming up to the ceiling and down to the floor. Patterns of light danced around faster than the eye could see, just leaving the impression that I'd missed something vitally important. No light reflected from the ceiling, though, and no light shone on it. It was as if it were simply gone, torn away by the light.

I didn't dare look at the floor. I could feel it beneath me, and that was as much as I wanted to know.

The furniture was gone now, too. Fireflies swarmed it under, and beneath their glow it just melted away. The banister still stood, I saw, leading up into infinity, but the stairs next to it were definitely gone. I didn't want to speculate as to where they'd disappeared to, but I didn't want to go there myself.

And now the fireflies were settling on me.

"Please," I said. "No." Not yelling, not screaming, just a quiet little request. Calm rained down on me, keeping me from crying out or defending myself. The universe was telling me this was inevitable.

More of them landed on me. I raised my hands, palms out, and a knot of golden light spun down into each one.

"Please," I said. "Not here. Let me go home."

I could feel them in my hair, crawling on my back, on my calves and down my arms.

"I'm going home now, I swear. Just let me go."

They were tickling their way up my neck, burrowing in my hair, forcing themselves into my mouth. Others covered my eyes, found their way up my nose, dived into my ears. They went down my throat, filling me up, and more kept coming. I was glowing from the inside now, filled with light that sputtered and sparked and made waves of itself all through me.

No, I thought. Not like this. Panic arrived late but in a hurry, driving me to try to stand, to crash myself against the wall, to scrape as many as I could off me. It was too late, though. There were fireflies under my skin, flowing through my veins, glowing in time with my heartbeat.

Then everything was a green-gold light that swallowed me up.

"Mr. Logan? I hate to bother you, Mr. Logan, but we're closing in five minutes, and I need to clean up down here."

I started violently and looked around. The basement was as I'd remembered it, ceiling and staircase intact. In front of me, the microfiche reader sat, squat and ugly and most definitely there. Overhead, the fluorescent lights flickered and shone, all save a single burned-out tube on the other side of the room.

There were no fireflies anywhere in sight—living, dead, or imaginary. Miss Moore, on the other hand, was standing at the foot of the stairs, tapping her foot impatiently and looking pleasantly irritated.

"Excuse me? I'm sorry, I didn't mean to stay this long." I stood, then I felt my knees go weak and reached out for the chair to support me.

Her expression changed in a heartbeat. "Are you all right?"

I nodded. "Just recovering from a few bad days. I'm sorry I took so much of your time. I really didn't mean to."

"It's perfectly fine. That's why I'm here." She crossed the room to where I more or less stood and took the microfiche folder in her hand. "Let me just put this away, and then I'll help you up the stairs. You look a bit peaked."

I waved her off. "No, no, I'll be fine. Really. As long as the banister's there." I took a quick peek at my watch and winced. "Oh, hell, the guy giving me a ride back must be pissed off."

"Oh." She looked embarrassed. "Sam Fuller actually came by looking for you. That was who you were referring to, right? He poked his head in and asked where you were. I told him that you seemed intent on what you were doing, and that I'd take you home." She blushed, or seemed to in the pale white light. "He seemed kind of relieved, to tell the truth. I guess he was in a hurry."

"His dog and I don't get along," I said, which was true enough as it went. "And thank you. You really don't need to do this, you know. I can walk back."

She looked down her nose at me. "Mr. Logan, you don't look as if you can walk across this room. I'm certainly not going to let you walk however many miles it is back to your farm."

"House," I corrected her, even as I took slow, careful steps across the basement. "It hasn't been farmed in years."

"Well then, your house." She dropped the fiche cards into the appropriate drawer and turned the key on it. "And the farm it's sitting on. Now you go on upstairs and sit in the reading area. I'm sure you can find something to read while you're waiting. It won't take me but a minute to take care of all this. After all, you're the first person we've had down here in three weeks."

I thought about arguing, but only for a moment. "You're the boss," I said, and I hauled myself up the stairs. Behind me, I could hear her tidying up in mysterious ways that, near as I could tell, involved re-arranging the chairs and pulling plugs out of walls. It was her business, though, so I didn't speculate on it too much.

The chairs around that low, round table that made up the reading area were a little too comfortable. I sank into one like a frog on a too-small lily pad, reaching like a drowning man for one of the magazines on the nearby table. My fingers closed on one and I pulled it in, and then realized I was looking at the back page ad.

I called myself a dumbass then flipped it around. The cover of *Carolina Woman* stared back at me, telling me that the ten most romantic spots in the whole state were inside waiting to be discovered, along with some helpful diet tips and a list of five up-and-coming companies in Charlotte owned by women.

"Terrific," I muttered. Rather than flail around again, I flipped it open and hoped Miss Moore would be done soon.

I was on the fifth most romantic place in the state—the beach near the Hatteras lighthouse, if you must know—when her footsteps sounded on the stairs. Moving fast, I tossed the magazine back on the table, then leaned back and closed my eyes like I was taking a nap.

"Number four is the Grove Park Inn, up in Asheville," she said from right behind me. "I don't agree with their top three, though."

"Hmm?" I asked. "You don't say."

"I do say," she corrected me, "and you're not the only man I've spotted pretending not to read that. Actually, I think more men read it than women. I think they're trying to do some scouting, or maybe get some ideas."

"Not me," I told her, and I flung myself out of the chair. "It was a simple matter of physics."

"Physics?"

I walked around the chair and gave her my best sheepish grin. "Yeah. I couldn't reach any of the others."

She gave me a quick little smile then pointed to the door. "Go on outside," she said. "I need to lock up and turn off the lights."

"I won't stop you," I promised, and I headed out the door. Behind me, she straightened magazines, flicked off light switches, and shut down the computer. Through it all, she worked with a tidy efficiency that wasn't so much graceful as it was precise. For Miss Moore, it seemed, if something was worth doing, it was worth doing as quickly and as neatly as possible.

Meanwhile, I leaned up against the outside wall and watched.

It took maybe another five minutes for her to finish up. She came bustling out the front door, apologizing for having taken so long. I laughed and told her that she was doing me the favor, and that she could take all the time—I nearly said "damn time," but caught myself—she wanted.

"Don't say that," she told me. "I just might." Then she locked the door and tugged on it once to make sure it held. It did, so she pivoted and started walking to her car.

It was easy to spot, as it was the only one still parked on the street. The sun was still well above the horizon, but the town had the feel of having gone to bed right after supper. Off in the distance you could hear cars, no doubt headed for one of the two bars or maybe the movie theater (all of three screens now, Sam had told me on our first trip in). Here, though, things were quiet.

"Hop in," she said. She pressed a button on her keychain to unlock the doors. It was some kind of Chevrolet, sensible and small and what the advertising boys called "sporty," which meant that it didn't have much in the way of trunk space. There were compact discs all over the front seat, for which she apologized, and a half-full bottle of Cheerwine in the cup holder.

"I wouldn't drink that if I were you," I warned as she settled into the driver's seat and pulled the seat belt across herself. "Cheerwine that's been sitting in the sun makes people hallucinate, shiver, and perform interpretive dances in public."

"Actually, I was going to offer you some," she said, shutting the door. She turned the key and the engine grumbled itself to life, masked in part by the hiss of the air conditioning and the last twenty seconds of a Nickel Creek song.

"Oops, I'm sorry. I forgot about the volume on that." She reached over and turned the music down. "I like to keep the windows rolled up and sing along."

"Why keep the windows rolled up, then?"

She shot me a quick smile. "Because I can't sing, that's why. Now, where am I taking you?"

"Home," I said, and thought about the word for a moment, "but I suppose you want actual directions."

"Those would help," she agreed, and she threw the car into drive. It swung smoothly out into the street as the next song started.

"It's real simple. You just want to find your way to Harrison Farm and head out of town. I'm a ways down on the left."

Ahead of us, one of the town's four stop lights turned red.

We coasted to a stop and waited, the engine humming. "So, just drive around and you'll tell me when you see it?"

I smiled. "Something like that. Look, I do appreciate this, but it is a ways out there, and I can walk. Besides, you don't hardly know me. Are you sure you want to do this?"

Adrienne—somehow, I'd started thinking of her that way since we'd left the library, despite the fact that she hadn't shown me any more familiarity in those few minutes than she had inside—shook her head with annoyance. "You do know, Mr. Logan, that it is sometimes permissible to let other people do you a favor. If you must console yourself, remember that Sam Fuller knows I'm taking you home. That should be sufficient precaution to make you feel better about my willingness to let a semi-stranger into my car. Not that I think you'd do anything untoward, mind you. You don't have that feel to you. Frankly, you feel more like the men who sneak peeks at *Carolina Woman*—a little shy, a little nervous, all hopeful that someone's just going to fall into their arms." She glanced over at me. "I'm not offending, I hope?"

"Not yet," I answered. "Though I'd wager I know a little bit more about women than you give me credit for."

"Oh, I'm sure you *think* you know something," she clarified. "But that doesn't mean you do."

Outside, the last of the buildings that marked downtown Maryfield sped by. Fields opened up on both sides of us now, knee-high corn and soy poking their heads up out of the soil.

I felt myself growing distinctly uncomfortable with the direction the conversation was taking—it felt a little too much like a letter in the sort of magazine I used to read in college—so I cleared my throat and made a deliberate effort to change the subject.

"How long have you been in Maryfield?" I asked. "I don't remember you from my last visit, and you sure as heck don't look like Miss Rose or Miss Lillian."

"They retired three years ago," she answered. "Miss Rose first. They were talking about moving to Florida, but they never got that far. I think they bought a house just outside of town and moved in together. You still see them in the grocery store from time to time. They're sweet ladies. They like to come in and check on me, and see if I need any help."

"And do you?"

"No, not really." She sounded sad. "We loan out almost as many movies as we do books these days."

"That's a shame. How'd you end up here, anyway?"

She laughed, then. "What is this, Mr. Logan, twenty questions? Careful, you'll run out before you know it."

"I never was any good at math," I told her, rolling down my window. "And I figure I've got at least fifteen or so left."

"Well, you've got at least one. I started here right after Miss Lillian retired. I'm from Banner Elk, up in the mountains. I got my degree in library science at Appalachian State, and then I applied for the job here. They hired me. There's nothing more to it than that, I'm afraid."

"Seems simple enough. Do you live in town?"

"I do. I don't even know why I drove today, except that I can't find my umbrella and with the way it rained the other day. . . ." Her voice trailed off and she shrugged. "It's a good thing that I did, wouldn't you say?"

"A good thing indeed," I agreed. "And now I'll stop being a nosy jerk. No more questions, I promise."

A new song started. She jabbed at the fast forward button, skipping it. "Sorry," she apologized. "I just hate that one. It's stupid and melodramatic and, well, never mind. This next one's better, I promise."

"Your car, your music," I told her. "I wouldn't care if you were playing 'Foggy Mountain Breakdown' backward to listen for secret messages hidden in the banjo line."

She shot me a funny look. "I think most people might have a problem with that, actually."

"I tried it with my Led Zeppelin records once. All I got out of it was something that sounded like 'funnurph nurgle beer.' Nothing vaguely evil about it. And your music is fine, honest."

"It's kind of you to say so." We rode on for a while longer in silence, doing that thing where you take turns looking over at one another but look away when it seems like the other person might meet your eyes.

It felt like high school all over again.

Finally, I saw the familiar chimney coming up on the left. "There it is," I said, pointing. "The next driveway is mine."

We pulled up in a shower of gravel then thumped to a stop.

"Thank you," I said, and I undid my seat belt. "And I know I've said that a lot today, but that one was important."

"You're welcome," she said, and she fiddled with the volume. I cracked my door.

"Look," I said, "it was a long way out here and it'll be a long way back. Do you want to come in for a while, have a glass of something to drink?"

She cut the engine and turned to look at me. "It's very nice of you to ask, Mr. Logan, but, like you're saying, it's a long drive back, and I'm not sure I want to do it in the dark."

"Then why'd you turn off the car?" I asked. "Come on, I won't bite. Honest."

"I was afraid you'd say that," she said, and she pulled the keys out of the ignition. "So why don't you give me the tour?"

"Gladly," I replied, stepping out of the car. "Welcome to my home."

I slammed the door behind me with a sound like a coffin lid coming down for the last time, and started walking toward the house. After a moment, she followed.

CHAPTER 16

"This is very nice," Adrienne said as we tromped up onto the porch. "It goes all the way back to the tree line?"

"Well past it," I replied, fumbling for my keys. "I own the whole patch of woods down there. I used to call it the Thicket when I was a kid. Now it's just something I don't have to mow."

"I think that goes for pretty much the whole property," she observed. "Why is that stand of pine trees out there by itself?"

I grimaced. "I'll show you later. It's not really the sort of thing that you can explain well."

She shrugged. "All right."

"Trust me," I said. The lock clicked, and I opened the door. "Welcome to the ancestral Logan estate." I stepped back away from the door and made a silly sort of bow. "After you."

"Oh, no." A smile thought about crossing her face. "It's your house. You should go first. It might be dangerous in there."

"You have no idea," I assured her, and I stepped in. A quick look around told me that the kitchen—toy soldiers and all—was just as I had left it, which was to say more or less fit for human habitation. Even the empties were lined up neatly against the back of the counter, and there weren't quite enough of them there to give a truly bad impression. "Sorry about the mess," I said. "I didn't know I'd be having company, except maybe Sam and Asa."

"That's quite all right." I could feel as well as hear her step into the house behind me. It was a pleasant sort of heat. "This is very nice. Did your mom decorate it?"

I nodded and stepped farther in. "Mother did, yes, though my grandmother did the basics. My grandfather built the house, you see, and Father just inherited it. I'm the third generation in here, more or less."

She stepped past me and did a little spin as she looked around. "Are you going to do anything with it?"

"I don't think so," I confessed. "Mother always had much better taste than anyone else in the family, except maybe when it came to Father. Besides, I'm not sure how long I'm going to be staying, and I don't want to start something I won't be around to finish."

"That seems like a sensible attitude." She stopped spinning, and I imagined that there was just a hint of disappointment in her voice. Then it was gone, and she was pointing down the long hall. "What's down here?"

I moved past her, careful not to touch. The kitchen was just wide enough to allow that, and I squeezed into the hallway. "The rest of the house. Do you want the grand tour?"

"That's why I'm here."

I turned to face her and took a few steps backward. "Well then, allow me to show you the Logan house, built on the ruins of the old Logan farmhouse, which was in turn built on the old Logan cabin, which, near as I can tell, was built on top of the old Logan family tent. We've been here a long time. Grandfather Logan built this particular place when he first got married. He married late and his folks had passed away, so he wanted a new place for his family—not to mention the fact that the old farmhouse was falling down around his ears. The rest was built in bits and pieces through the years, some when Mother moved in after she and Father got married, and some when I came along. There's no real plan to it, except that nobody in the Logan family ever liked visitors, so you won't see a lot of windows facing the road."

"There's one," she interrupted, pointing into the bathroom. "Seems an odd place, if that's the only one."

I stretched out and pulled the bathroom door shut. "It's not the only one, but it's close, and Mother said guests should get a little light for their washing up. Besides, the curtains are always drawn in there."

"They weren't that I saw," Adrienne contradicted me, her voice a little too bland to be serious. "You ought to be ashamed, if that's the washroom you're using. Someone might look in and see you."

"Someone," I replied with all the dignity I could muster, tentatively taking her hand to pull her along the corridor, "would have to be very lost and about nine feet tall. If'n Bigfoot wants to get a peek at my wares, then he's going to get a great view. Beyond that, I don't worry about it."

She giggled, and let me lead her farther on. "Is that the living room?"

I peered in. "Living, dining, knick-knack—you name it. It needs a good dusting before it's fit for company, though."

"I'm not company, I'm your ride," she responded. Her fingers slid out from between mine. Two steps and she passed me, picking up one of Mother's porcelain figurines. "This is very nice," she said, turning it over in her hands. "Where did it come from?"

I caught up to her and peered at the object she was holding. It was a porcelain representation of some kind of finch, red head and short beak and black wings all pressed back against a stocky little body. Mother had collected them, and there was an entire aviary set up in there for those who cared to look at it.

"Don't know, really," I said, and I gently took the figurine away from her. "Mother would haunt flea markets and estate sales for things like this, and every so often one would arrive in the mail. Father never liked them much, and I just knew that if I got close to them, I'd break one sooner or later. So I never learned too much about them."

"They're beautiful," Adrienne said. "Turn it over. The manufacturer's mark is usually on the bottom."

I did, and there it was. "Son of a . . . gun," I said. "Can you read that?"

She leaned in closer, which may or may not have been my intention. "No, I can't make it out."

"You could look a little closer," I offered.

Adrienne looked up at me. "I could," she said, and she took the bird back out of my hands. "You really ought to dust in here more." Carefully, she set it down on the shelf where she'd found it and strolled farther into the room.

She looked everywhere, picking out every bit of furniture and gewgaw that the generations of Logans had managed to accumulate and display over the years. Porcelain figures, Depression glass, lace doilies—each of them passed under Adrienne's scrutiny and met with her approval. After a while, I began to see the room through her eyes. It had been a forbidding place to me when I was younger, dark and full of things I couldn't or shouldn't go near. Now, though, I could start to understand why it was the way it was, why Mother had brought those things into the house and kept them there, and how important it had been to her to carve out a place like this in Father's home.

Finally, we came to the fireplace. Adrienne stood in front of it, leaning carefully on the mantel and looking down into the hearth. "How long has it been since you had a fire in here?" she asked, not looking back at me.

I stood behind her, my eyes carefully fixed on the chimney. "Not since Mother died, I'd guess. Carl might have done something. There's a pile of firewood around back, and it was dry when I got here. Maybe he's been using the place, not that I mind so much."

"Carl?" She didn't turn.

"Carl Powell. Friend of Mother and Father's. I hired him to be the caretaker when Mother died."

"Ah." She took a deep breath. "You should have people over here more, you know. It's too much house for just you."

"I'm not sure it is," I said softly. She turned and looked up at me, her expression asking for an explanation, but I didn't have one I'd care to give.

"Come on," I said instead. "Let me show you the rest."

With a long look behind her, Adrienne followed.

The rest of the tour was brief. My bedroom elicited a few giggles from her and a blush or two from me, especially since I hadn't made the bed or put away the previous night's laundry. A man ought not have a woman he's trying to impress see his boxers wadded up on the floor. Other rooms got fast inspections and faster explanations. Adrienne's interest was still back in the knick-knack room—that much was clear. I wasn't sure if I was pleased or bothered.

"That's it," I said when we'd gone through all the open rooms. "Can I get you something to drink?"

"No," she replied, and she pointed past me. "What's in there?"

I turned around to see what she was gesturing at. "Ah. Mother and Father's bedroom."

"Oh. May I see it?"

I thought for a minute. It certainly was presentable, and probably the nicest room in the house. It certainly wouldn't lower her opinion of me any to see it.

But it was Mother and Father's room, their private place. Aside from me (and Carl, my suspicious conscience reminded me. *That impression in the covers hadn't made itself*), no one had seen it since Mother's funeral. I'd known Adrienne—Miss Moore—maybe half a dozen hours.

Things were moving awful fast.

Maybe it was time things moved in a way I wanted them to.

"Certainly," I said. "Mother was always very proud of it. I reached out, put my hand on the knob, and turned it.

It wouldn't budge.

I flashed Adrienne a weak smile. "Hang on a minute. The door sticks sometimes." I put a little more strength into it and twisted the knob harder. Nothing happened.

"Do you need to unlock it?" Adrienne asked. "I always forget to do that when I lock my bedroom."

"I don't recall having locked it," I muttered through gritted teeth, both hands on the doorknob now. "As I said, sometimes it just gets stuck. The wood expands in the humidity and all that."

"It's okay," she said reassuringly, laying a hand on my shoulder. "I don't have to see it now. Maybe another time the door will cooperate a bit better."

"Maybe," I said reluctantly, and I let go of the doorknob. "I'll get that worked on in the meantime."

"That sounds like a good idea." She slipped her hand all the way back down to her side. "Now, could I have that drink you offered?"

I shot the door a look of pure hatred then turned my back on it. "Certainly," I said. "Beer, milk, juice, lemonade?"

"I don't suppose you have any Pepsi?" she asked as she led the way into the kitchen.

"Afraid not," I said. "Carl does my shopping for me, and I don't think he believes in that stuff. You'd think a man with no teeth wouldn't worry about tooth rot."

Adrienne laughed. "Maybe he knows something you don't. And a glass of water would be fine."

"Water it is." I walked over to the cabinet and pulled down a glass—an old Burger King collectible with Charlie Brown on it. "Ice?"

"Yes, please." The scrape of metal on tile told me she'd pulled out a chair; the hiss of air escaping a cushion said she'd sat down on it. I grabbed a handful of ice cubes from the fridge and dropped them into the glass. They hit with a musical tinkle, filling it halfway. I filled it the rest of the way with tap water, thought about a beer, and decided against it. I'd need a beer later, God knew, when I started really thinking about what had happened in that basement. As long as Adrienne was there, though, I didn't want anything in my system that would relax my control one little bit.

Women, as an acquaintance of mine during my college years had said, generally ain't impressed by nervous breakdowns.

I put the glass down in front of her and pulled up the next chair at the table. "There you go."

She took it, took a sip. "Aren't you having anything?" she asked.

"In a bit. Right now I'm not thirsty." I looked back over at the fridge. "Had myself a vanilla cola at Hilliard's today, and I'm still hanging onto that for flavor."

Adrienne grinned and took another sip. "I can understand that." A ring of condensation marked the table in front of her, and she reached out with one finger to trace designs in it. "Look," she said, "I do want you to know that I don't give all of the patrons rides home. You just seemed like, well, like you needed someone to talk to."

I nodded and watched her draw lines in the water. "I might, at that, though I'm not sure you want to hear some of the things I'd need to discuss. It's been a little awkward around here since I moved back, you understand."

"I think I do." She put the glass down and reached out, taking my hand in hers. Her fingertips were cold from the ice and wet from the condensation. They felt good against my skin. "This is a small town. It's tight-knit. It took me a while to fit in when I first came here from Boone, and I'm sure it's worse for you. Everything's almost the way you remember it, but not quite, so every step feels like the wrong one. Plus, you're all alone out here when your memory tells you it ought to have other voices. You never were by yourself much in this house as a child, were you?"

I shook my head. "No, I wasn't. Father traveled for business sometimes—he was an investor, mostly, though I never got a straight answer as to what he actually did for a living—but Mother was always here. When we traveled, we did it as a family, and then eventually I left. So I guess you're right on that, though sometimes I almost think I still hear them."

She stopped sketching on the tabletop and put her other hand atop mine. "That's not surprising, really. My parents died when I was about fifteen, and I still miss them terribly. For a while, when I went to bed, I'd listen real hard and sometimes I thought I could hear them telling me that everything was okay, and that I could close my eyes."

"That's terrible. I'm very sorry."

She shrugged. "Don't be. It was a long time ago, and it was nobody's fault, really. It was a car accident where someone's brakes failed and, well, everybody told me that it was over very quickly. I was taken in by an aunt, a sweet lady who was still waiting for her beau to come back from Vietnam. She decided that a librarian was an appropriate thing for me to be, and there you have my life story." Those gray eyes blinked twice, a little brightness at the corners, and she looked up at me. "I'm sorry, I don't usually tell people about that sort of thing."

I shushed her and fought the urge to clasp my other hand on top of hers. "It's okay. Thank you for trusting me with that."

Adrienne made a sound that was half sniffle, half cough. "You're welcome. I guess what I'm saying is that it's all right to miss them, but you do have to live your life."

"I thought I had been," I told her. "Moving up to Boston and all that. I'm back here because that stopped working out, and I'm trying to figure out what to do next. I'm not sure if being here is helping or hurting."

She patted my hand. "It's helping, I'm sure. Besides, you're brushing up on your library research skills. That can't be a bad thing."

Despite myself, I smiled. "True. It's just . . ." I hesitated.

"What?"

I shook my head. "Nothing. Not yet, anyway. There are a few things I need to figure out how to explain, that's all."

"Well," she said, leaning forward, "When you do, I'll be here."

"Will you now," I murmured, and I found myself being drawn toward her. Somehow, her glasses had found their way onto the table, and her eyes filled my view. They were mesmerizing, gorgeous; the sort to drive a man to clichés and acts of moonstruck stupidity. Drowning happy, Father had called it once when I'd asked him how he and Mother had met. You get pulled in and never want to come out.

Her lips parted, ever so slightly. I could hear her breathing—a soft counterpoint to the loud noises my heart was making. I half rose up out of my chair and leaned in farther toward her. She closed her eyes as we paused, a hairbreadth between us and a first kiss.

In the back of the house, something heavy came crashing down.

We both jerked back into our seats like we were on too-short leashes. Her hands pulled back from mine, accidentally backhanding the half-full water glass and sending it spinning into air. I reached for it, but it tumbled just out of my reach and shattered on the floor. Ice and water spattered everywhere, hiding shards of glass as they flew.

"Oh!" Adrienne looked so horrified I would have laughed, if I hadn't been about to cry. "I'm so sorry!"

I bit back a couple of inappropriate responses. "Don't be," I finally said. "It happens. Probably a squirrel getting in back there that made the noise. There's nothing to apologize for."

"But your glass . . ."

"Its time had come," I said simply. "It did have Charlie Brown on it, so it was bound to be unlucky." She made a move for the counter where the paper towels were kept and I waved her off. "No, no, no. Don't you worry about it. I'll clean it up."

"Are you sure?" She looked about sixteen and unsure of herself—surprised and scared all at once.

I nodded and got up out of my chair. "I am. Just sit tight for a minute and I will do just that."

She swept herself up out of her seat as well. "Actually, I should really be going. It's starting to get late, and I left some chicken out to defrost. If I don't get home soon, it won't be fit to use."

"All right," I said, and I tried to keep the disappointment out of my voice. "Careful where you step there."

"I will be," she promised, and she tiptoed through the mess with as much delicacy as she could manage. As she reached the door, she stopped and turned. "I don't know if this is too forward of me, but why don't you give me your phone number? That way, I can call and check up on you."

My voice as neutral as I could make it, I said, "Sounds good," and I scribbled it down on a napkin. She folded it in quarters neatly in a way I'd never been able to manage and tucked it away inside a pocket.

"I'll put this in my address book when I get home."

"You do that," I agreed. "Could I get your number as well? Just in case."

She smiled back at me. "Not yet," she said. "Maybe next time, Mr. Jacob Logan. Thank you for showing me around." She leaned in and kissed me on the cheek. "I'll be in touch."

Then she was gone. Out the door and down the steps and into her car in the blink of an eye. I stood there and watched as she started it up and backed out, all in one fluid motion. An instant later, she was on the road and disappearing behind a thin cloud of dust.

I could hear Nickel Creek faintly for a good twenty seconds after she was gone. I recognized the song, too. It was the one about the lighthouse missing its keeper, the one she had said she hated.

"Goddamn. I *don't* know anything about women," I said, and I eventually shut the door. I'd been half-hoping she'd change her mind and come back, or maybe I'd taken her words too seriously and didn't want to be alone in that house at that moment.

It didn't matter. The door closed smooth and easy, like it was supposed to. I turned my back on it and stared at the mess on the kitchen floor. Bits of Charlie Brown were everywhere, and the ice cubes were slowly melting away. That was good, as it would make the unpainted glass bits easier to pick out when I got around to it.

Better to let the process continue, I decided, and maybe some of the water would evaporate as well. Besides, in the mood I was in I was bound and certain to slice my finger open if I tried cleaning up now, so it was in everyone's best interest if I just let it be.

Instead, I stepped over it, heading for the back of the house to see what had come crashing down. I didn't believe it was animals, not for a minute. Most of me was tired, irritated, and unhappy with the turn of events. That part of me figured that it was just something old in an old house picking a real bad time to make its peace with gravity.

The rest of me was crazy and thought maybe, just maybe, it had been Mother.

The sound, I recalled, had come from the back of the house. I made my way down there, looking in each room for evidence of catastrophe. There was none. None of Mother's figurines were disturbed. Neither of the fireplace dogs had been knocked over. No chairs were on their sides or books were on the floor. And with each room that passed muster, my nervousness grew.

Finally, all that was left was the mudroom. The door was mostly closed—I hadn't exactly wanted to show off a washing machine to Adrienne—so I gently pushed it open with my right hand.

It moved a half an inch, then bumped into something on the floor. I shoved a little harder, and for my trouble I got resistance and the sound of metal sliding across floorboard. The door moved, at least, and I got maybe another forty-five degrees out of it before a *clang* and a *thunk* told me that whatever that mystery object might be, it was jammed in good and proper.

That was all right, though. The door was cracked far enough for me to slide past and get myself in there. I was curious, I confess, as to what the hell that thing could have been. I'd no recollection of anything in that room but the washer and the dryer, and a couple of bottles of detergent. None of that would have made the noises I'd heard. Hell, besides the washer and dryer, nothing in there was metal except the shelves up top, and those were bolted in.

I stuck my head around the door and reached up for the overhead light's pull cord. It took three tugs, but the thing finally came on, sputtering up and flickering like it was letting me know I'd better have a replacement ready to go soon.

I made a mental note and looked around. The shelf over the equipment was still there, still sturdily bolted where it ought to have been. There wasn't even any plaster dust in the air, the sure sign of falling shelving.

On the floor, though, was the shotgun. The same shotgun I'd tucked under my bed. It lay there, natural as can be, except that there was no way in hell it could have gotten there on its own.

It was there, though. No argument about that. I bent down and touched it. The barrel was cool, as if it had been sitting there a while. Carefully, I pulled it to me. In the light from above, I didn't see any prints on the steel. Whoever had moved it, if anyone, had been careful.

A sudden thought struck me, so I picked it up and cracked it. I'd fired both barrels near Carl (*all right, at Carl,* my conscience insisted) and I hadn't reloaded, so the chambers should be empty.

They weren't.

Very carefully, I closed it up and put the gun back down. Judging from its final resting position, the gun had been pointing straight at the outside door when I had come in looking for it, and that's exactly how I left it. Without a word, I yanked the light cord and shut the door, then backed away.

Five steps back I sat down on the floor, staring at the mudroom door. There were two possibilities here. One was that someone had come into the house, found the shotgun I'd hidden under the bed, found the shells (which were in no kind of obvious place) loaded the gun, and then tucked it in the back room, propping it up so that it would fall at an advantageous moment to keep me from doing something ungentlemanly with my new favorite librarian.

The related scenario, wherein someone had been waiting back there with the gun but had lost their nerve, didn't stand up to any kind of eyeballing. I hadn't heard the mudroom door open or close, and besides, why would anyone back there have wanted to run? After all, they were the one with the loaded gun.

No, either it had been carefully set up in back by an unknown intruder, or it had been done by someone in the house.

I was the only living person in the house. Adrienne hadn't been out of my sight the whole time she'd been here. The gun had been under my bed when I'd left.

"Mother?" I breathed, and then I dismissed the idea from my mind as impossibility.

She'd never touched the gun when she'd been alive. I could still recall fights she had with Father about keeping it in the bedroom. She wanted to keep the bedroom safe, it seemed, and was worried about an accident. Father replied that keeping the gun there was the best way to keep it safe, and around and around they went.

The mudroom, I recalled, was Mother's proposed alternate location for the shotgun. And if any man alive besides me knew that, it was Carl.

"Bloody hell." I stood back up very deliberately then made my way to Mother and Father's bedroom door. It was still closed, as it had been when I'd tried to show the place to Adrienne.

As I watched, something within the doorknob made a little, happy click.

All by itself, the door swung open.

"Oh, no," I said. "Not this time."

Hinges whined. The door swung wider.

"No, Mother," I said. "If you're there, and I don't think you are, you've made your point. Not in your house? Fine. I'd think you'd like her, though. She liked your things."

The door hung there for a moment, half-open, and then it swung shut with authority. The sound echoed through the house.

"All right. Be that way."

Nothing else happened, so I walked back into the kitchen and cast an eye on the mess on the floor. The ice had mostly finished melting, giving me less of a reason to put off cleaning the damn thing up. Less than thrilled at the prospect, I skittered my way around to the paper towel dispenser and tore myself off a few. Carefully, I dropped them on the puddle in the middle of the floor then went hunting for the broom.

I was maybe two thirds of the way through the cleanup, and mighty proud of myself for having mostly avoided jabbing myself with slivers of glass, when the phone rang. The timing was perfect: I'd just about closed in on a particularly tricky little shard and the shock of the noise startled me in just the wrong way. My fingers closed at exactly the wrong angle and I cursed mightily for a good ten seconds before I yanked the glass out of my thumb. A big red button of blood welled up where it had been, so I hoisted myself up and over to the paper towels, grabbed one, and pressed down to stop the bleeding.

The phone was unimpressed. It kept ringing.

"All right already," I snarled, snatching it off its cradle. "Yeah?"

"Easy, tiger," Jenna said. "What, did you think I was a telemarketer?"

"No, I . . ." My voice trailed off. "I just jabbed myself with some glass cleaning up something that broke, that's all."

"Whoops. You put Neosporin on it?"

"Not yet. It just happened five seconds ago, when the phone rang."

Oblivious to my sarcasm, Jenna pressed on. "No time to lose, then. Go on and take care of it. I'll wait."

Knowing this was an argument I had no chance of winning, I put the phone down on the counter and walked around the kitchen for what I figured was an appropriate amount of time. I counted ten seconds past that and then picked up again.

"Is it taken care of?" she asked.

I nodded then abruptly remembered I was talking on the phone. "All bandaged nicely, I promise. Now what gives me the pleasure of your conversation?"

"Honestly," she said, sounding a bit surprised herself, "I wanted to see how you were doing. You sounded a little freaky last time we talked."

"I'm fine," I reassured her. "Went into town today with a man who has a mean dog, then explored my childhood a bit further."

"Do tell." Jenna sounded relieved and amused, all at the same time. "Did you go to the soda fountain and put on a paper hat?"

"Hat, no. Fountain, yes. I'll take you when you get here. You'll love it."

"Oh, good." The words whooshed out of her. "I was afraid you were going to try to talk me out of it again."

"I know better," I said ruefully. "You'd show up anyway, and you'd be pissed off. So, do you want to hear about the rest of my day, or have your selfish purposes been realized?"

"Tell me all about it. The short version, though. The gory details can wait until Friday. Be warned, I'm going to interrogate you at length when I get there. You're leaving stuff out. I can tell."

"Oh can you, now?"

"Yes, I can," she replied. "Remember, I've seen you try to talk about financials. I *know* when you're lying."

Despite myself, I laughed. "That's why you got the job."

"Which one?"

"All of them. Now, hush and let me tell you a story."

Jenna snickered, a nasty sound. "You make it sound so dirty when you put it that way. But never mind, start talking."

I sighed. "If you're sure you're done with the stand-up comedy routine." There was heavy silence on the line for a moment, and a sense that those words had cut a bit deeper than I'd intended. "All right then. I hitched a ride into town with a friendly neighbor who turned out not to be so friendly. His dog got particularly unpleasant, and we parted ways when I got into town. I wandered around a bit and had a soda at the old pharmacy then went to talk to the reverend at my old church about what's been happening here. He was less surprised to hear about it than you'd think, and told me to come back to church. Then I went off to the library to look up this Officer Hanratty. I figured it was worth finding out a little about her before I started claiming police sarcasm."

"And what did you find out?" Jenna was all business now. That was one of the things I truly liked about her. When the time came to get down to brass tacks, she was as good as they got. The rest of the time, she was just brassy.

As opposed to, say, the sort of gentle courtesy you'd get out of a small-town librarian.

I forced that thought off to the side and made myself concentrate on Hanratty—the sort of exercise that could sprain a man's brain permanently. "She's an ex-Durham cop. Her husband, or ex-husband, was Sheriff's Office and got nailed by Internal Affairs. He cut a deal and they moved out here to 'revitalize' the local police force. A couple of years later, he left. She stayed and, if my source can be believed, started mainlining sweet tea."

"Interesting," she said. "Who's your local source?"

"The librarian," I replied. "Very helpful."

Jenna's voice was pure deadpan. "I'm sure she was. Anything else going on in the haunted house or scary handyman department?"

I hemmed and hawed a moment. "Shotguns that move themselves, doors that lock and unlock on their own, and strange noises. Other than that, not too much."

"That's enough, I think." She gave a low whistle. "Maybe you want to get that priest to take a look at that door, if not the shotgun?"

"Catholics have priests," I corrected. "I grew up with a preacher. And it's the door to Mother and Father's room. I'm sure they just want their privacy."

"You know, Logan," Jenna started and then trailed off. "I have a question for you."

"Ask," I told her, and I shifted the paper towel on my thumb.

It had developed a pretty impressive red stain as I'd been talking, and Jenna's earlier recommendation that I take care of it didn't sound half-bad any more.

"If I'm prying, I'm sorry, but did you ever notice that you never say 'Mom' or 'my mother' or 'Mommy' or anything like that? She's always 'Mother,' and your dad is always 'Father' and that's all there is to it. Very formal, when you think about it. It's like you're keeping them at arm's length, or under glass."

"You are prying," I said very softly. "But I'm not mad at you. I'd just rather not talk about that right now, okay?"

"Okay." She sounded hurt. "I'm sorry."

"I know." I took a deep breath, counted to five, and let it out. "We can talk about it more soon, when you're down here and you can see things first hand. You might understand some of it a little better. Right now, though, well, we're just going to miscommunicate and make each other mad, and I don't want that."

Jenna gave a sad little laugh. "In other words, get off the phone, woman."

"Something like that," I agreed. "But said with love."

"You southern charmer," she said. "All right. I'll call tomorrow night to check in, but no prying. I promise."

"Scout's honor?"

"I never got past Brownie, Logan. Don't push your luck."

"I won't," I said. "Good night, Jenna."

"Good night, idiot," she said affectionately.

I hung up then stepped over the remaining glass and water to make my way to the bathroom. The thumb was really bleeding more than it ought, and smearing some kind of medicine on it was sounding smarter and smarter.

A quick rummage through the medicine cabinet, one hand kept firmly on that swinging door, and I found what I was looking for. I pulled the paper towel off and did an awkward one-handed squirt of anti-bacterial goop onto my thumb, then wrestled a bandage onto it and pulled it tight.

"That ought to do it," I said, and I replaced everything neatly. "Now, let me finish in the kitchen, and then I can go to pieces about the fireflies in the library."

Nothing moved, opened, closed or slammed in response, so I assumed that I was cleared to proceed with my plan. Indeed, cleaning up took remarkably little more time. I knotted up the bag with the glass and tucked it inside another one, then decided to chuck the whole thing into the bin outside. No sense having sharp objects around the house unnecessarily, after all.

As I stepped outside, I realized how late it was getting. We were coming into high summer, so the nights started late and ended early, but even with that, the sun was hurrying toward the horizon. Adrienne's visit had been longer than I'd expected, it seemed. Night was coming on, a prospect I found I wasn't entirely comfortable with.

I tossed the bag into the bin with a jangle and tamped the lid back down when the sound of an approaching car made itself known. I looked up to see which direction the dust trail was coming from. Town, it seemed, headed out past me into the deeper hinterlands.

As the vehicle got closer, I recognized it. It was a truck, a white one.

Unless I was mistaken, it was Sam's.

It was. He zoomed past, slowing down only slightly when he passed my place. In the back, I could see Asa, his ears pinned back and his teeth bared. He watched the house as the truck rumbled along, staring in the way dogs have that says there's wolf in their family tree, and it's on a branch that hangs mighty low.

I stood there, not moving, and watched. The dust the truck raised rolled up and over me, then faded into the air. By the time it was gone, so was Sam, his truck melting off into the distance.

"That was mighty friendly," I mumbled to myself, and I turned back toward the house. Something nagged at me, though, something more than Sam's sudden turnaround.

It was only when I'd gone back inside that I realized what it was. I hadn't seen anyone else in the cab, but Asa was still riding in the back.

For some reason that worried me.

Dinner was a joyless affair, consisting mainly of a grilled baloney sandwich with mustard. Carl had gone heavy on the Oscar Meyer this time, but I wasn't feeling up to preparing anything more complicated. My thumb ached out of all proportion, and when I looked at the Band-Aid, it had a big red spot of blood in the middle of the pad.

I did the dishes, such as they were, and got myself a beer. Outside, the sun went down in a hurry. The sky sensed its mood and went dark right quick. Inside, I nursed my beer and waited for the sounds of the crickets and frogs to drift on up with the night.

I wanted to think about what had happened, but my brain was good and fogged. Mysterious shotgun movement? Fine. Doors that locked and unlocked themselves? Whatever. Officer Hanratty and her semi-mysterious past? Her own damn business.

The fireflies in the basement, though, were something else. The easiest explanation was that I had fallen asleep and dreamed the whole thing. Certainly Adrienne hadn't made mention of anything unusual when she brought me back to the real world. A hallucination brought on by my misadventures over the last few days was also a strong contender. You take enough knocks on the head, I figured, and disappearing staircases and magical lightning bugs really ought to manifest.

It hadn't felt that way, though. My eyes, when I checked them in the mirror after taking out the trash, didn't seem dilated. There was no strange taste in my mouth, nothing more than a little dull pain when I turned my head too fast. The lump from the fall I'd taken in the bathroom wasn't even noticeable unless you got up real close.

The other alternative was that something flat-out weird had happened down there, the latest in a string of flat-out weird things that had followed me since I'd left Boston. At this point, there was almost more evidence for the weirdness than there was for anything a man of science might understand, and that was troubling. A concussion, a man could take bed rest for. A dream he could wake up from. Magical fireflies crawling under his skin, however, were a horse of a different color.

"Crap," I said, and I took another sip of beer. It went down smooth and cold, and I realized just how hot the house was getting. Might as well go outside and not watch the fireflies, I told myself. At least there'll be a breeze.

I shoved the porch door open, a beer (one open, one not) in each hand, and strode out. The sky was already the deep shade of blue that jewelers use in velvet to make diamonds look good. Stars were out, plenty of them, and in the distance heat lightning flashed on and off. The rustle of the branches down in the Thicket was loud enough to hear, though the pine trees screened most of the wind off from the house.

It seemed peaceful enough. I settled into a chair and took another swig of beer. My view mostly faced downhill, toward the trees. As I expected, the land was dark and getting darker. I could almost imagine the land was a vast ocean, rolling up toward the rock of my home.

Home. When had I started thinking of the house that way? It was a good question, and I still wasn't sure the word fit. Mind you, I wasn't sure whether it was the house or me it wasn't right for, and that question bore some examination.

More beer followed, and soon it was time to crack the second one. There was an advantage to sitting out here, I decided. If there was one place on the planet where I wasn't going to be pestered by the fireflies, I had surely found it.

Chuckling to myself, I tried to plan the next day. The information about Hanratty was interesting, but I wasn't quite sure what I was supposed to do with it. Asking about her ex-husband didn't seem like a good idea. Maybe I could ask Carl. Invite him over for a beer or something like Adrienne had suggested. Ask his advice, maybe poke him a bit more about that promise he kept hinting at.

Maybe I could even get back into town. Talk to Reverend Trotter again, maybe stop by the library for a little more research.

"Easy boy, you're getting ahead of yourself," I said. "No sense rushing things, if there are things to be rushed. Besides, you need to get the house clean for company." I looked at the second bottle of beer, which had mysteriously emptied itself in a way that I suspected was connected to my current euphoria. "Right. Time to go in."

I lurched to my feet, leaving the beer bottles behind, and shuffled my way inside. Locking the door behind me was habit now, but I still double-checked. No sense taking chances, not now.

Bed seemed like a good idea, so I brushed my teeth, drank a couple of glasses of water, and stripped halfway down. Something gnawed at me as I did so, a fuzzy reminder that I'd forgotten something, but it was too late. Exhaustion and beer had taken over, and I could only plod my way to the bedroom and lay myself down, jeans and all.

I'll figure it out in the morning, I told myself, and I closed my eyes. Sleep pounced and carried me away.

The numbers on the clock told me it was three in the morning when I sat bolt upright in bed. I blinked, trying to figure out why the hell I'd woken up. The dreams I remembered weren't bad, just not the sort of thing I'd share with Adrienne or Jenna any time soon. A hand on my brow told me I wasn't soaked in sweat, neither. Something had jerked me up out of deep sleep like a fish on a line, though.

Overhead, dull thunder rumbled. It seemed as if the heat lightning had given way to the real thing, and more rain was on the way. I sat and listened, wondering if that was the case, but all I heard were distant drumrolls up above. Rain was coming, yes, but it was taking its own sweet time getting here. If that's what had awakened me, I was a lighter sleeper than I thought.

Another roll of thunder came and went, and I lay back down. "Go back to sleep," I told myself out loud. "It was nothing." I wadded up my pillow and folded my arms across my chest. Slow breaths told me I was well on my way.

Outside, something growled.

My eyes flew open. "What the hell?" I muttered, and I waited for the sound to repeat itself.

It did. Something was out there, something angry and hungry, and it gave a growl like something not of this world.

Softly, I swung my feet onto the floor and stood. "Son of a bitch," I muttered under my breath, and I took stealthy steps out into the hall. Maybe from there I could get a better sense of where the sound was coming from, or a better idea of what it was.

Another growl forced itself into my ears. It seemed to be everywhere, shaking the floorboards and rattling the windows. I turned in place, trying to get a sense of where it was coming from. Thunder mixed in with the sound, strengthening it and giving it a place to hide.

Through a window shade, I could see a brief flash. The lightning was getting closer, the thunder louder. The storm would be here soon.

The growling was getting louder, too. It seemed to be circling the house, moving from place to place. So help me, it felt like whatever was making it was looking for a way in.

I thought about that for a second. There were three doors and a whole mess of windows, most of them high off the ground. I couldn't do much about the windows, but the doors were more in my power. I sprinted to the kitchen and checked the door there. Locked. Smiling with grim purpose, I turned and hurried back down the hall. Every door I passed, I shut. Even if whatever it was out there got in a window, it would still have a door between it and me.

Bedroom door. Bathroom. Front door. Checked and locked. I went down the hall like a man possessed. Growls and thunder chased me along. One after another, they checked out.

The last door was the mudroom. I reached to open it then hesitated. The door was already closed, after all. I didn't need to open it, even if there were a door to the inside in there.

But there was a shotgun in there, too, and I suddenly wanted that in my hands very badly.

Gently, I turned the doorknob and pushed. The door slid open noiselessly. I could see the gun, gleaming in the dim light that came down the hall. Thunder boomed, but the growling, I noticed, had stopped.

Maybe it had gone away. Maybe there was nothing to worry about.

Maybe. I reached for the gun.

Something slammed into the outside door.

Startled, I fell back. The impact was repeated and the door shuddered. My hands stretched out instinctively for the gun as the door shook again, and a demon howl went up. Holding tight to the shotgun, I hurled myself against the door and threw my weight against it, just in time for another dull thud of impact. I could feel claws scrabbling at it, tearing into the wood. There was another slam, like a gut punch to the house, and then the rain came pouring down like the tears of God for His lonely children. It drummed down on the roof, thunder giving the sound accent and shape.

Outside, there was one last snarl, then silence. The only sounds were the voices of the storm, and the pounding of my heart. My hands were clenched tight around the gun, my eyes wide open and staring. I sat there in the dark, listening, not daring to move, not daring to believe that whatever it was had gone away.

Eventually, I slept, and the sounds of the rain washed my bad dreams away.

CHAPTER 17

I woke up with the shotgun still in my fingers, which is to say I woke up in a hurry.

I was still curled up on the mudroom floor, my back to the outside door. My back and my butt hurt like hell, and my fingers were cramped from hanging on to the gun so tightly. My head throbbed, and my neck made little popping sounds every which way I moved.

"Jesus, I feel old," I said. I used the gun as a prop to help me up. Daylight peeked in under the door, just enough to reassure me that the door itself was still set on its hinges and hung proper in its frame.

Holding the gun in one hand, I unlocked the door with the other. It stuck a little bit then came open. It swung in with a creak, and I gave a low whistle.

Something had done a number on it. The door itself was heavy enough—Grandfather Logan didn't believe in half-measures—but whatever had been howling outside last night had done its damnedest to get through it. Much of the paint on the lower panel had been clawed off, and the wood was all torn up. If I hadn't known better, I'd have sworn someone took an axe to it. Most of the splinters had been washed away by the rain, but there were still a few on the half-flight of steps that led down from where I stood. Some of them were a good four inches long.

The soldiers I'd placed out the night before weren't that big. I'd skipped the mudroom, I remembered, but thinking about that was nothing but foolishness. A gesture in the dark to make myself feel better wouldn't have done a damn thing, not against whatever had torn those gashes in the wood without half trying.

But I might set one in there anyway, once I'd dealt with other things. There was, after all, no sense taking chances.

Being careful not to disturb things too much, I took two steps down the stairs and looked at the ground around the base. The rain had turned it to mud, and old memories told me exactly how deep the mud around that part of the house could get. I had no intention of stepping in it, not if I could help it.

Besides, that would have messed up the very interesting prints that I could now see. The rain had blurred the outlines some, but the markings were still pretty distinct. Four toes, claw marks at the tip, and a broad pad in back—I knew that sort of print.

It was a dog. Damn big one, too.

I scooted down another step to get a closer look. The prints were near two inches long, the sign of a big dog indeed. They sank deep into the mud as well, which told me two things.

One, that meant the dog that had attacked my home last night was heavy as well as long.

Two, it meant that it stuck around a while after the rain started. I didn't find that very comforting, seeing as I now realized he'd been there long after I thought he'd gone. He'd been prowling around those steps, waiting for something.

Maybe even waiting for me to open the door.

I shook my head to clear the image and peered down at the prints. A closer look confirmed what I already suspected. There was only one set of prints here, even though there were a lot of them. That meant one dog and one dog only.

Leaving the door open was a calculated risk, but I didn't have my keys on me and I was afraid that if I went back into the house for them, I wouldn't be quite so willing to come out again. So, wearing jeans and nothing else, I left the door open behind me and set out to follow the tracks.

They weren't too hard to pick out. Here and there the ground had bare patches where the weeds had given up, and in those spots there were enough paw prints to keep me on the track.

They led, unsurprisingly, up to the edge of the drainage ditch, and that's where they vanished. I leaned out over the ditch, now graced with a fast-moving stream in its bottom, and checked the other side. Sure enough, there were a couple of prints, but not many, and they vanished into the gravel of the road.

I thought about hopping over myself, but decided against it. Not the way my luck was going, no sir. Instead, I walked down to the driveway, and then around to get myself a good feel for the road and how well it took prints.

The answer to that question was "Not well at all," and the gravel did a fine job of making me regret going out there barefoot. No, if the dog that had savaged my door had come out onto the road, there would be no way to pick up its trail again. It had vanished, though the heft of the gun in my hand made me think that maybe I wouldn't mind all that much if it came back. If it did, this time I'd be ready.

Satisfied and feeling my oats, I headed back to the house. Playing the mighty hunter for a few minutes was one thing, but the day was starting to get on, and I wanted a shower, a change of clothes, and a cup of coffee.

What I got instead was Officer Hanratty pulling into the driveway behind me, screeching to a stop so close I could feel the tiny bits of stone her car threw up bounce off the back of my legs.

For a moment, I considered walking back to the house, but that would have done me no good, not with Hanratty. So instead I let the gun drop then turned around to face her.

"Morning, Officer," I said. "This is a pleasant surprise. What can I do to help you?"

"You can put a shirt on," she said as she heaved herself out of the car. "And you can put the gun in the house. No sense scaring the neighbors."

"Yes, Officer," I said amiably. "Care to come in?"

She grimaced, a horrible thing to see first thing in the morning. "It's either that or I stand out here and yell, so why don't we do that?"

"Follow me, then." I traipsed around to the back of the house and up the mudroom steps. She followed me then gave a shout of surprise when she saw the door.

"What the hell happened here?"

"Dog," I said, pointing to the tracks. "Wild one tried to

get in last night. Tried real hard, too. Why do you think I'm walking around with this?" I patted the gun.

"I thought you were trying to blend in with the locals," Hanratty replied sarcastically. "Though you do seem to be doing a better job of it than the last time I saw you."

I thought about where Hanratty had come from, how long she'd been in town, and how she'd lectured me about what life was like here. I thought about saying something. Then I took a deep breath as quiet as I could and bit my tongue for a full ten seconds before trusting myself to speak. "Well, I fell asleep waiting for him to come back and was just checking his tracks before taking a shower. You might want to call animal control."

"Assuming the dog is wild, yes," she replied. She stood impatiently at the bottom of the steps. "Are we going to go in or what?"

"Going in," I said, and I did exactly that. Hanratty followed, and the stairs complained as she did.

I led her into the kitchen, past all the locked doors without comment. "Coffee?" I asked. She nodded, so I busied myself making a pot, double strength.

"So, what brings you out here at this hour?" I asked as the coffee brewed. "Good news on the car, I hope?"

She sank into a chair and drummed her fingers against the tabletop. "More or less. A couple of kids spotted someone driving it around town last night. They didn't get a good look at the driver, though."

"Not surprising." I poured two cups of coffee and brought them over to the table. "Cream and sugar?"

"Black," she replied. "At least until noon."

"Black it is." I shoved her cup in front of her. My cup hit the table a moment later and I took the chair directly across from where Hanratty sat. "So what part of town was the car spotted in?"

She pulled a notebook out of a pants pocket and flipped through a few pages. "Maynard and Hughes, according to the first witness. Right by the library building. It popped up across town a little while later then was spotted heading east and out of town. Needless to say, by the time anyone thought to call in, it was long gone."

I blinked and took a sip of coffee I didn't taste. "The library, huh? Weird."

"Yup. Especially since you were there yesterday, too."

Hanratty got one of my best long, slow looks, which didn't faze her a bit. "What's that supposed to mean?" I asked.

"Nothing," she replied, obviously having way too much fun with my discomfort. "It just means that the car was near the library, and you were near the library, and those are two very interesting facts."

I leaned back in my chair and held the coffee cup in front of me with both hands. "It could mean that the thief is stalking me. Makes sense after what happened the other day."

She nodded. "That's one possibility, certainly."

"I'd be interested in hearing any others you might have thought of."

"I'm still working that part out." She shifted in the chair, which groaned in protest. "I've got to examine all the possibilities, you know."

I nodded like I understood what the hell she was talking about. "Of course. That reminds me, I saw Sam Fuller go into the station house after he dropped me off yesterday. He say anything interesting?"

The officer locked her face into a frown and waggled a round finger at me. "That's none of your business, Mr. Logan."

I shrugged and slurped down more coffee. It was almost cool enough to drink, but I wasn't going to give Hanratty the satisfaction of a cough or a choke.

"Just curious. I like Sam. He's given me a couple of rides, and if he had some kind of trouble, I'd want to help out."

"Sam's got no trouble," she rumbled, emphasizing his name just enough to let me see the obvious comparison. "This may surprise you, but in a town like this, occasionally folks are just friends with the police and like stopping in to say hello sometimes."

"Oh, come off it," I sputtered. Hanratty looked up at me, shocked, but I didn't give a damn how shocked she pretended to be. The cat was clawing its way out of the bag, so I decided to give it a swift kick in the ass. "A town like this and folks like these—who the hell do you think you're fooling, Hanratty? You sound like you should be wearing a sandwich board for the local tourist bureau except, oh, wait, Maryfield's too damn small to have one."

"Very interesting, Mr. Logan." Her tone was guarded, and I nearly grinned when I saw her hands curl protectively, reflexively around the coffee. "But I'm not quite sure I understand where you're going with this."

"It ain't where I'm going, Officer *Lee*," I spat out. "It's where you've been. I don't know what the hell you're playing at, telling me all about small town this and small town that, but I don't really care for it. It's intimidation, is what it is, and I don't even know why. So why don't you cut that crap out and try to do some actual police work finding my stolen car, and I'll try to forget that you came running here from the closest thing this state has to a big city to hide out when things got hot."

"You don't know shit, Logan," she said icily, and she stood. "Remember that the next time you go shooting your mouth off about stuff you don't really understand." She put the mug down on the table. "Crappy coffee, by the way. You used to buy all yours at Starbucks, didn't you?"

"Preferred tea until I got back home," I said, standing up to show her I wasn't intimidated. "Can I show you out?"

"No, you can't." She marched past me to the kitchen door and put a meaty hand on the knob. "If there's any word on your car, I'll call."

"You do that," I said, and I sat back down. "Have a nice trip back to town, Officer."

The only response I got was the door slamming as she went out.

I waited until I heard the police car tearing down the road before finishing my coffee. Even then, I was half-expecting Hanratty to kick in the door and arrest me for malicious newspaper reading, or crappy coffee making, or maybe indecent exposure if she was feeling particularly creative. I knew I'd hit a nerve, and hit it hard. My guess was that most of the folks in town were too polite to try to find out anything about their new cop, and the rest too embarrassed to talk about it. Only a big city boy like myself—and I had to laugh at that description—was rude and brash and ornery enough to throw it in her face, never mind that she'd been applying a form of harassment that usually ended up involving the words "You ain't from around here, are you, boy?"

Well, screw her. Maybe there was something that I didn't know about her circumstances. In fact, I'd be shocked if there weren't. That being said, all I wanted out of her was a little public service, not lectures on my hometown or suspicious smirks or visits at odd hours.

Of more immediate concern was the fact that my car, complete with mysterious driver, had been spotted near the library. Maybe that was coincidence—by sufficiently loose definition two thirds of town was near the library, after all—but it still felt worrisome.

Frowning, I reached across the table for Hanratty's half-full cup and stopped.

Leaning forward, I could see something else on the table—a pair of black-rimmed glasses peeking out from behind the napkin holder. Hanratty couldn't possibly have failed to see them. Only I was that stupid.

No doubt Hanratty knew whose glasses those were. She probably knew every prescription in town, now that I thought on it, convincing herself that it was something small-town folks did. Hell, if someone convinced her that it was customary, she'd probably put on a Minnie Pearl hat and a smile, then go line-dance through the town square.

In the meantime, though, she had a bit more information on

my comings and goings than I wanted, and some on Adrienne's, too. The pieces of this puzzle weren't fitting together yet, but they were all on the same table, and I was getting the vague sense of an ugly-ass picture waiting to be formed.

There was nothing I could do at the moment, though, unless I wanted to pelt down the road in hopes of outrunning Hanratty's police car. With all due deliberateness, I took the coffee cups over to the sink and dumped Hanratty's out. After some fiddling with sponges and coffee grounds, I surveyed the kitchen and felt that it was good enough for the time being. My stomach wasn't settled enough for breakfast, not after last night's adventure and this morning's dust-up, so I just let the notion go and went around turning the house back into something habitable. That damned Nickel Creek song was in my head, and I found myself whistling bits of it off and on as I went.

But it was morning, with the sun shining and the night's rain gone. Even with a sore back from sleeping curled up on the mudroom floor, I felt better than I had in days. Maybe it was the mud between my toes, maybe it was the satisfaction of telling Hanratty off, maybe it was just the fact that, by the light of day, I just couldn't see ghosts and magical fireflies anymore. Maybe I'd start worrying about them again once the sun went down, but for now I had real flesh-and-blood problems to worry about.

Like, for example, the one that had nearly torn through my laundry room door.

It was pure coincidence that I was at the far end of the house, shutting the mudroom door and locking it, when the phone rang. I thought about letting it go, but curiosity got the better of me and I ended up running down the hall just in time to catch it.

"Hello?" I asked, a little breathless.

"Mr. Logan?" I heard Adrienne reply. "I hope I didn't catch you at a bad time."

I checked the kitchen clock. It was a quarter past nine—a perfectly reasonable time for someone to call. "Just an early time, that's all. I try to exercise my constitutional right to be a lazy son-of-a-gun these days." She started to apologize, and I shushed her. "Really, it's fine. What can I do for you?"

"Well, it's about yesterday," she said.

I let out an exaggerated sigh, full of the blues. "Why do I have the feeling you're not going to tell me you did some more research on my problem and found the one clue that will magically solve everything?"

"I'm afraid not," she replied, from the sounds of things smothering a giggle as she did so. "But I did leave my glasses at your house last night."

"That you did," I agreed. "And I'm going to be holding them for ransom. Leave three hundred dollars in small unmarked bills by the statue of Joe Johnston downtown, or you'll never see them again."

"Not on a librarian's salary," she said sweetly, "and in case you've forgotten, there is no statue of General Johnston."

I snapped my fingers, up near the phone so she could hear. "Damn. I knew there was a flaw in my cunning plan. So what now?"

She took a deep breath. "I was thinking I could come out

there to retrieve them after work, if that's all right with you. And if you don't mind, I could maybe bring some dinner along with me. Just to thank you for looking after the glasses."

"That's better than trusting my cooking," I heard myself saying. "I'd be honored."

"Great." You could actually hear her smile over the phone. "I'll be there around six thirty?"

"Sounds good to me," I told her. "I'm looking forward to it."

"Me, too," she said, and she broke the connection.

The next few hours were spent doing what no man in his right mind enjoys doing, which is to say tidying up in hopes of impressing a woman. There was something soothing about it, though, a pleasant change from all the worrying and hurrying and scurrying I'd been doing. By the time I was finished, everything except that scratched-up door looked presentable, which was no mean feat considering my state of mind.

At a quarter after six, I declared the place as done as it was going to get, and I moved to take care of the last two special items on the agenda. First was the shotgun, which I propped up in the mudroom with the safety off and the inside door closed.

Second came the door to Mother and Father's bedroom. I opened it, meeting no resistance. "Don't make me look bad this time," I said into the empty air, and then I propped the door open with a book off Father's shelf—a well-worn hardback copy of *Catch-22*. I'd never noticed it there before, but then again, there were a lot of things I'd never bothered to notice about Father.

I could explore them later, though. Now, I needed to wait for a pretty lady to show up.

✷

Show up she did, more or less on schedule. I was waiting on the porch when she did, feeling like a schoolboy. She was wearing a sundress all covered in pink flowers, neck cut high and hem way down low.

I hate the color pink. On her, it looked perfect.

In her hand, Adrienne had a brown paper bag, which I supposed held dinner. She bounced up the steps and smiled, holding the bag up like it was a treasure. "Fried catfish and slaw all right?" she asked.

"Perfect," I told her. "Come on in. I know the head waiter. He'll give us the best seats in the house."

We went in then, and she busied herself pulling the various foodstuffs out of the bag while I pulled out plates, glasses, and flatware. By the time I pulled the pitcher of lemonade out of the fridge, she had everything neatly portioned on the plates and was sitting, waiting for me.

"You're making me look bad here," I told her, and I settled in across the table from her.

"You look all right to me," she replied, putting knife and fork to her food. "How was your day?"

"All right," I told her around a mouthful of catfish. "I had a visit from Officer Hanratty this morning. She updated me on my car."

"That was nice of her." Cole slaw started disappearing at an alarming rate.

I nodded in agreement, not trusting myself to manage a

proper tone of voice. "Other than that, it was just housekeeping and being a bum. I find I rather enjoy that."

Adrienne looked past me out the window. "So does the grass, from what I can see. Going to mow that any time soon?"

"The grass ain't bothering me, so why should I bother it?" She looked stunned at that, like the idea of letting the grass grow hadn't even occurred to her. It was nearly enough to make me shoot lemonade out my nose. I swallowed hastily, coughing, and put the glass down. "Actually, I just don't know where Carl stashed the mower. It's not in the shed, 'cause I don't have one." And, when she looked at me in a way that said that answer wasn't quite good enough, I said, "I'll get around to it one of these days. Soon, even."

She was about to say something that I had hopes was approving when the phone rang. Instead, she turned to look at it. I did the same.

It rang again. *Jenna*, I thought. Crud. I'd forgotten all about her calling.

"Are you going to get that?" she asked.

"Nope," I told her, and I took another bite of catfish. "It's dinner time. I don't answer the phone during dinner. I also don't answer the phone when I have company. It's rude."

Third ring, this one somehow shriller than the last two.

"Is it now?" Adrienne arched her eyebrows, trying for one and getting both. "And that's your reason?"

Fourth ring. Jenna always hung up after five, I remembered.

"Yup." I nodded and looked down into my plate to keep from meeting her eyes. "Besides, I only have three jokes, and if I use them on the phone, then I can't tell 'em to you."

The fifth ring cut the air then cut itself off.

Silence.

Adrienne gave me an appraising look, one I couldn't read. "I'm sure they're good jokes, and they would bear repeating. Now finish eating. I've got red velvet cake in the bag still, and the frosting's probably all melted now."

"Yes'm," I said, and I went back to work on my catfish.

Dinner was long gone, replaced by conversation, when panic suddenly grabbed me. I turned to look out the window and felt my breath sink its hooks into the back of my throat. The sky had gone from powder blue to something getting on toward navy while we'd been talking, and I'd never noticed.

Last night, the dog had started hunting me in the middle of the night. What if it came back tonight?

What if it came back earlier? What if Adrienne were still here?

She noticed my distraction and followed my look. "It's getting late, isn't it?" she said more than asked. I nodded.

"That it is, and I know you have to work tomorrow. I'd hate to keep you too late just because I like to hear myself talk."

Adrienne tilted her head and gave me an odd look. "You know, any other man would be working overtime to try to get me to stay later. You certainly are a strange one."

"Too strange for my own good," I admitted, "and I'd love to keep you here as late as possible, except Hanratty's probably hiding in the shrubs with a video camera. Honestly, it's not that I don't enjoy your company, it's just that, well, maybe slow is a good way to go. With anything."

Her eyes narrowed. "This doesn't have anything to do with that phone call, does it?"

I shook my head, and I was pretty sure I meant it. "Cross my heart. That was a friend of mine from Boston who's coming in to town to help me sort out a few things. At least, I'm pretty sure it was. The other options are Hanratty or Carl."

"Or Sam Fuller," she added. "You're sure?"

I nodded. "Absolutely. I look forward to introducing you to Jenna when she gets down here."

She took a deep breath. "It'll be interesting to meet another friend of yours." While I chewed over what exactly she meant by that, she stood and carried her plate over to the sink. I watched her, silhouetted by the kitchen light in a way that was absolutely ordinary and absolutely beautiful.

I coughed and looked down at my plate. "You don't need to worry about that, you know. I'll clean up."

"Too late," she said brightly. "But if you want to be a gentleman, you can walk me out to my car."

"That I can do." I stood and walked to the door. "After you," I said, making a grand gesture I'd stolen from an old ZZ Top video as I pulled the door open.

"Thank you, kind sir," she replied, sweeping past me. I followed her across the porch and down the steps, a couple of seconds behind her the whole way.

When we reached her car, she stopped and turned. "Thank you for a lovely evening," she said, "and for taking care of my glasses."

"It was my pleasure," I told her. "Thank you for coming back out here, especially after last night."

She shrugged. "I told you—you ought not to be alone out here. It's plain to see. Whether it's me or Mr. Powell or you getting a puppy that's the answer, I don't know, but it's something to think about. Last night just proves it." Then, more shyly, "Besides, I like talking to you."

"I like talking to you, too." She didn't resist when I took her hands in mine, nor did she pull away. "And you can come out here any time you want. Honest."

She did pull away then, laughing. "We'll see how your friend from Boston feels about that." A second later she was in her car, waving from behind the windshield and starting up the engine. I stepped away so I wouldn't lose any toes as she pulled out, and then I followed her up the driveway to the edge of the road.

She waved one more time, flicked on her lights, then rumbled off down the Harrison Farm Road. I waited until I couldn't see her taillights any more, then gave the night sky a stupid grin and set about going back inside.

The house, seen from this angle, looked less like a house and more like a low hill, a kind of primitive fort huddling up against the night. It was a darker outline against a dark sky, with only a few dim lights through a few windows giving any sign that it was inhabited.

From around the other side of the house, a growl boiled up like smoke from a slow fire.

I suddenly remembered just where I'd left the shotgun, and I froze.

I calculated how far it was back to the house from where I stood, and how long it would take me to run it. Then I made a rough guess as to how long it would take a big dog to come charging around the corner, and decided I didn't like the answer.

"Good doggie?" I ventured hopefully. It growled again, louder now. Either it had gotten more pissed off, or it had come closer. The bulk of the house kept me from seeing which, and I didn't mind that one bit.

A quick look behind me told me that the road wasn't an option, either. There were no cars approaching in either direction, no one I could wave down and beg for protection. Running down the road was plain foolish. There was no way I'd outrun anything four-footed and angry, not on my best day and its worst.

That left running for the house, and luck.

I looked past the house, down to that dark line of pine trees. "Could use some help here," I said under my breath, and then I put my heels to use.

It was maybe fifty feet from where I stood to the steps leading up to the porch, and another couple yards past that to the still-open door. Not too far, I told myself. Head down, that's a good boy. My feet crunched on the driveway as I sprinted, my arms going like a windmill in a stiff breeze.

The growling changed to a howl, long and cruel. There was nothing mournful in this sound. This was a howl of murder.

I could hear the dog exploding out of whatever cover it'd been in, leaves whipping away from the force of its passage and branches tearing. The drum of its feet on the ground was loud enough to hear. How far away was it? Not far enough, that's all that mattered.

I tucked my head further down and ran faster. The light from the kitchen was just visible at the edge of my vision, pulling me on.

It let out another howl then, much closer than the first. It was playing with me, I knew, telling me it could catch me even if it didn't go all out.

Tall grass whipped across my shins as I took the last few steps toward the porch and leaped up the steps. My feet hit the wood of the deck with a thud as the dog came tearing around the corner of the house. I didn't look at it, didn't dare turn and lose any momentum. Instead, I threw myself forward, through the doorway and into the kitchen. My chin tucked into my arm to cushion the shock of landing, I hit the floor and skidded. Something stung my hand and I realized I'd hit one of the toy soldiers. I must have placed it on the floor before I went out, but now it was spinning, sliding away.

Claws tore into the wood of the deck behind me. I had one chance. Rolling on my side, I jammed my foot behind the door and kicked as hard as I could. The door swung forward.

I watched it. It seemed to go slowly, too slowly. It would never make it all the way.

Somehow, it swung shut. The click of the latch was like a gunshot, the dog slamming into it a second later like a cannon.

I lay back on the floor, panting. *Get up*, my mind told me. *Go get the gun!* But I couldn't move, knowing it was out there so close.

Claws scrabbled at the door, not furious like they had the

night before, but more like their owner was looking for a way in.

Different clicks, now. It was the sound of claws on brass. It had found the doorknob. It shouldn't be able to do anything with it, I knew. But it shouldn't have done any of this.

I sat up and pushed myself backward, away from the door. One hand closed on a chair leg, hoping I could fling it in front of me if I had to. My back tensed, waiting for the sound of the dog hurling itself against the wood.

Instead, I heard a whistle. The dog paused, and I swear I could hear it turn its head away. Then, calm as you please, it trotted away. *Click-clack-click* went its claws on the porch and down the steps, and then came the *swoosh* of a body moving through tall grass, going away.

All the air rushed out of me, and I collapsed to the floor.

In the distance, the dog barked, all its menace gone. It sounded happy.

"Screw you, too," I said, and I just lay there until all the sounds went away.

Eventually, I found the strength to stand up. A peek out the window told me nothing was out there, but I trusted that about as far as I trusted a Boston traffic cop with a ticket quota to meet. I locked the door then shoved a chair up under the handle. I thought about moving the table there as well, but that seemed excessive.

Then, and only then, did I pick up the phone to call Jenna.

She answered on the fourth ring, annoyed as all get out. "Yeah?"

"Hi," I said. "Did you call before?"

"I might have." She sounded deeply irritated. "What, are you screening your calls now?"

"No, just getting chased by wild dogs."

"Ah." I could hear the puff of her cigarette. "And I'm supposed to excuse you for that?"

"Come on, Jenna. It's been a hell of a day."

Breath hissed through her teeth, sharply. "They're all hellish days, Logan, or haven't you noticed that? You know what I think? I think that's not an accident. I think something's trying to keep you so busy you don't have time to think."

I blinked. "Never really thought about it that way."

"That's the point now, isn't it? So start thinking." She paused. "Look, I'm sorry. I'm just really worried about you, that's all. When you didn't answer, I was afraid something, well, something might have happened to you."

"It nearly did," I told her, "but not until later. I wasn't kidding about the wild dog. And thank you."

"You're welcome, I think." The Jenna I knew and relied on was back in control. "So dare I ask why you didn't answer, then?"

I coughed delicately. "I had company over."

There was a pause. "Oh did you, now?" Another pause. "Anyone interesting?"

"Just the librarian, I'm afraid," I told her. "She's very nice."

"I'm sure she is. Look, I don't want to keep you any longer—"

"You're not keeping me," I protested. She ignored me.

"I don't want to keep you. So, I'll see you tomorrow night,

and I won't bother calling before I get there?"

"You can meet her tomorrow if you want, honest," I said. "She was just out here for dinner."

"You're missing the point, Logan. As always," she told me, and then her voice softened. "But I'm still looking forward to seeing you. Good night."

"Good night," I said, and I listened for the click of Jenna hanging up. A moment later, it came. Maybe she'd been waiting for me to say something else. I don't know.

I placed the phone back on the receiver, and for the first time I saw how old and dingy it was. It was one of the first push-button models, and Mother had been proud when we'd gotten it. "Modern convenience," Father had joked, which annoyed her to no end. Father didn't see what was wrong with the old rotary dial phone we'd had, even when his fingers were getting too big for the holes. He'd dial using a pencil, a trick I tried and failed to master. Snapped a few pencils that way, though, which Father found amusing and Mother did not.

"Maybe I'll replace it," I said out loud, just to hear how it sounded. "Don't think that'll last too much longer, the way I've been going on."

I blinked. That sounded kind of like a long-term plan to me, one of those little details that creeps in when you've already decided on how the big things are going to be handled.

"Or maybe not," I said, more softly, and I stepped away, over to the window. "No sense rushing into things."

I could have sworn it was my imagination, but at that point I didn't know where my imagination lay any more. As I said those words, the house got warmer, like it was getting all puffed up and angry. It was like when you see a man lose his temper, and the red rises in his face and the heat just flows off him. That's what this felt like, that same sort of push and pressure.

The heat rose up and sweat broke out on my forehead. I wiped it away with my forearm and looked around for the cause, half expecting to see a fire in the corner.

There was nothing to see, just that sudden wet heat that wrapped around the house and everything in it. Getting outside seemed like a very good idea, so I flung the door open and staggered out into night air that was cooler than it had any right to be. A wave of hot air flowed behind me and boiled up into the night. I could see the heat haze pass in front of the stars.

Slowly, the air behind me lost its heat. Something was settling down, no doubt, though whether it was the furnace or something a little less reasonable I didn't know. I just knew that the night air felt calm and safe. It was funny, I know—with that dog running around, the porch was the last place I ought to have felt safe—but you could feel the dog's absence, like a wrong note had been taken out of a well-known recording, at least for a little while.

I don't know how long I stood there, but it was a good while. Up high, thin strips of cloud flew past, heading east. I watched them go, part of me wishing I could follow and the rest dead set against the idea. Behind me, the heat and pressure faded, and the house acquired a feel that was distinctly more welcoming. Mother, or whoever it was, had gotten it out of his or her system, and now I was being told I didn't have to stand in the corner any more.

Well, *thank you, but no*, I thought but didn't dare say. I'd be staying outside a little longer, and coming in on my own time. In the meantime, there was a night sky full of stars—if empty of fireflies—to admire.

Eventually, a yawn snuck up on me and told me it was time to head to bed. Tomorrow was promising to be a hell of a day, so there was no sense facing it at less than full strength. I gave the sky one last look, and then I drew my eyes down to more mundane things. Things like the trees down in the dark, the land, and the driveway—I scanned them all, half in hopes of finding something odd and half afraid I would.

Down on the driveway, something caught my eye. A brief flash of light, no more than a split second, drew me. I stared at the spot, not believing what I'd seen, and dared God to make it reappear.

It did. I swore softly, more at myself than anything else, and took cautious steps down off the porch. It took all my strength not to just hurry on over, maybe scaring off a miracle in the process, but somehow I managed.

And then, there I was, looking at a lone firefly. It shone dim, but shone it did, and it sat in the dirt on the side of my drive-way, on my land. As I got closer, it blinked more frantically, blinking on and off faster and faster.

Something had happened. A suspicion rose up in my mind as to what it was, and I quickly checked the ground just past where the firefly held its position.

There they were, faint but fresh. Tire tracks. Adrienne's tire tracks, to be specific, the ones she'd laid down that very night. They extended maybe three feet past where the firefly was, that far and no farther. That meant that where the lightning bug stood, she'd stood as well.

I thought about what that meant for a moment and didn't like any of the possibilities I came up with. Whatever was going on, I didn't want Adrienne mixed up in it. Even as I came to that conclusion, I knew it was too late. I might as well have asked the stars to stop shining. The forces that were bedeviling me weren't going to leave her alone, not any more.

Unbidden, the image of her face rose up in my mind. She was beautiful, of that there was no doubt. She was beautiful and young and charming, and a man with more of a sense of his own worth than I would have said she was falling hard for me. She was vulnerable, too—trusting in a way that made a cynic like myself want to protect her from the harsh things I'd seen and done.

The best way to do that, of course, would be to stay here. With her.

Carl's words in the Thicket came back to me, loud and clear. He'd talked about parts that didn't fit where they ought, and things that might happen to them. He'd left out one possibility, though. Maybe the shape of the place that part was supposed to go could be changed. A little work here, a little polish there, and suddenly everything would fit so right you'd never know the difference.

I felt sick. Nearly falling over, I dropped to my knees and picked up the firefly. It let me, holding still and shining dull and steady in my hands. Staggering, I walked it up to the property line and flung it into the air. It hung in the air a moment, then darted back past me and found its same spot on the ground.

There it stood, defiant and shining. One hand holding my gut, I lurched back down to it and looked down.

"Oh no you don't," I told it and whatever had brought it there. "Not like this. It's not fair. It's not right."

Then I brought my foot down, and ground it hard against the gravel and soil. When I lifted it, the light had gone out.

CHAPTER 18

Friday dawned ugly.

The skies were covered in clouds that had no business being there—thick thunderheads like you usually saw only in the afternoon heat. The air was heavy and sullen, and you could taste ozone with every breath. Rain was coming, but it was coming sulky. It would get here in its own good time, and the rest of the day was just going to have to suffer while it waited.

I stood on the porch and looked up at those gunmetal clouds and silently urged them to get on with it. The last thing I needed was Jenna getting delayed by the weather, or worse, trying to drive out here through a Carolina summer storm. Accidents had a way of happening during those, and that was under the best of circumstances. What I was facing now was anything but.

Inside, the house still simmered. The anger from last night was still there, turned down but not gone away. I could feel it with a single step over the threshold. It got stronger as you went into the house, too, and the door to Mother and Father's bedroom was almost hot to the touch.

If I'd had any doubts as to whether the house was haunted,

and if so, who was doing the haunting, they were gone now. "Leave Adrienne out of this, Mother," I said to the closed door, without bothering to try to open it. Nothing fell or crashed, but the heat didn't go away, either. I guess she was thinking about it.

That meant I had things to think about, too, which was why I was out on the porch and looking away down to the Thicket. Last night's revelation was still with me, sticking uncomfortably in my craw. Swallowing it was proving tough, which made me want to give it a chaser. And the more I thought about that, the more I realized there was only one thing I could do.

Call Carl.

Carl knew more than he was telling. Saying that was like saying that the sun came up in the east. But there was something else going on there, too. He'd been bending the last time we'd talked. Maybe I could get something else out of him, something that would help me make sense of what was going on.

Steeling myself against the pressure inside, I ducked back into the kitchen. After a gulp of cold coffee for courage, I called. The phone rang twice before Carl picked up, which is to say about two rings sooner than I was ready for him to.

"Yeah?" His voice was hard and suspicious, like he'd been waiting for the call and wasn't happy to be getting it. "That you, Logan? Speak up."

"It is, Carl." I swallowed and pulled together as many of my thoughts as I could. "I need to talk to you."

"Well, I don't need to talk to you none. What happened, you eat all your damn food already?"

I felt my lips curling into a grin. Same old Carl, which in its own way was a comfort. If he'd gone soft on me, I would have worried. "No, Carl. I'm doing fine. I just wanted to talk. I wanted to say thank you, too, but mostly I just wanted to talk."

"Thank you. Heh." His laugh sounded like dry leaves. "Nice thing to say, especially when you're trying to butter a man up. Don't thank me, Logan. I'm just doing my duty."

I crossed the kitchen and tucked the phone under my chin. "Your job ended when I came back, Carl. You've gone way above and beyond, even if I don't understand why."

He laughed again, without any joy in it. "That was a *job*, boy. I keep telling you that. Now why don't you stop dancing round the subject and tell me why you want to bend my ear?"

A felt a small jab of anger twist me up inside, as much from surprise as from hurt. I guess I really had been trying to say thank you, once I'd thought on it, and Carl's dismissing it made me feel low. "I really do want to say thank you, you know."

He snorted. "If you did, you'd say it to my face, not when you're hiding behind the phone and piling up questions to toss at me. Don't play hurt, boy. It doesn't become you. Just ask your questions straight and you might get an answer. You'd best hurry, though. I ain't long on patience these days."

My neck had a crick in it, so I switched the phone to my other ear. "Fine, if that's how you want it," I said, and I tried to phrase my questions in way that would draw answers, not whip-crack derision. "Look, I think I've got some idea of what's going on here. Maybe not with Hanratty or the car, but with the house, at least. I know you won't talk about that promise, so I'm not going to ask. I think I know why you wanted to talk to me down in the Thicket, though I'm not sure exactly how that works. But now, all of a sudden, things are getting mean here, and I don't know why. There's something wrong, and I want to make it right. How can I do that, Carl?"

There was almost silence on the end of the line, just slow breathing coming down the wire. "Boy," Carl finally said, "I'm not sure." More silence. "You remember what I told you down in the Thicket?"

"Yes?"

"You think on that real hard, son. Think on it the next time that pretty librarian smiles at you." He paused, and I could feel the tension in him as he tried to figure out what he had to say. "And I got a question for you."

That brought me up short. "For me?"

"Unless there's another jackass named Logan on the line, I'd reckon so. Now think about this, 'cause you'll only have one chance to answer it right. Get it wrong and, well, I wash my hands of you. I done my best."

"No pressure, then," I wisecracked. He didn't laugh, not that I had expected him to. "Hit me."

"Something's gonna hit you, all right," he said dryly. "Just answer this one for yourself. You don't need to tell me nothing. Think about your father, and ask where his place was."

It didn't surprise me when Carl hung up without saying good-bye.

I sipped more cold coffee and thought about the question. The more I did, the less it made sense. When my grandparents had died, the house had passed to Mother and Father. It was theirs. The deed, I knew, had been in both their names. The house had a sense of being solidly *theirs*, Mother's decoration over the base laid down by Grandfather Logan. No, it didn't make any sense. I put my coffee cup down on the table and steepled my hands under my chin. Whatever the hell Carl was talking about, it was too much for me, at least at this hour of the morning. I folded my hands and stared down at the tabletop. It really was damn ugly, now that I thought on it.

I blinked. That couldn't be it, could it? Every piece of furniture in the place was either inherited or picked out by Mother, except the table. Surely that couldn't have been what Carl meant. A quick look around the kitchen convinced me that the hunch wasn't quite right. It was very much Mother's room, really, and the more I thought on things the more I realized that they all were. Her touch was all over, from the front room to kitchen counters to the setup of the mudroom in back. This was her house, top to bottom.

Or maybe not. Toy soldiers told me differently, and the notion hit me like a thunderbolt. The one place Mother never went, the one place Father kept as his own—that was the attic.

Without thinking, I rose up out of my chair and walked down the hall to the attic entrance. That white string dangled in front of me, flapping in some draught I couldn't feel. It reminded me of the lure on one of those deep-sea fish that look like aliens or monsters. Those things had always held an awful fascination for me. I'd had nightmares about them as a child, imagining giant ones lurking in the ponds and waterways near the house, waiting for me.

I still took the bait. Reaching up, I yanked the cord down. With a squeal, the trapdoor opened toward me. My left hand held it steady, and my right let go of the cord to pull the ladder down. It looked old but sturdy, the wood dark with age and never painted. The steps seemed strong enough to hold my weight—they'd held Father's, after all—and so I trusted to luck and revelation, and I went on up.

It was smaller than I remembered, and the air was thick with dust. A naked bulb swung down from the ceiling, a chain hanging down from that, and that was all the light to be had up there. Two or three clicks were needed to get it going, and even once it lit up, it looked distinctly unwell. Hurrying seemed sensible.

A quick look around showed me boxes and dust. There were no footprints here, nothing that looked like a disturbance at all. Another time I'd ponder that, wonder how whoever had gotten the soldiers down had done it without setting foot up there. That was for another time, though. I was hunting the scent Carl had given me.

Patchy insulation lined the ceiling in places. In others, you could see the nails from the roofing driven straight through. They stuck out like thorns on a briar, and I reminded myself not to bang my head. Doing so would be unpleasant.

Something tugged me toward the far end of the room, and I let the feeling pull me along. That was the spot that was always forbidden, even after I'd been old enough to reach the cord. Father kept his things here in a locked trunk, the pieces of his life that no one else was allowed to see. I'd tried getting in once, thinking in my idiot teenager way that he was hiding dirty magazines, but the lock on the trunk defeated me. Father found out somehow, and that was about as angry as I ever saw him get. I never tried it again. Even when Father died, I left it alone. It was, I suspected, what he would have wanted.

This time, the lock was off. The trunk sat there, massive and black, and waited for me to open it. So I did.

Inside were papers, neatly bundled and tied off with red ribbon. Clothes, folded and tucked into plastic bags to protect them. Toys, ones I'd never seen. A baseball glove and a beaten-up ball, signed illegibly. Old pictures wrapped with rubber bands. And tucked in with the rest, a small book, bound in leather and tied around with a cord. A folded piece of paper poked out from one side. It was white and new, not yellowed like the rest that I saw.

This was what I was here for, I knew. Carefully, I pulled that book out and closed the lid behind it. There'd be time later to go through those things, maybe getting to know Father a little better in the process. I found myself looking forward to the prospect.

Right now, though, I had something to read.

I moved back toward the light and sat myself cross-legged on the floor. Carefully, I untied the leather cord. The book fell open to display pages filled with Father's handwriting. The paper, though, was marked with Carl's.

"Jacob," it read, and I realized with a shock it was the first time I'd ever seen him use my proper name.

You'll no doubt find this when the time is right. I don't know what your circumstances are, or if you'll ever come back to see this, but certain promises have been made that I believe will be fulfilled. Have a little faith, and read what your father has to say. Make of it what you will. The rest is up to you.

Below, it was signed in his hand, an economical collection of letters with as few curves as he could manage. I folded the note over twice then tucked it in my shirt pocket. Then, sitting under that sickly bulb, I started to read.

Father's book was not, much to my surprise, a day-by-day accounting of his doings. Instead, it was more of a journal, a collection of random writings. They dated from when he was fifteen or so to the years just before his death. The book itself was maybe an inch thick, made of heavy paper that was rough-cut on the edge. The cover was worn but sturdy, and the binding was stitched. This had been made by a man who wanted things to last, and owned by a man who took care of the things that were important to him. Even now, the leather of the cover was supple.

Not knowing what exactly I was looking for, I thumbed through the book. The earlier entries were in pencil; the later ones in ink. There were essays in there, and bits of poems both original and quoted. There were song lyrics and a few sketches that looked better than I would have guessed, including one of Grandfather Logan looking younger than I ever remembered seeing him.

Mostly, though, it was just observations on life and the things Father had seen. And so, lacking any better place to start, I turned back to the beginning and started reading.

He'd wanted to get away when he was young. That much

I'd known. What I hadn't known was that he'd done it.

The words he had for Grandfather Logan weren't kind. Cold was one of them, stern was another. He had respect for his father, but not a lot of love that I could see, and he couldn't wait to leave the house and the land.

I rubbed my eyes for a moment and winced. Some of the words Father used could have come out of my mouth, save one: respect. I'd never felt much respect for him, just confusion and anger. I could sense Mother's growing frustration with him, and made that my own. I couldn't get away fast enough, and I couldn't imagine a worse fate than being like him.

It seemed I was, though, or at least that I'd walked some of the same roads he did. College for him had been Chapel Hill, not Boston a thousand miles away, but it was somewhere else and that had been good enough. He'd gone, and he'd taken his own sweet time getting back while Grandmother and Grandfather Logan patiently waited. Those years were a blur of notes—a sketch of a street scene in Paris, some time in New York, mentions of women known and women lost. There was no mention of his work, though, or of Mother.

That changed when he came home. He'd come home after seven years away, grudging the time and the necessity. Grandmother Logan had fallen ill and would die soon after, but even so there was an air of wariness in the places where he discussed it. He loved his mother, yes, but there was something about coming home he'd dreaded. It hadn't been enough to keep him away, though. In the end, he'd come back to see her and say farewell, intending to make a short visit and then go.

Instead, the next twenty pages were about Mother. There was no more talk of returning to his wandering ways after that, just occasional wistful notes on things he wished he'd been able to see again.

I stopped at that point, frowned, and flipped back to read some of those passages again. He'd said something that nagged at me, and I was nearly frantic by the time I found the page I was looking for again.

"It seems," he'd written of Mother, "almost like she'd been waiting here for me all along."

I paused at that. What if she had been? What if she'd been the hook set in Father to reel him in and keep him here?

Who'd done it, though, and why? Not Mother, certainly— at that point she didn't know him, couldn't have known him. But if not her, then who?

Something cold started crawling up my spine as I thought about that question. Who'd wanted him back? Grandmother Logan? Maryfield itself? Who needed a Logan on this land?

I shook my head, trying to deny the thought. I was seeing ghosts and powers again when there was no need to. What if he just really loved her? Judging by those twenty pages, he did. I didn't have any answers, so I read on, looking for them.

I found the first mention of myself about ten pages on from that, and I nearly stopped reading. No man wants to know what his father really thinks of him, because every man fears not measuring up. As long as he can hear "I'm proud of you," the rest is just noise.

For years, I'd told myself I didn't care what Father thought.

It's why I tried to avoid thinking about him. Now, facing the truth of it, I knew those words were a lie.

Afraid of what I'd see, I turned the page.

And there it was in black and white, impossible to disown or deny. Disappointment. Dreams and wishes left unfulfilled. Self-doubt as he wondered if he was being a good father to me, pain as I drifted away from him, anger as he saw the contempt in my eyes. Woven through that were the growing seeds of discontent with Mother—the doubt, the worry, the feeling of being displaced in his own home.

He didn't talk much about the way he gained weight. I think it was just something Mother disapproved of, and that nearly broke my heart.

I read on, and my name disappeared from the pages. He talked about the Thicket a few times, about how he felt compelled to leave it be and the grief he took for that decision. He talked about missing me once, and those words were laced with a faint hint of envy. "He's gotten away like I thought I had," Father wrote. "His mother misses him terribly, and wishes every day he'd come home already."

And toward the end, there was much said about Carl. He and Father had never been friends, that much was true. Carl had been a suitor for Mother's hand when Father swept back into town and whisked her away, and Carl had never forgiven him for that. He was Maryfield through and through, a son of the local soil who couldn't imagine stepping past its borders. The years had softened and transformed his love for Mother, though, and through that Father and Carl made their peace. Father had seen his end coming and had wanted someone there for Mother and for the land. Carl accepted the responsibility—did it out of love for Mother and respect for Father being humble enough to ask. They'd even talked about me once. Carl said that Mother was afraid I'd never come back. Father was afraid I would, and that I'd never get away. He was proud of me, he wrote, proud of what I'd started to accomplish. He didn't want me to come home and stay, abandoning all I'd worked for.

Left unsaid was that he did want me to come home, if only to say good-bye. Left unsaid was any thought of his leaving the house to come and see me. That never seemed to be a possibility. This was his place, and he was bound to it.

Toward the end, he'd speculated a bit on things, on how he'd come home and why. He'd spent more time in the Thicket then, even though it was hardly an easy thing for him to do. There was nothing of what I'd expected, though. I'd read too many bad novels, I guess—I wanted there to be talk of ancient Indian burial grounds on the land, or curses cast or ghosts that haunted the place when Father was young. I'd wanted a mystic formula to give Mother peace, or a way to protect myself from her disappointment and anger. None of that was there. Father had been an investor, and a clever one, not a wizard or a shaman. He'd had his dark suspicions on why he'd been called home, but he didn't wander far down those paths. Instead, there was just a brooding feeling over how the spirit of the place didn't like its sons to wander, and a couple of jokes about the carrot and the stick.

I thought about my car, and about Adrienne, and about the dog outside my door at night. Carrot and stick, maybe. The picture was still too blurry for me to see.

Too quickly, I was at the end. I turned the last page, and didn't see what I'd hoped for. I'd wanted to see a note from him to me, a farewell or a benediction or an answer. Instead, there was a simple note in a shaky hand.

Elaine judged a man by his promises, and I'm afraid I haven't kept mine. I didn't put the stars on a string for her and I didn't pull down the moon to put it in her hands. I didn't take her to see Paris, though I got the feeling she never wanted to go. I didn't raise the son she wanted, or give her the daughter she would have loved. And I'm not sure I always loved her, though here at the last I find I still do. God have mercy on my soul and understand that I did the best I could, and forgive me for the times I fell short. Maybe some day I'll have the right words to ask her forgiveness as well.

Then, down at the bottom,

Here's hoping Carl has more sense than I did.

That's where it ended. I closed the book, almost reverently, and tied the leather around it again. I was tempted to put it back in the trunk, but instead settled for taking it with me as I climbed down, feeling sad and angry and a little bit afraid. I was going to need to read it again, that much was certain. Maybe this time I'd find more of what Carl had hinted was in there. That last page nagged at me, nagged at me hard, and I knew the answer was close. My feet hit the floor of the hallway, and

I absently folded up the ladder and closed the trapdoor.

Only then did I remember that I'd left the light on in the attic. Madder at myself than I ought to be, I reached up for the cord to pull the door back down. I'd just about reached it when I heard something that made my blood run cold.

Up above and undeniable, I heard the click of the light bulb's chain as something gave it a tug. The light disappeared from around the edges of the trapdoor.

"Thank you, Father," I said, and I walked away.

It was well after noon by the time I'd finished Father's journal, and the rain still hadn't rolled in. The air had a dead quality to it, and it stuck in the lungs like cotton candy. Overhead, the sky was the sick green-gray that made the neighbors think about heading down to their root cellars. I didn't think it was quite tornado weather, but the storm was shaping up to be a damn memorable one.

Choosing the better part of valor, I pulled out my one working flashlight and a few candles and stuck both them and some matches at strategic points throughout the house. Windows, the few that could be opened, were double-checked and shut tight.

The dishes and remaining cleaning only took a few minutes, and that left me at loose ends. I considered giving Father's book another read, but coming so soon on the heels of the first one, I didn't think it would do much good. Better to give it time to settle, to let my subconscious work on it.

That didn't mean I couldn't check out other options, though. There were all sorts of ways of dealing with ghosts, at least according to the stories I'd heard, and it was worth seeing what might work under these unusual circumstances.

And make no mistake, it was ghosts I was sure I was dealing with—spirits and memories and the power of a place that wasn't going to let me go. What swinging doors and moving shotguns hadn't convinced me of, the simple click of a lightbulb had. That much, at least, had become clear.

With that in mind, I picked up the phone and dialed the number for the church. An answering machine picked up after seven or so rings and informed me that the First Baptist Church of Maryfield was closed, but that if I left my name and number and a brief message explaining why the heck I needed to call the church in the first place, someone might get back to me sooner or later. There was a wait of about ten seconds, and then finally a beep.

"Hello? Reverend Trotter, this is Jacob Logan. I was wondering—"

There was a rattle and a click, the sound of the phone being picked up in a hurry. "Mr. Logan? Hello there, this is Doctor Trotter. I'm sorry—you caught me out of my office. What can I do for you?"

I hesitated, but only for a moment. "Reverend, do you remember what we talked about before?"

"We talked about a few things," he said mildly. "I assume you're talking about the notion your house is haunted, though. Am I correct?"

"That you are," I replied. "I actually had a kind of specific question about that. If I decided I wanted an exorcism, could you do it?"

I could almost hear him shaking his head. "If your father, may he rest in peace, had brought you to Sunday school more than once in a blue moon, you might remember that Roman Catholics do exorcisms. If you wanted me to come out and pray with you, well, that's a different matter. But before I did that, I'd want you to think about why you were asking me to do it. I'm not Terminix, son, and I'd be deeply offended if you treated me like you thought I was. If you decide your faith is there and you want some help, give me a call. If you want me to spray a little Jesus in the corners to clean the place out, well, I'm afraid that's not what I do. Does that help?"

"It does. Thank you," I said, and I hung up. My ears were stinging from the rebuke, in large part because that was exactly the sort of help I'd been hoping for, no strings attached. Whatever faith I had, it wasn't going to pray Mother out of her own home. She'd probably drive me off instead.

Thinking about Mother got me thinking about the state of the house in general, especially with company coming over. That led me to the realization that I hadn't actually set up a bedroom for Jenna, which led to a frantic search for clean sheets and the sort of general chaos that you see a lot on television and a lot less in real life. By the time I was finished with that, the sky had gotten noticeably darker and the taste of ozone in the air was broken-glass sharp. The kitchen clock read half past three, though by the looks of things a man might have sworn it was getting on sunset. I cocked my ear to listen for thunder in the distance, but didn't hear it. Outside, everything was still.

Experience told me the storm would start blowing up in

earnest in fifteen, maybe twenty minutes. The smart thing to do would be to settle in with a good book, and maybe a cold beer, and wait for the weather to do its thing.

Instead, I put Father's book and Carl's note on the table, and hustled myself out the door. There was someone I needed to talk to, and I didn't think it could wait. Not now, not after what I'd seen.

At the base of the porch steps I made a right, and hurried on down to that row of pine trees. They stood there, straight and tall and suddenly very fragile against the roiling clouds behind them. I did a quick mental estimate of how tall they were versus how far they were from the house, came up with an answer I could live with, and moved on past.

I hadn't been out to the stones since I'd slept at their feet. Now that I was here, I could almost start to see why. By day, the headstones looked much the same as they did by night, which struck me as a bit worrisome. Consecrated gravestones ought not to be that dark by day, even a day like this one. They seemed to drink in the light around them, and they looked thirsty for more.

Overhead, the thunder finally decided to rumble. I stood there waiting for the rain and staring down at the graves. "Is there anything I can do to make you more comfortable?" I asked, not really caring if I got an answer. "If there is, do me a favor and tell me, all right? No more clanging and banging and supernatural hoodoo. It scares the ladies, Mother, and you always did want me to meet a nice girl."

Then, I waited. Neither Mother nor Father said anything, but the rain picked that moment to start coming down, and come down it did. I trudged back up to the house in a reasonable downpour, the raindrops thrumming against the earth and grass in a steady rhythm. I didn't hurry. I'd be soaked by the time I got to the house anyway. Besides, the water was cool on my skin, and I was in no rush. Jenna wasn't due for hours yet, and the only thing to do in the house was some combination of worry, pace, and try to figure out what the hell Father had been talking about.

Halfway up the slope to the house, I saw the Audi. It was rolling past the house headed in toward town, moving at a good clip. Sheets of water were already spraying up behind it as it went.

I took a fast step forward and then caught myself. I wasn't going to go chasing it, not this time. Instead, I just kept walking, taking a casual look as it cruised past. It slowed as it rolled on by, long enough for me to get something of a look at the driver. The windows were fogged to hell, but there was a sense of a shape in there.

A large shape.

Suddenly, I found myself wondering what exactly Officer Hanratty was up to at that moment. Tearing my gaze away from the car's retreating taillights, I forced myself to go back up the steps and into the house. Still looking out the window, I picked up the phone and dialed the Maryfield police.

"Police," a disinterested voice with a heavy Carolina accent said in my ear. "How can I help y'all?"

"Is Officer Hanratty there?" I asked politely.

"Hang on just a minute. Lemme see if she's still here." I heard a click as the phone hit the tabletop, and then faintly, the same man's voice calling, "Hey Jerry, is Hanratty still here?" There was a pause, and then, "Well, damn. Who'd have thought?"

There was a moment's fumbling on the other end of the line, and then the helpful officer picked back up. "Nope, she's gone for the night."

"Oh, well." I did my best to sound disappointed, and did a fair job of pulling it off proper. "Do you know when she left?"

" 'Bout an hour ago, I think. Something about a date, if'n you can believe that." The man sounded frankly disbelieving, and I couldn't say I blamed him. It would take a brave man to tame Officer Hanratty.

"Well, thank you," I said, hoping to end the conversation.

"Can I take a message?"

I could feel my polite demeanor starting to crack. "No, that's all right. I'll just call back tomorrow."

The officer on the other end of the line was just determined to be helpful. "She ain't going to be in then, either. Try Sunday after church."

"I will," I told him through gritted teeth. "Thank you very much. You've been very helpful."

"Not at all, sir," he said, and he hung up. I blinked and did the same. It was a hell of a change from my first call to that station, and I wondered why. Maybe I just got a different officer this time, or maybe something else had changed.

Another mystery. I was getting kind of weary of them, truth be told. A man can only handle so many unanswered questions at a time before he decides to stop looking for answers.

I looked at the clock. There were another couple of hours

before Jenna was due, so I made myself a sandwich. I washed it down with a cold beer, then tidied up and sat at the kitchen table to wait. Outside, the rain poured down, steady and dull. Even the thunder had settled in to a quiet rumble.

My eyes closed on their own. *Just a little nap*, I thought. *It's raining out. I'd hear the dog if it came 'round. No sign of Mother for hours. Everything's fine.*

I jerked bolt upright to the sound of fists hammering on the kitchen door. My back and neck were both wound tight in all the wrong places, so when I stood to get the door it felt like someone had run a wire down my spine and plugged it in.

"Coming," I shouted, and I stumbled toward the door. Faintly, through the wood, I could hear Jenna. She was using her lovely voice to curse a blue streak, a series of words I did not think Mother would have approved of coming from a young lady.

I fumbled with the latch and pulled the door open. Jenna stood there, soaking wet with her bags in her hands and murder in her eyes.

"About goddamned time, Logan," she said by way of greeting, and she shook her head so that water flew everywhere. Her hair, which had hung well past her shoulders the last time I'd seen her, was now cut short, and that, along with the weariness from her travel, lent her expression a severity I hadn't often seen in her.

"Good to see you too," I said. "Want to come in?"

"Do I want to. . . ." She sputtered for a moment, stopped, and laughed. "No, I think I'll stand out here and enjoy some more fine Carolina weather. Jesus, Logan get the hell out of my way already."

I grinned and did just that. "Welcome to my home," I said as she did a most unladylike stomp inside. "Can I help you with those?"

She dropped her bags on the floor and shrugged out of her jacket. It landed with a wet slap and immediately started leaking water in all directions. "Not unless you want to toss them in the dryer. Good God, you live way out in the middle of nowhere. Another few miles and I'd be in Tennessee."

"You've got a ways to go before that, I promise," I said, smiling. "Come here. It's good to see you."

"Careful, I'm soaking," she replied, but she gave me a soggy hug anyway. "God, it's good to see you, too."

Neither of us said anything for a moment, her head resting against my shoulder. I could feel the water soaking through my shirt but I didn't mind. It *was* a fine thing to see her. Even wan from the road and pissed off, there was an energy to her that I hadn't felt in a while, something alien to this place but which part of me recognized and responded to. It felt good.

Finally, we broke apart and each took a step back. I looked her up and down, and she did the same to me. She spoke first, though.

"God, Logan, you've gone native. T-shirt, jeans, minimal work with the razor—when's the mullet going to be done growing out?"

"Thursday next," I told her. "I'll go put on some Skynyrd and you can make yourself right at home. Or"—and I paused dramatically—"I can take this stuff down to the guest room, and you can dry off and change."

"I thought I'd do that here instead," she said with a wicked look. My jaw must have dropped, because she burst out laughing. "Oh, Logan. You are so adorable when you're trying to deal with women. Don't worry, I was just kidding, honest. Now, where are you hiding me?"

"Right this way," I said, and I picked up her bags. They were both wheeled carry-ons, flat black and packed to the gills. Each of them weighed far more than they had any right to. "Unh. You know, you're supposed to pack light clothes to come down here, it being hot and all."

"I did," she said with a smirk. "It's the shoes that are heavy. Now lead on, or I'll just stand here and drip."

"Yes, ma'am." I started down the hall. "I can give you the grand tour later, or just point stuff out now."

"Don't bother," she said, following behind. "I'll just poke around to find what I need. Besides, it's not that big a house. I can probably figure out where everything is."

"More or less," I admitted, though something in her tone stung. "There are a few things you might not want to figure out on your own."

"Like what?" she asked as I stopped at the guest room door and put her bags down.

"Like where I've got the shotgun." I opened the door. "This is your room for the duration. The bed's comfortable, the sheets are clean, and the drawer space might be sufficient unto your needs."

She wriggled past me and into the room. "It'll do," she said after a quick scan. "Very rustic."

I looked around at the decoration like I was seeing it for the first time. Tan walls with a floral border up top, wooden furniture, which Father had helped his father make, a handmade quilt on the bed and a lamp on the nightstand that had been old when I was a child.

"Rustic," I said quietly. "That's one word for it."

"Relax," she said. "It's fine. I love it. Now scoot. I'm going to get out of these wet things, and if you wanted to watch, you had your chance in the kitchen." She shooed me out, then seized her bags and shut the door behind her.

I shook my head and headed back to the kitchen. It was, after all, where I kept the beer.

Jenna joined me maybe half an hour later, dressed in a red blouse and black skirt that matched her lipstick and her hair, respectively. Outside, the evening had come down hard. We'd gone from afternoon to night without any warning, and as the rain kept hammering down, it just got darker and darker. Lighting zipped and zapped off in the distance, little flashes of light instead of the big bolts a storm like this usually sent racing across the sky.

"Nice weather you got here," she said dryly, pulling up a chair. "Got any more beer?"

I hooked a thumb over my shoulder. "In the fridge."

She gave me a look. "You're not going to be a southern gentleman and get it for me?"

"I figured you're one of them liberated Yankee women and can get your own damn beer." I gave her a smile to show I didn't mean it. "Besides, you can get me another one while you're up."

"There's no football game on, you know," she said in a tone that read "warning," but she got up and went to the refrigerator anyway. She snagged a couple of longnecks, twisted the lid off hers, and sat mine down in front of me.

"Thank you," I told her, and I opened it. "Sorry it's not microbrew."

Jenna shrugged and sat down. "Contrary to their marketing department's belief, Sam Adams is not the water of life. I have been known to drink a Bud or two in my time." To prove it, she took a long swallow and set the bottle down expertly. "So," she said. "What the hell is going on?"

I stared at my beer without touching it. "You want the whole thing, or just the stuff that's happened since the last time we talked?"

She gnawed on her lip as she thought about it. "Just the new stuff, and anything I might have missed."

"Okay." I took a deep breath, let myself have one sip of beer. "The short version is that I'm pretty sure that Mother's ghost is haunting this place. Father's too, though he's a lot less obvious about it. Carl's mixed up with them somehow. He's mentioned rather prominently in Father's journal, which I found up in the attic. So are a lot of things."

"Like what?" she prompted.

"Like the fact that he left home for college. Came back a few years later with no intention of staying for more than a couple of days."

"Sort of like you?"

"A lot like me," I admitted. "Anyway, he met Mother and stayed. Moved back into the house, got married, and stayed. There's more in there, but I'm still figuring it out."

Jenna nodded. "Anything else?"

"Well, let's see." I started ticking things off on my fingers. "There's a dog of some sort out there that comes by every night, and I think it's trying to kill me. Damn near clawed through the mudroom door the other night. There's my stolen car, which I saw driving past the house again this afternoon. There's Officer Hanratty, who's acting weirder and weirder. The fireflies are still acting pretty weird themselves." I paused.

"And the librarian you promised I could meet?" Jenna's eyes met mine.

"She's about the one thing in this that isn't screwed up," I said, but I looked away as I did.

"Uh-huh. We'll tackle that later." She drummed her fingers on the tabletop. "That's an awful lot to be going on for little old you, don't you think?"

I gave a half-hearted shrug. "I guess. Like you said, I've been running from one thing to another so fast I haven't really had time to try to put it all together. I mean, if I'd come home and no one liked me because I was an outsider, fine. I could deal with that. Take stock, make plans, move on—I would have been out of their hair in a few weeks at most. But this. . . ." I shook my head. "There's something Carl told me that's making a scary amount of sense right now."

"What is it?" she asked, patting my hand reassuringly. "I thought Carl wanted your guts on a stick."

"He's warming up to me," I admitted. "Now he occasionally calls me 'son' instead of 'boy.' It's a big deal. But anyway, he told me that the town, or something in it, wanted me to stay, and that if I didn't quite fit, it would, well, it would make me fit."

"That sounds ominous." She didn't move her hand, but she stopped patting mine. "What do you think it means?"

"I don't know, but I've got a few ideas." I looked around, struck by a sudden feeling that something was watching. The spot between my shoulder blades started itching, and I lowered my voice without thinking. "It's like there's too much Boston in me, you know what I mean? Too much for me to fit in here. And whatever this thing is, it'll do what it takes to get that out. So far, I think it's just been trying to beat it out of me. All stick, no carrot."

Jenna leaned back and killed half the beer left in the bottle. "Interesting. And where do your mom and the fireflies fit into this?"

"I don't know. I just don't know." I held up my hands, helpless. "She always wanted me to come back and stay, but this. . . ." I trailed off. "I don't know."

"Well, you're not lying about that, at least." I started to protest, but she held up her hand. "Uh-uh. I know you better than that. You're not telling me everything, and I'm guessing most of the stuff you're leaving out involves your librarian."

"Adrienne," I corrected.

"The prosecution rests," she said with a smirk. "I'm sure you'll tell me when you're ready."

"Whatever." I took a swig of beer. It tasted like water.

"So, what do you think?"

"I think," she answered carefully, "that there is in fact an awful lot going on here, and you've got more of the pieces than I do. I will tell you that you sound and look different than you did a week and a half ago. If this place is working on you, it's working fast. I also think that you were right before you started overthinking this, and that your groundskeeper—"

"Caretaker," I interrupted

"Hired help," she swept on, "is behind whatever the hell is going on. Come on, Logan. Do you really think the whole town is all about you? That's the big city in you talking. These people have their own lives. They weren't just waiting for you to come back so they could hide in your attic and play boogedy-boo."

"Maybe," I said grudgingly. Now that I'd accepted Doctor Trotter's idea about ghosts, I was holding tight to it. And Jenna, well, she hadn't read Father's journal.

She leaned forward. "And I've been thinking about your Officer Hanratty. We should go see her tomorrow."

"She won't be at the station," I responded. "Called today to check."

"My dear Jacob." She shook her head in that condescending way I'd gotten in too many meetings. "If you're there, she's somehow going to find an excuse to check her voicemail or do some paperwork or something. Oh, she'll be there. I'll bet a dinner at the No Name on it."

"No bet. I know better."

"Good boy." She killed her beer then looked across the table at mine. "Are you going to finish that?"

"Depends." I shrugged. "Do you want it?"

She reached for it. "No, but I'll drink it anyway. After the landing and the drive out here, I'm ready for straight Jack if you've got it."

"I think I gave away the hard stuff after Mother died, but you're welcome to check to see if I missed anything." I wrapped her fingers around the bottle and shoved it toward her. "Go ahead. Price of the beer? Tell me about your trip."

Jenna looked at me, and then she pulled the bottle to her like I might decide to take it back. "Bad weather means delays and a rough landing. That was a pain in the ass, but I could deal with it. The drive out here was what really beat me with a stick."

"Oh?"

"Yeah." She sipped pensively, and then she made a face. "I take it back. I want some good beer. We'll pick it up tomorrow."

I nodded. "You're driving, which means I get to start on them early."

"Bastard." She stuck out her tongue briefly then rubbed her eyes. "And the drive out here was just . . . tiring. It's a long drive, you know. It's not easy to follow some of these state highways, either, especially not in rain like this."

I nodded. "So just a hard drive, then?"

"Well . . ." Her voice trailed off. "Mostly."

"Mostly?"

She looked down at the tabletop. "Mostly. I think your stories are getting to me, because I swear it felt like something was, I don't know, pacing me the whole time, especially once I got close. The feeling just got stronger."

"Interesting," I said softly, and I thought about the sensation of being watched I'd had, just a few minutes before. "What else you got?"

She shook her head, violently. "No. I think that's enough, don't you?"

Abruptly, she stood. "Look, I think I'm just tired. Tomorrow we'll get up, we'll go into town, we'll meet your scary police officer, and we'll start getting this straightened out, all right? Right now, I just need sleep."

I shoved my chair back and stood to face her. "That sounds like a hell of an idea. I have to warn you, though."

Her voice was shot through with sudden weariness. "What? You've told me about the ghosts. Did you miss one?"

"It's the dog." I grabbed the bottles from the table and headed for the sink. "I'm not kidding when I say he's coming after me."

She nodded slowly. "Yes, but he's outside and you're inside."

"And so are you," I reminded her, "and he's tried to get in twice." I put the bottles down in the sink and turned to face her. "So help me, Jenna, if you hear *anything*, call me. Wake me up. Get me out of bed and point me at the shotgun."

"I'll do that," she promised, her face pale. She tried to smile. "Sounds like I should be staying with you tonight. It would be safer."

"I'm not so sure about that," I said slowly. "Getting far away from me might be the safest thing."

"Poor dear." She tiptoed over to me and planted a kiss on the tip of my nose. "Even your ghosts are confused. Now go to bed. If the monster dog shows up, I'll just escort it to your room and go back to sleep. Good night, Jacob."

"Good night." I gave her a brief hug. "Pleasant dreams."

"You too," she said, and she disappeared down the hall.

Much to my surprise, sleep came easy. It didn't come restful, though. Half a dozen times, I found myself sitting bolt upright, shaking and sweating from nightmares that took me apart and spun me like taffy. I couldn't remember them, but then again I didn't want to.

I'd sit there in the dark, heart pounding, and listen for the creature at the door who'd stalked me the last two nights, straining to hear it over the rain and the sound of my pulse.

Nothing. It seemed the rain had warned it off, or maybe it just had someone else to terrorize. It didn't matter to me. It was three in the morning and then some by the time I finally drifted off to sleep for the last time.

And as I did, one last nightmare grabbed me and pulled me under.

In it, I saw Carl. He was withered and old, and his eyes glowed with insect light. He was standing down on the edge of the woods, and he had a hand out to beckon me to him. I took it, and it was cold and dead but filled with a terrible strength. He pulled me into the Thicket then, into that strange place where we'd spoken, and the fireflies came with us. "They've been waiting," he said. "They're very angry with you."

They descended upon me then, came down like a plague out of the Bible.

And me? I stood there and welcomed them as they crawled inside my eyes, as if it were penance for my sins.

Wake up, I told myself. *It's just a dream!* But the fireflies wouldn't let me go, and I fell down into the cold grasp of the gold-green light.

CHAPTER 20

It was still raining in the morning, a thin drizzle that came and went. The sky was a lighter shade of gray than it had been, but that was about all that could be said for it. Here and there sunlight tried to punch its way through, but all it did was give hints of color behind the gray—pale yellow and sick, tornado-sky green. There wouldn't be any long walks in the fields today, that was for damn certain.

I rolled myself out of bed and into my bathrobe then edged the door open as slowly as I could. It creaked a bit, low and long, but hopefully not enough to wake Jenna. On careful tiptoes, I made my way down the hall and into the kitchen to brew some coffee and hopefully pull myself together while I was the only one awake in the house.

Naturally, Jenna was sitting at the table when I got there. She looked mighty pleased with herself, in part because she'd gotten up first, and in part because she had two steaming cups of coffee strategically placed and ready to go.

"Morning," she said pleasantly, and she tucked her hands into her bathrobe pockets. She looked refreshed and cheerful. Apparently the previous night's hardships didn't have any lingering effects.

"Mmmm," I replied. "What the hell are you doing up at this hour?"

"Reading," she replied, and she laid Father's journal down on the table.

I stared at it, then at her. She was smiling.

"Where did you get this?" I asked. I could barely see. My eyes were full of a red haze and my throat felt tight.

"It was just lying out here," she said. "I figured that since you left it out—"

"I didn't," I said. "I put it back in my room last night. It should have been there this morning."

"Well, I didn't go into your room looking for it, if that's what you're asking." She sounded annoyed. "Really, Logan, what's the big deal? It's a journal. So what?"

"It's Father's journal," I choked out. "Until yesterday, I didn't even know that it existed. I just read it for the first time. There are things in there that I never knew about him. Things about him. Things about how he felt about me."

"Ah," she said, and she offered me the journal. I snatched it out of her hands and shoved it into a bathrobe pocket. "Should I not have done that?"

"No, no . . . yes. I don't know. I don't know how it got out here." I felt my hands curling into fists. "That was for me."

"Maybe it was for us," she said softly. I pretended I didn't hear her, and I counted to ten silently. I counted another ten after that, and then I busied myself with breakfast. When I turned with the plates, Jenna was gone, and the shower was running.

I shrugged, sat down, and started eating.

The morning was chilly, though outside the heat had started to rise. I offered Jenna the tour of the house; she said she'd seen it while I was sleeping, and she didn't sound impressed. For my part, I was still angry over Father's journal, and by the time we'd both settled down and washed up, it was getting on eleven.

I suggested going into town, and both of us agreed that it was better than staying cooped up in the house all day with each other.

We made our way through the wet grass to where Jenna had parked her rental car. It was a Ford convertible, one of those things that were passing for Mustangs these days. The paint job was a slick shade of green that the eye wanted to slide off of, which seemed to me to run counter to the main reason you'd drive a convertible.

She'd pulled down near the end of the driveway, so it was a short walk from the house. A couple of clicks and beeps from the keychain unlocked the doors, and I slid myself in on the passenger side. "Hope you don't mind my driving," Jenna said as she got in. "They wouldn't take my word that my alternate driver was too busy being chased by ghosts."

I just shook my head, and she gave me a long look. "Are you still mad about the book thing? Look, I'm sorry. I just thought maybe I could help. I didn't mean to offend you."

"You shouldn't have looked at it," I said softly. "But that's no nevermind right now. I'm sorry, too. You're right, this place is working on me, and I'm not sure that's a good thing. Let's go into town. I promised you a vanilla cola that would curl your toes."

"They're pre-curled," she said tartly, but her face was still worried as we pulled out onto the road and headed into town.

The drive in was mostly silent. I was still angry, and she was afraid of getting me angrier. On occasion, I'd point out some local landmark or other—not that there were many to note—and she'd nod or say something inconsequential. Not one joke about cow-tipping, though, which surprised me to no end.

By the time we rolled into Maryfield proper, I'd forced myself into a better mood. The rain had mostly stopped, and the sun was starting to peek through the clouds.

"Look," I said as we rolled past the police station, "I'm sorry if I've been a jerk. It's just that the book meant a lot to me. I never knew a lot of that stuff about Father, and it felt like it was our secret, something he and I shared. Having anyone else read it a day later; it just kind of hurt."

"I should have figured something like that." She sighed. "So let's say our sorrys and move on."

"Fair enough. Do you want the grand tour of Maryfield?"

She pulled in to a parking space a block down from the station. "Why not? Walking tour? I didn't notice a gym at the house, so I could use the exercise."

I didn't have an answer to that, so instead I got out of the car. She got out a moment later, and then she pointed.

"What?" I asked.

"Who's that?" she asked. I looked where she was pointing, and there was Hanratty. She was scurrying toward the station, looking left and right as she did.

"Well, I'll be damned," I murmured, and I took a few steps toward her. "That's the cop I was telling you about. But she's not supposed to be here today."

Jenna favored me with a smirk. "What did I tell you?" she chided. "Now let's go catch her." She hurried forward with that big city walk of hers, the one that radiated "get out of my way; I make more money than you do." When she used it, people usually obeyed, most times without even knowing they were doing it. I hurried after her, which was the other effect it had.

Maybe Hanratty heard the sound of my shoes on the concrete, or maybe she just felt the tidal wave of Jenna's approach. Either way, she stopped, turned, and saw me coming. Then, with an amazing bit of grace, she turned on her heel and stalked off the other way.

"Officer Hanratty!" I called. "Can I talk to you?"

She ignored me, walking faster. Across the street, people turned and stared. Nobody chased Hanratty in this town. Nobody.

Which was as good a reason as any to stop doing it myself, just before I passed in front of the police station doors. Jenna came to a halt a few steps later, then turned to glare at me.

"Why did you stop?" she asked. "We were catching up."

I pointed to the building to our left. "I really don't want to be seen chasing a police officer in this town, particularly not when all her coworkers are right at hand. There could be a misunderstanding."

"Misunderstanding." She grinned without humor. "Quaint."

"That's one word for it," I allowed. "Now, can I show you the shrine of my childhood?"

She bowed extravagantly. "Lead on, Macduff."

"Lay on," I corrected her. "Even us country hicks learned that."

"Asshole," she said, and then she hooked her arm inside mine. "Come on. You owe me a vanilla cola, right?"

"Right," I told her, and I led her off toward Hilliard's.

We almost didn't make it. Halfway down the block, Jenna spotted the franchise place that had opened up next door and her eyes got wide.

"Ooh, lattes," she cooed, and she started dragging me forward. "I could kill for a latte. How about it?"

"No, no, no," I said, and I dug my heels in. "You can get that back in Boston, and probably better made, too. I said I was showing you my home town, not prefab you can see anywhere."

"But Logan," she said, and there was a hint of pleading in her voice. "Your coffee sucks."

"So I've been told," I agreed. "And the best cure for that is a hand-drawn vanilla cola. Come on."

"Oh, fine." She looked at me, and her pout promised murder. "Is that where we're going? The place with the Notre Dame sign?"

I squinted at our destination. "What are you talking about?"

She pulled her arm out of mine and pointed to the sign over Mr. Hilliard's front door. "Gold. Green. Notre Dame colors. Every good Boston College alum knows and hates those colors."

I shrugged. "Sorry. To me, they mean Hilliard's. And besides, I went to UMass Boston."

"I know, and I like you anyway."

I reached the door first and held it open for her, the bell hanging from the handle jangling to announce our passage. Mr. Hilliard was behind the counter, hand-drying a glass.

"Mr. Hilliard," I said as I came up toward the soda fountain. Jenna's head was on a swivel, looking back and forth like she didn't know where to start. "I think I need two vanilla colas, if you could see your way to making them for us."

He turned, saw Jenna, and raised an eyebrow. "I might be able to do that, Mr. Logan. Sit yourselves down, and introduce me to your friend here."

"Certainly," I began, but Jenna cut me off.

"Hi. I'm Jennifer Conlon. Mr. Logan and I used to work together, back in Boston." She held out her hand to him. He stared at it for a moment like it had made a rattling sound in the woodpile, and then he gingerly shook it.

"How do you do, Miss Conlon," he said with a voice like a sock full of gravel. "Welcome to Maryfield, and to my establishment. I hope Mr. Logan is taking good care of you."

"Oh, he is," she said, too fast. "He's the same gentleman he was up north. Hasn't changed a bit."

Hilliard blinked. "Oh, hasn't he? I'll go draw you those sodas now." He turned and stared at me. "On the house, in honor of your friend gracing us with her visit." And with that, he turned and headed for the back of the store. "Need more syrup," he called over his shoulder before disappearing into the stockroom.

"Jenna!" I whispered. "What are you doing?"

"Trying to be polite," she shot back. "And just so you know, he's got a handshake like a dead fish."

I thought about trying to explain how what she'd said would be all over town before we finished sipping our sodas, but something kept me from it. Something in the way Hilliard had looked at me after Jenna had said I hadn't changed, when we all knew that wasn't true. Instead, I just settled for, "He's getting on in years. That's all."

"Uh-huh," she said. "Vanilla cola. Right."

Mr. Hilliard emerged from the back a little while later, a container of what I assumed was vanilla syrup in his hands. "Sorry about that, folks," he said. "This will just take me a minute to set up."

"That's fine," I told him while Jenna shot me a furious look. "We've got nothing but time."

"Good, because you're going to need it." He set about fiddling with the fountain, while I watched and Jenna fumed. Eventually, all the tubes were connected to Mr. Hilliard's satisfaction, and he slowly and carefully drew us our sodas.

"Ladies first," he said, and he set Jenna's down in front of her. He waiting for her to take a sip, the straw bent precisely to the right angle, before putting mine down in front of me.

"It's . . . very sweet," Jenna said around sips. I turned to look at her, my lips wrapped around my straw, and nearly sent an explosion of laughter down into the bottom of my glass. The poor thing looked so surprised. Of course it was going to be sweet. Too late, I remembered that her tastes ran to Diet Coke and suchlike, and that the level of sugar that was standard in a drink around here was liable to put her into a coma.

"You don't have to finish if you don't want to," I whispered, while Hilliard watched us like a hawk from across the counter.

"No, no," she gasped. "It's . . . just not what I'm used to."

She tried valiantly, she did. A few more sips, each one scrunching her face up more, while I drank mine slow and easy. Hilliard said nothing, just bustled around back there as if we'd suddenly become unworthy of his attention.

"Thank you, Mr. Hilliard," she finally said, and she pushed her half-full glass away. "It was lovely. I've never had anything like it."

"I'll guess you haven't," he said, even as he reached for my empty. "Enjoy your time in Maryfield, Miss Conlon. I'm glad you came to visit us."

"Thank you," she said, sliding out of her seat and heading for the door. I looked back and forth helplessly, and then I followed her out.

Jenna had somehow managed to assume a pose that said she'd been waiting for hours when I caught up with her on the sidewalk, despite the fact that she was maybe ten seconds ahead of me. "Jesus, Logan. How can you drink those things?"

"Through a straw," I said, and I held up my hand to forestall the inevitable explosion. "Look, I'm sorry. I grew up on them, so they taste great to me."

"It was like shoving sugarcane right into my pancreas," she said, shaking her head. "I tried, Logan, I really did, but if I'd finished that thing, my teeth would have melted on the spot."

The urge to defend the honor of the esteemed Mr. Hilliard

rose up in me, but I tamped it down, tamped it down good and hard. If I was going to show Jenna the lure of Maryfield, I couldn't afford to get into a fight with her about it.

At least, not until she'd seen it all. Then, maybe, we'd have some words.

Doctor Trotter wasn't at the church when we strolled past, but we did run into him across the street from my old school. We'd been up and down the few square blocks that made up the town's main strip, skipping the library but precious little else. I could see from her expression that Jenna was less than impressed, and that the town's charm was lost on someone used to bigger, faster, and more.

"Where is everyone, Logan?" she asked at one point. "It's Saturday. Shouldn't there be people around, or something?"

"I don't know," I said, and I didn't. "I remember it being a little more lively than this, but it's prime growing season. Maybe they're working the farmer's market over in Winston-Salem."

"The whole town?" she said, but she let it drop.

Doctor Trotter saw us coming from across the street, and he jaywalked with practiced ease to intercept us. "Jacob. How are you? Who's your friend?"

"Jenna Conlon," I said before Jenna could jump in, and I got an elbow in my ribs for my trouble. "She's visiting me from up north."

"I see," he said, in a way that indicated that maybe he saw more than there was to see. "A pleasure to meet you, Miss. Don't be too hard on our Maryfield. It's all we've got."

"It's very nice," she said, about the first time I'd seen her even near a loss for words. "Logan is just showing me around."

"Good." He chuckled. "Maybe it will jog his memory a bit. Goodness knows he could use a refresher." He turned to me, then and his smile faded. "Really, Jacob, I'm a little surprised at you."

"Me?" I squeaked. "Why?"

Doctor Trotter frowned. "From everything I hear, you've got all sorts of troubles going on out at your place. It's not polite to invite a guest into a troubled home, Jacob Logan. It can get uncomfortable for them to come into a . . . situation."

I stood there, my jaw fair hanging open, while he turned back to Jenna. "Sorry you had to see that, Miss, and it's no reflection on you. I just expect better of a Logan, that's all."

"Logan?" she said in a tiny, strangled voice, "I think I left something back at the house. Can we go now, please?"

"Of course," I said. "Doctor Trotter."

"Jacob, Miss Conlon." He nodded. "Have a good day." He walked off, and Jenna stared after him.

"Logan. . . ." she started, but she trailed off, wordless.

"I don't know what the hell that was about, either," I said. "But you're right. Let's go home."

"Home," she said. "Yeah. Let's go there."

"I'm sorry," she said as we walked into the kitchen. "I can see why you wanted to leave this place, Logan. I'm less certain why you came back."

"Cheap real estate," I joked, but my heart wasn't in it. "Look, Jenna, I know this isn't Boston, but there're things here that mean something to me. Things that helped make me who I am."

"Things you left behind," she corrected, and she shivered. "Do we have to always talk in the kitchen?" she asked. "Can we go somewhere else?"

I nodded. "There's the living room, but no one ever really used it for talking."

"Perfect," she said, and she walked away.

I caught up with her as she dropped herself down into one of Mother's high-backed chairs. "Comfy," she said, and she patted the armrest. "Sit yourself down, too. You're making me nervous."

I paced back and forth behind her. "That's good," I said, "because I'm nervous. I'm nervous about the ghost, I'm nervous about my car, I'm nervous about that dog, I'm nervous about the fireflies—"

"And you're pissed off at me," she finished.

I stopped and stared at her. "Well, yeah."

"That's the plan," she said. "If you're pissed off, you'll usually do something. It's been driving me nuts, Logan, listening to you talk about this. Everything's happened *to* you. Why didn't you just shoot the stupid dog? It was on your land. No one would have said boo."

"I don't know," I said, truthfully, and I sat down on the floor in front of her. "I honestly don't."

"That's interesting," she said. "You think you've got too much city in you to use a shotgun any more?"

"It just didn't feel right." I shook my head and thought about Carl, and the kick of the shotgun in my hands. "No, that's wrong. You know what? It never even occurred to me. I had the shotgun in my hands the first time, but I never even thought about using it. Hell, I could have put both barrels through the mudroom door and shredded whatever was on the other side of it. Instead, I just held it."

Jenna nodded. "Do you really belong here any more, Logan? I mean, look around. This house is a tomb, this town is dead, and this place is trying to kill you. Why stay?"

"This house is my home! It's where I grew up, and this town is what made me," I shot back.

She half-rose out of the chair. "It made you leave. Why come home at all? You could have gone anywhere. I know how much you got when you liquidated everything. You could have done anything. Why back here?"

I blinked and looked up at her. "Because I thought I should," I finally said. "Because once upon a time, I promised Mother that I would."

"They're dead, Logan." Her eyes flashed with anger and a little extra brightness the edge in her voice couldn't explain. "You don't have to keep those promises."

"Yes, I do." My voice was a whisper. "You always keep your promises to Mother."

She blinked and sat back. "That's what your father said, in the book."

"I know."

Her voice was almost pleading now. "He left, Jacob. Just like you did."

"He came back."

"He didn't want to. I think he wants you to go. You ever

think about that? About how maybe it's his ghost, not hers, trying to get you out of here?"

I stood and turned away from her. "It doesn't matter, anyway. I'm here for a while no matter what. There's the car insurance to take care of, and things to tie up, and new arrangements to make with Carl."

She shook her head. "Just sell the place. Go."

"No. You don't sell family land." I walked over to the mantel and picked up one of Mother's knickknacks. It was a porcelain hummingbird, painted bright colors that seemed out of place. "You know why I always call them Mother and Father?"

I could hear Jenna stand and take a few cautious steps toward me. "No. Why?"

"Because I always felt I was theirs more than they were mine. Does that make any sense, any sense at all?"

"No," she admitted, and she slipped her arms around me from behind. "But it doesn't have to, if it makes sense to you. I'm sorry, Logan. I'm not trying to make fun of things that are important to you. I was just hoping that I could get you to see them that way, so you could go. I think you should leave. I think you should leave right now. You can take care of the insurance and everything else from the road. Something here's not right for you. It's not safe."

I closed my eyes and just let her hold me. "It hasn't harmed me yet, whatever it is."

She exploded. "It's nearly killed you how many times? And yet you stand there and let it come after you again and again. Why aren't you more worried, Logan? What do you know that I don't?"

I turned to look at her and cupped her face in my hands. She was, I thought, very beautiful at that moment, as beautiful as Adrienne had been.

"I know this place," I said softly, and I kissed her forehead. "All right. I'll come away with you in the morning. You've got a week off? Let's drive around Carolina. We'll go to the Outer Banks, or maybe up to Asheville. I'll show you the sights. You might even find something to be impressed by."

Tears leaked from the corners of her eyes and ran in slow tracks down her face. "Don't joke about this, Logan. I'm scared for you."

"I'm not joking. We'll go. At the end of the week, bring me back and I'll see what I want to do next. But tomorrow we go."

She smiled then, a brave smile, and crushed herself against me. I held her for a while, and then I gently made some distance between us. "Now, more important stuff. Shall I make dinner?"

"God, no." The old Jenna was back, the tough one who wasn't afraid of anything. "I remember your cooking when you had good ingredients to work with. Down here, I can only imagine what you'd whip up."

"Baloney tartare," I said, grinning as she punched me in the arm. "Come on. Let's see what we've got."

Dinner took longer than expected, due in large part to the odd assortment of ingredients I had lurking in the icebox. By the time we agreed on what to make, it was dark; by the time we finished, it was getting on eleven o'clock.

"Not bad," I said as I dumped the plates into the sink. "We make a good team."

"We always did," Jenna replied from her chair. "As long as you remembered who was in charge."

"My house, my kitchen—I'm in charge."

"Keep telling yourself that and you'll sleep nights," she said, and she laughed. "On a more serious note, do you think that dog will come back tonight?"

I shrugged. "I don't know. Maybe." I jerked a thumb in the direction of the mudroom. "Shotgun is down there, if you want to shoot it instead of waiting for me to try."

"Don't tempt me," she said. "Sit down for a minute. We can do the dishes later."

I shook suds off my hands and pulled up a chair. "You have a point. Besides, I've been thinking about things, and I might have come up with something."

She sank into the chair next to me. "Do tell, O mysterious one."

"Bear with me," I told her. "This is something I've never told anyone, and I can't say that I'm proud of it."

"Uh-oh." She moved her chair fractionally closer to mine. "Confession time."

"Sort of," I agreed. "Now, this is going to sound stupid," I said, and I caught myself. "Of course, it all sounds stupid."

Jenna nodded. "So why stop now? What's this great revelation you've had?"

I took a deep breath. "Did I ever tell you what Mother said about fireflies?"

Her eyes unfocused as she tried to remember. "That they

were sort of tour guides into heaven? I think you told me that at a party in Somerville once, after you'd gotten well and truly plastered on Ketel One and OJ."

"Oh, right. That party." I did my best to avoid blushing at the memory. "But you've pretty much got it right. She thought that they guided angels to righteous souls and showed them the way back to heaven."

"Cute." Jenna drummed her fingers on the table. "Did she actually believe that, or was it a story to keep you from bringing nine zillion bugs into the house?"

"They're beetles, not bugs," I corrected her. "And I don't know. She might have. That's where it gets weird."

"Weirder," Jenna corrected. "Spill the details."

"When Father died and we put in his stone. . . ." My voice trailed off and I started again. "After Mother had said her good-byes at the graveside, I went back out there. The stone was crawling with lightning bugs. Hundreds of them. And I brushed every last one off. The ones who kept coming back, well, I killed them."

"Cripes," Jenna breathed. "And you think—"

I held up my hand. "I'm not done yet. When Mother died, I did the same thing. No fireflies on her grave, not a one."

Jenna got up and turned away from me. "For God's sake, Logan, why?"

"Stupid reasons," I said. "With Father, it was because I was angry at him, angry that he'd wasted his life and been none of the things a boy wants his father to be. With Mother, it was different. It was like she could find her own way to heaven, and I'd be damned if I'd let some insect grab the credit. I had faith in her, you know?" I exhaled sharply, a sound that might have been a sob leaking out with the air.

"That was a pretty unrighteous thing to do," Jenna finally said. "Not that any rational human being would believe that firefly crap, but still, you don't mess with your parents' gravestones. You just don't."

I shrugged. "I guess. It was a long time ago."

"Five years for your mother," she shot back, and she sank back down into her chair. "This makes a bit more sense now. The firefly stuff, anyway."

"It does, at that," I nodded. "But it's hard to believe, you know?"

"Tell that to the ghost in the bedroom," she said wearily. "You can't do anything the easy way, can you?"

I shook my head. "Nope. Never could."

"What you need," she said cautiously, "is someone to take care of you, because you're clearly not capable of doing it yourself."

She looked as if she were going to say more then, but a knock on the door interrupted her.

"Who the hell is that?" Jenna asked, half-rising out of her chair. "It's kind of late for the neighbors to come over for a cup of sugar."

"The neighbors wouldn't come over here after dark if the devil and all his personal injury lawyers were chasing them," I replied, edging my way over to the door. I pulled back the shade a little bit, enough to see who was out there.

It was Adrienne, wild-eyed and clutching a bag, and behind her, like the Angel of Death, was Hanratty.

I unlocked the door. "Jacob, who is it?" Jenna asked, but I didn't answer. Instead, I opened the door and stepped back, and Adrienne and her escort tumbled in. Without a word, Adrienne collapsed into my arms and started sobbing. Hanratty stared at me with undisguised contempt, while Jenna looked back and forth with an expression that slowly hardened into pure granite.

I stroked Adrienne's hair and murmured that it was going to be all right, that she was safe. It didn't seem to do any good, but it didn't seem to do any harm either, so I kept it up until Hanratty impaled me with a look.

"Mr. Logan," she said in a tone that chilled the room nicely, "I am very sorry to disturb you at this late hour."

"It's fine," I said, raising my head and my voice. "My friend and I"—I indicated Jenna with a nod, which she returned— "were just talking. What can I do for you?"

She snorted. "For me? Nothing. For her"—she jerked a thumb at Adrienne—"it remains to be seen." With surprising gentleness, she detached Adrienne from my arms and led her over to the table. "You got any coffee or Wild Turkey or something you can give the girl? Can't you see she needs a little help here?"

Jenna sprang into action before I did, hurrying over to the stove and starting a pot of Folgers. "Jacob, what's going on here?"

I looked back and forth. Jenna was fussing by the stove while Hanratty was crouched next to a shivering Adrienne. Her eyes were huge and dark, what Mother used to call "raccoon eyes." Only then did I notice what she was wearing: a rain slicker over an ankle-length bathrobe, and slippers on her feet. They were fuzzy slippers, no less, with bunny noses and big floppy ears. One of them was scorched a bit along the left side.

Two and two suddenly came together in my brain, and I do believe my jaw actually dropped. "Don't tell me," I started, and then Jenna elbowed me out of the way.

"Coffee," she announced, and put the cup and saucer right in front of Adrienne. "Now, what happened?"

It was Hanratty who answered, which didn't surprise me one bit. "Around eight o'clock tonight, we got a call that Mr. Logan's missing car had been seen on Maynard Street, heading north. Miss Moore here"—she indicated Adrienne—"maintained an apartment on the first floor of a three-story building at the intersection of Maynard and Blount."

"Maintained?"

Hanratty glowered and nodded as Adrienne gratefully sipped her coffee. I could see her hands shaking.

"Maintained," Adrienne said. "It's . . . it's not there any more." And she burst out sobbing again. Jenna moved to comfort her while Hanratty fixed her eye on me. "Your car, you will be interested to know, has been located."

"I don't like where this is going," I said. "What *happened*, Hanratty?"

Her voice took on a more formal, clipped tone. "At a quarter past nine this evening, an officer was dispatched to the vicinity of Maynard Road to see if your car could be intercepted. As he approached the intersection of Maynard and Blount, he heard a crash and saw flames ahead of him. At that time, he turned on his siren and hurried to the site, where he spotted your car. It had apparently been driven at high velocity into the wall of Miss Moore's apartment, and had managed to punch through that wall into her bedroom." She looked quickly over at Adrienne. "If she hadn't been off brushing her teeth, it probably would have killed her."

"Jesus," I said softly.

Hanratty nodded. "Something like that. The fuel tank went up properly right about then and the building started to go with it. Gas heat, you know. Officer Bates was able to clear the building, including Miss Moore, and call for backup and the fire department. The fire was brought under control, but Miss Moore's apartment was rendered uninhabitable."

"Oh, that's terrible." I looked over to where Adrienne sat. She and Jenna were murmuring to each other. "Is she all right?"

"Shook up, but that's all. The paramedics from County General said she's fine physically. We had them take a good long look at her, have no fear, and that was before we took her statement."

"Of course." The words came out of me in a rush. "I'm just glad she's all right." A sudden thought struck me. "What about the driver of the car? Did you catch him?"

"That's the interesting thing," Hanratty drawled. "There wasn't one."

"What? That's impossible."

She nodded. "You're right. But there was no sign of a driver in the wreckage, nor was there any description from eyewitnesses of anyone fleeing the area. No prints were lifted from the wreck, though considering the shape it was in that's hardly surprising. A wreck like that, normally we're picking up what's left of the driver with a vacuum cleaner. You don't expect to find prints on something burned out that badly."

"Well, at least the insurance company will finally listen to me," I said distantly. "No witnesses?"

Hanratty shook her head side to side slowly. "Not a one. Best guess we've got, honestly, is that the driver started the car toward the apartment and then bailed out onto the pavement. If he'd been in the car when it hit, he would have been a pulled pork sandwich by the time it burned out. No chance of survival, much less one of getting up and running off without being seen."

I nodded. "So what now?"

"Now," Hanratty said with immense satisfaction, "I get to ask you to account for your whereabouts between nine and a quarter past that hour this evening." She took out her notepad and opened it with a flourish. "Speak clearly, please."

"Oh, for God's sake." I turned my back on Hanratty and went over to the sink, looking for some clean water to wash out the rotten taste in my mouth. "I was here, all right? With Jenna the whole time."

"Don't say anything without a lawyer, Logan," Jenna said, as if on cue. She looked up from Adrienne, who seemed a bit calmer, and she glared at Hanratty. You could hear the sparks crackle then, in that old-time Frankenstein movie sort of way. I saw Adrienne draw back an inch without thinking about it, and I'm pretty sure I did the same. "She's just trying to mess with you."

"And you are?" Hanratty asked, a great fat cat sitting in front of a brand-new mouse hole.

"Jennifer Conlon." The words came out pure ice.

"Your business here?"

"I'm visiting Mr. Logan."

"And your relationship to him?"

"If I say 'purely sexual,' will you put your pencil down already? I'm a friend, here to visit, and I was with Mr. Logan the entire evening. The only time he was out of sight was when he went off to take a leak, and even then I could hear him." She crossed her arms and leaned forward. "Now are you done trying to mess with Jacob, or do you have more bullshit up your sleeve, Officer? There's a girl here who's an obvious wreck, and you dragged her out here into the howling wilderness just so you could play bad cop? That's fine police work, it is."

Hanratty put the pad down, and for a moment I actually thought she might try to arrest Jenna. "Actually, I brought her here because she insisted on it. She was going to drive, but I didn't think she was in any shape to do so, and so I gave her a lift." She favored Adrienne with a look. "Honey, would you mind telling this nice lady here your version of this?"

Adrienne nodded then drained the last of her coffee. "I'd gone to bed, actually—my bed was right up against the wall—when I realized . . . I realized I hadn't brushed my teeth. So I got up to do that and then all of a sudden there was this . . . this *noise*. I thought something had exploded, so I ran back to see what it was, and everything was on fire. So, so, so I grabbed a handful of clothes, 'cause they were the only things I could reach that weren't already *burning*, and then I ran. There was a policeman outside and he was yelling at people to get out, and someone was screaming, and then someone put this on me to cover up, and I just sat down on the curb and watched."

"The bag is mine," Hanratty added wryly. "You're probably going to need to take her shopping tomorrow, though I don't think the fire department's in a hurry to get the slicker back." Jenna shot her a look, and she subsided. "Keep going, child."

Adrienne sniffled. Jenna handed her a tissue from somewhere, and there was a champion bout of nose-blowing before she could continue. "Thank you," the librarian said. "I'm so sorry for disturbing your . . . your visit with Mr. Logan."

"Jacob's already disturbed," Jenna answered automatically. "Now, keep going. I'll freshen up your cup." She shoved back from the table, took the mug with a disapproving look, and put the flame under the kettle. I sidled over to the cabinet that held my meager condiment selection and pulled out the sugar, which Jenna took wordlessly.

Adrienne, I could see, was watching us with big eyes. "I really am sorry to interrupt," she said. "But I didn't . . . I mean, my whole apartment was gone, and everything in it, and I didn't have anywhere else to go, so I thought maybe I could stay out here for a while." She took a deep breath. "Until I found someplace else. It wouldn't take long, I promise, and I wouldn't touch anything, and. . . ." Abruptly, she collapsed down on herself, miserable.

"Of course you can stay," Jenna said. "Now stop crying. You don't have the complexion for it." Gracefully, she dunked too much sugar and too much milk into the coffee, and then she stirred it. "Drink this, and then we'll have a look at what you brought, and get you into something that smells a little less like soot. You've got another bedroom you can make up, right Logan?"

I nodded, not trusting myself to say anything.

"Good." Jenna plowed on. "Now Officer Hanratty, is there anything else you need to do here, or are we finished?"

Hanratty lurched to her feet. "Honey, we're just getting started. Come on down to the station tomorrow and I'll take formal statements from you and Mr. Logan. Then I can get him the paperwork he needs for his insurance." She turned to me. "You'll need to identify the car, of course."

"Of course." I moved the kettle to a cold burner and thought desperate thoughts about a beer. "What time should we be down there?"

"By noon," Hanratty answered. "I'll let myself out, as usual. Good night." She marched over to the door, then turned and said to Adrienne, "You call if you need anything, okay?"

Adrienne nodded, huddled in on herself in a way that was heartbreaking to see. "I will. Thank you."

"Just my job," Hanratty said, and she stalked out. The door slammed shut behind her.

The echo of the door hung in the air for longer than it had any right to, nearly until I heard Hanratty drive away. Then, and only then, did we move around the kitchen again. The tension drained out of the air, and I could feel those steel bands around my chest loosen up, just a touch.

Jenna put her cup down on the table with a clank. "That was special, now, wasn't it?"

"Hanratty's a charmer, like I told you." I rummaged through

the cabinet and came up with some ancient Sweet'N Low, just in case. "Do you want anything else to drink, Adrienne?"

"No thanks." She didn't sit, but rather hovered, her eyes constantly flicking to the door and the night outside.

"I think formal introductions are in order," I said as I poured hot water and instant coffee into a cup of my own. "Jenna, this is Adrienne Moore. She's one of the librarians here in town, and she's been a big help to me in all this mess. Adrienne, this is Jenna. She's a friend and business associate of mine from Boston."

"Nice to meet you," Adrienne sniffled.

"Don't let him fool you with that 'business associate' bullcrap. I worked for him, and then ran screaming for the hills." Jenna grinned, genuinely, and patted Adrienne on the shoulder. "Now finish your coffee and then we'll get you taken care of."

"I'm all right, really." Adrienne put her cup down and stood. "I'm just very tired."

"Of course you are. Now take that ridiculous raincoat off, and let's put you to bed." Jenna gave me a look that clearly said, "Get your ass in gear," and I figured it out about a second after anyone with a brain would have.

"Right, right." I hastily dropped my cup into the sink and made a grab for Adrienne's bag. "Come this way. We'll figure out where to put you, get you some towels and everything, no worries."

"You're very nice to let me stay here," Adrienne said, with considerably fewer sniffles as she followed me. "I know it's a big imposition."

"No," I told her. "It's a big house. Besides, it's good to have someone out here to protect me from Jenna and her razor-sharp tongue."

"Just for that, you sleep alone tonight, Logan," Jenna said, and I could hear the sharp intake of Adrienne's breath. "Oh, relax, I'm just kidding. Now where are we going to put you?"

"Right this way," I said, and I suddenly stopped. To my left was the door to Mother and Father's bedroom. It was open, and as I watched, it swung open wider. "Oh, no," I breathed.

Jenna squeezed past Adrienne to stand next to me. "How about here?" she said, and she barged in. I followed her, my heart going a hundred miles a minute.

"Are you nuts?" I hissed once we'd crossed the threshold. I flicked on the light and gestured. "This is my parents' room. She can't sleep in here."

"The bed's made up," Jenna said mildly. "Saves us some work. And did you realize you just called them your parents? That's a first, I think."

"Never mind that," I said. "She can't stay in here. Things have been happening in here, or haven't you been paying attention?"

"The door was open," Jenna said. "The door was *opening*. You saw it too. Your mother wants her in here."

"I know," I said softly. "That's what scares me."

She smiled at me. "Smart boy. Now go get her bag."

Adrienne was standing in the hallway, her arms folded across her chest. holding herself tightly. "Adrienne? You'll be staying in here, if that's all right?" She nodded, but didn't say anything. "I'll be right across the hall," I said, more softly. "You can leave the door open, and I'll leave mine open, and if you need me, just come get me, all right?"

She nodded again. I stepped closer, and when she didn't move away I pulled her to me. She didn't resist, but she didn't open her arms, either, and I could feel the tension in her body. "It's going to be all right, I promise," I told her. "You're safe here. I'll take care of you. And besides, I don't have any other cars."

She didn't laugh, but I could feel her smile a bit. "I'm just afraid," she whispered. "Do I have to sleep in there?"

"Just for tonight," I promised. "Tomorrow, we can figure something else out. But nothing will happen tonight, I swear."

"Nothing else, you mean." And there was a spark of the Adrienne I'd first met. "All right. I trust you. I hope you're a light sleeper, just in case."

"Just in case what?" I said, and I waggled my eyebrows even though I knew she couldn't see them. "I'll stand watch outside your door all night, if you ask."

She actually laughed then. "You're terrible," she said, and she disengaged herself from my arms. I stooped to pick up her bag and followed her into the bedroom.

Jenna had already turned down the bed and fluffed the pillows. "You should be comfortable in here, dear. Jacob, why don't you run out to the kitchen and clean up. I'll see about getting Adrienne here something to sleep in, and maybe something for tomorrow."

"As you command." I put the bag down next to the bed. "Towels are in the closet next to the bathroom. First come first served on the hot water in the morning. I'll see you tomorrow."

Adrienne shot me a look of pure gratitude. "Thank you, Jacob," she said, and she shooed me out.

I shut the door behind me, carefully. Nothing odd happened as I did, though I did hear a burst of laughter from Jenna that would have scared small children, had there been any around. Down to the kitchen I went, and I made a great show of puttering around with mugs and dishwashing soap. When everything was as clean as it was likely to get, I set up the drying rack and took myself to the door. There I looked out at the night and wondered if the dog would visit.

An hour or three later, Jenna joined me. "Hi," I said without turning around.

"Hi," she replied, and she leaned on my back. "Whatcha looking at?"

"Nothing, and that's good." I shook my head. "I keep on wondering when that damn dog is going to come back."

She shifted slightly, and I was suddenly aware of her body pressing against mine "Maybe there are too many people here for him, or he got picked up by animal control."

I laughed. "Around here, animal control is firing a warning shot and giving him a chance to run. No, he's still out there. I can feel it." I turned and felt her slide off me. "The scary thing is, I don't know why he's out there. All the rest of it—well most of the rest of it—I'm starting to understand. But the dog? I don't know."

She gave me a look that could best be called appraising. "How serious are you about all this, Logan?"

"Dead serious, Jenna. I can't afford to be otherwise." I pulled out a chair and swung it around, then sat myself in it and leaned over the back. "Mother's trapped and wants me back here. I don't doubt any more that she's here or that she's real. Father's stuck here, too, and I think he's trying to help me. Carl's tied up with both of them, and the town's working with Mother whether they know it or not. Hanratty, well, she's just a cast-iron bitch—"

"Don't be too hard on her," Jenna said, much to my surprise. "I think I know what's going on there."

"Oh?" I gestured to a chair. "Pull up a seat and tell me about it."

"You said she followed her husband here, and then he left?" I nodded. "She stayed, though. Why?"

I shrugged. "Never gave it much thought. Maybe she liked Mr. Hilliard's ice cream?"

"Looks like, but that's not what I'm thinking. She stayed. She made herself a part of the town."

"Man, did she ever," I grumbled. "She was lecturing me on what it's like to be from here."

Jenna stabbed the tabletop with a finger. "Exactly. She gave up a good job to come here, and then she *chose* to stay. I think she's become more town than the townies, just to vindicate the decision she made to come here. She moved here, and by God, she's staying."

The light dawned. "And all of a sudden I come here, I don't want to be here, and the town tries to pull me in. Damn, that must be busting her balls."

"That's one way of putting it." She gave a thin smile. "So don't be too mean to Hanratty, even if she is a cast-iron bitch. She got dealt a lousy hand, and she's been bluffing with a pair of threes for years. Oh, and she's got a gun."

I chuckled. "All right, I'll try to play nice. She doesn't make it easy, though."

She shook her head. "No, she doesn't. Though it was nice of her to bring your little friend out here."

I felt myself blushing. "Adrienne? How is she?"

"Dead asleep," Jenna answered. "Which is not surprising. She's had a hell of a day. I know if I had a strange car drive into my bedroom, I'd be a wreck. No pun intended."

"None noticed," I told her. "That whole thing worries me."

"Oh, really? What part?"

"Two things, actually." I adjusted myself in the chair and found myself frowning. "One is the driver. I caught a glimpse—just a glimpse—of the driver yesterday. He—or she—was big. Really big."

"You thought it was Hanratty." It wasn't a question.

"I had my suspicions," I confessed.

Jenna leaned back. "But if your friend's story holds, that's impossible."

I nodded. "She wasn't supposed to be on duty today, so what she was doing at the apartment is an open question. Then again, in a town like this, everyone pitches in at a moment like that. But if we can trust her and Adrienne, the large, heavyset driver just . . . vanished. And that leaves one suspect."

"And that is?"

"Father," I said.

Jenna looked unconvinced. "Hmm. Wasn't he trying to help you, or so you thought?"

I stood and started pacing. "That's what I thought. Maybe

this is his way of trying to help. If Adrienne's the bait the town is dangling, and Father doesn't want me to get caught the way he did. . . ." I let my voice trail off.

"That doesn't sound like your father, Logan," Jenna said in a very small voice. "He wouldn't . . . no. I don't believe it."

I shrugged. "Maybe death changes a person. Then again, Mother could have gotten a hold of him. He never really could say no when she insisted. I don't know."

"That may be for the best. So what's the other thing?"

"The toothbrushing," I said.

Jenna stared at me, incredulous. "She forgot to brush her teeth. So what?"

"Do you really think Adrienne ever forgets to brush her teeth? Come on, she's wearing bunny slippers. But this time, she forgets just in time to get out of the way so that Father can drive my car into her bedroom and wreck the joint. . . ."

"Forcing her to come out here, where presumably you two can get to know each other better. Very devious, Logan. I'm not sure whether to applaud the ghosts of your parents for being sneaky, or you for having a subconscious that came up with it." Jenna's expression was grim. "So, how do you feel about it?"

"About what?"

She shook her head. "Assuming you're right, and there's been enough weird stuff going on that I'm willing to at least entertain the notion that you're right, how do you feel about being set up by your dead mother?"

"I don't know," I said truthfully. "It's all rather confusing. Hell, the first time Adrienne was out here Mother knocked stuff over to ensure there'd be no hanky-panky. It was the old 'not in my house' routine, I guess. Or at least, 'Not yet.' I always was a sucker for reverse psychology."

"Are you sure it was your mother?"

I blinked. "Oh," I said. "You think Father did it instead, to keep me off the hook?"

Jenna shook her head. "I don't think anything. But as long as we're willing to entertain the possibility that you've got ghost problems, it makes a certain amount of sense."

"And it fits with what Carl said," I said softly. "Where was my father's place? Damn."

Jenna gave a soft, low laugh. "Poor Jacob. All you wanted was some time to be alone, and all of this lands on you." She stood. "She's a nice kid, Jake. She's not you, though. I know you well enough to know that. Make your own choices, when it actually comes time to make them."

She rubbed her eyes and yawned. "And now, I'm for bed. I'll see you in the morning. Hopefully the ghosts will let you be for the rest of the night."

"Good night," I said quietly. "Thank you for coming down, Jenna."

"Don't thank me yet," she said. "I've only been here one day. I could still screw everything up."

"You don't screw things up," I said, and I let myself grin. "Occasionally, you just set up things that are screwed."

"Like this," she said, and she headed off into the dark of the house. "Good night."

"Good night," I said again, and I wondered about the dog.

CHAPTER
21

I spent a few more minutes puttering around before deciding that, as usual, Jenna had the right idea. Lights went out one by one, windows and doors were checked, and I made my way to bed. True to my word, I kept my door open, which meant sleeping in a t-shirt and sweats. No sense scandalizing Adrienne if she did come running in the middle of the night, and no sense giving Jenna more to laugh about than absolutely necessary.

Sleep came hard that night. I kept on hearing something like thunder in the far distance, though the rain had stopped all those hours before, and every creak and groan the house made was like shouting in my ears. Across the hall, I could hear Adrienne breathing, regular and soft. The sound rasped on my eardrums out of all proportion, and by one in the morning I was resigned to the hopelessness of it all.

I swung my feet out of bed and onto the floor, figuring to go into the kitchen and read. My left hand found a book on the night stand, and I padded out into the hall. The urge to check in on Adrienne rose up, but I strangled it in its cradle and instead tiptoed down the hall, away from where the women were sleeping and out into dim yellow light.

Deciding against coffee, I drew myself a cup of water instead. The book was one I'd bought in Boston and brought down with me, a legal thriller about a two-fisted lawyer who seemed to solve most of his courtroom problems by getting into gunfights. I was halfway in and still hadn't figured out what the hell was going on, but at that hour of the night, I didn't particularly care. Sipping from my glass, I settled in at the table and tried to find my place.

I'd just managed to locate it when something went *ratta-tat-tat* on the window. I turned to see what it was, and there was Carl, pale as death and looking twice as hungry. He saw me looking back at him and grinned, then motioned me over urgently.

For a moment, I just sat there, thinking it was a dream. Besides, he didn't look the sort of thing you hurried over to, not at that hour and looking that way. The skin on his face was drawn tight across the bone, and his eyes were brighter than they had any right to be. In Boston, they'd say he was on something. Here, I was more worried that he'd gone off.

Cautious in my movement, I walked over to the window. "What do you want, Carl?" I asked, mouthing the words wide so he'd understand me without my shouting. I didn't want to wake the women by bellowing through the glass, and I wasn't sure I wanted to open the door and let Carl in.

After all, it was pretty damn late.

In answer, Carl pointed downhill. "Come on out, boy," he said, loud enough for me to hear him clearly. "We need to talk."

"We can talk right here," I said. I threw a look over my shoulder to see if Jenna or Adrienne had woken up. Not yet, it seemed, and for that I was thankful.

Carl shook his head. "No we can't, son. Grab the book and come with me." I picked up the novel I'd been reading, and got a snort of disdain for my trouble. "Not that one, son. The other. Now come on. There's no time to lose."

I shook my head. "No, Carl. I'm not going. I'm not leaving those two alone to go traipsing down into the Thicket, not at this time of night."

A single cabinet swung open then slammed itself shut. It sounded like a gunshot.

"She wants you to go, son," Carl said through the glass, grinning. He held up a lantern. "I'll lead you down there safe, I swear. Just pick up the book and come along."

I turned away from him and stared at the cabinet. It didn't move again. The spot between my shoulder blades itched; Carl staring into it, I guessed.

The thought struck me that he'd be standing out there all night, if necessary, and probably the next night, too. He'd be there as long as it took, because that was Carl's way, and he'd made a promise. Might as well get it over with, then, I told myself. Once and for all. Even if it kills me.

"Fine," I said abruptly, and I moved to the door to let Carl in. Something crunched underfoot as I did so. I looked down.

It was a toy soldier, facing out. I was pretty sure it hadn't been there before. "I'm sorry, Dad," I said under my breath, and I opened the door. Carl stood there, intense and unblinking. I took a step back, a little disturbed and not able to hide it.

"Come on," he said, and he motioned impatiently.

I backpedaled one step farther. "Let me go get the book, and the shotgun."

"Just the book," he said, and he stayed on the threshold. "You won't need the gun, Jacob. Not tonight."

"Are you sure? There's a dog out there that—"

"Never mind the dog," he said, with a voice like hitting a stone wall. "I told you, I'll take care of you. Or are you doubting me?"

I looked down at his shoes. They were muddy. Maybe he'd heard about the dog from Hanratty. Maybe he'd seen it, skulking around the boundaries of my land. Maybe he'd—

No. Enough maybes. It was time to go and finish things, and time to take Carl at his word. After all, it was what had gotten us all into this mess.

"No, Carl." I said. "I'm not doubting you. Just being cautious."

"Caution's good. Knowing when to leave it behind is better." He beckoned with his free hand. "Get moving, son. We're running out of time."

I backed away. "Don't come in, now. You hear?"

"I'll wait," he said, and he looked down at my dead soldier. "Not sure I'd be entirely welcome inside, anyhow."

I hurried down the hall to my room. The book was there. So was a notepad and a pen, and while I might be damnfool enough to go on this adventure, I wasn't damnfool enough not to leave some evidence of my whereabouts. If nothing else, it would give Hanratty something to go on if I went missing, and if she decided to do anything about it.

Quickly, I walked over to the small table that served as a desk and grabbed myself a piece of paper. The first two pens I pulled out of the pencil cup were dead, and I nearly tore a hole through the paper trying to write with them. The third one, though, finally worked, so I wrote my message as quick as I could.

"Gone to the Thicket with Carl," it read. "No need to worry. I'll be back by dawn."

I didn't sign my name. That and the fact that I said "no need to worry" would get Jenna wound tighter than a cokehead's pocket watch. She wouldn't come after me, though. She'd be smarter than that. She'd stay here, hunker down, and be ready for what came after.

Which is exactly what she wouldn't do if I flat-out told her to stay. Then she might follow, being the contrary sort she was, and I didn't relish the idea of her trying to find her way through the Thicket in the dark.

Besides, Carl had promised to protect me. He didn't say a damn thing about anyone else.

Father's book was where I'd left it, on a shelf next to a piggy bank that I hadn't put a penny into in years. I grabbed it and stuffed it into a baggy pocket, then walked out to face Carl in the doorway.

"I'm ready," I said. "Let's go."

"No, you're not," he replied. "But we'll go anyway."

I had nothing to say to that, so I just stepped out after him. The door shut on its own behind me, not that it surprised me that it did so, and off we went.

The grass was still wet as we moved downslope toward the Thicket. Overhead, a high wind pushed clouds across the sky in a hurry, but down where we walked it was still. Carl went first, his lantern held high and his pace steady. I followed close behind, determined not to lose him in the dark. I carried the book in my left pocket, my hand over it to make sure it didn't slip out. I looked back at the house once. It sat there, quiet and peaceful, dim lights showing through a couple of windows. It could have been anyone's home, anywhere.

I turned my back on it and hurried to catch up with Carl.

We passed the pine trees without slowing. I'd figured Carl would want to stop there, maybe make some sort of gesture to Mother and Father, but he didn't break stride. "Keep moving, boy," he called back to me. "You'll see them soon enough."

"That doesn't inspire confidence, Carl," I huffed, but I kept going. Truth be told, I didn't even look.

We made good time across the field and into the Thicket proper. Carl ducked and weaved around branches as he went, leaving no trace of his passage. I wasn't quite as graceful, but I made my way in decent time, following the yellow glow of that bobbing lantern. At times, it almost reminded me of something, but then a branch would swing back and smack me across the face, and I'd lose track of whatever I'd been thinking of.

The trek through the woods wasn't as hard as I'd figured. I'd anticipated spending half the night hacking our way through briers and odd bits of mountain laurel, but the route was mostly clear. I won't say the trees pulled themselves out of our way, not exactly, but low-hanging branches didn't seem to hang so low, and creeper vines always seemed to be hanging just out of the way. It wasn't easy going, mind you, just not as tough as it could have been.

The moon was hanging just over the tree line when we finally broke into the clearing where Carl and I had spoken before. Thin light made it down through the trees around the clearing. A little more glow made its way through the top of the clearing itself, but the moon wasn't high enough to do much work that way. Instead, a few Coleman lanterns sat on the ground, casting long shadows across the grass with white light. A man could get blinded one moment and lose himself in the dark the next.

And there they were, waiting for me.

Carl was in the center, of course, holding his lantern high so it painted his face like a scarecrow skull long past its season.

Reverend Trotter was to his left, looking pale and thin, his hands pressed together around a Bible and his eyes pointed straight down at the ground.

Mr. Hilliard stood to Carl's right, looking like he'd grown straight up out of the soil with leaves in his beard. He was dressed for work at the store, but in his hands was a piece of weathered wood that might have been as old as the trees around us. He shifted it back and forth, his hands turning it over and over again.

Two cops stood one on either side of the semicircle, their hands on their guns and their faces unreadable. Other faces from town, half-remembered or long unseen, stood there unblinking, watching me.

No Hanratty, but somehow it made sense for her not to be

here. This was a business for men, I could feel that in my bones, and she had no place in this circle.

And there, right in front of Carl, was Sam Fuller.

He knelt down on the ground in the center of that gathering, one hand holding Asa by the collar and the other scratching the hound behind the ears. The dog sat, alert and easy, ears down and tail wagging.

Sam looked up at me, and there were tears in his eyes. "You were supposed to shoot him," he said, in a voice that broke my heart. "Why couldn't you just shoot him?"

"Sam," I said haltingly, "I don't know what you're. . . ."

Asa's head came up, and in an instant it changed. He bared his teeth in a wicked snarl, a chainsaw growl rising up in his throat. And in his eyes, buried deep against the black, was a spark of firefly green.

I stumbled back a step and Asa surged forward—Sam's hand on his collar was the only thing holding him down. Then the glow faded and Asa was Asa again, his muzzle drooping with confusion.

"I don't understand," I said, and I looked from face to face. "I never wanted to hurt Asa, not one bit. What do you want from me?"

It was Mr. Hilliard who spoke, his voice rumbling up out of him like smoke from a cave. "We've all been trying to tell you, one way or another. Bits and pieces of it, hoping you'd put it together. You were supposed to be a bright one, after all. All the teachers said so."

I shook my head. "I don't know what you're talking about. Look, I just came back for a little while. I was going to just get my head together and move on. That's all."

"It doesn't work that way, Mr. Logan," the reverend intoned gravely. "What you want is the smallest part of this. Your father's book should have taught you that."

Behind me, I could hear footsteps on grass. The circle had closed around me. There was no way out, not now.

"Father didn't want to come back here, either," I said. There was low laughter at that, though as I looked from face to face I couldn't tell who was doing the laughing. "If he hadn't met Mother—"

"But he did," Carl said. "He came back, and he met her, and he stayed. That's what was supposed to happen. And now you've come back."

"And you've met her," one of the cops chimed in.

"What, Hanratty? No thank you," I joked. No one laughed. Not at that.

Carl put the lantern down and took a step forward. "Don't play the fool, Logan. It doesn't suit you all that well. This is where you belong. You've fought it, and it's cost you a little. A car ain't much, not in the grand scheme of things. Keep fighting, and it'll cost you more. A man can only swim upstream so long before he gets tired. Much easier to go where the water takes you, don't you think? Safer, too."

"Are you threatening me?" I asked softly. "I don't respond well to threats."

"You don't respond well to much of anything," Hilliard said. "But Carl doesn't make threats. He states facts. You do know what you're facing, Logan, don't you? You do know what you're standing on the brink of?"

I reached my hand into my pocket and closed my fingers around Father's book.

"I know a bit," I said cautiously. "I know Mother's in the house, and Father, too. I know fireflies won't come onto my land, and I think I know why. And I know there's a woman asleep up in that house who doesn't deserve to be used like you all want her to be. Is that what you wanted to hear, all of you? Is that what I'm supposed to know?" I was shouting by the end of it, not that I cared. Birds rustled up out of trees from the noise and Asa whined, but the men around me stood silent.

"You don't know anything," Carl finally said, when the last flutter of wings had died away. "You've got all the pieces in your hands and you'd rather line them up by which has the prettiest picture than try to put them together. Think about something bigger than you for once, boy." The last word was filled with venom. "You're right, your parents are still here, and that's why I'm here, too."

"The promise," I said, realization washing over me. "You promised them you'd take care of me."

"No." His voice was cold and flat as stone. "I promised your mother I'd see you back here and set you up proper. Make you see that this was where you belonged, even when my gut told me that wasn't necessarily so. And all the time, she was there watching. You got no idea, son, none at all."

My eyes met his. Neither of us looked away. For a moment, it was if there were only the two of us there in that circle. "You've done your job, Carl. You've kept your promise. Now let me make my decision. Let me go."

"I'm afraid I can't do that," he said, and he looked away.

"What she wants, she gets. You know that. She wants you kept here. You got no choice at all."

"It's a house, Carl. I can just walk away."

"You think that, don't you? What are the odds something hasn't happened to your friend's car by the time you get back from this place? If you try to walk, what makes you think a wind and a rain won't come up and drive you back into the house? Call for a way out, and that phone line will go dead. You should just be thankful she didn't ask me to cut it before."

I walked toward him, getting angrier with every step. "What the hell are you talking about, Carl?"

He set the lantern down and crossed his arms over his chest. "You know damn well what I'm talking about, boy. I'm talking about keeping you locked up in that house while she had time to work on you, to hook you and drag you in, to make you want to stay and think it was your idea all along. I didn't steal your damn car, boy, but I damn sure made it so you couldn't track it down once she had your father take it. Brought you food so you wouldn't leave the house, tried to keep you inside those walls so you'd settle in 'cause it was the only thing you could do. Don't go looking for that cell phone in the tall grass, neither. You won't find it no more. Hell, I had to talk her into letting you go into town at all, and then I was only able to 'cause it was a way to get you into that pretty young thing's arms. Don't you see, son? You've been given every chance to go along with this. Why keep fighting?"

I shook my head. "And the time I almost got led to my death? Who was driving the car that day, Carl? How'd you know to find me?"

"You were supposed to take to your sickbed, Mr. Logan," Reverend Trotter interrupted. "And someone from town would come to tend you. Unfortunately, you seem to have inherited the Logan family constitution." He looked thoughtful for a moment. "Your father was a tough bastard before you, you know. We had much the same problem with him."

I turned to face him. "That's not in the book."

"Oh, yes it is." He nodded solemnly. "If you know how to read it. Understated man, Joshua was, and in his way as stubborn as you are. But in the end, he realized he belonged here, and in exchange for his acceptance, he received a few . . . dispensations. Like the love of your mother, for example."

"That's impossible. Stupid. And even if Carl's trying to keep some bullshit promise"—Asa snarled at that, and Sam didn't seem too eager to calm him this time—"why are the rest of you here? Is this the secret town council? You going to show me the dark rituals that only I can perform, as the last of the Logans? Come on, give me something better than that."

"It's not quite that," Hilliard said, "but there's a little truth to it. The town doesn't like giving up its own, you see, but some folks belong here more than others. Logans belong here," he said, and his eyes met mine, "the same way that lady friend of yours doesn't. And sometimes, well, when the circumstances are right, the town can take more of a hand in things."

He shook his head, sad for me, or maybe for himself. "Your mother was out here a long time by herself. I think the land learned to listen to her, or maybe she listened to it, the same way it talked to your grandmother back in the day. It doesn't matter. You made her a promise that you didn't keep, and that gave her something to cling to. Carl made a promise he did keep, and that's why we're here. We've all made the promise, too, Jacob. Told your mother we'd help bring you back. She insisted on it, really—there should always be a Logan on Logan land, and she was quite the traditionalist. Helped her adjust to life with your father, to be honest. And believe me, it's a promise we'd all rather be shut of."

"It's just a promise. Words."

"That's what a promise is to you, boy, and that's what brought us to this place." Carl's words were full of scorn. "You gave out promises free as air, and never kept a one. Fair broke your mother's heart, you did, always promising to come home and never doing it. She lived on that hope for years, and you let her wither on it. Promises have weight, boy. They have consequences. And if you make 'em the right way, to the right person, they're stronger than death."

I opened my mouth to scoff, but Hilliard interrupted me. "Carl's got cancer, Jacob. Doctors said it should have killed him years ago. She wouldn't let him go. Reverend Trotter? His heart's bad. Dead tissue, they said. Shouldn't be able to keep beating. She makes sure it does."

"And you?" I said softly.

"Don't ask," he replied, in a way that filled me with shame. "Death would be welcomed in my house, at any hour of any day. But she's not letting us go until the deed is done." He looked left, then right, all around the circle. "You can help let us go."

I blinked hard, tears doing their damnedest to fill up the corners of my eyes. "It's impossible. This is Mother, right? The little woman who couldn't get Father to stop eating, couldn't get me to come home. How can she do this?"

"That was all you ever saw of her." Reverend Trotter corrected me, gently. "That's not all she was. She was a strong woman, and a brave one, except maybe where you were concerned directly. And death changes people, changes them more than even you'd think, especially when you're trapped someplace you don't belong. Bargains are made, you see. Deals are struck. Prices paid."

"The fireflies," I breathed. "O God, the fireflies."

"The fireflies," the reverend echoed.

"Makes you feel good, doesn't it?" That was Sam Fuller, his eyes full of hate. The force of it hit me like a shot to the gut, the pure brute fury of it. I'd been wrong to think we could ever be friends, not with that kind of hatred in him.

Not that I wasn't sure I didn't deserve it.

He took a step forward, stalking me. "You ever think on what you did, Logan? Ever think on what it cost? Brave man, to shoo the fireflies off her stone? Well, they've been waiting to do their duty. Been waiting ever since, and your folks been waiting with them."

I took another step closer to Carl. His gaze measured me up and down, registering what I was doing, but he didn't move. "Why do you care, though, Sam? My sin, not yours. My parents"—the words were oddly hard to say—"not yours."

"My friends," he answered simply. "My neighbors. Waiting on your mistake. And when I got to talking with you and realized you didn't belong here, I realized that all these good men had suffered for nothing, and I'd be suffering along with them."

He scratched Asa under the chin. "There's two ways to bind you to this place, you see. Two ways to seal the bargain. Love and blood. We've been trying both." He looked away. "The love was Adrienne's. The blood was supposed to be Asa's. You haven't taken either."

"My God, Sam, I'm sorry. I'm so sorry," I said, and I turned to look around the circle. "All of you, I am so goddamned sorry. I wish I'd known. I wish...."

"You made your promises," Mr. Hilliard rumbled. "You did know, deep down. You always knew."

"So how do I make it right?" I asked. "What do I do?"

"Two ways to make it right," Carl answered, his toe kicking at the edge of the lantern's base. "The pleasant way is to go back up to that house and whisper some sweet words to a kind girl who's asleep."

I shook my head. "No. If I court her, I court her myself. Not like this. It ain't fair to her, same as it wasn't fair to my mother."

Carl shrugged. "Then there's one other way. Sam?"

Fuller stepped back, away from his hound. Asa sat there, docile, his tail thumping the ground in slow measured beats. "I'm ready," he said, his tone giving the lie to his words.

"Asa?" I asked.

Fuller nodded. "Kill him. Now. He won't fight." He shuddered, fighting back what sounded like a sob. "Only reason he went bad on you was to try to get you to shoot him. Make you do it in self-defense."

"No." The murmurs rose up around me, confused and angry. "I'm not doing it."

"You got but two ways to do it, son," Carl said. "And if you won't take the easy path, you need to take this one."

"Why didn't you let me shoot you, then, the last time we were down here." He flinched at that, and I saw an opening and kept right on pushing. "Why'd you dodge when all this could have been over, and no one the wiser?"

He stood there, suddenly frail. But only for an instant before the Carl I knew was back again, my tormentor come to lead me the last mile. "Killing me wouldn't have done it," he said softly. "My blood's not quite right any more. The sap from a dead tree won't flow right, if you take my meaning."

"Or maybe you weren't quite ready to give up living yet," I said, trying to sound braver than I felt.

"If only," he said, and there was a world of heartbreak in those two words. "Now, which will it be? You've got to decide here, and you've got to decide now."

"Bullshit," I spat out into his face. "I can go right back to that house and decide for myself if I want to stay, without any magic fireflies or sacrifices or supernatural shotgun weddings or any damn thing else. I ask that girl to marry me like this, and in thirty years the same thing will happen all over again. And I'm not killing my neighbor's dog, not with him standing there and not for this. It's a wicked thing to ask of a man."

Carl smiled and nodded, and then he decked me. I went over like a sack of bricks, the book flying out of my hand. "That's very noble, son. Damn stupid, too. Is a dog's life worth more than a man's?" He stepped forward and delivered a kick to my ribs that knocked the breath out of my lungs. "Is it maybe worth holding your mother's immortal soul out of heaven?"

I scrambled to all fours, just in time to get a boot under the chin. My head snapped back and I tumbled to the edge of the ring. Strong hands shoved me back into the center, back toward where Carl was waiting. Behind him, Asa sat calm as a statue, watching.

"It's not right," I cried out, and I took a swing. Carl ducked under it and planted his fist in my gut. I doubled over, and he brought both hands down on the back of my head. I went down, my chin hitting the ground hard enough to rattle my teeth.

Around us, the other men in the circle were strangely silent. No cheering, no shouting, not a word of encouragement or dismay. But every time my back brushed the outside of that ring, they pushed me back in.

"You angry yet, boy?" Carl taunted. "Angry enough to fight?" I didn't answer, throwing a series of punches at his torso instead. He blocked them all, but missed the straight kick I leveled at his knee. It staggered him and drove him back, but it didn't wipe the grin off his face. "Angry enough to get your hands dirty?" I rushed him to press the attack, but he met me with a flurry of punches. I blocked some of them and caught some others in the face. The taste of blood filled my mouth; I spat once and lowered my shoulder into Carl's rib cage.

He was light enough to go over easy—the cancer, I guessed—but getting him down was one thing, holding him down was another. He got his arms up, one hand on my windpipe, and we rolled around on the ground kicking and gouging like wildcats. He choked off my air; I hacked at his wrist and bent his bony fingers back. He went to gouge my eyes; I slammed my forehead into his and snapped his head back.

"Good, boy, good," he muttered with a bloody grin, and then I was somehow on top of him with my forearm across his throat and his right hand pinned down into the grass. He smiled up at me. "You're ready to do what you have to do."

"I'm not going to kill, Carl," I told him.

"Oh, yes you will," he assured me. "Or I'm going to kill you and keep you here that way. She'll be happy with that, in the end." With his free hand, he pointed up to the night sky. I looked up. Thousands of fireflies danced there, perching themselves on tree branches and casting a glow that didn't dare reach the ground. "You'll do it with them watching, because you'll do it to protect yourself. I just proved that—to them, to you, to everyone." He looked slowly around the circle. "And if I'd kept pushing, you'd have kept swinging. It's in you, Logan."

"No, it ain't." I rolled off him and pulled myself to my feet. My ribs ached and my face was covered with cuts and scratches. My mouth was filled with blood, and the knuckles of my left hand were scraped raw. Carl, down there on the ground and smiling like a skull, didn't look that much better. "If it were in me, you'd be dead right now."

"I just didn't push you hard enough," he said, and he coughed. Slowly, he got to his feet and planted himself in front of me. "You fought pretty hard anyhow, and that's just for your worthless skin. What'll you do," he asked, and he looked past me, past the ring of men, out into the Thicket and uphill, "to protect someone else."

"No," I said. "Don't."

He ignored me. "Sam?" was all he said.

"Of course," Sam replied. "Asa, go get 'em."

Asa's eyes went flat and cold, and that green light sparked in them. Maybe it was a reflection from the fireflies up above, but I don't think so. He growled low in his throat, and then he leaped forward, teeth bared and spittle dripping down. I braced myself for the hit, threw my arms up in front of me, and waited.

He bounded right past me, howling, and out of the circle. In an instant, he was lost in the underbrush, headed uphill.

Headed toward the house.

"Son of a bitch," I swore, while Carl cackled behind me.

"That's it!" he said. "You'll spill that blood now, won't you? Go git 'im!"

"You bastard," I said, suddenly calm with the knowledge of what I had to do, and I reached down for the Coleman lantern. "You goddamned bastard."

"You won't need the light," he said, still grinning. "Just follow the sound."

I swung.

The base of the lantern caught him just under the jaw with a solid crack. I could hear bone snap, could see things moving under his skin that weren't meant to move that way. He spun around once, eyes wide with surprise, and fell to the ground.

I stepped over to him, and then I swung it again. It connected with the side of his head, and this time, the sound it made was a grinding crunch. I didn't care. I just held up that lantern, burning bright through all that, and stared down at the wreck of Carl's face.

"Maybe it is in me after all," I said. "Fine. I've shed blood. Now call him back."

"Can't," Sam said, but he didn't move. None of them did.

"Like I told you . . . can't be . . . my blood," Carl wheezed. "Mine's already . . . spoken for." And he laughed—a horrible, wet sound.

"You'll be wanting this." Hilliard stepped forward and handed me the length of wood he'd been holding. "With Asa, it might come in handy. The lantern's too heavy to run with, anyway."

I took it and looked up at him. "Time's a-wasting," he added, and he pointed to Carl. "We'll stay with him. Don't worry about that. Now go do what you have to do. For your mother, for your father, for those women in that house. For all of us. Go."

"Go," they all murmured as one, and the back of the circle opened for me. In the distance, I could hear Asa howling.

The lantern fell from my fingers and rolled onto its side. I spun around, looking at each and every one of those men, looking for another way out of this. Their faces told me there was none. My eyes finally met Reverend Trotter's. He stared back at me, sad and knowing.

"Son," he said, "God go with you. Now run."

I ran.

CHAPTER 22

This time, the trees seemed to be holding me back. Up ahead, I could hear Asa. His howl was enough to wake the dead, and he gave it often, leading me on. Sometimes it sounded like it came from behind the next tree, sometimes from a mile away.

I was pretty sure he was waiting for me. Didn't trust that hunch enough to bank on it, though, so I ran. Ran with my head down and that walking stick Hilliard had given me tucked under one arm, ran through the creepers and the vines and the low-hanging branches that caught my clothes and tore at my hair and pulled me back, ran even when I didn't know quite where I was running to except in the direction of that howl.

Suddenly, I was out of the trees and looking uphill at the line of pines that hid the house from view. My breath rasped in my lungs, hot and painful as I stood there a moment. Around me, the fireflies rose up in a swarm, lighting my way. Halfway up the hill, I could see a dark shape moving fast. Moving toward the house.

Asa.

I started running again.

The cloud of fireflies moved with me, casting long green shadows on the grass. I ignored them as best I could, throwing myself up the slope. Up ahead, Asa vanished around the bend past the pine trees and closed in on the house proper.

I ran faster. Another dozen steps and I heard the first explosive thud as the hound threw himself against the damaged door, and the first angry snarl as it refused to give.

"I'm coming," I called out, though I knew no one in the house could here me. "Hang on, I'm coming."

Somehow, I covered the ground. All I remember is a series of blunt, harsh sounds—my feet against the turf, the pounding of my heart, and the battering of Asa against that weakened door.

He saw me when I was maybe a hundred yards from the house, shaking his head from another failed attempt to batter his way indoors. As he caught sight of me he stopped and turned, looking up to meet my eyes. I stared back and started running right at him, that walking stick raised high.

He waited a second then charged back at me.

We met there on the grass, a little closer to halfway between us than I would have guessed likely. Asa leaped up at the last moment, his muzzle open wide and his teeth gleaming. I threw my arm in the way just in time, and his jaws closed on it instead of my throat. I gave out a yell of pure pain, but still managed to slam the dog down against the ground. He didn't let go, so I tried to bring that walking stick down on him, hard. The angle was wrong, though, and what was supposed to snap ribs instead glanced off.

He let go, rolled away, and bounced back to his feet. I saw

blood on his muzzle and felt the same dripping down my arm. The pain was white lightning shooting up and down from my fist to my shoulder. I ignored it and shifted the walking stick into a two-handed grip, crouching low and growling right back. Inside the house, I heard shouting and doors slamming. Jenna would take care of things, I told myself. Jenna's got it under control in there.

Asa charged again. I swung my weapon at him, but he dodged and went for the back of my ankle. I backpedaled enough that he barely missed, then the back of my calf hit him and I went over. He was on me in an instant, with only that length of wood keeping his teeth away from my throat. I twisted it left, then right, his strength matching me in every-thing I did. His paws tore at my chest and belly, trying to disembowel me, and all I could do was curl up and try to roll, to get my weight on top of him.

Finally, I wrenched the shaft out of his mouth and slammed it against the side of his head. Asa let out a whine of pain and staggered back, his ears flat against his skull and his eyes nar-rowed. We circled each other, me trying to get between him and that weakened door, him intent on me but still eyeing a way past. "Come on," I said, and I thumped the heavy wood against my hand. "Come on, boy. You're gonna get the stick."

His response was a blood-chilling howl that went up to the skies. Behind him, the moon sank red down to the horizon. His claws tore at the dirt as he crouched, impatient and angry.

From the house, I heard a click. Asa heard it, too. His ears shot up and his head turned, away from me and toward the porch.

Toward the kitchen, I knew. Toward the door that had just been unlocked.

"Oh, no," I breathed, and I charged.

Asa was getting ready to spring away from me, and I caught him half-turned. The swing I took had no poetry in it, no grace. It was just a desperate man with a length of wood trying to beat something he hated to death, pure and simple. It caught Asa broadside, and I could feel ribs snap under the impact. The follow-through took me off-balance, though, and I stumbled. Asa swung his head back to me and bit down on my hand. Bones crunched under the pressure, and I saw, rather than felt, myself drop that walking stick. It rolled away into the grass, useless. With my other hand, I pounded Asa in the face as hard as I could, again and again. He snarled, twisting his head to tear chunks of flesh out of me while I whimpered and hammered at him as best I could.

It was the blood that saved me then. Too much of it was flowing out of my hand, I guess, choking Asa as it pooled down in his throat. He made a sound that was half cough, half bark, and let me go, a gobbet of red liquid flying free as he did so. I fell backward, clutching what had been my hand. I tried to get up, but he butted me with his head, and again I went over.

He stood over me then, looking down with his fangs bared. "I was supposed to kill you," I said, fear and pain and sadness all mixed up in me. "I guess I'm sorry."

"Don't move, Logan," Jenna said from somewhere off to my right, and she pulled the lead trigger.

There was a click and, a half-heartbeat later, an explosion louder than thunder.

Asa's head disintegrated in an instant. A hot wind blew over me, pellets grazing my skin as they rushed past. I blinked, unable to move.

"Go down, damn it," she said, and she fired again.

Asa's headless corpse collapsed in stages, its blood running down into the ground.

"Jenna?" I whispered. "Is that you?"

Her face appeared in front of me, the shotgun falling from her hands to rest on the ground beside me.

"It's me," she said. "Jesus, Logan, you're a mess." She was crying, tears pouring down in a hot rain. "I can't leave you alone for a minute. I mean, just look at you."

"I don't want to, thanks," I said weakly, and I got a half-hearted chuckle out of her for my efforts. "Help me up. Please."

"Screw that," she said, and she looked back over her shoulder. "You stay right where you are. I'm gonna go get my car and we're taking you to a hospital. What the hell happened to you, Logan? What's going on?"

"Promises being kept," I mumbled, and I tried to sit up. "Adrienne?"

"Safe and sound and locked into that bedroom, scared half to death," Jenna assured me. "Now lie down. Relax. I'll be right back."

"Okay," I said, and I sagged back onto the ground. I could hear her footsteps move off, and I closed my eyes. The ground was cool against my back as I wrapped my torn hand in my shirt, pressing as hard as I dared to stop the bleeding. Everything was all right, I told myself. Everything was over. Everyone was safe. I lay back and listened to the footsteps.

Footsteps. Lots of them. More than Jenna could be making by herself.

I heaved myself up, my stomach nearly emptying itself as I did so. "Jenna!" I called out.

"Way ahead of you, Logan," she said, but there was a note of fear in her voice, and I could see why. It was the men I'd spoken to in the Thicket, the men who'd made that pledge to Mother to seal my bargain with the land, no matter what. They were past the pine trees now, closing in on the house and moving fast. Carl was leading them.

His face was swollen and distorted, leaking blood in a couple of places and misshapen in others, but he was moving at a steady clip that was more frightening than a full-on sprint would have been. The others moved behind him, spread out in a wedge like a flight of geese headed south in a hurry.

They were headed for Jenna, though. Quickly and with a stride full of purpose, they were coming for her.

"Jenna!" I called out desperately. "Get in the house! Lock the doors!"

"I won't leave you!" she said, caught between the house and the car. "They're gonna kill you, Logan!"

"They're not after me," I said. "Not any more. Go!"

She hesitated a moment, and then she ran for the house. I reached out for the shotgun and used it as a crutch, hauling myself to my feet. I checked the chambers, just to be sure, and had my worst fear confirmed. They were empty.

Resigned, I jammed the muzzle into the ground and leaned on it. It had saved me once, now it could support me as I waited.

I didn't have to wait long. Jenna had barely slammed the door when Carl and his men covered the last bit of that long slope, up to where I stood. I held myself up as best I could and regarded them.

"Carl," I said. "It's over. Go home. Go see a doctor. Just go."

"I can't do that, Jacob," he said. "Blood or love, and you let someone else spill the blood." Behind him, I could see Sam Fuller. A dead man might have worn that face, some Egyptian king buried long ago. It showed nothing but the grave.

"I'll make my own choice," I said. "Get off my land." Overhead, the fireflies danced, frantically. Faces half-formed in the cloud the fireflies made of themselves, and then vanished away in a heartbeat. Other shapes showed themselves, too, things I didn't want to think too hard about.

"It ain't your land properly yet." Carl shook his head slow and wistful. "Not until you seal the deal. And you know what that means now."

I knew exactly what he meant, and my blood ran cold at the thought. If Adrienne was going to bind me to this place, then the next logical step was to get rid of the rival, real or perceived. To get rid of Jenna.

"You're not hurting Jenna," I told him. "You'll get to her over my dead body, and if you do that, you'll never be free of Mother. You want that, Carl?"

"He ain't so dumb after all," one of the cops cracked, and there was low, nasty laughter.

"Dead body ain't too far off," another man said. "Step aside easy and you won't get hurt."

"And if I don't step aside?" I raised the shotgun.

Carl stared at out at me with one good eye and one gone crazy from broken bones and blood. "Then we beat you within an inch of your life, kill your Yankee tramp, and let Adrienne nurse you back to health. You might even learn how to walk again some day. No leaving after that, I promise you. None at all."

I leveled the gun at him. "You're not going past me, Carl."

"Your barrels are full of mud," he said mildly. "You've been up north too long. No man who cares about his gun treats it like that. 'Sides, we heard the shots. It ain't loaded now, is it?"

"You ready to take that chance?" I asked.

"No chance 'tall," he replied as he stepped forward.

I rammed the shotgun forward as hard as I could into his chest and pulled both triggers, hoping for a miracle. I got no miracles, but Carl did stumble back into Sam Fuller's arms, and the two went down in a heap. Mr. Hilliard surged past them, though, and one of the cops came up on my left, and even as I swung the gun like a club back and forth, I found myself giving ground.

"Keep him busy, boys!" Reverend Trotter stood at the back, urging them on. The rest of you, get into that house! Hurry!" I tried to fight forward through the press, but numbers bore me down. Someone stomped on my broken hand and I screamed. From around the corner of the house, I could hear breaking glass and splintering wood. Someone was going in through the kitchen door the hard way. Faintly, I could hear cursing—Jenna's and someone else's. She'd found the knife block, near as I could tell, and was making a fight of it. But even with three men holding me down, there were still more than enough to take her. It was only a matter of time.

Another man came down on my legs, pinning them, then a third man threw himself across my chest. I struggled best I could, but there were too many of them. Someone wrenched the shotgun out of my fingers, then reversed it and slammed the butt into my face. I felt my nose crunch underneath the blow. Fresh blood flowed down into my throat, filled my mouth, and spilled down over my face. I gasped for air, and Sam Fuller put his boot down, lightly, on my throat.

"Hold still," he said in his dead, angry voice. "Hold still and it won't hurt any more. Hold still and it will all be over soon."

I could still hear Jenna, cursing like a wildcat. Something was breaking in the kitchen, more glass and maybe some furniture. They were in the house now. Even if she kept retreating, there was only so far she could go. Fuller was right. It would be over soon. A small part of me hoped that Adrienne had fainted, that she wouldn't be hearing or seeing any of this.

Another part of me wondered what the hell Mother—my mother—was thinking of all this. If this was what she wanted, what she truly wanted for her son. Somehow, I didn't think so. At least, that's what I wanted to believe.

Fuller's head jerked left, as he stared up at the house. "What the hell—" he asked, but the sentence never finished. Glass exploded outward, streaks of yellow-green lightning arcing between them as they scythed outward. Men went down, clutching at a dozen razored slashes. Fierce light crackled in the air.

The pressure on me suddenly eased as the men holding me fell away. I rolled myself over, spat blood onto the ground, and propped myself up as best as I could to see what the hell had just happened.

There was Adrienne. She was half-climbing, half-floating out that broken window, surrounded by a sickly green glow. There was blood on her feet from the glass, and more dripping down her fingers. The light mixed in with the streams of red, wrapping itself around her and mixing with them until I could have sworn it, and not blood, was flowing in her veins. It flared strong around her eyes, her hands, and over her breast. Her hair whipped out behind her, tossed by an unseen wind, and she was dressed simply in a white cotton nightgown, ankle length and modest.

One of Mother's, I realized, and for an instant, my heart damn near stopped. The hair on the back of my neck stood up, and I smelled ozone sharp and clear.

She was on the grass and walking toward them, the broken glass taking a terrible toll on her bare feet and her not noticing it.

"Not like this!" Adrienne shrieked. "It wasn't supposed to be like this," and suddenly I could hear Mother's voice overlaying her own. The two of them spoke in some terrible harmony, each echoing the other and making weird music of their voices. "This is not what I wanted. Not what you promised!"

Carl staggered past me, long red slashes across his face and arms from the glass.

"Elaine, let us finish this," he begged, and he dropped to his knees. "Please. Then you can rest."

"This isn't what I asked for, Carl," she whispered. "You promised to protect him, to bring him home."

"He needs protecting from himself!" Carl's voice was frantic now. Behind him, the other men slowly backed away. No sounds came from inside the house, which I prayed was a good thing. "He was going to leave again. He was doing everything wrong. This is for his own good!"

"This is for my own good?" I asked, and I held up my hand. I could see white bone through torn skin, brown dried blood cracking as I reached toward Adrienne. "Please, Mother. Not this. Not any more."

She turned toward me, her eyes shining bright. "Jacob?" she asked. "My darling boy, is that you?"

"It's me, Mother," I said. "Please. Make it stop."

"You never came back," she said, walking closer to me. Carl, forgotten, blinked wordlessly beyond her. "You promised and you promised, and you never came back."

"I know," I said. "I was wrong. Punish me if you have to—I was a bad son, a liar. I know that now. I deserve it. But let Jenna go. Let them all go, Mother. Please."

"You'll stay?" she asked, and it was all Mother now, Adrienne's voice gone somewhere I couldn't and didn't want to imagine.

"I'll try," I told her. "I can't promise any more."

"Elaine," Carl began, and Adrienne turned toward him, cold fire dancing in a halo around her. "Let us do what we have to do. It needs to be finished."

"It's finished now," she said, in a voice of infinite sadness. "I keep my promises too, Carl. Always and forever."

And with that, the green-gold light came up from inside and around her and swallowed us all.

CHAPTER 23

"They're dead?" Jenna asked. "All of them?"

"All the ones who are still here," I said, too tired to keep the pain out of my voice. "The others . . . gone. The ones who'd been kept past their time? Here." I pointed with my good hand at the bodies stretched out on the ground. Dr. Trotter was there, and Mr. Hilliard, and Carl, and Sam Fuller. They looked peaceful, even with the slashes and tears. Around them, bits of broken glass reflected weak starlight. The fireflies that had followed in their train were gone, though, and I found I missed them. Dawn was an hour off, at the very least, and the sky was still dark. "I think my mother let them go."

"Your mother," she said, like the words tasted funny in her mouth. "Strange to hear you say that."

I shrugged. "It's the truth. How's Adrienne?"

"Sleeping it off inside. I don't think she knows what happened, but poor thing, she's terrified. Her feet. . . ." she started, and then her voice trailed off. "They weren't as bad as they looked. Just so you know."

"Thank God," I breathed. "Thank you for taking care of her."

She gave me a hard look. "You could go inside and comfort her, you know."

"I could," I agreed. "But I don't think I can comfort anyone right now. Except maybe the two people I should have given that to a long time ago. Help me up?"

She reached down and clasped my hand in hers. There were vicious cuts on her arm, I could see, and I wondered what else had happened in that house that I didn't know about. Maybe she'd tell me, someday.

The two of us managed to pull me up, somehow. Our hands stayed intertwined longer than absolutely necessary, then slipped apart, and I turned to face her.

"Jenna," I started to say, but she put a finger on my lips.

"Go do what you have to do," she said. "Talk to them. I'll be in the house when you get back. Then we can talk about what happens when the sun comes up."

I nodded, and started the slow trudge down the hill to where my parents lay buried. Jenna was right. There were things I had to say to the dead before I could talk to the living.

It took longer than expected to reach the graves, each step a new kind of agony. But at last there I was, looking down on them in sorrow and regret.

Lacking any other path to take, I spoke to them. "Mother," I said. "Father. If you're here. If you can hear me. I'm home. I should have come back sooner, I know, but it wasn't home for me for a long, long time. I don't know if I can stay, either. You know that. I'll keep the land, I promise. It'll always be in the family. I love you. I miss you. I wish I'd been a better son, but I am the man I am. And I wish I could see fireflies here again." Then my throat pulled itself tight, and any other words I could have said would have found themselves wrapped up in tears.

"I love you," I said again when my throat finally stopped catching, and I headed back to the house. Through the pine trees, I could see the lights of the kitchen come on. Jenna was no doubt busy making coffee inside. Maybe Adrienne had woken up. There was glass to sweep up and damage to assess and a phone call to the police to make and maybe even some deep dreamless sleep to dive into.

Slowly, but with rising speed, I walked toward the light.

Hanratty was there within the half hour, with half the emergency vehicles in the county following behind her. The noise woke Adrienne, who stumbled out into the kitchen wrapped in a blanket and an old shawl of my mother's. Her eyes were wild, and I knew right then that she'd never spend another night in this house.

"Mr. Logan?" she asked haltingly. "Jake? What happened. *What happened?*"

"It's all over," I said. "I promise."

She saw my hand then, still bleeding through the torn up old shirt we'd wrapped around it, and the bloody rags we'd wound around my arm. She saw the wreckage of the door, the broken glass still on the floor and the shattered furniture. She saw Jenna standing there like a hawk, and past her paramedics moving stretchers with covered bodies on them. Hanratty's voice carried over the racket, bellowing orders.

Adrienne's jaw dropped. Her eyes widened and she started

shaking. "No," she whispered. "What did you do, Jake? What did you *do?*"

"Adrienne. . . ." I started, and I reached out for her.

"Leave me alone!" she screamed, and she ran back down the hall. A door slammed a moment later.

"I think I'll be taking her out of here," Hanratty said as she walked up the porch. "Trouble does have a way of finding you, doesn't it, Mr. Logan?"

I stared at her. "I'm too tired for games, Officer Hanratty. Just take care of her, okay? She means a lot to me."

"You got a funny way of showing it." Hanratty snorted, but she didn't push it any further. "I suppose you have an explanation for all this?"

"Not really," I admitted. "I could tell you what happened, but you'd never believe it. Besides, the autopsies will show that Carl Powell died of cancer, and Reverend Trotter of heart disease, and you don't want to try to figure out what they were doing out here in the middle of the night anyway."

"You'd be surprised," she said softly. "Have all the promises been kept?"

I blinked. "In their own way. I think. How'd you know?"

"I know what's going on in this town," she said. "It's my job. You'll be staying, then?"

"I don't know. I'll give it a shot and see what happens."

"Good enough," she said, and she turned to Jenna. "He's not a total asshole, you know. You could do worse."

"I could," she agreed, as she shot me a look I chose not to read.

Hanratty yawned then, a sound like one you'd hear in the

wrong end of a zoo. "I'd better take Miss Moore out of here. Maybe get her feet looked at, and her hands, too. You two," she added conspiratorially, "might want to get out of sight while I do so. She looked a bit upset."

"That she did," Jenna noted. "Come on, Logan. Let's get some air."

"Good thought," Hanratty said. "Go let the folks at the ambulance check you out while you're out there. 'Specially you, Logan. That hand looks nasty. You might even think about a trip to County and some time in a hospital bed. I'll expect you in town to make a statement when you're feeling up to it." She cocked a sharp stare at us both. "You *will* come in and make a statement, won't you?"

"Promise," I said, and I nearly swallowed my tongue trying not to laugh. Hanratty gave a snort.

"Fine, whatever." Hanratty said. "Get out of here already so I can take that poor girl somewhere else."

I nodded, not trusting myself to speak. Jenna took my arm, the good one, and we stepped through the broken door together.

Dawn was coming up slow and wary, like it wasn't sure it wanted the job. The sky overhead was clear, but where the sun was rising there were ragged strips of cloud, just starting to glow red. Out in the fields, the creatures that normally went to bed with the day were uneasy. You could hear it in their calls—ragged choruses of croaks and chirps, all the rhythm lost. It reminded me of a good old big city traffic jam, with everyone leaning on their horns all at once and no one getting anywhere.

"So you're staying," she said.

"For a while," I told her, and I leaned gingerly on the railing. "I have to, you know. I think it will be better here now, though."

"It might be," she said grudgingly. "The house feels . . . different."

"Breezier," I said, and we both chuckled. "No, I think you're right. I think they're gone. My father went with her when she decided it was time to go. I hope they're where they need to be."

"You'll know tonight."

"I will?" I looked at her. "How?"

"Look for fireflies," she told me. "If they're back, it's over."

I smiled at her. "You know, you're right. I never would have thought of that." I blinked then, as I realized what she was saying. "You're going back? Today?"

Jenna nodded. "Today. It's been interesting, Logan, but I have to tell you, this isn't the restful trip I was looking for. I'm sure you'll be fine, but I can't stay here, not for a while. Maybe once you get things back together, I'll come back down and we'll give it another shot."

"I'd like that," I said, and found that I meant it. My good hand slid toward her on the rail. After a moment, she took it and gave it a squeeze. "I'd like that a lot."

"I might, too," she said, and she kissed me.

We broke apart after a long moment, and I blinked. "Hurry back," I said, only half joking.

"I just might," she said in a quiet voice I'd never heard from her before. "Now come on, let's get your hand looked at. And your arm. And your nose. And, Jesus, Logan, I hope you still have insurance because you're just a mess."

"COBRA," I told her. "And you're an absolutely beautiful mess."

"Smooth talker," she said, even as she led me down the steps toward the paramedics.

EPILOGUE

It was evening when Jenna left, her rental car roaring down the road in a plume of white smoke that somehow didn't feel like a good-bye. I watched her go, feeling better than I had in a long time, and kicked off my shoes. It seemed like the right thing to do, and I wasn't going to argue with an urge like that.

They'd kept me in the hospital 'til the next morning, much to my surprise and Jenna's worry. She'd decided to stick around long enough to see that I made it home safe and sound. "But not a minute more," she warned me as they loaded me into the ambulance, and she even sounded like she meant it a little bit. Then she followed us to County, and damned if she didn't sit five feet off the ambulance bumper the whole way there.

The prognosis on my injuries was mixed. My nose was reparable, or so the doctor said, but I was never going to be quite the same handsome devil ever again. Having a chunk of your face knocked a few degrees off line will do that for a man.

The news on my hand hadn't been quite as good—there were some crushed bones to go with the severe lacerations.

They had to do surgery to put the jigsaw puzzle inside my fist back together, and then they slapped my arm in a cast up to the elbow to make sure I didn't mess it up again. The doctor also stuck me with a rabies shot, just in case, and gave me a stern talking-to about the way I took care of myself. I took it all as best I could, too tired and too numb to wiseass back at him.

Jenna, for her part, was fine. Scratches and cuts and a bruise here and there—she took care of herself, as always. She sat by my bedside and watched me sleep, or at least that's what the nurses told me when I woke up and she was gone. She didn't come back until morning—pale, tired-looking, and ready to get me out of there come more hell or high water. And, at my bedside, she'd placed one crushed, crumpled toy soldier.

Hanratty's questioning of both of us had been perfunctory, not that I'd expected much else. Details would have raised too many questions. Instead, the town would discreetly mourn the loss of some of its leading citizens, pick up, and move on. Carl, it turned out, had a considerable sum of money that he'd willed to the upkeep of the Logan property, and specifically to the perpetual care of my mother's grave. I told Hanratty I wasn't sure I'd be using it, and she gave a massive shrug. "No sense in letting it go to waste," she said, "especially after what you went through with him."

"He went through more with me," I said, and I let the subject drop. There'd be enough time to deal with that later. There'd be enough time to deal with a lot of things later.

Adrienne, on the other hand . . . well, I didn't know what happened to Adrienne. Nor did I ask, though I wanted to. Hanratty dropped a couple of hints that she'd gone back to her family in Banner Elk for some peace and quiet, and she strongly discouraged any follow-up on the matter.

And then Jenna brought me home, said her long good-byes, and drove away.

I waited until the last plume of dust was out of sight, and then I stepped off the porch and felt the cool wet grass between my toes. This was my land. I belonged here. Every step I took told me that it was right.

In front of me, the fireflies danced. I could see them lighting my way in swirling clouds of light and steady pulses in the grass. I took special care not to step on them as I walked down to the pine trees and beyond. It wouldn't do to harm any fireflies, not now. It just wouldn't do.

The graves were waiting, like they always had been, just past the trees. Father's stone had lines of lightning snaking along it, bolts of yellow-green power that wriggled and writhed and winked out when you least expected it. The same lines of fireflies that covered his grave snaked through the tall grass that grew there and shone up to heaven. Mother's stone was different, a soft glow from a hundred lights shining low and steady all at once. It told the angels, "Here I am. Come get me. Come bring me home."

Up above, the skies were bright and clearing. There was a quarter moon sitting overhead in a patch of open sky torn from the clouds around it. The rain had long since gone, but I didn't mind. It had rained enough since I'd come home. I wanted to see the stars.

I smiled and turned back to the graves. "Good-bye, Mother," I said. "Good-bye, Father. I'm sorry. I did love you, you know. I wish I'd shown it better." They didn't answer, not even in that fever-dream way I'd imagined they might. They were gone, thank God, gone home to wherever good people who try hard and love strong are supposed to go. Off in the distance, frogs sang and crickets chirped, and every so often I could hear the wind. No voices, though, and when I spoke, the night swallowed up the sound right quick.

That was fine. It was over. The fireflies were proof of that, all the proof that I needed. I nodded to each stone then pivoted on my heel to head back up toward the house. It had been a long day in a series of long days, and I was bone tired.

As I turned, though, I noticed something. Lightning bugs were everywhere, happy and oblivious. One even landed in my hair. Except . . .

Except there was one bare patch left without them. It was six feet by three feet, just the right size for a grave, and it was right next to where my Mother rested. No fireflies danced on it. No fireflies would cross its boundaries.

I took a deep breath and rested my hand on a tree to help steady me. No fireflies there, not for me. A slow look around my land showed me sparks of light everywhere else. They'd come back, all right; they'd come back like they'd never left.

Save for that one spot, that one bare patch of black night resting so close to Mother's gravestone it made my heart ache. There was a message for me there, a message written in light and shadow.

That grave they marked out was mine, and not a one of them would guide an angel to it.

I'd planned, even after all this, to stay through the end of the year then move on come next spring. This was my land now, my home, but I still needed to mcve on. The difference was that I'd come back to it, and both the land and I knew it. No matter where I went, I'd come home. Maybe Jenna would join me, maybe she wouldn't. That was for the future to tell, though, to unwind in its own way and its own time.

That's what was written in my blood and in my bones. And the fireflies? They knew that once I came back, I'd be staying.

Forever and ever.

Amen.